Praise for
MARY GENTLE

"A rare narrative talent."
C.J. Cherryh

"A fine writer."
Marion Zimmer Bradley

"A major talent at work."
Interzone

"Colorful and inventive . . .
Gentle writes with considerable energy and vividness."
New York Newsday

"She is a writer who knows politics and human nature and gives the reader an exciting romp to boot."
Julian May

"My profoundest gratitude to Mary Gentle for creating such a marvelous world and all the myriad wonders."
Anne McCaffrey

Other Books by
Mary Gentle

A Secret History: The Book of Ash, #1
Carthage Ascendant: The Book of Ash, #2
The Wild Machines: The Book of Ash, #3
A Hawk in Silver
Scholars and Soldiers
Rats and Gargoyles
The Architecture of Desire
Left to His Own Devices
Grunts!
Golden Witchbreed
Ancient Light

MARY GENTLE

LOST BURGUNDY

THE BOOK OF ASH, #4

An Imprint of HarperCollins*Publishers*

This is a work of fiction. Names, characters, places, and incidents are the products of the author's imagination or are used fictitiously and are not to be construed as real. Any resemblance to actual events, locales, organizations, or persons, living or dead, is entirely coincidental.

EOS
An Imprint of HarperCollins*Publishers*
10 East 53rd Street
New York, New York 10022-5299

Cover art by Donato Giancola
ISBN: 0-380-81114-6
www.eosbooks.com

First Eos paperback printing: December 2000

Printed in the U.S.A.

10 9 8 7 6 5 4 3 2 1

Note to the Reader

Since both political and historical considerations have led to separate publication of the four Books of ASH, this note is intended to bring the reader up to date with the three previous volumes: *A Secret History, Carthage Ascendant*, and *The Wild Machines.*

Ash, a fifteenth-century mercenary captain, is inextricably caught up in the Visigoth invasion of Europe from North Africa. She has discovered that her "saint's voice," the Lion who guides her in battle, is in fact the transmission of the Visigoth *machina rei militaris* or "tactical computer." Ash's twin—the Visigoth general called the Faris—was bred to hear the *machina* at long-distance, and Ash has discovered that she was discarded from the same experiment.

Determined to destroy the *machina rei militaris* in Carthage itself, Ash attaches herself to the only remaining European power still fighting against the Visigoths: Burgundy, led by its ruling Duke, Charles. At the disastrous battle at Auxonne, Ash is captured, injured, and taken as a prisoner to North Africa.

In Carthage, she is imprisoned, awaiting vivisection by the Visigoth lord Leofric, breeder of herself and the Faris. Her husband, the turncoat German knight Fernando, attempts to kidnap her on behalf of another Visigoth lord, Gelimer, by taking her on a hunting expedition outside Carthage, among the pyramids. There, she calls on her "voice" for help—and meets only silence.

Threatened with immediate execution at the coronation of the new King-Caliph, Ash tries to forcibly download information from the *machina rei militaris*. She hears not one, but many voices: not the *machina*, but other voices, which call themselves "the Wild Machines." For centuries they have guided the military strategy of the Visigoth Empire, speaking covertly through their only channel, the *machina rei militaris*. Their goal is to see Burgundy wiped off the face of the earth—she does not know, and cannot yet discover, *why*.

Simultaneously with their voices, an earthquake collapses the palace, and she escapes; together with her priest, Godfrey, who is killed as they flee through the old Roman sewers. Emerging into the open, she meets her own men coming in on the planned raid to destroy the *machina rei militaris*. The raid fails. Ash sees an aurora over the pyramids, and realizes that these are "the Wild Machines." She is compelled to go toward them, but her men forcibly rescue her from their summons.

Ash and her men retreat back across the Mediterranean to find the rest of the company. As they trek toward Burgundy, she hears the voice of dead Godfrey, in her head, in the *machina rei militaris:* his personality uploaded to it at the moment of his death.

The rest of the company are in Dijon, trapped along with the Burgundians by the Faris's besieging army. Ash is given a promise by the injured Duke of Burgundy that, if the siege holds, he will order his remaining forces to mount a second attack on Carthage. She brings her forces into the city.

Calling a parley with the Faris outside, Ash tells her what she's learned—that the Faris has been bred from a line of wonder-workers, not only to speak with the *machina rei militaris*, but to make a miracle that will wipe humanity off the face of the earth. For some unknown reason, Burgundy must be destroyed before the Wild Machines can trigger the Faris into this act, over which she will have no control. They are interrupted by news that the injured Duke is dying. The Burgundians request that the Faris allow the hunt by which the Burgundians choose their new duke. Terrified, the Faris agrees.

Ash and her men, together with the company's disguised woman surgeon, Florian, ride out of Dijon on the hunt. Ash finds herself following a miraculous milk white hart with a golden collar: the Heraldic Beast of Burgundy. She "hears" the Wild Machines' joy as Duke Charles dies, and sees the sun dim as they attempt their "miracle." Simultaneously, she finds that Florian has cornered the hart—now a mundane, pink-eyed albino animal. Florian kills the hart. The miracle fails.

Florian, hailed as the new Duchess of Burgundy, tells Ash that the Burgundians have for generations bred their own defense against wonder-workers—someone in whose presence no miracles can occur. Florian, now, is all that stands in the way of the Wild Machines' destruction of Burgundy, of Europe, and perhaps of all humanity—while she lives.

And Florian is outside the shaky safety of the one city that still withstands the Visigoth conquering legions . . .

This fourth and final volume completes the translation of the controversial Sible Hedingham manuscript.

[Original e-mail documents found inserted, folded, in British Library copy of 3rd edition, *Ash: The Lost History of Burgundy*, (2001) — possibly in chronological order of editing original typescript?]
[previous e-mail missing?]

Message: #350 (Anna Longman)
Subject: Ash
Date: 15/12/00 at 03.23 a.m.
From: Ngrant@

format address deleted
other details encrypted by
non-discoverable personal key

Anna--

I know. It seems unbelievable. But it appears to be nothing less than the truth. No previous survey shows this sea trench. Not before we started looking here.

Isobel brought one of the tech people to the meeting I've just come out of, and showed us downloaded satellite surveys. Not that there are many, the Tunisian military being as sensitive as any other military—but what we have are unambiguous.

Shallow water here. No deep trenches below the 1000 metre mark.

And yet, our ROVs are down there now, as I'm typing this.

I don't like this, Anna. The Middle East and the Mediterranean have been far too closely surveyed to say, now, that this could all be down to lost or misinterpreted evidence, distorted analysis, fake documents, or fraud.

I cannot genuinely deny this. According to recent satellite scans, and according to British Admiralty charts, the seabed where we found the trench used to be flat. Not silt, not a trench; nothing but rock. God knows, given the submarine warfare in the Mediterranean sixty years ago, the Admiralty charts are pretty substantive! It isn't a geological feature anyone could have missed.

I have just suggested, in Isobel's meeting, that we look for seismograph readings: there may have been a recent earthquake. She tells me that's what she's been doing over the last ten days: pulling in all the favours she has with various colleagues, to check the most up-to-date satellite reports and geological surveys.

No earthquake. Not so much as an undersea tremor.

I'll post to you again when I have had some time to think this over—it's only been a few hours since Isobel called her meeting; she and her physicist colleagues are still at it, talking into the small hours of the morning.

I went up on deck. Looked into blackness, tasted wet air. Tried to come to terms with this idea—a hundred ideas going around in my own mind—no: I'm not making sense.

One line of Florian's haunts me. Mediaeval Latin translation can be hell—is 'dn' an abbreviation for _dominus_ or _domina_;masculine or feminine? Or is it in fact 'dm', for _deum_? Context is all, handwriting is all; and even then a sentence may have two or three perfectly viable different translations, only *one* of which is what the author wrote!

I _know_ the 'hand' of Fraxinus/Sible Hedingham: I have for eight years. I can't realistically make it read anything else.

What Floria says *is* "You hunted a myth. I made it real."

--Pierce

Message: #199 (Pierce Ratcliff)
Subject: Ash
Date: 15/12/00 at 05.14 a.m.
From: Longman@

format address deleted
other details encrypted and
non-recoverably deleted

Pierce--

Physicists?

Just checked back in your mailings, and yes, you did mention this before. I missed it. Why has an archaeologist like Dr Isobel got physicists with her? Is it purely a 'social' visit, Pierce? It doesn't look like it.

I really don't want to ask this, but I need her to mail me to confirm what you're saying.

I wouldn't take one person's word for this. Not even my mother's.

--Anna

Message: #365 (Anna Longman)
Subject: Ash
Date: 15/12/00 at 06.05 a.m.
From: Ngrant@

format address deleted
other details encrypted by
non-discoverable personal key

Anna--

The physicists? Tami Inoshishi and James Howlett: Isobel's friends from artificial intelligence and theoretical physics. I suppose they're here quasi-unofficially, at her request? They've been offering help to the expedition—they desperately want to get the Stone Golem up, and off-site, for examination—tests at CERN, the whole works.

I've been trying to talk to them, but they're astonishingly dismissive. Or perhaps preoccupied. The strange thing is that Ms Inoshishi isn't at all interested in the concept that the machina rei militaris may be a primitive 'computer' of some sort, and Howlett isn't really interested in the golems that we found at the land site.

What they *are* interested in are my chronicle texts, and the seabed surveys.

They seem very interested in the concept of evidence changing.

What I find disturbing, I suppose, is that when I speculate that the nature of the del Guiz and Angelotti documentary evidence may have undergone some kind of a _genuine_ change, they take me seriously.

Talk to me, Anna. You're a person who's not here, not caught up in the enthusiasm. Do I sound mad to you?

--Pierce

Message: #202 (Pierce Ratcliff)
Subject: Ash
Date: 15/12/00 at 06.10 a.m.
From: Longman@

format address deleted
other details encrypted and
non-recoverably deleted

Pierce--

Are Ms Inoshishi and Mr Howlett there in an official capacity? It sounds as though they are colleagues of Dr Napier-Grant there in a private capacity. Is she going to report back to her university soon? What's going to happen _officially_?

Pierce—what do _you_ think of all this? My head is spinning.

--Anna

Message: #372 (Anna Longman)
Subject: Ash
Date: 15/12/00 at 08.12 p.m.
From: Ngrant@

format address deleted
other details encrypted by
non-discoverable personal key

Anna--

I don't think. I have nothing like enough evidence as yet to allow me to think.

Anything else would be unfounded speculation.

I'm going to be busy with the people here; I will get back to you as soon as I can.

And I'm going to continue translating.

I have a further section of reasonably adequately translated material from the Sible Hedingham ms., I'll attach the files with this message.

I need to resolve some of the apparent anomalies in the next part of the text. I feel that I cannot say anything definite until the whole of the Sible Hedingham ms. has been translated.

--Pierce

- -

Message: #204 (Pierce Ratcliff)
Subject: Ash
Date: 15/12/00 at 10.38 p.m.
From: Longman@

format address deleted
other details encrypted and
non-recoverably deleted

Enough shit, Pierce (pardon my French). Enough havering, enough sitting on the fence—

You've got Dr Isobel's friends there on the ship, she obviously thought it was important enough to call scientists in; there are maps that don't show the site you've found on the seabed; Pierce, _what do you believe is happening_?

Enough academic caution. Tell me. Now.

--Anna

- -

Message: #376 (Anna Longman)
Subject: Ash
Date: 15/12/00 at 11.13 p.m.
From: Ngrant@

format address deleted
other details encrypted by
non-discoverable personal key

Anna--

I am forced to believe a whole series of self-contradictory facts.

—That the Angelotti and del Guiz texts have been classified as 'Fiction' for the past fifty years—and yet, Anna, when I last consulted them a few months ago, they were shelved under normal Late Mediaeval History.

—That the 'Fraxinus' text is a genuine fifteenth century biography of Ash, that has enabled us to find evidence of post-Roman technology in a 'Visigoth' settlement, and the ruins of a 'Carthage' on the Mediterranean seabed—and yet, that when we study the previous sixty years of surveys, there is no geological feature on that seabed that matches the one we have found. And there has been no recent seismic activity that could have produced it.

—That a "messenger-golem" with wear-marks _on the soles of its feet_ can be classified, by a reputable department of metallurgy, as a fake made after 1945—and now as a genuine artefact with its bronze cast between five and six centuries ago.

Because I've now actually seen the report, Anna. What they're presenting isn't an apology for a mistake.

It is two sets of readings, two weeks apart, that imply completely different conclusions.

The altered status of the 'Ash' documentation is one thing—I've been e-mailing curators: there are known artefacts no longer in display cases, the 'Ash sallet' has vanished from Rouen, both the helmet AND the catalogue entry.

What is missing is not half so disturbing as what is here.

You see, Anna, I had begun to have a theory. Simply, that there was *something* that needed explaining.

I'll be honest. Anna, I KNOW the 'Ash' documents were authentic history when I first studied them. Whatever I may have said about errors of re-classification, you will remember that I found myself completely unable to explain it in any satisfactory way. I think that I _had_ almost come to believe in Vaughan Davies' theory out of sheer desperation—that there actually has been a 'first history' of the world, which was wiped out in some fashion, and that we now inhabit a 'second history', into which bits of the first have somehow survived. That Ash's history was first genuine, and has now been—fading, if you like—to Romance, to a cycle of legends.

So I had reached a conclusion, before the last ten days. I had thought that, since neither Ash's Burgundy, nor the Visigoth Empire in North Africa, had any evidence that hadn't been thoroughly discredited at that point—well, how could I say this to you? I had begun to think that perhaps they *were* from a 'previous version' of our past, growing less real by the decade. A previous past history in which the text's 'miracle' *did* take place. In which the Faris and the 'Wild Machines' (or whatever it is those literary metaphors represent) triggered some kind of alteration in history. Or, to put it in scientific terms, a previous past history in which the possible subatomic states of the universe were (deliberately and consciously) collapsed into a different reality—the one we now inhabit.

Vaughan Davies' theory is just that: a theory. And yet we have to find truth somewhere. Remember that, whatever he is now, when he was a young man he _knew_ Bohr, Dirac, Heisenberg; if the biographers are to be believed, he debated with them on equal terms. He did not know—and nor have I been much aware of, until I talked to James Howlett today—the work of the succeeding scientific generation on quantum theory and the various versions of the anthropic principle.

Perhaps I've taken on too much of the mediaeval world-view: to find a respected physicist listening to me seriously when I ask if 'deep consciousness' might change the universe—I find it unnerving! I try to follow James when he talks about the Copenhagen interpretation and the many-worlds model . . . with rather less than the average numerate layman's understanding, I fear.

Although even he, with all his many-branching multiverses from each collapsing quantum moment, can't answer two questions.

The first is, why would there be only _one_ great 'fracture of history', as Davies called it? Mainstream quantum theory calls for continuous fracture, as you once wrote to me: a universe in which you simultaneously perform every action, moral and immoral. An endlessly-branching tree of alternate universes, from every single second of time.

And, even if that point were adequately answered, even if we knew that only one great quantum restructuring of the universe had taken place, as some versions of the anthropic quantum model demand—that by observing our universe now, we have in a sense _created_ the Big Bang 'back then', and what we observe of the cosmos now . . . Anna, why would there be evidence _left over_ from before the fracture? A previous state of the universe has *no* existence, not even a theoretical one!

James Howlett has just looked over my shoulder, shaken his head, and gone off to fight with his software models of mathematical reality. No, I dare say I don't give even an adequate layman's explanation of what he's been trying to tell me.

Perhaps it's because I'm a historian: despite the fact that we experience only the present, I retain a superstitious conviction that the past exists—that it has been _real_. And yet we know nothing but this single present moment. . . .

What I had suggested to James Howlett was that the remaining contradictory evidence—the Angelotti and del Guiz manuscripts—would be anomalies from previous quantum states, becoming less and less 'possible'—less *real*. Turning from mediaeval history into legend, into fiction. Fading into impossibility.

Then, you found the Sible Hedingham manuscript, and Isobel's team found the ruins of Carthage.

I've been so deep in translation work—when I haven't been glued to the images the ROVs are transmitting—that it didn't occur to me to think.

No, I didn't want to think.

It wasn't until today, just now; until James Howlett said to me—"I think the important question is, why are these discoveries appearing?"

And I immediately, without thinking, corrected him: "*Re*-appearing."

If there has been a 'previous state' of the universe, if we are a 'second history'—if any of this is even possible, and not utter nonsense—then that 'fading of a first history' cannot be the whole story. What we've found—the ruins of Carthage on the floor of the Mediterranean Sea, and the machina rei militaris: the Stone Golem—were they actually *here* before this December?

You see, Vaughan Davies notwithstanding, I can't begin to formulate a theory that accounts for why some of the evidence should appear to be *coming back*.

Anna, if this is true, then things are still changing.

And if things are still changing, then this isn't "dead history"—_it isn't over_.

--Pierce

PART ONE

16 November AD 1476–25 November AD 1476

THE EMPTY CHAIR[1]

[1]Sible Hedingham ms part 3.

I

SLEET BEGAN TO blind her the moment they rode out of the forest and galloped for Dijon's northwest gate.

Wet ice whipped into Ash's face as she spurred the pale bay, under a sky clouding up from gray to black, mixed rain and sleet slashing down.

"Get her into the city!" Ash bawled over the gathering storm, throat hoarse. "*Now*! Get her through those fucking gates: *go*!"

She crowded in, riding knee-to-knee with Florian—Christus Viridianus! *Duchess* Florian—and the rest of the mounted Lion men-at-arms, the soaked swallowtail banner cracking overhead.

Sudden hooves thudded, cutting up the sodden earth behind her on the road down to the bridge over the moat. A stream of warhorses and riders went past and around her, in Burgundian blue and red and draggled plumes—*de la Marche's men*! she realized, a hand on her sword hilt.

Come out to escort us in.

Enclosed in that armed safety, they thundered back between the paths, trenches, barricades, and buildings of the Visigoth camp—between the chaos of Visigoth troops running in all directions—new, wet mud spraying up from ironshod hooves.

Just before the narrow bridge, the horses slowed, milled about; and she hit the pommel of her saddle in frustration. Two hundred mounted men. She stared at their backs, swore out loud, turning the pale bay with her spurs, gazing back into the slashing sleet and rain that now hid the Visigoth camp, hid everything more than fifty yards away. No more than ten minutes to get through this choke point, over the bridge, through the gate; but an aching wait, fretting itself into half an hour in her mind.

Visigoth mounted archers! she anticipated. As soon as they sort themselves out . . . —No, not in this weather.

The skin at the nape of her neck shivered.

It'll be golems, with Greek Fire flamethrowers, like at Auxonne—we're bunched up here, we'll fry like wasps in a fire!

The stress of the wait made the pit of her stomach hurt. Moving again, at last—men shouting, horses' hooves: all echoed under the arched stonework of the city gate. The breath of the animals went up white into the wet air. She swung her mount around, following Florian's winded and limping gray gelding, was briefly aware of the darkness in the tunnel of the gate, and then burst out into drenched daylight, Antonio Angelotti grabbing at her bridle.

"The Duke's dead!" he yelled up at her, face streaming with rain. "Time to change sides *now*! Madonna, shall I send a messenger out to the Carthaginians?"

"Stop panicking, Angeli!"

The high steel-and-leather saddle creaked as she sat back, shifting her weight to stop the bay dancing sideways across shattered, flooded cobbles.

"There's a new Duke—*Duchess*!" she corrected herself. "It's Florian. *Our* Florian!"

"Florian?"

From behind Angelotti, Robert Anselm growled, "Fuck!"

Ash wheeled the lathered gelding, bringing it under her control. Every instinct swore at her to muster her men now, abandon all baggage but the essential, and leave this city to the natural consequences of a bungled transfer of power.

How can I? Her fist hit the saddle pommel. *How can I!*

"Demoiselle-Captain!" Olivier de la Marche rode in close, leaning across from his warhorse to clasp her arm, gauntlet against vambrace. "See to the defenses of this gate! I give you authority over Jonvelle, Jussey, and Lacombe; take up your place from the gate here, north along the wall to the White Tower! Then I must speak with you!"

"Sieur—!" She did not get it out in time: his chestnut stallion was already clopping away into the downpour, in with his men-at-arms.

The crossbowman Jan-Jacob Clovet, taking the bay's reins from Angelotti, shrugged and spat. "Son of a bitch!"

"Now is that putting the mercenaries up the sharp end, as usual? Or is that giving us the place of honor, because it's going to be hit hardest when they come?"

"God spare us from ducal favor, boss," Jan-Jacob Clovet said fervently. "*Any* fucking duke. *Or* duchess. Are you *sure* about the doc? She can't be, can she?"

"Oh, she can! Florian!" Ash bawled.

De la Marche's sub-captain and his men brought steaming, caparisoned warhorses between her and Florian, shouldering the woman surgeon and her broken-down mount out and across the devastated zone of the city behind the walls, heading at the trot for the ducal palace.

"Florian!"

She caught one glimpse of Floria del Guiz' white face, between the pauldrons of the armored knights surrounding her. Then the household of Olivier de la Marche closed in.

Shit! No time!

Ash spun the uncooperative bay on its heels, facing the gate again.

"Angeli! Thomas! Get 'em up on the walls! Rickard, warn Captain Jonvelle—the Visigoths are gonna come right over those fucking walls behind us!"

ii

"WHY DON'T THEY come!"

Ash stood at a slit window in the Byward Tower, squinting out into slanting water. Rain splintered down onto the walls of Dijon. The tower's flint and masonry breathed off cold.

Rain beat in: solid, intense storm rain. Rivulets ran down off her steel sallet and visor. Her breath and body warmth made the safety of armor stickily humid, despite the biting cold wind.

" 'Nother couple of hours, it'll be dark." Robert Anselm shouldered into the window embrasure, his rust-starred armor scraping against hers. "Fuck, I thought the whole fucking rag'ead army was coming in after you!"

"They should be! If I was them—there's never been a better chance—!"

The thunder of the city gate shutting behind them still tingles in her bones.

"Maybe they're having a mutiny out there! Maybe the Faris is dead. *I* don't know!"

"Wouldn't you . . . know?"

Carefully, she probes in that part of her soul that she shares. Almost beyond hearing, there are voices—the *machina rei militaris*, Godfrey, the Wild Machines? For the first time in her life she can't tell. And there is an echo of that intense pressure, subliminally sensed, felt in the bones, that racked her when the hart was hunted and the sun dimmed in the autumn sky. Voices as weak, or weaker, than at that moment of the unmaking.

"There's been some . . . damage, I think. I don't know what or to who. Temporary, permanent—I can't tell." In fear and frustration, Ash added, "Just when we could do with hearing Godfrey, right, Roberto? Hey, maybe the Faris *has* died! Maybe her *qa'ids* are running around like headless chickens trying to sort out the command structure: *that's* why they haven't attacked . . ."

"Won't take 'em long." Anselm put his face to the stone aperture, his hard, armored body shifting, trying to make out anything beyond the misty walls of the city. "I've had the muster roll called. There's two of our officers still missing. John Price. Euen Huw."

"Shit . . ."

Ash peered out of the gap between tightly mortared stones. Her breath made gray plumes in front of her face. The intensity of the lashing water came in bursts, slapping the stone rim of the window. She did not flinch back.

"Price isn't even a fucking cavalryman . . . Nobody's to go out after them." Her voice sounded curt in her own ears.

Anselm protested, "Girl—"

Ash cut him off. "I don't like it any more than you. Nothing happens until we can see what's going on. The Duke's *dead*. This city could fall apart from the *inside*, any second! I want a command meeting with de la Marche; I want to see Florian! After that, maybe we'll send a man out through one of the postern gates."

Anselm, grimly sardonic, said, "We got no idea what the fucking ragheads are doing. *Or* the Burgundians. You don't like it. Nor do I."

The hissing slash of water against stone increased. Ash pressed up closer to the slit-window, hands braced against the cold stone to either side. Across the empty air, she realized she was seeing only a few yards of broken earth.

She shifted as far to one side as she could, to let Robert cram in beside her. He hawked, spat, white mucus spraying the stone sill.

"At least this shitting weather gets in their powder, and stretches the siege-machine ropes . . ."

Promptly as he spoke, a shrill whistle and roar sounded, each man in the tower room flinching, automatically. Ash jumped down from the window embrasure and clattered to where she could see out of the door. A faint thump, and a glow through the rain, down in the ruined part of the city, made her skin shiver by what it implied.

"Rain's not going to stop the golem-machines," she said. "Or the Greek Fire."

Robert Anselm did not move from the window. After a moment, she strode back and stepped up to rejoin him.

He grunted. "They got Charlie's funeral going yet?"

"Fuck, who's going to tell *us* anything!"

"You heard anything from the doc?"

Ash took her gaze away from the shrouded gray lumps on the puddled earth beyond the moat—discarded ladders, dead and bloated horses, one or two corpses of men. Slaves, probably, not thought worth the recovery. All a uniform mud gray; all motionless.

"Roberto—whatever it means—she *is* Duchess."

"And I'm the fucking King of Carthage!"

"I've heard the Wild Machines," Ash said, her gaze steadily on him. "In my soul. And I've seen them—I've stood there while they shook the earth under my feet. And I saw Florian's face, and I *heard* them, Robert—they tried to make their devil's miracle, and they were stopped. Cold. Because of her; because of our Florian. Because she made Burgundy's Heraldic Beast into . . . meat."

On his face, what there is visible of it under sallet-visor and sopping-wet hood, she sees an expression of cynical disbelief.

"What that means to the Burgundians, I don't know yet. But . . . You weren't there, Robert."

Anselm's head turned. She saw him only in profile now, looking out from the window-slit. His voice gravel, he protested, "I know I fucking *wasn't there*! I *prayed* for you! Me and the lads; Paston and Faversham, up on the wall—"

Push it or not? she wondered, diverted. Yes. I need to know how bad it is: I'm going to depend on this man.

"If you'd come on the assault, you might have seen what happened on the hunt. You bottled out."

Jerking round, his face red, he jabbed a finger two inches from her breastplate. "*You don't fucking say that!*"

She was aware that the escort and banner men-at-arms by the tower door looked over, signaled them with a gesture to stay where they were.

"Robert, what's the problem?" She loosened and removed one gauntlet, and raised her bare hand to wipe at her wet face. "Apart from the obvious! We've seen shittier sieges. Neuss. Admitted it's better being on the *outside* . . ."

His confidence was not to be got by humor. His expression closed up. This close, she could see the hazel green color of his eyes, the thread-veins on his nose and cheekbones, sallet and shadow making his face unreadable.

Ash waited.

A renewed wind took the rain in great gusts, beating

against the walls like surf. Ash is momentarily reminded of the sea beating against the cliffs of Carthage harbor, below the stone window-slits of House Leofric, is conscious of a similar great void, the other side of this wall, vast empty air, filled with freezing gray torrents. Faint spray dampened her cheeks. She reached up, with a left-hand gauntlet that—despite being scoured in sand and rubbed with goose grease—was already orange-spotted with rust, and tilted her visor down.

"What is it, Roberto?"

The man's body beside her crushed her farther into the window embrasure as he heaved a great sigh. He looked out at the ever-moving rain. He spoke, at last, with an apparent acceptance of her right to make demands of him:

"I didn't know if you were alive or dead after Auxonne. No one could get any news of your body being picked up off the field. I expected to see your head on a spear. Because if you *were* dead, the Goths were going to show your body off, damn fucking sure!"

His voice became quieter, barely audible to her, never mind to the men-at-arms by the door.

"If you were a prisoner, they'd've shown you in chains . . . You could have been off in the woods, wounded. You could have crawled off to die. No one would have found you."

He turned to look at her. The rain made him squint, under his raised visor, flesh creasing around his eyes.

"That was how it was, girl. *I* thought you'd been shoveled into a grave-trench, without being recognized. Those fire throwers . . . A lot of the men came back saying bodies were burned black. Tony said you might have been taken prisoner at Auxonne and carted off to North Africa, because of how interested they were at Basle in getting hold of you. But they wouldn't care if they'd had to take a *dead* body. Scientist-magi give me the willies," Anselm added, with an unself-conscious shudder.

She waited, listening to the slash of rain on flint, not prompting him.

"Three months, and then—" His gaze fixed on her. "You *had* to be dead, there was no other way to behave—and then, out of nowhere, three days ago, a message on a crossbow bolt—"

"You'd got used to leading the company."

His hands slammed into the wall either side of her, pinning her into the window embrasure. She glanced down at the steel of his arms, then up into his face.

Spittle sprayed from his mouth, dotting the front of her livery tabard. "*I wanted to come to Africa!* I *didn't* want to stay in Dijon! Sweet Green Christ—What do you *think* happened, girl? I had John de fucking Vere saying, the Duke's sending half the company to Carthage, I need a man I can leave in command *here*—"

The men at the tower door stirred uneasily. He broke off, deliberately lowering his voice again.

"If you were anywhere, dead or alive, it had to be Carthage! Only I didn't have a fucking choice! I got ordered to stay here! And now I find out you *were* there, *alive*—"

Ash reached up and put her hands on his wrists and gently tugged them down. The steel of his vambrace was slick with rain, cold against her one bare palm.

"I can see Oxford doing it that way. He'd need to take Angeli, for the guns. You'd been my second-in-command, you *were* in command, there wasn't anyone else he could leave behind with safety. Robert, I could have been dead. Or if not dead, then anywhere. You were right to stay here."

"I should have gone with him! I was sure you were dead. I was wrong!" Robert Anselm punched his fist hard into the flint lining of the window embrasure. He looked down at his scratched, dented gauntlet and absently flexed his fingers. "If I'd pulled the company out with me, Dijon wouldn't be standing siege now, but I'm telling you, girl, I should have come to Carthage. For you."

"If you had," Ash said, measuring the thoughts out in her mind, "we might have taken House Leofric. With that many more men and guns. We might have destroyed the Stone Golem; we might have broken the only connection the Wild Machines have with the world—the only way they can do their miracle."

His eyes flicked toward her, small behind the incongruously long lashes.

"But then"—Ash shrugged—"if you hadn't been here, Dijon might have fallen before you'd got as far as the coast—then the Duke would have been executed, and we'd know by now what it is the Wild Machines are going to use the Faris for. Because they'd have done it, three months ago!"

"And maybe not," Anselm rumbled.

"We're *here*, *now*. What does it matter what you didn't do? Robert, none of what you're telling me explains why you didn't come on the attack against the Faris today. None of it tells me why you've lost your bottle. And I need to know that, because I depend on you, and so do a lot of other people here."

She was frank, forcing herself to mention fear aloud. What she saw on his face as he turned his head away was not shame.

He muttered, "You went out expecting to be killed."

"Yes. If I had, but if I'd killed her—"

So quietly she almost missed it, Robert Anselm interrupted. "I couldn't ride out with you today. I couldn't see you get killed in front of me."

Ash stared at him.

"Not after three months," he said painfully. "I held masses for you, girl. I grieved. I carried on without you. Then you came back. *Then* you ask me to ride out and watch you get killed. That's too much to ask."

The slash of rain against flint-embedded walls grew heavier. Streamlets of water dribbled down between the planks of the roof above, splattering them and the floorboards irrespectively.

I know what to say, Ash thought. Why can't I say it?

"So," he said harshly, "this is where you relieve me of my rank, ain't it? You know you can't trust me in combat anymore. You think I'll be watching your back, not doing my job."

Some tension in her reached crisis. She snapped, "What do you want me to tell you, Robert? The same old stuff? 'We can *all* get killed, here and now, anytime, better get used to it'?

'That's what we do for a living, war gets you killed'? I can sing that song! Six months ago, I'd have said it to you! Not now!"

Robert Anselm reached up and unbuckled his helmet, dipping his head to remove it. The helmet lining and his body heat had left his stubbled head slick with sweat. He breathed out, hard.

"And now?"

"It hurts," Ash said. She pressed her bare knuckle against the wall, grinding skin against stone, as if the physical pain could give her release. "You don't want to see me hacked up? *I* don't want to send you and Angeli and the others up on the walls. I brought these guys back through country like nothing on earth! I don't want them getting cut up raiding the Visigoths' camp, or whatever idea de la Marche is going to come up with when I see him. I want to hold us back, go sit in the tower, out of the bombardment—*I'm starting to be afraid of people getting hurt.*"

There was a long pause. The rain grew louder.

Robert Anselm gave a small, suppressed snuffle. "Looks like we're both in the shit, then!"

As she stared at him, startled, he burst into a full guffaw.

"Jesus, Roberto—!"

The snuffle caught her by surprise. An emptiness in her chest made her choke, spurt out a giggle, laugh, finally, out loud. It would not be denied: a bubbling thing that made her sputter, wet-eyed, unable to get a coherent word out.

Shuddering to a rumbling halt, Robert Anselm reached across, putting his arm around her shoulders and shaking her.

"*We're* fucked," he said cheerfully.

"It's nothing to laugh about!"

"Pair of fucking *idiots*," he added. His arm fell away as he straightened himself up, plate sliding over steel plate. His eyes still bright, his expression sobered. "Both of us should get out of this game. Don't think the ragheads are going to give us the option, though."

"Fuck, no . . ." She sucked at her knuckle, and a trickle of blood. "Robert, I can't *do* this if I'm afraid of people getting hurt."

He looked down at her, from where he stood on the flint steps. "Now we find out, don't we? Whether we're good at this when it's *really* hard? When you *have* to not care?"

Her nostrils are full of the smell of wet steel, his male sweat, sodden wool, the city's midden heaps far below. Rain spattered in, spraying her cheeks with a fine, freezing dew. As the wind gusted sharply, she and Anselm turned simultaneously toward the arrow slit again.

"There's nobody in charge in here. They must know that! *Why* isn't she attacking now!"

She sent a stream of messengers to the ducal palace in the next hour, who came back one after another with word of not being able to get through to the new Duchess, to the Sieur de la Marche, to Chamberlain-Counselor Ternant; with news of the palace being a chaotic horde of courtiers, undertakers, celebrants, priests, and noblemen, simultaneously torn between arranging a crowning and a funeral.

"Captain Jonvelle told me something!" Rickard added, panting, soaked to the skin in the cold wall-tower's room.

Ash considered asking why he had stopped to gossip with de la Marche's Burgundian captains, saw his bright face, and decided against it.

"Saps. The ragheads are still mining. His men can *hear* them! They're *still* digging!"

"Hope they *drown*," Ash growled under her breath.

She spent her time pacing the crowded floors of the Byward Tower, among men armed and ready to go out if the walls were threatened, a lance here and there being sent out to watch, to listen, for anything that might be seen or heard in devastating rain.

Forty miles south, down that road—cold darkness, twenty-four hours a day. Given what surrounds Burgundy's borders . . . Is it any wonder we're getting shit weather here?

"Boss . . ." Thomas Tydder, elbowed forward by his brother Simon, looked at her from under streaming dark hair. When he spoke, a drop of water hanging off the end of his nose wobbled. "Boss, is it true? Has Saint Godfrey deserted us?"

Ash signaled Tydder's lance leader to leave him be.

"Not deserted," she said firmly. "He speaks for us now in the Communion of Saints, you know that, don't you?"

Relieved and embarrassed, the boy ducked his head in a nod.

Past him, Ash caught sight of Robert Anselm, Roberto's features utterly impassive. Automatically, she prodded at her soul, as a man may prod in his mouth for a tooth that has been drawn and has left only a tender, unfilled gap.

Stepping closer, Anselm murmured, "Is he right?"

The thunder of the falling rain has concealed her whisper, every time she speaks aloud to Godfrey, to the Stone Golem, even—*Christus*!—to the Wild Machines themselves. Anselm knows, though.

"Still nothing I can understand," she said succinctly.

"Lion and Boar preserve us," Anselm rumbled. "Is that good or bad?"

"*Fuck* knows, Robert!"

The frustration of waiting seared through her: she would have welcomed anything, even the anticipated thump of siege ladders and flood of Visigoth men over the city wall. She stomped toward the tower's open doorway.

The roar of fuse-flames and the shatter of clay pots echoed along the wall, and blue-and-yellow fire spread in a ripple across the stone surface of the parapet and burned unhindered by the torrential rain. All the leather buckets of earth and sand that lined the walls grew sodden and too heavy to lift.

Ash signaled her men to leave it alone and watched the gelatinous flaming mixture gradually washed over the flagstones and down the inside of the city walls. *There's nothing much left to burn down there anyway: we won't have a city fire.*

Some forty minutes or so before she judged the last light might leave the iron gray, pelting sky, two very solidly built Burgundian men-at-arms appeared in the tower doorway, with a slighter man between them.

"Boss!" Thomas Rochester, running along with them—ducking at every embrasure, stumbling into the dark shelter of the tower—bawled a report. "Euen's back!"

Heads turned in the tower room, and all along the rows of Lion men-at-arms settled in the brattices, and behind merlons, in the pouring rain, men crowding to see the small, wiry figure trot along the stone parapet in Burgundian custody.

"He's one of ours, Sergeant." Ash broke into a tremendous grin. "Son of a *bitch* . . ."

The Burgundians saluted, a little cautiously, and made their way back out into the rain. Ash gave a laugh of sheer relief at the bedraggled Welshman dripping water, shivering in the icy wind, but with a grin brilliant enough to shine through the growing twilight.

"Somebody get this idiot a cloak! Euen, in here!"

She waited as one of the baggage women handed Euen Huw a bowl of tepid soup.

"You're wet, Euen . . . *really* wet."

"Came in through a water gate, didn't I?" he said gravely, soup spilling down his unshaven chin. "Down by the mills. Swam the moat. Some Burgundian bastard nearly nailed me with an arrow, too. They keep a good watch down there."

"Information," Ash said.

Euen Huw sighed, leaning back against the flint-embedded wall and relaxing with immeasurable relief. "When we were out on that hunt? I got as far as the raghead camp, see, all ready to take out their boss, but no one was with me. Then they Carthaginian bastards all come back in a hell of a rush; I got separated from my lance, and it's taken me the rest of today to sneak back out of their camp."

Ash pictures the man with his betraying livery stuffed into a bundle, eating (and no doubt, drinking) with Visigoth freemen and slaves and mercenaries, paying close attention to camp rumor and official statements.

"Jesu Christus! Okay. First thing. Are they deploying for an attack?"

"Can't tell, boss. I had to come out through the siege-engine park, didn't see what they was doing up the north end."

Ash frowned. "Is the Faris still alive?"

"Oh, she's alive, boss, she just fell over, that's all."

" 'Fell *over*'?"

"A God-touched fit,[2] boss. Foaming! They say she's back up again now, but a bit groggy."

Unaware that she was scowling, Ash thought, *Shit! If she'd* died, *all our problems would be solved*—!

"Someone said she gave orders she was going back to Carthage, then she canceled them," Euen added.

A hope that Ash was not aware of holding shriveled up, in that second.

So much for her going back and persuading House Leofric to destroy the Stone Golem.

Ash did not say *Godfrey*? The unnerving unintelligibility in her mind, constant now for five hours, built toward unbearable tension in her.

"Her officers hate it, though." Euen's black eyes twinkled. "By what I heard, every one of their *qa'ids* is hoping he's got enough support to make him commander in her place."

"Well, isn't that a nice little morale problem for them?" Her mock sympathy was transparent enough for Euen Huw to chuckle. "That's why they haven't mounted any full assaults?"

"Maybe it'll be down to 'starve us out' now, boss." The Welshman looked thoughtfully at the scraped-clean bottom of his bowl and carefully placed his spoon in it. "Or blow up them walls. Tell you something, though, boss. I nearly didn't make it back here. Never mind dodging Mister Mander's boys, and our Agnes Dei—the ragheads are reinforcing their perimeter guards all round the city."

"They can't sew the whole place up. Too much ground to cover."

Euen Huw shrugged. "Jack Price might know more, boss. I saw him in with their spearmen. He back yet, is he?"

"Not yet." Ash shifted, noting Rickard at the tower door, and two or three lance leaders with him, obvious questions on their faces. "Get your lads to make you comfortable, Euen. That was some trick you pulled." She let him turn away before she said, mock-casually, "Good to have you back . . ."

---

[2]A better translation might be 'epileptic fit'?

"Oh yes." The Welshman lifted his arms, encompassing all the pounding rain, fire-scarred stone, and demolished houses of the besieged city. With breathtaking sarcasm, he said, "Can't think of anywhere I'd rather be, boss."

"Yeah, well." She grinned back at him. "You never were too bright."

Slow darkness fell: the rain continued to pound.

There was no word from the ducal palace.

The Faris isn't attacking. *Why?*

What have the Wild Machines done to her?

She went back at last to the company's tower, where her pages snipped her points, unshelling her from her armor, and slept a black sleep without dreams of boars. Before dawn she was up and armored again, blundering around in the candlelit darkness to the noise of thunder and sleeting rain, riding out with the next shift of men-at-arms to the walls.

An hour or so after an indistinguishable dawn came—the rain growing brighter—she and an escort rode back through the streets of Dijon. Visibility was no better in this morning light: rain bounced back up off the cobbles, everything more than twenty yards off was a mist. Heading toward the ducal palace, they got lost.

Her nameless pale bay warhorse picked its hooves delicately up out of shit. The rain that flooded the streets flooded middens, too. Ash wrinkled her nostrils at the acrid stench, guiding the horse carefully on the thin film of liquid muck that spread over the cobbles.

Jan-Jacob Clovet lifted a soaking wet arm. "Down that way, boss! I recognize that tavern."

She grinned at the crossbowman who, having been with the part of the company that stayed in Dijon, had an intimate knowledge of its inns, taverns, and ordinaries. "Lead on . . ."

She spent two hours not getting into the ducal palace to see Floria del Guiz, or the Viscount-Mayor, or Olivier de la Marche; being asked to wait among crowds of civilian and military petitioners by embarrassed Burgundian men-at-arms at whom she did not choose to shout, since they were obeying the orders of people much like herself.

But at least there *are* people here. They haven't stolen the arms, the plate, the linen, and the furniture, and legged it over to the Visigoths. Good sign?

Back at the city wall, she had to stand aside for a procession of her men coming down, two Greek Fire casualties with them, and Father Faversham treading the wet stone steps carefully in their wake.

He put his hood back from his bearded pale face, gazing down at her. "Captain, will Florian come back to the hospital soon? We need her!"

I didn't even *think* of that.

Every muscle in her body ached, the rain seeped in and made her silk arming doublet sodden, and a film of rust browned the Milanese white harness. She shook her head, giving a great *whuf*! of breath that blew the rain out of her face.

"I don't know, Father," she said. "Do what you can."

Treading up the rain-slick flint steps to the Byward Tower again, she thought, *That isn't the only reason I've got to talk to Florian! Shit, what's* happening *here?*

Toward Nones,[3] a runner brought her back from patrolling that corner of the city that includes the northwest gate and two towers of the northern wall. She stopped briefly with bowed head in the rain as one of the Burgundian priests led prayers for the feast of St. Gregory.[4] Entering the Byward Tower, she was momentarily free of the spatter of rain on armor. She climbed up the stout wooden steps to the top floor, emerging out into the water-blasted air, where Anselm and his sub-cap-

---

[3]3 P.M.

[4]Two saints by the name of Gregory have a feast day in November: Gregory *Thaumaturgus* ("the Wonderworker"), d.c. 270, and Gregory of Tours, d.c. 594. Both feast days occur on 17 November. The events of this text therefore *must* take place within the first forty-eight hours after the 'hunting of the hart'.

tains stood at the crenellations, in draggled Lion liveries turned from yellow and blue to black by the rain.

"It's easing off!" Anselm bellowed, over the noise of the wind.

"You say!"

Walking forward, she did feel the drenching hiss of the rain lessen. She stood beside Anselm and looked out from the tower. Across the empty air, she realized she was seeing several hundred yards more of broken earth, to the rain-shrouded movable wooden barriers protecting the Visigoth saps.

"What the fuck is *that*?" she demanded.

Visibility shifted. She became aware of the shrouded gray lumps of Visigoth barrack-tents, five hundred yards north of the city walls, and the glimmer of gray brilliance beyond that marked the Suzon River, emerging from the concealing rain.

Beyond Dijon's moat, beyond the no-man's-land of ravaged ground between the city and the enemy, something was new. Ash squinted. In front of the Visigoth tents and defenses—wet, raw, obviously newly turned—great banks of earthworks surrounded the north side of Dijon.

"Fucking hell . . ." she breathed.

"Fuck," Anselm said, equally blankly. "Trenches?"

Men moved, as the rain lessened. Emerging from trenches, mud-soaked and exhausted, hundreds of Visigoth serfs were collecting in the open spaces of the enemy camp. Even at this distance, she could see some men holding others up.

She could just see that they were kneeling, to be blessed.

Brightly visible, animal-headed banners and eagles bobbed between the canvas walls. Arian priests with their imaginifers[5] walking in the muddy lanes between the tents, in procession—the sound of cornicens[6] shrilled out. As she watched,

---

[5]In Roman military terms, the legionary who carries an image of the emperor. Presumably the text implies the Visigoth imaginifers carried images of the King-Caliph.

[6]Puzzling! Mentioned in the Roman army of Trajan's era, as players of curved horns—but of course this may be Visigoths using a Roman term to legitimise some ritual musicians of their own.

armed men came piling out of wet, sagging canvas shelters, to also stand and wait for a blessing. *More than one procession*! Ash realized; her eye caught by another imaginifer down toward the western bridge.

The incessant noise of rain thinned, died. Ash stared out through her steaming breath at a light gray sky, and high, moving cloud. At the expanse of river, river valley, and enemy camp, sodden under the afternoon sky.

"Frigging *hell* . . ."

Her gaze came back to the earthworks. Beside her, Anselm's sergeant snarled to keep order among the escort. Anselm gripped two merlons and leaned out between them. She turned and stared to the east, trying to take in as much of the camp outside the city as she could see.

"Son of a bitch," Robert said flatly, at her ear.

Over on the west bank of the Suzon, men were taking covers off siege machines; she could see crews winding the winches. Golem-crewed Visigoth trebuchets hurled rocks in high arcs—she could not see where they were landing; south, probably; stone splinters shrapneling the streets. It was not what she looked at.

Dozens of palisade-sheltered trenches zigzagged out to the east, and to the west. She stared out at great mazes of diggings, shored up in the wet, rank upon rank of them, stretching along as far as she could see.

Ash leaned herself out, to see as far as possible either side.

"Even if they dug for the last forty-eight hours—!" Anselm broke off. "It's impossible!"

"Disposable serf labor. They don't care how many hundreds they kill." Ash slammed her palm against the stone. "Jonvelle heard digging! It wasn't saps. It was this. *Golem-diggers*, Robert! If they used everything—"

She sees again the marble and brass of the messenger-golems in the Faris's tent: their impassive stone faces, their tireless stone hands.

"—who knows how many golems they've got! *That's* how they did this!"

There is no break in the walls of thrown-up earth, no interrupted part of the trench system that now zigzags from the

Suzon clear across these acres upon acres of land north of the city wall, maybe clear to the Ouche River in the east. And they have chained boats across the river at *this* bridge, too.

"Robert." Her voice was dry; she swallowed. "Robert, send a runner to Angelotti, and to de la Marche's *ingeniatores*. Ask how far these earthworks and trenches extend. I want to know if they do cover the east and the south, the way it looks like they do."

Anselm leaned back from staring westward, at the earthworks defending the siege-engine camp. "No breaks that I can see. Christus! They must have worked through the nights—"

Ash sees it, as if she has been there: the bent backs of serfs, digging wet dirt, illuminated by Greek Fire torches. And the stone golems that man the trebuchets and the flamethrowers and carry messages, all of them set to digging—stone hands invulnerable to pain, unmindful of any need to rest.

Surrounding the entire city.

The horns of the cornicens shrilled through the wet air, and she heard the voice of a cantador chanting.

"They've got patrols going into all those defenses." Robert Anselm lifted a plate-covered arm, pointing. "Bloody hell. Looks like most of a legion."

"Fucking Green Christ!"

Even at Neuss, there were men who could slip the siege lines in either direction: gather information, desert, spread treachery and rumor, raid the besieger's supplies, attempt assassination. There always are. Always.

This isn't a normal siege.

Nothing about this has ever been normal!

"We're going to have hell's own job getting anybody past that," Ash said. "Never mind sallying out for any kind of attack."

She turned away from the battlements.

"I'm going back to the palace. You, you, and you: with me. Roberto—we *have* to speak to Florian."

iii

AS THE RAIN eased off, a chain of men-at-arms passed rock-damaged beams and rafters up the steps from the city below, jamming the makeshift wooden struts in wherever hoardings could be reinforced. Antonio Angelotti, apparently oblivious to the stone splinters now spraying off the outside walls and the thud and boom of Visigoth cannon fire, lifted his hand in greeting, standing back from his crews running cannon up the steps to the parapet.

"I wish I were an *amir's ingeniator* again, madonna!" He wiped dripping yellow-and-blue-dyed plumes away from his archer's sallet, out of his eyes, smiling at her. "Have you seen what they've done out there? The skill—"

"Fuck your professional appreciation!"

The broad excitement in his smile did not alter as another chunk of limestone slammed into the wall ten feet below the battlements, shaking the parapet under their feet.

"Make us up more mangonels and arbalests!"[7] Ash raised her voice over the noise of the men. "Get Dickon—no—whoever's taken over as master smith—"

"Jean Bertran."

"—Bertran. I want bolts and rock-chuckers. I don't want us to run out of powder before we have to."

"I'll see to it, madonna."

"You're coming with me." She squinted a glance at the clearing afternoon sky, judged how fast the temperature fell now that the sky was clearing. "Rochester, take over here—unless it's a Visigoth attack, I don't want to hear about it! You keep Jussey under control, Tom."

---

[7]Mangonels: military catapults—crew-served weapons, of various sizes. Arbalest—a siege-size crossbow, usually frame-mounted.

"Yes, boss!"

A continuous shattering bombardment began to split and crack the air—great jagged rocks the size of a horse's carcass; iron shot that fissured the merlons of the battlements. Ash braced herself and walked down the dripping steps from the wall to street level, Robert Anselm, Angelotti, and her banner-bearer behind her. She hesitated for a moment before mounting up, gaze sweeping the demolished open space immediately behind the walls.

"Feels more dangerous than the fucking *battlements*!"

Angelotti inclined his head, while settling his sallet more firmly on his damp yellow ringlets. "Their gunners have got the elevation for this area."

"Oh, joy . . ."

She touched a spur to the bay, which skittered sideways on the wet cobbles before she hauled its head around and pointed it toward the distant, intact rooflines of the city. Giovanni Petro and ten archers—all drawn from men who had not been to Carthage—fell in around her, bowstrings under their hats in this wet, hands close to falchions and bucklers, wincing away from the sky as they strode though the rubble. The leashed mastiffs Brifault and Bonniau whined, almost under the bay's hooves.

Robert Anselm rode in silence over the sopping ground. He might have been another anonymous armored man, one of de la Marche's remaining Burgundians, but for his livery. She could read nothing of what she could see of his expression. Angelotti glanced up continually as he rode, letting his scrawny mount put her hooves where she might—calculating the ability of enemy gunners? The sky began to turn white, wet, clear; with a tinge of yellow on the southwest horizon. Perhaps two hours of light left now, before autumn's early sunset.

Florian. The Faris. Godfrey. John Price. Shit: why don't I know what's happening with any*body!*

Inquiries have brought her no information, either, about a white-haired hackbutter of middle age, in borrowed Lion Azure livery. If Guillaume Arnisout came into Dijon in yesterday's mad rush, he's keeping quiet about it.

What did I expect? Loyalty? He knew me when I was a child-whore. That isn't enough to bring anybody over to *this* side of these walls!

"Will we get in to see the doc?" Anselm pondered.

"Oh, yeah. You watch me."

The wreckage of homes and shops behind the gate is deserted—work teams of citizens and Burgundian military have cleared paths through the burned and battered buildings, pulling them down completely where necessary. Making a maze of deserted ruins. There is no wall left standing higher than a man's height.

"I want some of the lads down here. Make this lot into barricades. If the ragheads take the northwest gate, we might hold them if we've got something to anchor a line-fight on."

"Right." Anselm nodded.

She rode at a walk, not risking laming the gelding. *If they get us, they get us*. The slam and shatter of rock two hundred yards off made her flinch. Another dark object flashed through the air: high, close. She tensed, expecting a crash. No noise came.

Giovanni Petro's sharp face creased. "Fucking *hell*, boss!"

"Yeah. I know."

The escort straggled out in front and behind, automatically spacing themselves. She nodded to herself. A cold wind blew in her face. Rain still ran off the wreckage of masonry and oak beams. Shifting her weight to bring the pale gelding around the corner of a half house, she saw four of the archers clustered around something—no, *two* things, she corrected herself—on the earth. Petro straightened up as she rode forward, hauling the mastiffs back by their studded collars.

"Must have been that trebuchet strike, boss," the Italian grunted brusquely. "No missile. A man's body; come down in two places. The head's over here."

Ash said steadily, "One of ours."

Or else you wouldn't be giving it a second look.

"I think it's John Price, boss."

Signaling Anselm and Angelotti to stay on their horses, Ash swung herself out of the war-saddle and down. She side-stepped around the men picking up a severed torso and legs from shattered cobbles.

As she passed the two crossbowmen, Guilhelm and Michael, their grip slipped. A mass of reddish blue intestines plopped out of the body's cavity, into puddles. Fluid leaked away into the water.

Without looking at her, Guilhelm mumbled, "We ain't found his arms yet, boss. Might have come down someplace else."

"It's all right. Father Faversham will still give him Christian burial."

Beyond them, a woman in a hacked-off kirtle and hose knelt in the mud, her steel war-hat tilted back, crying. Her face shone red and blubbered with weeping. As she looked up at Ash's approaching clatter, Ash recognized Margaret Schmidt.

Margaret Schmidt held a severed head between her hands. It was recognizable. John Price.

"Look on the bright side," Ash said, more for Giovanni Petro's ears than those of the crossbow-woman. "At least he was dead *before* they shot him over the walls."

Petro gave a snort. "There's that. Okay, Schmidt—put the head in the blanket with the rest of him."

The young woman lifted her head. Her eyes filled again with tears. *"No!"*

"You fucking little cunt, don't you talk to *me* like—!"

"Okay." Ash signaled Petro, jerking her head. He moved reluctantly back to the work detail shifting Price's body. She was aware of her mounted officers watching. She saw how the woman's fingers were pressing into the flesh of the severed head. Dried blood patched her skin and kirtle front.

Not dead *that* long before they shot him over, then.

She called back to Anselm, "Need to check if he's been tortured." *Could he have told them anything worth hearing?* Then, more gently, turning back to Margaret Schmidt: "Put him down."

The woman's gaze went flat and cold. Anger, or fear, sharpened her features. "This is somebody's *head*, for Christ's sake!"

"I know what it is."

Full Milanese armor does not easily allow squatting. Ash went down on one knee beside the woman.

"Don't make an issue out of this. Don't make Petro have to hand you over to the provosts. Do it now."

"No—" Margaret Schmidt looked down into features beaten purple and bloody, but still recognizable as the Englishman John Price. She sounded on the verge of throwing up. "No, you don't understand. I'm holding somebody's *head*. I saw it come over us . . . I thought it was a rock . . ."

The last time Ash looked at John Price's face with any attention, a half-moon whitened it on the bluff above the Auxonne road. Weathered, drink-reddened, and full of a cheerful confidence. Nothing like this butcher's shop reject in the woman's hands.

Forcing a sardonic humor into her tone, Ash said, "If you don't like this, you'll like Geraint ab Morgan's disciplinary measures a lot less."

Tears ran over the rims of the young woman's eyes, seeped down into the dirt on her face. "What are we *doing* here? It's mad! All of you, walking around up there on the walls, just waiting for them to come again so you can fight—and now they've got us *trapped* in here—!" She met Ash's gaze. "You want to fight. I've seen it. You actually *want* to. I'm—this is somebody's head, this is a *person*!"

Ash slowly got to her feet. Behind her, Petro and the other archers had unwrapped somebody's bedroll, held it between four of them, now, with a burden dragging it down. The bottom of it was already stained and dripping.

"He was not interrogated," Angelotti called. "Only killed, madonna. Spear wound to the belly."

"Ride on!" she called. "Get over in cover!"

Angelotti spurred his horse. Anselm leaned from the saddle, said something to Guilhelm, who took the bay's reins and stood waiting as the rest of Petro's squad moved off. Ash turned back to Margaret Schmidt.

Why am I wasting time with her? One half-assed crossbow woman?

Ah, but she's still one of us . . .

Ash spoke over the noise of orders and horses' hooves.

"This isn't the first time you've seen a man die."

Margaret Schmidt looked up with an expression Ash could not place. An utter contempt, she realized. *An expression I've grown used to not seeing—at least: not directed at me.*

"I worked in a whorehouse!" the woman said bitterly. "Sometimes I'd step over someone with his throat cut, just to get into the house. That's thieving, or somebody's grudge; they didn't volunteer for it! To kill someone they don't even *know*!"

Ash felt her shoulders and back tense, steel-hard, under her steel armor, expecting the strike of another missile in these wrecked streets.

Keeping her voice from going thin with an effort, she said, "I'll take you off the company's books. But first you're going to pick up John Price's head and take it to your sergeant. Then you can do what you want."

"I'm leaving now!"

"No. You're not. First you have to do as I say."

Carefully, Margaret Schmidt put the severed head down on the wet earth in front of her. She kept a proprietary hand on the matted hair. "When I first saw you in Basle, I thought you were a man. You *are* a man. None of this matters to you, does it? You don't know what it's like in this city if you're not a soldier—you don't know what the women are afraid of—you don't think about anything except your company; if I wasn't in the company, you wouldn't waste ten minutes on me, or what I do, or don't do! That's all that matters to you! Orders!"

Ash rubbed at her face. Half her attention on the sky, she said quietly, "You're right. I don't care what you do. If it wasn't for the fact that I've seen you up on the walls, fighting in Lion livery, and you're *new* to this—you'd already be with Messire Morgan, so fast your feet wouldn't touch the ground. But as it is, you do what I say. Because if *you* don't, there's a chance someone else might not."

"And I thought Mother Astrid was a bitch and a tyrant!"

It was melodramatic, no less genuine for being so; and Ash might have smiled, in another situation. "It's easy to call someone else a tyrant. It isn't so easy to keep armed men in order."

The blond woman's breath came raggedly into her throat. "You and your damn *soldiers*! We're trapped in this city! There are families here. There are women who can't defend themselves. There are men who've spent their life keeping shop: *they* can't fight either! There are priests!"

Ash blinked.

Margaret Schmidt coughed, wiped her mouth with her hand, and then stared at it, appalled, as the head of John Price rolled over onto its side on the broken cobbles.

A bluish film covered the eyes.

Ash—with a memory of Price's capable hand steering her down into the moonlit underbrush, pointing out the Visigoth fires—felt her breath suddenly catch. *Robert was right: this is when it's too hard.*

A crow flopped down, all in ruffled black feathers, landed three yards away, and began to hop sideways toward the severed head.

Margaret Schmidt lifted her head and wailed, as unselfconscious as a small child. She might not be more than fifteen or sixteen, Ash suddenly realized.

"I want to get out of here! I wish I'd never come! I wish I'd never left the soeurs." Tears streamed down Margaret's face. "I don't understand! Why couldn't we leave before? Now we'll never get out! We'll *die* here!"

Ash's throat tightened. She could not speak. For a second, fear shifted in her gut, and her eyes stung. A quick look showed her her banner far toward the undamaged houses; even Guilhelm, holding her horse, was out of earshot.

"We won't die." *I hope*.

Tears cutting the dirt on her face, Margaret Schmidt reached out toward the severed head. She pulled her red, wet fingers back, shuddering. "You! It's *your* fault he's dead!"

Ash swatted at the crow. It bounced back, in a flutter, and landed on the churned-up cobbles, stalking from side to side, one black eye watching her.

"In the end, it is," she said, and saw the woman gape at her. "Pick the head up and bring it. *Everybody's* scared. Everybody in Dijon. We're just safer in here—your shopkeepers and farmers and priests, too."

"For how long!"

Ten minutes? Ten days? Ten months?

Ash said carefully, "We have food enough for weeks."

As the woman hung her head, Ash thought quite suddenly, *She's right. I'd say this to her—or to Rickard, if he was frightened. But I wouldn't say it to either of them if they couldn't use a sword or crossbow. I wouldn't bother. What does that make me?*

"No one *wants* to fight." Ash attempted to see the kneeling woman's face. "It's just better to be attacking someone with a close-combat weapon than it is being blown off the wall by cannon." And as Margaret Schmidt's head came up, Ash added, "Okay: not much better."

The woman coughed, making a sound that could have been both a laugh and a sob. She got up off her knees and picked up John Price's severed head, scooping it up in her ragged knee-length kirtle.

"This is better than fucking men for money." Margaret Schmidt looked up from what she held in her skirts and kicked a piece of broken brick at the crow. It hopped a few paces away. "But not *much* better. I'm sorry, lady. Captain Ash. Do you think I should leave your company?"

Dismay went through her. *Here's another one who thinks I have the answers!*

But then, why shouldn't she think that? I go to some lengths to sound as though I do. All the time.

"I'll . . . talk to Petro. If he says you're up to standard, you can stay."

Ash watched the woman hold her bunched skirt squeamishly and turn her head to look at the lance and its sergeant.

What should I tell you? You're safer with us than as a civilian, if the Goths overrun Dijon? You could just be killed, not raped and killed? Yeah, that's a much *better option.*

Why aren't you with Florian? What damn idiot ever convinced you that you wanted to be a mercenary soldier?

"Give that to Petro," Ash said. "He's not angry with you. He's angry because John Price was a mate of his."

By the time they got within three streets of the ducal palace, evening dimmed the sky. They could not move for people. The gables of the houses—still dripping—were hung with great swaths of black velvet. The insignia of the Golden Fleece[8] hung from every building. Anselm and Angelotti, in mutual and unspoken habit, rode ahead of her banner, pushing a way through the people as a man breasts the waves of the sea.

A drenched tail end of cloth, easily eight ells long, trailed across her and dripped water down her harness as she rode under it. Velvet that might—she thought—have been warm, worn against the cold. *Shit, what a waste! What do they think we're going to do this winter!*

If the Goths come over the walls today or tomorrow, there *isn't* a "this winter" as far as these people are concerned.

The pressure of bodies pushed Petro, Schmidt, and the rest of the escort against the bay's flanks: she quietened it, moving on. Her gaze went over the mass of hats and shoulders as she passed through the people jammed between buildings here. Ahead, a flurry of men in black—dozens of them!—read from lists and shoved people bodily this way and that.

Anselm leaned down from the saddle to accost one. The man pushed past him, stared up at the Lion Affronté, made a mark on his scroll, and called up to Ash: "After the Sieur de la Marche! Remember that, demoiselle!"

"Bloody cheek." Robert Anselm let Orgueil drop back a stride, to ride beside her. "What now? We can't get through this."

Torch-fire flickered, growing stronger as the wet light failed. Down in the street, it was already dark; only the sky above the tilting rooftops held some pale brightness. Approaching the edge of the crowd at the road junction, Ash saw black-robed torchbearers—holding people back.

She squinted into the dusk. "We need to see Florian. More than these damn Burgundians do!"

Between the lines of fire, chaplains and equerries, in black cloth, cleared a way from the direction of the ducal palace, holding the center of the road clear. Tears streamed down the faces of people close by. Ash glanced the other way down the street—*to the cathedral*? she thought, trying dimly to call

[8]An order of chivalry founded by Duke Philip of Burgundy.

back memories of the summer, and riding there with John de Vere and Godfrey.

Nothing but a mass of packed heads, hats pulled off to show respect, a crowd everywhere so thick that she abandoned any idea of riding through it to the palace now, or sending a messenger on foot.

"It's the funeral!" she realized. "This is Charles's funeral, now. They're burying the Duke."

Anselm appeared singularly unimpressed. "So—what next?"

"Where have they given us precedence?" She tapped her gauntlet on the pommel of the saddle. "After de la Marche—he was Charles's champion. After the noblemen; before the rest of the men-at-arms. Does that sound good to you, Robert?"

"Oh yeah. Sounds like they might *not* do what the Faris did to her Frankish mercenaries—stick 'em out in front, get 'em chewed up. *If* we're still signed up with Burgundy."

Antonio Angelotti shifted his chestnut mount back, flicking his head as water dripped down from the gabled roofs above him. The torchlight made chiaroscuro of his icon-face under the sallet's silver brilliance.

"Our surgeon will be at the funeral if she's Duchess now, madonna."

"Oh, you worked that one out, too?" Ash smiled, shakily. "Enough messing about, right? They want to bury Charles—fine. I'm sure he'd rather they were keeping Dijon out of Visigoth hands. They want to crown *Florian*, for fuck's sake? Also fine—but they'd better bloody get on with it. We have to plan now. Plan what we can do."

"If there is to be a coronation, following this . . ." Angelotti shrugged.

"We need," Ash said, "to know who's really in charge, now. Because we've got decisions to make. This siege only needs the lightest shove, and it's all over. And . . . whatever else happens, Florian has to stay alive."

The last light faded, down in the narrow streets. Clergy and citizens, court servants and doctors and secretaries and sergeants at arms came past; and Charles's sovereign-bailiffs and *maîtres de requêtes* and *procureurs-générals*, their liveries and black garments illuminated by torchlight. The remaining noblemen—those few who are not with the army in the north or rotting outside Auxonne—walked in long black robes, bearing a pall of gold. It became dark, and the pitch torches made the street pungent. Too many torches surrounded it: Ash could not look into the flames and see the coffin when it passed. Dazzled, she recognized one of the abbots walking in its wake, and two of Charles's bastard brothers; and then glimpsed, at the back of their personal attendants, red-and-blue livery—de la Marche, he and all his noble companions riding horses in black cloth caparisons.

Ash spurred the gelding and rode, determinedly, in de la Marche's wake, as the funeral procession moved through the streets of Dijon, followed the black-draped, lead coffin into the cathedral.[9] She took up a place standing by a pillar, not far behind the Burgundian nobility. Every few minutes, as unobtrusively as possible, de la Marche's military aides approached and whispered to him: messages, she guessed, from the wall. Petro, stationed by the door, filtered news from her own runners: the northwest, at least, still unassaulted.

She sweated through chants and anthems. The coffin stood with embalmed heart, and embalmed entrails, each in its own lead casket on top of it, on a bier draped to the ground in black velvet, with four great candles at the corners.

The chants lasted past Vespers,[10] past Compline.[11] She sweated through the requiem mass, which began at midnight in the nave that was hung with black cloth. Fourteen hundred candles burned, their beeswax sweetness stifling in the enclosed air—at the sides of the nave, men were using bollock-dagger hilts to punch holes in the glass of the ogee windows, and let out the unbearable heat.

Twice, she slept kneeling. Once, Anselm's tactful hand on her pauldron shook her awake, and she nodded at him, and

---

[9]In fact, Charles the Bold had no such formal obsequies after the battle of Nancy. This funeral seems more like the one accorded his father, Philip the Good, in 1467, nine years earlier.

[10]6 P.M.

[11]9 P.M.

swallowed with a stale mouth, helped when Angelotti covertly passed her a costrel of wine. The second time, as another mass began, she felt herself slide off into unconsciousness, without any ability to stop herself.

She woke, leaning against Angelotti, still strapped into metal plates, with every muscle and bone in her body hurting.

"Green Christ!" she muttered under her breath.

That was drowned by the swelling anthem from the choir that had woken her, sound shredding the last remnants of sleep and the candle-hot air. Robed men moved in ritual patterns. Beside her, Anselm got to his feet in respect and reached down and hauled her upright. Numbness in her knees and legs gave way to searing pain.

The lead coffin of the Grand Duke of the West passed down the nave: Charles called the Bold, Philip's son, John's grandson; heir of Burgundy and Arles; being conveyed down into the crypt by four green-robed bishops and twenty-two abbots.

A pale light shone at the windows that was not candlelight. Dawn: pale, clear, and the bells for Prime ringing out of double spires across the city, as the choir in the great cathedral fell into final silence.

Ash covertly flexed her bad knee, shifted her leg, thought *Green Christ, never sleep in armor in church!* and glanced behind to see where her page with her helmet was.

"Madonna!" Angelotti pointed down the nave. She turned her head, staring.

Beside her, Anselm frowned, looking around uncertainly.

In the dimness of dawn and the few unextinguished candles, a tall, slender woman came down between the high, soaring multiple pillars of the cathedral. Throngs of officials and courtiers trod at her heels. She was not young—not far from her thirtieth year, perhaps—but still beautiful in the way that court women are. The black brocade and velvet of her robes brightened the green of her eyes, the gold of her hair. Looking at the fair-skinned face under the finest of linen veils—a little freckled across the cheekbones, but clean—Ash thought *Doesn't that woman there look like my husband, Fernando?* before she hitched air halfway through a breath, stared, heard Anselm swear, and realized *That's Floria!*

Her feet were moving her before she properly realized it. Neither awake nor alert yet, Ash stepped out in front of the procession. *I planned this last night. What the fuck did I think I was going to say!*

"Florian! Never mind all this." Ash gestured, cannon and couter scraping as she waved her arm to take in all the cathedral, the court. "I'm calling an officer meeting. *Now*. We can't wait any longer!"

Green eyes and stark fair brows stared out at her from under a padded headdress and translucent veil. A momentary, unexpected embarrassment made her stop speaking. So difficult, looking at this woman, to picture the long-legged, dirty-faced surgeon who gets drunk with the baggage-train women, and who squints through a hangover to sew up wounds with threaded gut and reasonably steady hand.

In a voice equally awkward, Floria del Guiz muttered, "Yes. You're right . . ." and stared around at the grief-stricken crowds, as if at a loss.

Behind her, a green-robed abbot murmured, "Your Grace, not here!"

The noise of footsteps made the nave loud and murmurous. Automatically, in the presence of so many clergy, and still not recovered from sleeplessness or exertion, Ash touched her breastplate over her heart.

"So." She stared at Florian. "Are you Duchess? Is it anything more than being the nobles' puppet? We need to talk about keeping you alive!"

Florian, in woman's clothing, stared back, saying nothing.

Quiet in Ash's mind as snowfall, Godfrey Maximillian's voice whispered, perfectly clearly:

—Child?

IV

ASH CAUGHT AT Robert Anselm's shoulder. Morning, the eighteenth of November—she is still, at some deep level, in shock. Ignoring Florian's rapid words to the nobles around her, she is conscious only of a memory of influence, pressure, force.

"Godfrey!"

Some official leaned over Florian's shoulder, whispering urgently.

"Perimeter defense!" Ash was briefly aware of Petro and his archers surrounding her, facing outward, not drawing weapons in a holy place, but ready. She put her hands over her face and whispered into her cold, steel gauntlets:

"Godfrey—is that really you?"

—Ash, little one . . .

This is nothing like the previous strength of his voice in her mind. This is as quiet as wind through bare branches, as soft as snow falling onto other snow. Momentarily, a scent comes to her—resinous pine needles; the raw, rich, dungy smell of boar. She sees no vision in her mind.

What's happened to you!

With that same internal sense that she is performing some action, she *listens*. As she has always listened, when she has called the voice of the Lion, the Stone Golem, the *machina rei militaris*.

—Ash.

"Godfrey?" She hesitated; asked again. "Godfrey?"

—Weak beyond measuring, and a little broken, child, but, yes. Me.

"Green Christ, Godfrey, I thought I'd lost you!"

—You heard silence, not absence.

"That's . . . I couldn't tell!" She shook her head, aware that men surrounded her, her own and others; and that Florian was giving loud, clear instructions. She did not know what the woman said.

—Now, you hear me . . . And you fear, too, that you will hear the voices of God's Fallen.

"I don't think the Wild Machines are anything to do with God!"

—Everything that comes, comes to us by God's grace.

So weak—as if he's far from her, farther than can be measured in distance. The tiles under her slick-soled boots are granular with dawnlight. She glimpsed them sparkle, between her steel-armored fingers.

There is a hand under each arm: there are men walking: there is someone—Florian—ahead of her, leading the way. To where?

Outside, the new, cold, damp air pricks at her covered face.

"Can you hear the Wild Machines?" Ash demanded. "I heard them after the hart was hunted, and then— Are they there? Godfrey, *are they*!"

—I have been hurt, and recovering. There was an immanence: a great storm began to break, then nothing. Then confusion. And now there is you, child. I heard you calling to me.

"Yes, I . . . called."

Godfrey's voice, that is the *machina rei militaris*, says:

—I heard you weeping.

She woke herself with soundless weeping, two nights before; voiceless enough that it disturbed neither Rickard nor any of the pages. Woke, and put it out of her mind. Sometimes, on campaign, it happens.

She stumbled, hands dropping from her face, had a momentary glimpse of freezing early morning outside of the cathedral, de la Marche's armed ducal household escort, the great boxy carriage of the Duchess; and then she is lost, again, in interior listening.

"Are they still there?" she insisted. "The Wild Machines, Godfrey! *Are they still there?*"

—I hear nothing now. But nor did I hear their passing, child. I have not heard them die.

Silence, but not absence.

"We'd *know*, would we, if they were gone? Or—damaged?"

Suddenly intense, Ash uncovered her face, breathing cold air, eyes watering at the approaching bright white walls of the ducal palace. Anselm and Angelotti still had a hand under each mailed armpit. She staggered as she walked. Pages followed with the horses. Now the sky has cleared, it is becoming very cold.

"No. How could I know? Why would I? Shit, that would be *too* easy . . ."

—All I hear is their silence.

The dispersing funeral crowds in the Dijon streets passed unnoticed. So did the muttering of her men superstitiously watching their commander talk to her voice—*but not*, she reflects, *the voice they are used to thinking of—"Saint" Godfrey, good grief!* She ignored everything, ignored Anselm and Angelotti half-carrying her into the palace between them, forcing every part of her strength into the weak contact.

"They did try to do their miracle. I felt it, when the Duke died. They tried to trigger the Faris. It wasn't even aimed at me, and I felt it!" A bare awareness of steps intruded itself: she stumbled up them. "And I heard their . . . anger . . . *after* the hunt ended. If they're not damaged, not destroyed—shit, for all I know, they can do that again anytime the Duchess dies!"

—Duchess?

No mistaking the very human bewilderment in her shared soul, Godfrey to the life.

—Margaret of York is Duchess, now?

"Oh, her? Hell, no. She's even missed her husband's funeral!"

Ash sounded sardonic, even to herself. The edge of a stool banged into the back of her greaves. She sat, automatically. "I was hoping she'd turn up. With about ten thousand armed men, for choice, and raise the siege! No, Widow Margaret's still somewhere in the north. Florian's the Duchess."

—Florian!

Somewhere close, there is a familiar, exasperated snort.

"Godfrey, have you heard the Faris since the hunt—is she sick? Is she sane?"

—*She lives, and is as she was before.*—The ghost of an old amusement, as if Godfrey Maximillian is forgetting what it is like to laugh.—*She will not speak to the* machina rei militaris.

"Does she try to speak to the Wild Machines?"

—*No. All the great Devils are silent . . . I have been shocked, deaf, dumb . . . How long?*

Ash, aware now that she sits in a high tapestried chamber, that there are Burgundians speaking at high volume, that the woman who looks like Florian appears to be overriding them, said, "Forty-eight hours? Maybe an hour or two less?"

—*I do not know what their silence may mean.*

The voice in her head did not fade; it suddenly became silent, as if weakness drained it away. She still had a sense of him, something priestly, Saint Godfrey, infusing the sacral parts of her mind.

If I could make *them hear me—the Wild Machines . . . Shit: not yet: I have to think!*

She blinked her streaming eyes, and realized that she was looking out of the windows of the Tour Philippe le Bon, Burgundy's quarreling courtiers and military men filling the room with noise behind her.

Morning in the same building, if not the same room, in which she last saw Charles of Burgundy. This lower chamber has the same great carved limestone hearth at the end, fire burning fiercely against the early bitter cold. The same blond floorboards, and white-plastered walls covered with tapestries. But an oak throne stands upon a dais in the place where his bed is, in the room above.

A sudden pang went through her, which had not been there all the night they were burying him with masses and prayer. *Shit:* another *one dead.*

Fuck Carthage!

Anger brought her to herself, brought some respite from the cold silence in her head. *It isn't good business to get involved.* Heat from the blazing hearth intruded, made her conscious of her silk doublet and woolen hose that have been rain-saturated and dried again on her in sleep, of armor whose bright surface is glazed thick with rust, of the immense ache and cramps of her body.

"You all right?" Robert Anselm said, standing over her.

"Same old same old. I'll live. Where's Florian?" She reached up, caught his armored forearm, and pulled herself to her feet. The room tilted. "Shit."

"Food." Anselm strode off back into the chamber.

The clear, brilliant cold light stung her gritty eyes. She is looking out from the window of the Tour Philippe le Bon. Up past the towers that her company occupies, dawn shows her iron-walled wagons axle-deep in mud, wheeled into place in the Visigoth camp to protect Greek Fire throwers covering the approach to the northwest gate.

"Eat that."

Anselm's hand shoved a torn crust of bread into her hand. The smell of it brought saliva into her mouth and a great rumble from her gut. She ripped the crust with her teeth, and said as she chewed, "Thanks."

"*You* ain't got the fucking sense." A grin. "Fuck me, what a bunch of wankers. 'Scuse me while I sort this out."

He left her side, moving back into the crush of courtiers. A raw female voice snapped Ash's head around:

"A *petit conseil*[12] first! Messire de la Marche. Messire Ternant. Bishop John. Captain Ash. The rest later! Everyone else *out*!"

Florian: her exact tone when yelling at some deacon late in bringing her linen bandages and gut. Straightening up, the tall woman in black robes stalked away from the long table, across the room. Men stood back from her; bowed as she passed.

One man's voice snapped, "I protest!"

Ash recognized the Viscount-Mayor, Richard Follo; thought *But he has a point, there should be some merchant representative,* and then *How much of a "Duchess" can Florian be!*

One of de la Marche's aides and two of his captains began

---

[12] 'Little/small council'.

moving people toward the chamber door, in the way that armored men can move an unarmed crowd without ever having to draw sword. A whole slew of officers, sergeants at arms, servants, household retainers, equerries, surgeons, secretaries, ex-tutors, minor captains, and financial administrators were rapidly ushered out.

"Ash—" Floria del Guiz suddenly glanced across the emptying floor and shook her head at three Burgundian equerries who were attempting—with no success—to escort a suddenly monoglot Robert Anselm and Antonio Angelotti out of the chamber. At her signal, the equerries in ducal livery bowed and backed out of the room. None of them looked at Olivier de la Marche or Philippe Ternant first, for confirmation of the order.

That's—interesting.

A pantler bowed his way past Florian, and servers with dazzling white linen for the oak table followed, and a dozen men with silver dishes. Floria del Guiz turned and strode the remaining few steps toward Ash, with a stride not used to wearing a robe and underrobe long at the front. Her slippered toe caught the fur-trimmed hem of the black velvet overrobe. She stumbled, her feet tangled in glorious cloth.

"Watch it!" Ash reached out, grabbing very solid weight, stopping Floria from falling. She stared into the so-close, so-familiar, face. She realized that she smelled no wine on the woman's breath.

"Merde!" Florian swore in a whisper. Ash saw her gaze flinch away from the mass of men around them.

Ash let go of the tall woman's arms. Florian's tight sleeve snagged the edges of her gauntlet plates as the woman got her balance. Florian reached down to shake out her skirts, exposing an underdress of silver brocade all sewn with sapphires and diamonds and silver thread, and tugged at the high belt, settling it under her bustline. The high-waisted black velvet snugged tight over her shoulders, arms, and torso. Under it, brocade laced at the front in a vee over a shift of so fine a linen it was translucent to the pink flesh of her breasts beneath. As a surgeon, Floria del Guiz stooped; as a woman in court mourning, she stood very tall and very straight indeed.

"Christus Viridianus, why couldn't I look like that in my wedding dress?" Ash said wryly. "And you're telling me Margaret Schmidt turned you down?"

The flash of a glance from Florian's eyes made Ash think *That was overhearty. Jesus. What do I say to her?* Something about Florian standing in front of her in women's dress unsettled her. *Maybe seeing her with Margaret Schmidt wasn't so odd when she looked like a man.*

As if what Ash had said had not been spoken, Florian demanded, "In the cathedral—is Boss hearing voices again?"

"I heard Godfrey. Florian, I think he's been—hurt, somehow. As for the Wild Machines . . . nothing yet: not a fucking word."

"Why not?"

"Yeah, like I'd know. Godfrey doesn't think they're dead—if that's the term. Maybe they're damaged. You're Duchess. Why don't *you* tell *me*!"

Floria snorted, as familiar as if she had still been surgeon, still been in a sagging, blood-boltered tent back of some field of battle, digging steel out of meat.

"Christ, Ash! If *I* knew, you'd know! Being 'Duchess' doesn't help me with that."

They had made her wash, Ash realized; no dried blood under her fingernails.

"We have to talk, 'Duchess.' " Ash glanced up at the tall woman—Florian's fair hair scraped back under her horned headdress to expose a broad white brow, left hand now automatically holding up the front of her overgown, folds of velvet falling gracefully down.

Difficult to believe she's a surgeon; you'd swear she'd stayed a noblewoman all her life.

Ash realized the woman was perfectly conscious of how many people were watching her—watching both of them, now.

Automatically turning her back toward the crowd to conceal her expression, she caught Florian's reflection in the chill, leaded window glass. A long-featured woman in court splendor, Valois jewelry bright at her neck and wrists and veiled headdress, only the dark marks in her eye sockets hinting at confusion or exhaustion. And beside her, crop-haired, in field-filthy plate, a woman with scarred cheeks and stunned eyes.

"Give the word," Ash said abruptly. "I'll get you out of here. I don't know how, but I will."

"You *don't* know how." The woman gave her a sardonic grin that was all Florian, all surgeon, a grin familiar from a hundred months under canvas in the field.

"There's no military problem that hasn't got a solution!" Ash stopped. "Except the one that kills you, of course . . ."

"Oh, of *course*. The Wild Machines," Florian began, and a woman crossed the emptying room and stepped between Ash and her surgeon, narrow eyes tight with fury, interrupting without any hesitation.

It took Ash a second to recognize Jeanne Châlon, and another second to realize she herself was looking around for men-at-arms to have the woman removed.

Jeanne Châlon said shrilly, "I have ordered you funeral bake-meats—they brought me two saddles of mutton, a boiled capon, tripe, chitterlings, and three partridges—it is *nothing* fit for a Valois Duchess! Tell them we must be served more, and more fitting food!"

Ash finally caught Roberto's eye, jerked her head. Floria said nothing, giving her aunt a little push toward the chamber door.

"The lady is right!" Olivier de la Marche's baritone cut through the chamber. "Bring better food for the Duchess." He gestured to the servants.

Ash caught a look close to triumph as the other woman walked away.

"You let her in here?"

"She's been kind to me. The last two days. She's the only family I have."

"No," Ash said, reflexively, as to any member of the Lion Azure, "she isn't."

"I wish this was like organizing the surgeon's tent, Ash. In the tent, I know what I'm *doing*. Here, I have no idea what I'm doing. I just know what I *am*."

The servants and pages had almost finished setting the table: the odor of wine sauce brought water into Ash's mouth. Anselm arrived, heavy tread making the boards creak, Angelotti at his armored shoulder. Both men looked at the surgeon with deliberately blank faces.

Moving rapidly, Floria stepped up onto the dais, laying a hand on the carved oak arm of the ducal throne. "I *know* what I am. I *know* what I do."

Standing over the bleeding body of the hart, hearing her surgeon say *I maintain the real*: all this is startlingly clear to Ash. Not to these two of her officers—nor are they Burgundian.

" 'Ow?" Robert Anselm demanded.

"I don't know *how* I do it, or why!" Exasperated, Florian met his gaze. "It really doesn't matter what you call it! Except that it does. They call it 'being Duchess' here. *They* believe I'm their Duchess. Ash, if we leave, this town falls." She stopped, corrected herself. "If *I* leave."

"Are you sure?" Antonio Angelotti asked.

Florian kept her gaze fixed on Ash. "Do I have to tell *you* about morale?" Her fingers tightened on the arm of the throne. "I don't want this. Look at it! Talk about *Welcome to the hot seat*[13] . . ."

The surgeon lifted her head, gazing down the chamber. Ash saw her look at the old chamberlain-counselor, at de la Marche, at a bishop, at the departing servers.

"If I didn't know what I am, I'd run. You know me, Ash. I might just run anyway."

"Yeah. You might. If only into a bottle."

Florian took her hand away from the ducal throne and the waxed oak that she had been stroking with one clean thumb. She stepped down from the dais again, standing between Anselm and Angelotti. It was clear to Ash that they would not be approached, not while the surgeon made her desire for pri-

---

[13]In the text's original mediaeval Latin: 'the siege perilous'.

vacy apparent; that, if anything, broke the surface tension of her sleepless exhaustion, made her think again *This place is on borrowed time—one of my company's tied here—what do I do?*

Ash looked desperately around the long bright chamber, at the still-clustering men in rich robes and armor, at the food set out on the sun-bleached cloth.

"When I made the hart . . ." Florian looked down at her scrubbed hands, as if she expected to find them bloody. "It hurt Godfrey."

Ash met her gaze, seeing something there that might have been self-blame. "He's recovering, I think."

"So maybe whatever happened damaged the Wild Machines. Destroyed them."

"Maybe. But I wouldn't count on it. I heard them after the hart was dead."

Robert Anselm grunted. "If we're very, *very* lucky, they were damaged . . ."

Picking up his words, Angelotti completed: ". . . if what happened when the hunt aborted their miracle *hurt* them, madonna. So: if they *are* damaged . . . they might recover tomorrow. Or it might take fifty years. Or we might be fortunate: it might never happen."

Florian looked questioningly at her. Ash shook her head.

"Godfrey says he hears 'silence, not absence.' I can't make myself believe they're gone. They might not even be hurt. Who knows why they're silent? The only way we can be safe is to act as if I'll hear them again tomorrow."

A bare forty-eight hours of funeral, lack of sleep, and the sheer impact of the Burgundian court; all this made Florian seem subdued. She drew in a breath, twisting the bezels of the gold rings on her fingers, and looked up at Ash. Her expression was the same as it had been in the wildwood, soaked in hart's blood, staggered by the certainty of her knowledge.

"Would we have heard," she said, "if the sun had come up on the other side of the Burgundian border, in the past two days? Beyond Auxonne?"

"Oh, *shit*." Anselm's disgusted bellow made the remaining Burgundian noblemen startle and shift back toward the hearth end of the chamber.

"Yeah, you got it. *Euen*. Shit! Euen Huw," Ash explained to Florian. "He was out in their camp. He'd have brought the rumor back in with him. Something like that would be through the raghead camp inside fifteen minutes!"

Ash shrugged. The steel of her armor squealed, rust scraping off with the movement.

"I'm being dumb. If *that* had happened, the Goths wouldn't care about being overheard by me, they'd use the Stone Golem to tell the Faris! And Godfrey would have told me. If there was sun over Christendom, now, we'd know. It's dark. And if it's dark, the Wild Machines are still with us."

"Either that, and they're silent," Florian said, "or the darkness is permanent without them."

"Better hope not," Ash said grimly. "Or next year's going to be hell."

"So nothing's changed. Whatever you're not hearing from the Wild Machines."

"Then why am I not hearing it!"

Angelotti ticked off words on his powder black fingers with surprising, delicate grace: "No Duke. Perhaps a Duchess. Still dark. No assault on the walls. No threats from the *Ferae Natura Machinae*. If there is a pattern, madonna, I can't see it."

Ash ignored the crowd and clatter behind her.

"They may have reasons for silence. They might be hiding damage. How can we know? It's what I really hate," she said. "Making decisions, on not enough information. But there's never enough information. And you have to make the decisions anyway."

She took a breath.

"We need to ensure Florian's safety. That comes first. Burgundy or no bloody Burgundy, Duchess or no Duchess, Florian is what's stopping the Wild Machines—" She broke off. "Unless there *is* no need, anymore—"

Florian smoothed her robe down, with long-fingered, spotless hands. The sheer linen of her veil concealed nothing of her expression, only misted it, gave it paradoxical clarity.

"Out in the desert," she said.

"What?"

"You forced them to talk to you. You told me."

Angelotti nodded. Robert Anselm's scowl, unconscious, was almost a snarl.

"So do that now," Florian said. "Find out. I need to know. Am I doing what Charles did? Am I the obstacle? Am I maintaining the real *against* anything?"

"When I tried it before the hunt—they'd learned to shut me out of their knowledge." Ash hesitated. "But they still *spoke* to me."

If I think about it, I won't do it.

There is a brief second of memory in her mind: of the Lord-*Amir* Leofric's face when she drew the words of the *machina rei militaris* into her soul, and of the bitter chill sand outside Carthage as she hits it, facedown, the first time that she did more than listen to the Wild Machines. When she wrenched knowledge from them, all in a heartbeat.

Inside herself, she prepares. It is more than passive, more than emptying herself for voices to come; she makes herself a void that pulls, that compels itself to be filled.

Closes her eyes, shuts out the tower room, Florian, Roberto, Angeli, directs her speech beyond and through the *machina rei militaris*, hundreds of leagues away, in Carthage:

"Come on, you motherfuckers . . ."

And *listens*.

A faint sound, in the shared solitude of her soul; no more than an unwilling whisper, overlaid by Godfrey's anguish. A voice, woven of many voices, heard now for the first time since the hart lay bloody on the turf in front of her:

"PLAN WHILE YOU CAN, LITTLE THING OF EARTH. WE ARE NOT YET CAST DOWN."

The chamber wall felt bitter cold, cooling her scarred cheek where she leaned against the masonry.

"Let me take that, boss."

Shifting, she realized Rickard stood beside her, prizing her sallet out of her hands. She let him take it. With a sigh, she straightened, and let him unspring the pins on her pauldrons, and remove the rust-starred shoulder defenses. He tucked the plates under his arm. Awkwardly, he unbuckled her belt and took sword and scabbard, staring at her anxiously.

"Boss . . ."

She turned her back on him, moving with greater ease. The window's reflection showed her the chamber, Anselm somberly speaking to the rest of the Lion escort as they left, Antonio Angelotti with one beautiful hand resting on Florian's arm.

I'd forgotten. Even after three days, I'd forgotten. How—their voices feel, speaking to me.

She reaches out. When she touches her fingers to the glass, it is bitter cold through the linen of her gauntlets.

From here, in this morning light, she sees Dijon's heterogeneous walls and towers from high inside the city. White-plastered masonry here, missile-smashed brick there; the blue-gray flint of a tower by the mills still pouring black smoke into the air. The city below her is a mass of red-tiled roofs. South, between the double spires of a hundred churches, she can see the Suzon snaking away in a white gleam, between the wooded, gray limestone hills. The air is empty of birds. Distant church bells ring.

She can see nowhere—the banks of the western river, the ground beyond the moat, the road running up toward the western bridge—that is not blocked by newly turned earth. The Visigoth's ditches and banks, so small from up here, the pavises and mantlets set up along them barely visible. Distant cornicens sound in the enemy camp.

It is as if there is a precipice now, a verge in her mind, beyond which is a drop more vertiginous than this one from the tower. And in that depth, the presence of voices.

Robert Anselm, his voice bluff with shock and mordant humor, said, "We'll take it there's no fucking *good* news, right?"

That's the first time he's seen me speak to the Wild Machines.

Shit, Robert, I wish you'd come to Carthage!

"You got *that* right . . ."

What she seeks for is the welcome numbness of action, her old ability to cut off self from feeling. The closest she can come is to maintain an interest in watching her hands, which are shaking.

"Madonna." Angelotti reached out and took her arm, drawing her with surprising strength into a walk. She stumbled across the oak boards, past the hearth, caught her balance as the Italian master gunner shoved her into one of the chairs lining the long table—and stepped back, gracefully, to give Florian his hand and seat the Duchess of Burgundy almost as swiftly.

"Eat," he said. "And drink—madonna Florian, there must be wine?"

With shaking hands, Ash unbuckled her gauntlets, dropped them heavily onto the linen cloth, and reached for one of the gold, ruby-studded goblets.

She was aware of Burgundians seating themselves—few now: the chamber very empty—and servers and pantlers complaining about lack of ceremony; but all she wanted was the thick sting of wine on her tongue. When served meats, she took the plate much as she would have done in camp, and did not realize until whole minutes later that she was stabbing up mutton not with her eating knife, but with her bollock dagger.

Ah, that's mercenaries for you . . .

The taste of onions, and ortolan,[14] and pease pottage in her mouth; their weight in her stomach; all this and she began to be aware of herself, her surroundings, the sheer solid reality of linen, table, armor, doublet, plate. She belched.

They can't reach me. No more than they could when I spoke to them before the hunt. All they can do is speak.

"I don't know if they're damaged or not." She spoke to Florian through a mouthful of frumenty,[15] spattering the linen. "How would I tell? But they're there."

"Oh God."

Not like Florian to sound devout, Ash observed, and put down her spoon, and wiped her bare finger around the all-but-

[14]The garden bunting: a bird known as a table delicacy.
[15]Wheat boiled in milk, with cinnamon and sugar.

empty bowl, and sucked on the last sweetness as she looked at Floria del Guiz.

Florian said, "That makes me Charles Valois."

Ash, instantly grimly cheerful, said, "Look on the bright side. Now there's four hundred of us determined you're going to stay alive." She glanced down the table at Olivier de la Marche. "Make that the better part of two and a half thousand."

"It isn't a joke!"

"Don't think about it." Ash softened her voice. "Don't think about it. Think about staying alive. That's normal: everybody wants to do that. Don't think about what happens if you die—"

"The Faris does her miracle. The Wild Machines force her." Florian spoke in a strained undertone. "Burgundy's a wasteland. And then so is everything—"

"*Don't* think about it."

Ash closed her dirty hand over Florian's, tightening her grip until she knew she must be hurting the surgeon.

"Don't think about it," Ash repeated. "You can't afford to. Ask Roberto. Ask Angeli. If you think about what depends on you, yourself, you'd never be a commander, never make yourself crucial to any assault. Just assume you'll stay alive, Florian. Assume that we don't care *what* we have to do to keep you that way."

In Robert's growling agreement there is only loyalty; Angelotti's swift glance has more in it of awareness, of Carthage—and of Burgundy, too, as his blond curly head turns, briefly looking at Olivier de la Marche, at Philippe Ternant, and the bishop.

"I wonder if you have to stay in Burgundy?" Ash speculated. "I wonder if we have to be in this siege?"

Floria lowered her voice. "Ash, like it or not, I *am* who they're going to call Duchess now."

"Yeah," Ash said, "I know. I don't see a way out of that."

This is my damn surgeon we're talking about here!

She felt Florian's hand shift in hers, and released it. Red marks imprinted the skin. The woman took her hand back, flexing her fingers in a gesture that somehow had nothing of the feminine about it.

Florian's gaze went to the great fire in the hearth, tended by the palace servants. "Jesus, Ash, I'm not a Duchess!"

"Say that again," Robert Anselm mumbled, grinning, and showing threads of beef caught in his yellowing teeth. "Barely a sawbones!"

Florian's tone approached more normality than Ash had heard from her since the cathedral:

"Fuck you, Anselm!"

"Pleasure. Thought you weren't that way inclined?"

"I get more pussy than you do, you English poof! Always have."

"He's not a poof, madonna." Angelotti slid his hand under Anselm's tassets. "Worse luck!"

Robert Anselm clenched his fist, made as if to slam his armored elbow into the gunner, and then sat back on his chair. "Go on, you little wop cocksucker. Only time you're going to feel a *real* prick!"

Florian, bright-eyed, and putting her elbows on the table, remarked, "I don't know—he *is* a real prick, why shouldn't he feel like one?"

Ash gaped, cringed, and stared frozen-faced down the table at the Burgundian nobility, her palms wet with sweat.

They stared back, faces bewildered.

Ash managed to show her teeth in a desperate smile.

Olivier de la Marche inclined his head in bemused courtesy.

Hang on. Her smile remained fixed. She replayed the quick-fire exchange in her head. *Roberto started that one in English—Kentish English at that—and she followed him—thank Christ!*

Without change of expression, she remarked through her teeth, "I can't take you bastards anywhere!"

"Of course you can." Florian, her shoulder muscles relaxed, reached out and touched her bare fist to Anselm's arm, Angelotti's breastplate. "Twice. The second time to apologize."

Ash saw their relaxation, the unspoken bond between them. Surgeon, gunner, and commander: all as it might have been in the company's tents, anytime these five years. But now, seen for the first time after Florian's forty-eight hours of separation.

Fuck, we needed that. But everything's still changing.

She grabbed for the goblet and held it up to be filled. Wine's steadying warmth burned down her gullet. "Okay! Okay, we need to plan what we're doing. Florian, you get any of the messages I sent up to the palace yesterday?"

"Eventually." Florian spoke with a kind of contained amusement that could hide any embarrassment or panic that a surgeon-turned-Duchess might be feeling. "When they'd come through a dozen secretaries."

"Shit, what a way to run a duchy!"

"Think yourself lucky. De la Marche says most of the lawyers went north with Margaret. Before Auxonne."

Ash leaned on the table. "You haven't left the Lion Azure. Not yet. Not until you tell me you have."

Florian's expression was momentarily unreadable.

"We need to know your status. What 'duchess' really means—what sort of Duchess does Olivier de la Marche think you are? If there's one person in this city who holds command of the Burgundian military forces right now, it's him, not you."

Florian glanced toward Olivier de la Marche. Ash saw him interpret that as a summons, abandon his place. He walked up toward the head of the table. She thought she saw a slight unsureness as he looked at Floria, but de la Marche's lined face broke into a beam, seeing Ash.

"Jeez, he ought to like his Duchess, but I didn't know *I* was that popular . . ."

Florian's face, under the sheerness of the veil, clearly showed exasperation. "Boss! You know what we've—what the company's been doing, these last two days. And you. Up on the walls. Backward and forward across the no-man's-land behind the northwest gate. Out there getting shot at."

"Oh, yeah, I was forgetting," Ash said dryly. "Not that we

have a choice! Hell, even Jussey and Jonville have been giving us good backup . . ."

Olivier de la March, coming up to the Duchess, bowed stiffly to her. He kept his gaze on Ash. "How could they not?"

It took her a moment to realize that it was a rhetorical question spoken with transparent honesty. She looked questioningly at him.

"You bear the sword that shed the Hart's Blood," Olivier de la Marche said. "Every man in Dijon knows that."

" 'Bear the sword'—" Ash broke off.

"I did use your sword." Florian's closed lips moved; she might have been trying to smother a wild grin.

"You nicked it off me because you didn't have one, and it was the only one to hand!" Ash swung her gaze back to de la Marche. "Green Christ! So she used my sword. So what? She might as well have used a sharp stick, for all the difference it would have made!"

De la Marche's face crinkled, lines around his eyes that weather and laughter had put there. Something more sophisticated overlay the honesty in his expression, perhaps pleasure at her refusal to capitalize on an apparent advantage.

"And *anyway*," Ash added, "it's been cleaned since. Or if it hasn't, my pages are going to have sore arses!"

Her hand went out. From his place at the wall, Rickard jumped forward, presenting her sword hilt-first. She seized the leather, thumbing the blade an inch out of the scabbard's friction grip. The gray of the metal was uncolored by anything except the silver abrasions of a new sharpening, ordered after the hunt. Nothing marred the razor sharpness of the edges.

"*Was* it this one? Or was I still borrowing yours, Robert?"

"Oh, it was your wheel-pommel sword, madonna," Angelotti put in. "The Faris had just sent it back. I swear we thought you were going to sleep with it."

"*Thank* you; that'll do!" She slotted it home. Rickard stepped back, grinning.

De la Marche, ignoring both the presence and the familiarity of her sub-captains, said, "This fact remains, Demoiselle-Captain: your sword spilled the Hart's Blood. Do you imagine any man in the city thinks less of it because it is a tool, and you keep it clean and sharp for its proper use? Go out into the street. To 'Hero of Carthage,' you will hear added 'Hart's-Blood,' and 'Sword of the Duchy.' You are no longer a mere mercenary captain to the people of Burgundy."

Ash smothered a snort, aware of Robert Anselm's profane exclamation beside her.

"These titles are all marks of God's grace," de la Marche said. "A standard is only silk cloth, Demoiselle-Captain, but men are maimed holding it and die to defend it. The Duchess is our standard. I think, despite yourself, you are becoming one of our banners."

All humor left her expression. She was aware of Anselm's stillness, Angelotti's gaze, and the attention from farther down the table, and from the men and women clearing the remains of the meal.

"No," she said. "I'm not. *We're* not."

The big Burgundian turned, and bowed very formally to Floria del Guiz. "With your permission, Your Grace?"

Equally formally—equally uncomfortably—Florian nodded.

A sudden realization hit Ash. With difficulty, she kept her expression unchanged.

Shit! He can cope with *me*—I might be a woman in man's clothing, but I'm a soldier. He can pretend I'm a man. Florian . . . he's seen Floria as Florian. And she's a civilian. And he doesn't know how to treat her. How to see her as Duchess.

And, currently, he's the most powerful man in Dijon.

"Demoiselle-Captain, your *condotta* died with my lord the Duke." De la Marche paused. "You have four hundred men. You have seen what lies outside the city now—the new trenches. In the normal way of things, I would ask you to sign a new *condotta* with Burgundy, and I would expect you to refuse."

Robert Anselm said rhetorically, "Nice when they 'ave confidence in their town, ain't it!"

De la Marche glanced once at Floria del Guiz, and continued. "The 'hero of Carthage' will get no contract with the

Carthaginians. Your *men* might, under one or other of your *centeniers.*[16] However, they choose otherwise. I am commander of the late Duke's household knights: I know what it is to have men believe in their commander. Demoiselle Ash, it is a responsibility."

"Too fucking right it is!"

She was not aware, until his lined face creased in a smile, that sleeplessness had betrayed her into speaking the thought out loud.

"Demoiselle-Captain, we have a successor to my lord Charles. Her Grace the Duchess Floria. Your surgeon. In view of this—"

Robert Anselm interrupted harshly. "Let's cut the crap, shall we?"

Ash shot him a glance. *Shit. Next time we're going to play "hard-man thug" and "noble commander," you might warn me!*

Anselm said, "We're stuck in here because the rag'eads hate Ash, the guys won't dump her as captain, and now our doc is Duchess—but this town *is* going to fall, Messire de la Marche. It's just a matter of time. If you think you're getting our services for free, just because we're stuck in here at the moment, you got another fucking think coming!"

His discourtesy echoed off the whitewashed ceiling. Olivier de la Marche's expression did not change. Mildly, he said, "Your remaining *condotta* is with the English Earl of Oxford, who may well be dead, by now. I have a proposal to put to Demoiselle-Captain Ash."

A swift glance at Florian's face showed only bewilderment. Either this isn't something he discussed with her, or forty-eight hours of chaos have knocked it out of her head. *Shit, I wish I was prepared for this!*

Ash rested her hands on the oak table, flexing her cramped fingers. Every line of the roping on her gauntlet cuff was picked out in brown rust now, and she let herself follow the

---

[16]In the Burgundian army under Charles the Bold, *centenier* refers to a captain commanding a company consisting of a hundred soldiers.

lines of dinted steel for a moment, where it lay, before looking up at the man across the table.

"And your proposal is?"

Olivier de la Marche spoke. "Demoiselle Ash, I want you to take my place as commander in chief of the Burgundian army."

V

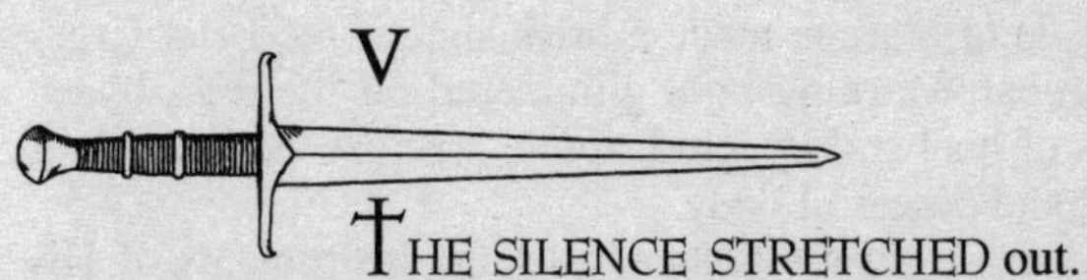

THE SILENCE STRETCHED out.

Neither Anselm, Angelotti, nor Florian spoke. The old chamberlain-counselor, Ternant, leaned across the foot of the table to whisper something to the bishop, but too quietly to be heard over the crackling of the hearth-fire. The Burgundian servants froze in place.

Her wooden chair screeched back as Ash surged to her feet. The noise, and her raised voice, made the servants and guards stare.

"You're *crazy*!"

The big Burgundian nobleman laughed. It had a note of delight in it. Perfectly seriously, he jabbed one blunt-fingered hand at her chest.

"Demoiselle, ask yourself! Who came back triumphant out of the very bowels of the enemy's capital, Carthage? Who fought their way undefeated across half Europe, bringing our new Duchess to us? Who arrived, miraculously, *just in time*: before the very day that Duke Charles of the Valois died!"

"What!" Ash slammed a bare hand down on the table's surface. The noise whip-cracked around the ducal chamber. "You're *shitting* me!"

"And who guarded our Duchess when the hunt rode, saw her safe to her fate, and gave into her hand the very blade with which she made the Hart?"

"Fucking *hell*!"

Stepping back from the table, Ash took two quick strides, swung around, faced the Burgundian:

"We didn't 'come triumphant' out of Carthage! We retreated out of there as fast as we could *run*! We *barely* made it north to you from Marseilles, one step in front of the Visigoths—I think we've been routing back across Europe since Basle! And as for *when* we got here—" She shook her head, cropped silver hair flying. "Haven't you guys ever heard of coincidence! And I'd like to have seen you try to *stop* Florian hunting! Green Christ up a fucking Oak Tree!"

Olivier de la Marche made a brisk sign of the Briar Cross on his surcoat. Morning light glimmered off the reds, blues, and golds of his heraldry, cloth spotless across the breadth of his armor and powerful body.

"God doesn't always bother to let the instruments of His purpose know what they are, Demoiselle-Captain. Why should He? You've done everything He desires."

Ash, at a loss, gaped at him.

Angelotti, from where he sat, murmured, "Mother of God . . . !"

"And," the Burgundian commander added, "doubtless you will continue to bring about His desires."

"You're the army's commander, de la Marche; you've been that for years, they've seen you in tourney and war—even if I agreed to this idiocy, nobody's going to follow *my* orders as Captain-General of Burgundy's army!"

"But they will!"

Now de la Marche turned away, walked a few steps with his hands clasped behind his back, and then came back to stand before the table at which Florian sat. His gaze flicked over the Duchess, ranked Ash's sub-commanders as not pertinent to the discussion, settled again on Ash.

"They *will*," de la Marche repeated. "Demoiselle-Captain, I've told you why. You've been up on the walls. Go down into the streets, if you don't believe me, and listen to the legend you have become! We believe that God sent you to bring our Duchess to us, when otherwise all would have perished when Duke Charles died. The men of Dijon believe that you will fight for us, against Visigoths you have already beaten once, and that while you fight, this city will not fall."

Philippe Ternant got up and walked toward them, supporting himself with one veined hand on the table, the bishop at his other elbow. "It's true. I've heard them."

"You have a glamor, now," de la Marche persisted. "As Joan the Virgin had for France. It is for you, now, to be a Joan of Arc for Burgundy. You cannot deny that this has come to you."

Oh yes I bloody can—

Looking away from Olivier de la Marche, she intercepted the glance first of one of the servers in white doublets, and then of the guard he stood next to. Both men's faces wore a naked, painful hope, no protection of cynicism.

"Uh-uh." Ash raised her hands in front of her, palms out, as if she could block the Burgundian Captain-General's words. "Not me. I've seen this parcel and it's ticking . . ."[17]

"You have a duty—"

"I *don't* have a duty! I'm a fucking *mercenary!*"

Panting, frustrated, Ash glared at the man.

"I didn't ask for this! It's a pile of crap! Eight hundred men's the most I've ever commanded—"

"You would have myself and my officers, Demoiselle."

"I don't want them! This ain't gonna happen! Dijon's nothing to me, Burgundy's nothing to me!"

Thunderously, de la Marche roared at field volume, "*We believe in you whether you like it or not!*"

"Well *I* didn't bloody ask you to!"

Screaming up into the big man's face, Ash found herself breathless, robbed of speech by his expression.

Suddenly quiet, Olivier de la Marche said, "Do you think I *want* you as Captain-General, girl? Do you think I want to stand down? I was Duke Charles's man for longer than you've been alive. I've seen him write ordinance after ordinance, turning the armies of Burgundy into the best in Christendom—and now half of them lie dead at Auxonne, no man

---

[17]I have freely translated a textual difficulty.

knows what is passing in Flanders, and inside these walls there are a bare two thousand men. I find it hard to believe that anyone except myself is to be trusted with the defense of this city. And yet I find it harder to believe that God has not sent you. You are here, now, to be our oriflamme.[18] How can I object? God *demands* your service."

Her breath came hard, but she sounded casually cynical. "So He might. He hasn't bloody paid me yet!"

"This is not a joke!"

"No. It isn't." Finding herself behind Florian's chair, Ash stopped pacing and turned to rest her hands on the blond woman's shoulders, velvet warm under her palms. "It isn't a joke at all."

"Then—"

"Now you listen to me." Ash spoke quietly. She waited, until it forced the armored Burgundian noble to stop bellowing and listen.

Ash said, "Burgundy doesn't matter. *Florian* matters."

Under her hands, Florian stirred.

Ash said, "It's not important if we leave Dijon, and you guys get massacred, and Burgundy's conquered by the Visigoths. All that's important is that Florian stays alive. All the while she's alive, the Wild Machines can't do a damn thing. And if she dies, it won't matter about Burgundy either, because none of us will be around to know about it: you, me, the Burgundians, or the Visigoths!"

"Demoiselle-Captain—"

"I can't afford the time to be a hero for you!"

"Demoiselle Ash—!"

"Hey. It's not like I'm the only one with charisma." Ash grinned, crookedly, finding some emotional balance as she faced him. "Aren't you the tournament Golden Boy? And—oh, what about Anthony de la Roche? He's charismatic—"

"He's in Flanders," de la Marche said grimly. "You are here! Demoiselle, I can't believe that you would defy God's will in this way!"

---

[18]Originally the sacred banner of St. Denis.

"You're not listening to me!"

As she was about to shout—to scream, in sheer frustration, *Florian*!—she heard Robert Anselm's voice from beside her.

"You ain't thinking, girl."

He put heavy, broad hands on the arms of his chair and shoved himself up onto his feet. Armor clattered. He made the unconscious body adjustment that settles harness into place, and faced Ash.

Robert Anselm jerked a thumb at the windows. "You want to be sure Florian stays alive? With that lot out there? What's better than being in charge of the whole damn Burgundian army?"

Ash stared at him.

"Jesus wept, Robert!"

"He may have a point, madonna."

Ash smacked her hand into her fist. "No!" She swung around, facing Olivier de la Marche. "I'm not taking on your damn army! I've got to have the option of taking Florian out of here."

She found herself actually watching de la Marche's nostrils move, flaring as he inhaled, sharply, and bit off whatever he was about to say.

"You never went to Carthage," Ash said, more gently. "You've never seen the Wild Machines—"

"She is our Duchess!"

"That doesn't *matter*, you idiot!"

Antonio Angelotti stood up, forcing himself by that movement between Ash and Olivier de la Marche. Ash backed away a step, her throat raw, glaring at the Burgundian nobleman.

Angelotti reached down and touched the saints' medals looped around the wrist of his fluted German gauntlet, and made a point of looking at Ash for permission to speak.

Breathing hard, she finally nodded.

"Your Grace," Angelotti spoke past de la Marche, to the bishop. "Does the Duchess need to stay within Burgundian territory?"

The bishop—a round-faced, dark man with some of the

Valois look—appeared startled. "Now that is rank superstition."

"Is it?" Ash came immediately to Angelotti's defense. She ignored de la Marche's thunderous frown. "Now is it? I *saw* somebody make a saint's vision into a solid piece of meat and blood. And now you all say she's your Duchess. You got some nerve telling me my master gunner's question is superstitious!"

"It shows a certain lack of thought." The bishop let go of Philippe Ternant's elbow and steepled his fingers, touching them to his small, pursed, delicate mouth. "How could my late brother Charles have made war, or pursued diplomacy, if he couldn't leave the territories of Burgundy?"

"Well . . ." Ash realized that her face felt warm. "Yeah, okay. Now you mention it."

"The *hunt* must occur on Burgundian land." The bishop bowed to Florian. "And within a certain narrow space of time. If our Duchess—pardon, Your Grace—were to die outside the borders of Burgundy now, news would not reach us in time, even if the city still stood. Then, no hunt, no new Duke or Duchess, and . . ."

He finished with an eloquent shrug, and a glance at the pale early-morning sun beyond the glass.

"So Dijon must stand, and the Duchess with it!" Olivier de la Marche blew out a harsh breath. "It's clear to me, Demoiselle Ash. Your surgeon is our Duchess, now. And you are destined to be our commander in chief, not I. Our Pucelle."

"I am *not*—" Ash hauled her voice down from a squeak. "Not your goddamn commander in chief!"

Deep frustration wrote itself in the lines of de la Marche's face. He glared at her, then at Florian—and then looked away from the Burgundian woman, fixing his gaze on Ash again. "It's true our Duchess has been your surgeon. Does this mean you won't follow her?"

"She hasn't stopped being my surgeon yet! Messire de la Marche, I know what Florian is. I'm far from convinced that makes her a Duchess. And I know what a factious nobility's like. This city could fall in a second!" Ash jabbed a finger at him. "Exactly *how* many of your knights and nobles believe Florian is Duchess?"

For the first time, de la Marche appeared staggered. He did not speak.

"Florian, take a look out of the window." Ash smiled grimly, not taking her eyes off de la Marche. "That should concentrate your mind. Now tell me who *is* in charge here, now Charles is dead."

When the surgeon spoke again, her voice held a raw honesty, and she talked as if de la Marche and Ternant and the bishop were not present.

"It's me. I'm in charge."

Ash snapped a look over her shoulder, startled.

"I thought I wouldn't be. That I'd be a figurehead. It isn't like that." Floria's face altered. "It's ironic. I ran off to Padua and Salerno when all I had to be afraid of was being married off like all the other noble broodmares. Now I'm trapped, but because I'm the heir and successor to *Charles de Bourgogne*! And I *am*. I am, Ash. These people are doing what I say. That's frightening."

Breathless, Ash muttered automatically, "Too fucking right!"

At the surgeon's sardonic look, she added:

"Florian, I *know* you. You've got no more idea how to rule a duchy than my last turd! Why should you have? But if it's 'Yes, my lady, yes, Your Grace . . . ' "

"Yes," Florian said.

Moved by some personal impulse that she would not have given way to, before, off-balance in some subtle way, Ash muttered, "Sweet Christ, woman, you don't know when you're well-off! You have no idea of what it's like to have to *prove* your right to authority, day by day by day. Because you hunted the hart. And that *makes* you Duchess."

"Hunting the Hart made me what I am. *Nothing* makes me a Duchess!" Floria's long, strong fingers clenched, her knuckles white. "I have to be stepping right into the middle of other people's political games here! I can only know what other people tell me. I need all the help I can get. People I trust. Ash. You're one of them."

Ash shifted uncomfortably in her armor, overwarm in the fire-heated stuffiness of the tower room. She looked away from Florian's expression, aware that it demanded something of her.

"There's you. There's the company. There's Messire de la Marche." Ash shook her head. "There's Burgundy. There's Christendom—I can't get my head around that one. *Everything . . .* All I know is, I have to keep you alive, and I have to get us to some point where we can fight back." Now she looked up at de la Marche. "And you want me to be some Sacred Virgin-Warrior. I'm not from bloody Domremy,[19] I'm from *Carthage*! I'm slave-born. Green Christ! Get a grip!"

"*You* get a grip." Florian stood, in a graceful sweep of velvet. She put her hand on Anselm's vambrace. "I'm with Roberto on this one. You've told me often enough. Men win when they believe they can win."

"Aw, *shit*—"

Antonio Angelotti seated himself again, and said thoughtfully, "You would need to talk to our officers and men. The Lion Azure should not turn into the Duchess's Household guard . . ."

Olivier de la Marche grunted. As Ash looked up at him, the big man said, in a normal speaking voice, "My apologies, Demoiselle-Captain. Naturally, a commander must speak to his men. How soon can you do this?"

" 'How soon'!"

There was no echo of her incredulity on their faces.

She looked first at Florian. Nothing to be read there. A drawn anxiety shadowed Philippe Ternant's features; the bishop's round face was unreadable.

"You are no longer just a mercenary commander," Olivier de la Marche repeated. "Not to us. If you wanted to, demoiselle, you could make a play for power here. That would split the city. I *offer* you the command, instead. Captain over me,

---

[19]Actual birthplace of Jeanne D'Arc.

with me to use my authority when you're not on duty, the responsibility to be yours, as well."

At his last word, his lips curved up; he looked for a moment much as he must have done as a young champion of Charles's household, riding in the great tournaments of Burgundy: a careless prowess that does not need to consider itself, matched with an awareness that loyalty is simple and men are complex.

"If we don't last out more than two or three days more," he added, "I will share the disgrace with you, Demoiselle-Captain; how is that for an offer?"

She held his gaze, aware that not only Florian, but Robert and Angeli also watched her, that the chamberlain-counselor and the bishop now had identical expressions of hope.

"Uh . . ." she wiped her hand across her nose. Angelotti sat with his helm in his lap, smoothing the rain-draggled plumes into order. He shot a glance at her from under gold brows. Having known him and Anselm for so long, she did not need to hear them speak their opinions aloud.

"You have at least to *tell* your men," de la Marche said, "that every man in Dijon demands this of you. And my men are waiting for your answer now."

Christ, do I actually have to take this seriously?

Fuck . . .

"You'd be putting a mercenary commander in over Burgundian nobles," she said slowly. "I don't want to find myself involved in some internecine war *inside* Dijon, with the Visigoths still there outside!"

Olivier de la Marche nodded assent. "The worst of all worlds, Demoiselle."

"What are you going to do about factions and political infighting?" Ash nodded toward her surgeon. "Florian isn't even a Valois. It's a good fifteen years since she's been noble!"

Florian spluttered, hand up to her veil, muttered something indistinguishable, but in entirely familiar, cynical tones.

"And then," Ash said, "you're adding me."

"The Turks have their Janissaries,[20] do they not? We're only men," Olivier de la Marche said, "and you're asking the wrong man about factions, Demoiselle-Captain. I'm a soldier, not a politician. All the politicians are in the north; my lord Duke sent them there with Duchess Margaret, before Auxonne. God and His Saints protect her!"

"But Florian," Ash began.

"I'll tell you now, Demoiselle-Captain. Duchess Floria will have all the loyalty that men gave to my lord, Charles. This is *Burgundy*. We're only men, and men of honor are prone to quarrel. But we are pious men, we recognize a woman sent by God to us; she *is* our Duchess."

Into the moment's silence that followed, he added, "And you: God sent you to us, also. Now, Demoiselle Ash—what will *you* do?"

Five hours later, she returned to the Tour Philippe le Bon in highly polished armor and clean Lion Azure livery. Heads lifted as she entered the room, interrupting the last of the noon meal. She nodded briefly, let Anselm and Angelotti move ahead down the table, and let Rickard take his place at the wall with her sword and helmet. She strode to the head of the table and sat in the empty chair waiting beside Floria del Guiz.

"*Well?*" Florian demanded, under her breath.

"You got any more of that frumenty? I could really go some of that." Ash coughed. "And mead. Anything with honey in. My throat's *ragged* from talking to that lot."

"Ash!"

"Okay, okay!" A quick glance showed her a couple of dozen of de la Marche's commanders at the table, and two abbots with the bishop, all staring with the same intense curiosity as the servants. "Just let me *eat*."

Florian grinned, suddenly, and signaled to the servers. "I'm not keeping Boss from her food. Bad things happen when you keep Boss from her food . . ."

---

[20]Slave troops, often attaining high rank.

As the servers came to table, the Duchess of Burgundy reached out with long-fingered hands, helping herself and Ash from the dishes. Ash flicked a glance at the pantler's and butler's expressions. *Ah, shit! She's got them. I've done that one . . .*

What she saw was not disdain for such nonnoble acts, but a kind of pride in their Duchess's blunt military manners.

Ash reached for a plate the right weight and color to be gold. Unused to the noble luxury of a chair, she caught her armored elbows on the chair arms. She scooped up the wheat and honey gruel in a metal spoon—an oddly different taste to eating from a horn spoon—and shot a gaze down the table.

Anselm and Angelotti ignored her, seizing on the last of the food and eating with the fast, single-minded determination of soldiers, the gunner's fair head close to Anselm's shaven pate as they simultaneously leaned back to call for more wine. Next to Angelotti, the rheumy-eyed Chamberlain-Counselor Philippe Ternant ignored the meat on his plate in favor of a rapid, whispered conversation with Olivier de la Marche, his eyes on Ash. Beyond the ducal champion, Ash saw the same middle-aged man in Episcopal green who had been present at dawn.

Unable to speak with her mouth full, she raised her eyebrows at Florian.

"Bishop John of Cambrai," Floria murmured, mouth equally full. She swallowed. "One of the late Duke's bastard half brothers. He's a man after my own heart; there's never enough women in the world for him![21] He's another reason I need you here. We've got business with him later. Whatever you've decided. Ash, *what does the company say*?"

Ash studied the bishop: round-faced, with black velvet eyes, and soft, matt black hair growing around his tonsure, and only the Valois nose to mark him as an indisputable child

---

[21]I have regularised the text, which indiscriminately refers to him as 'Bishop Jean' and 'Bishop John' of Cambrai. There appears to be some independent evidence for Floria's comment in this text—Bishop John's funeral mass, in 1480, was attended by a total of thirty-six of his illegitimate children.

of Philip the Good. She shook her head at Florian, pointing at her mirror-polished gorget and her neck.

"Better in a minute."

"In your own damn time . . . What state is the infirmary in?" Florian demanded. "How's Rostovnaya? And Vitteleschi? And Szechy?"

Anything to put off the moment. Ash stopped chewing, swallowed; sent her mind back to the infirmary in the company tower. "Blanche and Baldina are running it, with Father Faversham. Looks okay."

"What would you know!"

"About Ludmilla—spoke to Blanche—she says the burns aren't healing."

"They won't if the stupid woman keeps trying to stand her duty up on the walls!"

"Your Grace," de la Marche interrupted.

Ash did not look at the surgeon-turned-Duchess; she kept her gaze on the men lining the long table. Abandoning ceremony, they ceased eating, the officers looking toward Olivier de la Marche.

He rumbled, "Your Grace, with your permission—Demoiselle-Captain Ash, what have you decided?"

The spoon rattled as Ash set it down on the gold plate. She kept her gaze momentarily on the rich, warm glow of the metal. Then she lifted her head to see them all silent, all staring.

Sudden sweat made her arming doublet sodden in the time that it took her to stand up.

"They voted." Her voice sounded both thin and hoarse in her own ears.

An unbroken silence.

"It all comes down to what keeps Florian alive longer. You'll die to keep Florian alive. So will we. Different reasons. But we'll both do whatever it takes."

A cold nausea pierced her. She leaned her fists on the table, to keep herself from dizzily sitting straight back down.

"If that also means me as your 'Pucelle,' to boost morale—well: whatever it takes."

Their eyes are on her: men of Burgundy, in their blue-and-red livery with the bold St. Andrew's crosses. Men she knows—Jussey, Lacombe—and men she knows only by sight, or not at all. She is conscious of her cleaned-up armor, her bright livery—and of her short-cropped hair, and the scars on her cheeks.

No. She watched the faces of men in their mid and late twenties, a few of them older. *It doesn't* matter *what I look like—they're seeing what they want to see.*

She switched her gaze back to de la Marche.

"I'll take the position of commander in chief. You'll be my second-in-command. I'm in."

Voices broke out. She heard it as a confused babble.

"There are two conditions!" Her voice cracked. She coughed, glanced around the room, fixed her eyes on Olivier de la Marche, and started again. "Two conditions. First: I'll take this on until you get somebody better—when Anthony de la Roche comes down from Flanders, this job's his. You want a Burgundian with leadership and charisma: that's him. Second: I'm here in Dijon only until we can carry the fight to the enemy: kill my sister the Faris, because she's a channel for the Wild Machines' power, or attack the Wild Machines themselves."

For a moment, she is dizzy with it: the desire to leave this battered, claustrophobic city. Even the memory of the horrific forced march from Marseilles is distanced, now, beside the chance of getting *out*.

"And if we can get your Duchess—our Florian—away safely at *any* point, we're leaving this town to the ragheads. On that basis," she said, "and with the vote of the Lion Azure—I'm here."

The babble of voices resolved itself to two things: a cheer, and the explosive profanity of one of the abbots. Men all around the table stood up—one abbot's green vestments swirling as he stalked toward the door—but the men in breastplate and hose crowded around her, grinning, speaking, shouting.

De la Marche strode up to her. Ash scrambled back from

the high table. The Burgundian knight reached out, grasping her hand, and she managed to keep herself from wincing aloud.

"Welcome, Demoiselle-Captain!"

"Pleasure," Ash muttered weakly. Her knuckles ground together. As he released her hand, she hid her fingers behind her back, massaging painful flesh.

" 'Captain-General' !" two knights corrected, almost simultaneously, one curly-haired and unknown to her, the other a thick-set man, Captain Lacombe, away from duty on the northwest wall.

Captain-General of Burgundy. Shit.

Instead of leaving her, the fear intensified, nausea turning to cramps in her bowels. She kept her face as expressionless as she could.

Farther down the table, Angelotti winked at her. It failed to steady her.

Well, it's done now. I've said it.

Formal chivalric introductions passed in a blur of names. She stood, surrounded by men mostly a head taller than herself, talking at the tops of their voices. Looking back, she saw the remaining abbot and the bishop monopolizing Florian.

The curly-haired knight's gaze followed hers. He might have been twenty-five, old enough to have killed and ordered killed any number of men in battle, but what was on his face as he watched Floria was a shining awe. Sounding contrite, he said suddenly, "Two of you blessed by God—I'm glad you're our commander, Demoiselle-Captain Ash. You're a warrior. Her Grace is so far above us—"

Ash lifted an eyebrow and shot him a glance at about shoulder height. "And I'm not?"

"I—well, I—" He blushed, furiously. "That's not what I—"

As if he were one of her own lance leaders, Ash said, "I think the phrase you're looking for is 'oh shit!,' soldier . . ."

Lacombe snorted, and grinned at his younger companion. "Didn't I tell you what she was like? This is the Sieur de Romont, Captain Ash. Don't mind him, he's a dork in here, but he fucks those legionaries every time they come across the walls."

"Oh, I'm sure he does," Ash said dryly. Meeting Captain Romont's pleased and blushing gaze, she thought suddenly of Florian in the camp outside Dijon's walls: *call it charisma if you like . . .*

The first smile tugged at her mouth.

I'd like to see de la Marche copy my command style.

And then, her eyes on Lacombe and Romont and the others: *If I get this wrong—if I'm not up to this job—all of you will be lying dead in the streets. And soon.*

She turned, walking to the table and putting her hands on the back of her chair; and as if there had been an order given, the *centeniers* of the Burgundian forces returned to their seats and waited for her to speak. She waited until Florian sat down.

"I'm not a one-man show." Ash leaned on the chair back, looking at each of the faces around the table in turn. "I never have been. I have good officers. I expect them to speak their minds. In fact"—she looked across at Anselm and Angelotti—"most of the time I can't shut the bastards up!"

It was not the laugh that warmed her, but the unmistakable body language of men settling down to listen. Their expressions held cynicism, hope, judgment: *This is standard commander bullshit, we've heard it all before*, mixed with *We're in deep shit here, are you good enough to get us out*?

Burgundy may be different. But soldiers are soldiers.

Thank Christ I'll have de la Marche.

"So I expect you to talk to me, to keep me up to date with what's happening, and to relay what I say to you to your men. I don't want us blindsided by trouble because some dipstick thought he didn't have to tell me about a problem, or he thought his guys didn't need to know what the command people are saying. I don't have to tell you we're hanging by a thread here. So we need to get it together, and we need to do it fast."

There were perhaps two, out of the twenty, who still automatically looked at Olivier de la Marche after she had finished speaking. She mentally noted faces, if not yet names. *Two out of twenty is* fucking *good . . .*

"Okay. *Now.*"

Ash left the chair and paced, primarily to let them get a clear view of her newly polished, expensive Milanese harness, but also to look out of the tower window, at the antlike movements of the Visigoths beyond their trenches.

"What we need to know is—why the fuck have they given us three days to talk about this?"

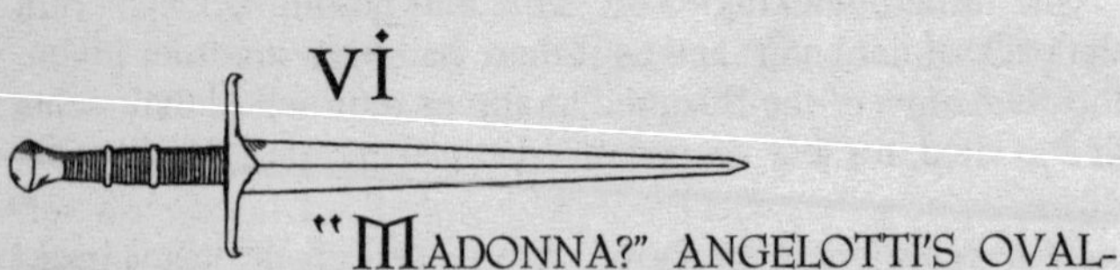

VI

"MADONNA?" ANGELOTTI'S OVAL-lidded glance took in everybody gathered at the table.

Ash briefly explained, "My *magister ingeniator*,"[22] and gestured him to speak.

"The new golem-built entrenchments are a fathom deep, at least, and the same wide. In some places the lines are three deep. Any attack would have to throw down fascines and pavises and boards, to cross the ditches. There will always be time now for the Visigoths to sound the alarm and deploy to meet us."

Ash saw heads nodding among the Burgundian *centeniers*.

Angelotti added, "I've spoken with the Burgundian engineers. Those dug-outs go clear over to the Ouche, in the east; and they continue all the way down the broken ground over on the east bank." He shrugged, eloquently. "We can't break out in any direction, *madonna*! This was worth their three days. *If*—"

About to interrupt, Ash found herself interrupted:

"Is a ditch that important, for God's sake?" Florian leaned forward, as she has done in tents from northern France to southern Italy, arguing with Ash's command staff.

"It stops us sallying out." Robert Anselm hit the table with

---

[22]'Combat engineer'.

his fist. "But it's crazy! Why are they worried about that? They can *take* this city. Right now! You look out there! They'll lose a lot of men—but they'll do it."

Imperceptibly, Olivier de la Marche nodded.

"A ditch *is* important." Ash waited until Florian's attention came back to her. "Trenches. Trenches are defense—not attack. Florian, they've got the Wild Machines behind them, urging them on. What we need to know is, why have they spent forty-eight hours digging, not attacking?"

Now Florian nodded, too, green eyes intent, and Ash prodded the oak tabletop with her finger for emphasis.

"*Why* dig? Why *not* attack? I can make a guess why—and if I'm right, we're going to have a little time."

Lacombe's flushed face took on a look of hope. Ash surveyed the other Burgundian officers. "The Faris has stopped the assaults on the walls. She's sticking to bombardment. She's dug entrenchments round the *whole fucking city*—"

"Do you not hear her orders?" de la Marche interrupted. "Does she not speak with this Stone Golem that you, too, hear?"

"G—Saint Godfrey told me she doesn't speak to it now. If he's right, she hasn't used the *machina rei militaris* since I went into her camp and spoke to her, before we came into the city. That means she isn't listening to Carthage . . . And I'm willing to bet I *am* right: that last attack she put in on the northwest gate, before the Duke died, she must have done that without the Stone Golem."

"They so nearly took the gate!" the elderly chamberlain-counselor Ternant protested. "Was that the act of a madwoman?"

"It wasn't smart." With the bull-necked Lacombe and the other *centeniers* already interrupting, Ash raised her voice over theirs and pursued the point. "She made a feint on the wall where we were, and when it looked like we were pushing it back, she put Greek Fire down on her own people. Oh, I know *why* she thought sending van Mander's company would work—she thought it would freak out my guys who'd fought beside him before. They're hard bastards; it'll take more than that. And then she thought that dumping Greek Fire on us and van Mander when his assault was failing would clear the wall and let her attack with her Visigoth troops and win. But it was a bad mistake. She killed her own mercenaries. There isn't a Frankish soldier in Dijon who'll go over to the Visigoths now."

Memory flashed her back to the wall. Not, as she might have expected, to Ludmilla Rostovnaya rolling, body on fire, but to the face of Bartolemy St. John as she shoved fourteen inches of steel dagger into his eye socket and blood soaked the velvet cover of his brigandine. *I was there when he ordered that one from the armorer. And now Dickon Stour's dead, too.*

Into the silence, Ash said, "The *machina rei militaris* would have warned her off doing that—I know it would, because it would warn *me* off it, if I ever thought anything like that was a good idea!"

She grinned. It was not clear from the expressions around her whether they were worried by the lack of divinity of their Pucelle's voices, or reassured by her military acumen.

"The Faris isn't using the Stone Golem. I'd bet money she *won't*, now. She knows that anything she reports, any tactical advice she asks for—we'll hear it, too. Even Carthage is keeping silent. She can't get orders from them, now. For the moment—she's on her own."

"And?" Olivier de la Marche prompted. "What does this mean, Demoiselle-Captain?"

She has a brief memory of the Faris, profile illuminated by the lamps in her headquarters, hands resting in her lap, the nails on her fingers chewed ragged.

"She's frozen up. *I* think she's terrified of making mistakes. She knows the Stone Golem is overheard. And she knows the Wild Machines are there. That simple. She can't pretend they're not there anymore. She knows what they can do to her—could do." Ash frowned. "So she can't ask for battlefield advice. And she's too scared to do it alone."

Bishop John said quietly, "And do they still have their

power, demoiselle: this *machina plena malis*,[23] these Wild Machines?"

There was silence, except for the crackling of the fire in the hearth. The Burgundian officers turned, one by one, to look at her. The green-robed Bishop of Cambrai touched his fingertips to the Briar Cross above his heart.

"I hear them." Ash watched expressions. "They could be damaged, and lying about it. But we can't afford to bet on it. And, having spoken to them once, at your Duchess's request, I don't plan to do it again—if nothing else, it works both ways: whatever the Wild Machines say to me, the Visigoths will know. They only have to ask the Stone Golem, and it'll repeat every question I ask." She nodded an acknowledgment to de la Marche. "The less the Wild Machines know, the better. The less House Leofric and the King-Caliph know, the better."

Lacombe's friend Romont put in, "Does King-Caliph Gelimer know about these . . . 'Wild Machines'?"

"Oh yeah." Ash grinned at him, in morbid humor. "They call the light over the King-Caliphs' tombs the 'Fire of the Blessing.' *'Arif* Alderic told me that, in the Visigoth camp." Restless, she began to pace again, thinking aloud. "Up to now, the Faris has kept quiet about the Wild Machines, but—if I was her, I might not. If the Visigoths believed her, they might just say, 'hey, we have a whole lot *more* tactical machines on our side.' Their morale might go up!"

Anselm scowled. "Yeah. They're fucking stupid enough!"

"The last time I saw the Faris, at the truce, she admitted to me that she heard the Wild Machines. She had a fit, when the hunt happened—I think she's shitting herself. By now she knows there's a successor to Duke Charles. *She* can't be sure the Wild Machines are damaged. As soon as the Duke's successor dies—sorry, Florian—the same thing is going to hap-

---

[23]*Machina plena malis*—'a contrivance full of evils'. Used punningly in the text to refer to a 'contrivance' in the sense of a trick or snare, as well as a constructed device.

pen again. She's going to make a miracle for the Wild Machines. The Faris is going to be used . . ."

A look went between Olivier de la Marche and Bishop John: it might have been something as simple as fear.

"She's jammed her head up her arse," Ash said brutally, "and she's waiting for the problem to go away. It isn't going to. And it would be a good idea if we didn't jam *our* heads up *our* arses, too!"

Another of the *centeniers* spoke in a heavy northern accent. "If she does plan to let cold, and hunger, and time do her siege work, without attacking, then, we have time to plan."

Ash rested her armored hand on his shoulder as she reached the chair in which he sat. "Even if she is, Captain—one of her *qa'ids* could take over tomorrow. Then we're fucked."

De la Marche nodded.

Meeting his gaze, moving on, the oak boards creaking under her, Ash said, "Say that the Faris continues to soft-pedal—Carthage will get increasingly shitty with her. *They* still want Burgundy's surrender. They don't want any more of a winter campaign than they're already stuck with. . . . King-Caliph Gelimer's in charge, *Amir* Leofric is sick—I don't know how much weight this Sisnandus carries. How long will it take before Gelimer sends a—" Ash paused; said sardonically, "—a more 'conventional' general out to replace the Faris? Anything from two to four weeks. Assuming a new commander hasn't left already. And *he'll* follow orders and attack. What," she added to de la Marche, "is the matter?"

Olivier de la Marche started, and wiped his hand over his mouth. When he removed it, there was no trace of a smile. "You appear to have a sound grasp of the situation, Demoiselle-Captain."

Ash put her fists on her hips. "Yeah. It's my job."

Someone at the far end of the table laughed out loud in brief appreciation. She could feel the balance of the room shift, the very beginnings of a prickly dislike that anyone—even de la Marche—would think of denigrating the Maid of Burgundy.

"If I'm right"—another glance out of the bright windows—"she's going to sit behind that ditch she's dug, and wait for us to starve. They won't let her do that indefinitely. We could have anything from fifteen minutes to four weeks before things go pear-shaped." A quirk of her mouth. "If we had enough food for four weeks . . ."

Olivier de la Marche's expression became absorbed in calculations. He broke off, looked up at Ash again. "So. She has experienced *qa'ids* out there. They might give her advice; she might get her confidence back. She *might* use the *machina rei militaris* to devise a plan to take this city—although she hardly needs to."

"Oh yeah. Any of that. I said I think we have time—I don't think we have very *much* time. Okay . . ." Ash began to point at random around the table: "Suggestions."

"We might take a leaf from their *magister ingeniator*'s book," Antonio Angelotti said, unexpectedly.

Ash paused, staring at him. She put out of her mind the suddenly overwhelming fear that she might have committed herself wrongly, that four hundred men—two and a half thousand men, now—will suffer from this decision. She responded to the new atmosphere in the room. *Now we can make plans.*

"Go on, Angeli."

"A sap," the Italian gunner said. "Let me look at the ground up in the northeast quarter of the city. We might dig a sap out under the wall on that side, west of the wet ground on the bank of the Ouche, under their northern camp. We might get *madonna* Florian out that way. Then the Duchess is preserved, even if Dijon falls. And"—he looked at de la Marche—"you can get to the north and fight back."

Olivier de la Marche blinked. "Mining for such a distance? Under those ditches; under their camp? And deep enough not to be overheard? That would take a phenomenal amount of time and timber, Messire Angelotti."

Robert Anselm murmured, "Sounds good to me . . ."

"Okay: that's one." Ash snapped her fingers. "Next. You!"

Captain Romont, startled, blurted out, "Send men out with grenades and powder. We could burn their stores!"

"If we could get to them." Ash glanced at the bright glass of the chamber's windows. "We know from Godfrey that she has three legions up north, fighting at Bruges and Antwerp and

Ghent; she's only got two legions here to feed, one understrength. And she can keep on shipping food and Greek Fire over the Med. . . . Although that gives her fucking long supply lines to cope with."

Anselm grunted. "Enough to give them problems?"

"It's just possible *we* could wait *them* out. They didn't expect not to be able to live off the country when they got here. I don't believe that they expected darkness to cover Iberia—all their fields and farms there. But even if Iberia's under the Penitence, now, they've still got Egypt, and they've had twenty years to prepare for this."

Momentarily, she sees not the weak sun outside the tower window, but the frozen blackness of Lyons and Avignon, the snow falling in Carthage.

The half of Christendom that didn't starve this harvest is going to starve next year. There is going to be famine. Just, too late to help us here.

"Any sabotage we can do is a plus. And the next!"

One of the *centeniers*, barely more than a boy, grinned. "We've got some captured liveries, Demoiselle-Captain! I have men who are brave enough to try getting through those trenches in disguise. It's no lack of chivalry to sabotage the enemy."

Ash just stopped herself saying *And it isn't chivalrous when you come back by trebuchet, either*.

"If you can get men out," she said grimly, "what they have to do is kill my sister."

Bishop John's expression showed extreme distaste. He said nothing. Nor did Philippe Ternant—the old man, after a meal, and in this warm chamber, might have been asleep. There was no distaste or disinterest from the officers.

"Take the Faris out, and the Wild Machines are stopped cold. I suspect the Visigoth army is, too. Okay, we'll discuss this one in detail in a minute—we should send out some two-man and four-man teams, and try to assassinate her, but it won't be easy. The ragheads can have patrols in those ditches twenty-four hours a day—"

"But if we could do it!" de la Marche exclaimed. "It would prevent their miracle; it would throw the legions here into confusion; it might save Dijon, or buy us time to break out, or time enough for the army in the north to march here!"

Another of the *centeniers*, whose name she could not remember, said acidly, "*If* you know where she is, my lord. She may have withdrawn her HQ to the rear of the enemy camp. She may have withdrawn it to a nearby town or fortress. I grant you, spies may tell us where she is—but we have to retrieve them first."

"Okay." Ash stopped pacing, now at the far end of the table, looking down at the seated Burgundian knights. "Okay: any more?"

"Send out heralds."

The voice was Florian's. Ash glanced back at her in surprise.

"Send out heralds. If you're right, the Faris knows something's badly wrong. She might talk to us. Negotiate."

Ash thought de la Marche's face held a certain scepticism, but he said mildly, "There are the heralds of the ducal household, your Grace. They stand ready."

"Any more?"

Robert Anselm rumbled, "We could do a mass assault, if we could get over those fucking trenches, boss—but I don't even know what strength of troops there are in the city, total?"

Thanks, Roberto.

"Okay, that's a good point." Ash's circumnavigation of the long table brought her back past Florian to her own chair. She leaned on the tall, carved-oak back, looking across at Olivier de la Marche. "You want to give the overall picture here?"

"Demoiselle-Captain."

Olivier de la Marche fumbled at ink-stained lists on the tablecloth, in front of him, but did not look down at them. He kept his gaze on Florian—weighing her, Ash thought suddenly—contrasting this exiled Burgundian noblewoman with the man he had followed through battle and court for so many years. *And Charles has only been dead two days. Christus, how he must miss him!*

Philippe Ternant opened lizard eyes, and said, perfectly alertly, "We are not the strength we were. At one time, Your Grace, I might have offered you a hundred chamberlains, with myself as first chamberlain; a hundred chaplains under your first chaplain—"

Olivier de la Marche waved the old man to silence. Ash could see acknowledgment of the respite in the glance that went between them.

Grief almost indistinguishable in his tone, de la Marche said, "We had high casualties at Auxonne. Your Grace, before that field, I could have offered you two thousand men as your personal household troops alone. Forty mounted chamberlains and gentlemen of the Duke's chamber died with the standard at Auxonne; and of four hundred cavalry, fifty survive."

The atmosphere around the table changed, the men's expressions taking on more weight, more memory. Feeling how it did not exclude her, Ash realizes: *I have been watched, up at the northwest gate. And at Auxonne, too.*

De la Marche said, "I myself led what survives of sixteen one-hundred-strong companies of mounted archers and household infantry back to Dijon. There are three hundred of us."

He kept a steady gaze on Floria del Guiz.

"We lost our bombards, serpentines, and mortars on that field. Of the army itself, there died men-at-arms to the number of one thousand, one hundred, and five—" He looked down at the slanting ink lines on the paper he held. "Mounted archers, upwards of three thousand; crossbowmen, one thousand or less; the archers on foot, eight hundred; the billmen, fifteen hundred or more."

Romont, Lacombe, and two or three of the other officers stared down at the table.

Florian said nothing. Ash saw her lips move, soundless. Hearing it listed made her own gut turn over, remembering that half-dark wet morning scarred by Greek Fire. *It must be worse*, she thought, *for a surgeon who only sees the result of such numbers, and never the butchery that brings it about.*

"Your Grace, I may still offer you your *archier de corps*, but there is one captain now, and not two; twenty men, not forty. They are your bodyguard; they will die to keep you alive. For the rest, I have restructured the companies of

Berghes and Loyecte and Saint-Seigne." He nodded acknowledgment to those *centeniers*. "If I could make up twenty full companies in Dijon now, I would count us rich. What strength we have is knights, foot archers and arquebusiers, and billmen, in the main. No more than two thousand men."

"The Lion is down to forty-eight lances," Robert Anselm put in. "Mostly men-at-arms, archers, and hackbutters; some cannon. The company's light guns are still in Carthage. Unless the ragheads shipped them north, and they're out there in the artillery park."

Angelotti gave him a filthy look.

De la Marche said, "We have scouts enough in towers and on the walls to give us warning of where an attack will come. If every man attends to the trumpets and standards, we can deploy our companies well enough to cover an attack against any part of the walls. Perhaps two attacks at once." He opened his mouth as if to complete the thought, and stopped.

We had a hard enough job holding one gate against one attack. They've got the manpower to put two full-strength attacks in at once, or three.

And we've got far too few troops for a breakout.

Ash shifted herself up off the chair back, careless of scratching the golden oak; steel plates sliding, tassets shifting on buff leather straps. A fierce restlessness kept her from sitting down, kept her on her feet and moving. "I want the companies' duties rotated. Nobody gets the same section of wall for more than twenty-four hours."

Lacombe scowled up at her as she passed. "They will say, demoiselle, that you do that to spare your own men—and mine—their constant danger at the northwest gate."

"They can say what they like." Ash halted. "I don't want the ragheads knowing which Franks they'll be up against, and I don't want anybody getting used to the Visigoth unit they're facing. I don't want familiarity—that's when men start getting bribed to open postern gates. So we'll do it my way, okay."

He nodded briskly. "We'll see to it, Demoiselle-Captain."

"That's 'Captain.' Or 'Captain-General.' " She grinned. "Or 'boss.' "

With enough eye contact to make it seem a small contest of

wills, Lacombe said—as if he had not cheerfully been saying it for forty-eight hours now, up on the walls—"We'll see to it, boss."

Her silk arming doublet is clammy, under her armor, with new sweat. Two thousand five hundred men, and all the miles of wall to be guarded—!

"Okay," she went on smoothly, walking around to de la Marche's seat. "So now let's move on. Messire, when I sent Father Paston to you, before the hunt—I know there was one Visigoth report from Flanders." She spoke over the rising mutter of interest. "By that time I was dictating in my sleep! Let's have your clerk or mine read it out. We need to know now what chance we've got of the northern army raising this siege—and I think it was a very recent report?"

De la Marche frowned, fretting among the papers piled on the desk. A tonsured clerk got up from beside the Bishop of Cambrai, searching more of the papers. Ash sensed movement, shifted, and Rickard, blushing, reached past her and took a document from the heap.

"Father Paston's hand, boss," he explained. "Shall I read it?"

He automatically looked at Ash; Ash, as automatically, nodded permission; and only afterward saw the surgeon-Duchess's expression of quiet amusement. Ash noted it had gone right past the *centeniers*, too.

The boy seated himself at the table, close to a patch of bright sunlight, and spread out his folded sheets of paper. Ash admired the neat chancery hand, upside down.

"This is something Godfrey heard, in the *machina rei militaris*?" Florian herself reached for wine and poured it into her cup, not bothering to call over a page. De la Marche frowned, caught between social embarrassment—*a Duchess should not do this!*—and an inability to criticize his sovereign.

"Yeah. A Visigoth report, from before the Faris stopped using the *machina*."

Florian tapped the table with the foot of her goblet. "So. Does it tell us about Duchess Margaret? Who are her forces, where are they, who is she fighting?"

Memory of dictating this, in the early hours, sparked a memory. Ash said, "Strictly speaking, it'll be Margaret of York, Dowager *Duchesse de Bourgogne*, now."

Are we going to have trouble because Charles's daughter Marie ought to inherit? She watched the Burgundians' faces. *No. Florian hunted the hart. Look at them: they're unshakable.*

Ash signaled to Rickard. The boy ran his fingers down one sheet of paper, his lips moving, until he reached the part he wanted to read aloud. " 'The town of Le Crotoy fell to us, this day, the thirteenth in the sign of the scorpion.' "[24] Aware of the captains listening, his voice strengthened. " 'Glory to the King-Caliph Gelimer, under the hand of the One True God, who will remember that our treaty with the Frankish king, Louis, forces him to help us. Since the Burgundian town of Crotoy is close to the French border, we bid him allow us to cross his territory, and to resupply our legions, which he did. And therefore we fell upon the men in Crotoy.' "

"Devious little fuck!" Ash muttered. "Louis, I mean."

Olivier de la Marche cleared his throat. "I know my lady Margaret had planned to write to Louis, as she is sister to the English king as well as Duchess of Burgundy, and beg him to come to her aid. The Spider long supported both sides in the English wars. There was a chance he'd change his allegiance from the Anjou woman[25] to York, and to us. He has made overtures to King Edward, her brother, since he took the throne, and is paying him a pension."

"He's not going to bolster up Anglo-Burgundian power on the French borders," Florian said, and as they stared at her, shrugged and added, "I've listened to Messire Ternant and my other counselors. Louis sees the Visigoths as a useful counterweight to Burgundy and the English."

---

[24]c. 3rd November? If this is the astrological sign of Scorpio.

[25]Margaret of Anjou, wife of the English king Henry VI; funded in some of her attempts to regain the crown for her husband or her son by Louis XI of France. In 1476, Margaret is reported as just having been ransomed from England, and present in the French court.

"And the French will expect the King-Caliph to hold what he's conquered," Ash added. "They'll be shit-scared, right now, about the darkness—they'll know it's spread everywhere, even to Iberia, where Carthage gets its grain. Louis's probably hoping the Visigoths can take it away!"

"Can they?" Rickard broke in. He flushed. "Sorry, my lord de la Marche—"

"Rickard's one of my junior officers, my lord," Ash said smoothly. "I let everybody speak in officer meetings. Then I make my own mind up."

Floria spoke to the boy. "Rickard, I think if the Visigoths could take the Eternal Twilight away, they'd have done it by now."

Lacombe and a couple of the others—Berghes? Loyecte?—grunted knowing agreement.

"Carry on," Ash directed.

Rickard read without hesitation from the cramped lines. " 'The Frankish woman and her forces fell back from Le Crotoy, and it is likely she will make for Bruges, Ghent, or Antwerp. Be aware, great Caliph, that in Ghent, because of the trouble to her that her Chancellor has been, she was forced to disband the estates there.' "[26]

"Who's the Chancellor?" Ash looked at Ternant.

Florian cut in. "Guillaime Hugonet, Lord of Saillant, Chancellor of Burgundy." She spoke as if she had memorized the name. "I'm told he's good at raising taxes. She can pay that army. He's a good orator . . . Apparently he was with Margaret before, in Flanders and Brabant."

Philippe Ternant inclined his head in agreement.

"Hugonet may be good at keeping the northern army funded and in the field," Olivier de la Marche snarled, "but even under war conditions, I doubt that anyone will put up with him! The man made innumerable political enemies in

---

[26]The Flemish part of the Estates-General: representatives of the cities and provinces there. In fact, these events appear to closely parallel the history of the early part of 1477, after Duke Charles's death in battle at Nancy.

Ghent and Bruges. A hard-liner, demoiselle. If Guillaime Hugonet has made the lady Margaret disband the Estates, that means the cities will be in a ferment."

"I guess Anthony de la Roche is still her military commander?" Ash speculated.

Another of the *centeniers* exclaimed, "He's one of our late Duke's father's bastards. He ought to be loyal, if nothing else!"[27]

Ash caught Florian's eye. She had no need to say *professional rivalry*; it was plain from the surgeon-Duchess's expression that she deduced exactly the same thing.

"Rickard?"

" 'The Frankish woman has yet an army, by virtue that she is pious in her heretic religion. Know, great Gelimer, that she does not swear, either by God or the Saints; that she is said to hold mass wherever the army travels, three times a day; that she has with her her musicians, choir, and has mass sung. She travels always as befits a lady, riding sidesaddle, always chaperoned by priests. My heart is cold, King-Caliph, when I tell you how much support she has among the common folk, who still revere her husband's name.' "

"This was a fortnight ago?" Captain Romont murmured. "I wonder how long he held his command after this report got back to Carthage?"

Ash grinned at the curly-haired knight, and gestured for Richard to read on.

" 'The Frankish woman has with her some eight thousand men—' "

Someone at the far end of the table whistled. Ash glanced in that direction and saw men grinning. *Eight thousand! Now there's a reassuring figure . . .*

" '—all in Burgundian colors, and at first under the com-

---

[27] Anthony de la Roche was taken prisoner at Nancy, in January of 1477, when Charles the Bold was killed. Rather than staying loyal to Margaret, or indeed to his half niece Mary of Burgundy, he transferred his allegiance with breathtaking haste to Louis XI, and thus retained his lands in the conquered duchy.

mand of Philippe of Croy, the Lord of Chimay, but after his death,[28] under command of Anthony, Duke's bastard, Count of La Roche. This man, great King-Caliph, is a notable soldier. In battle, he has been in command of the ducal banner, and often was deputed to act as regent for the dead Duke. He is her first chamberlain, and men say that she holds him dear in her heart, for that, when they held tournament to celebrate her wedding to his half brother Charles, he was gravely injured, wearing her favor—' "

"Oh, spare me!" Florian sighed.

Ash chuckled. "I like this one. He picks up all the gossip."

"Eight thousand men," Olivier de la Marche repeated.

More soberly, Ash said, "About the same number that we've got sitting outside the walls. Doesn't she get more? Rickard, where's the next bit?"

The boy shuffled through four sheets of paper, bringing one to the top of the pile, and smoothing it out. He squinted at the black lettering.

" 'I have heard—under the One True God to your ear, King-Caliph—that when she had dismissed the councils of her common people, she was forced to ride personally from city to city, to The Hague, Leiden, Delft, and Gouda, to raise more men. But I do not fear to tell you that she has a scant one thousand more.[29] Rumor says she has made these cities melt down all their bells to make new cannon. Our three legions push north and east, hard in her pursuit now, and before long there will be more victories to gladden the heart of Carthage.' "

"Before long," Ash said, "that man will be digging latrines. Christus! I can see why the Faris wanted to be up north, not here. That's where the action is!"

---

[28]In fact, the Lord of Chimay was taken prisoner at the battle of Nancy, on 5 January 1477, and after being ransomed, returned to loyally serve Mary of Burgundy and her heirs, in Duke Maximillian's court.

[29]In the winter of 1476/77, raising troops for her husband, Margaret is reported as having raised another four thousand men from these towns.

"I see that both you and she wish to meet each other on the field of battle, Demoiselle-Captain. That is commendable fire and courage." Olivier de la Marche reached out with one fleshy hand and patted Floria's arm, oblivious to the look of dry humor on her face. "However, this tells us of one minor victory for them, but Lady Margaret and the lord of la Roche leading an army—this is good news!"

"It's good news fourteen or fifteen days old." Ash drummed her fingertips lightly against her leg-armor. "It's too early to say for sure, but if the *Mère-Duchesse* has had another fortnight since this, and she hasn't been defeated—we could see her coming south."

Into the optimistic silence, Florian said:

"There's no mention of Lord-*Amir* Leofric. Or the Faris herself. Or the *machina rei militaris* itself."

"No. The reports the other way—to the Faris—have said nothing. . . . I don't know who this 'cousin' Sisnandus is, who took over the House after we left, after the earthquake. I don't know if Leofric's more seriously injured than I first thought." She momentarily forgot the *centeniers* of the Burgundian army, staring unseeing into distance. "But remember, nothing's happened to make the *King-Caliph* distrust the Stone Golem's strategic advice. As far as he's concerned, all this is a sign of God's favor! If it's still telling him 'take Burgundy'—that's what he's going to do. Damn: we need Margaret's army here *now*!"

With the last word, her frustration broke out; her hand went up and came down flat on the table, with a hollow gunshot sound. Rickard twitched, and wiped his squinting eyes.

"Suppose God grants the *Mère-Duchesse* the defeat of the legions in the north." Olivier de la Marche swept extraneous papers aside and uncovered a map. "It will not be easy to feed her men, away from the rich cities, but suppose Lady Margaret's commander commandeers boats, Demoiselle-Captain. Rivers will bring them south faster than a forced march. There is still sunlight over Burgundy. The Meuse and the Marne will not have frozen." He bowed his head toward Florian. "Your Grace, if they can win in the north, they *can* come to us. God send them a victory!"

"Soon would be nice," Ash remarked wryly. Over his chuckle, she said, "Okay: we talk about this, we make initial deployments, we wait for Margaret, we see if we can kill the Faris before she gets here. Anything anyone thinks has been left out?"

Silence.

Antonio Angelotti said languidly, "Just one thing, boss. May we stop holding council in the Tour Philippe, at least in daylight? *Every* Visigoth gun team out there's using it as a marker for target practice!"

The *centeniers* laughed, one man leaning over to speak to another, two knights sharing ale from the server's jug; and her stomach clenched, painfully.

Don't be stupid, girl!—it's obvious from this window—you can see they're not trying to deploy for an attack yet. I don't need to be up at the gate . . .

I can't leave these guys yet.

Green Christ, am I going to spend all my time now talking?

"Boss need to hit something?" Florian queried, with acid penetration.

"Boss isn't going to get the chance, is she?" Ash continued to look, to memorize faces: *Romont, Loyecte, Berghes—no, the skinny-legged one in Gothic arm defenses is Berghes—* "Because that isn't what the Big Boss does, is it?"

"You're not the Big Boss," Florian said briskly. She raised her voice for attention. "Right. The Duke stayed here in Dijon. It didn't help him. If digging a long tunnel is what it takes, dig one. Start it now."

Rickard automatically began to scribble on a sheet of paper.

Floria added, "They could attack us at any time. So send out the heralds. But send out—was it the Sieur de Loyecte's men? Yes. Them too."

"Florian—"

De la Marche said, "Your Grace—"

"It's my responsibility."

The surgeon-turned-Duchess held up a pale hand. For all the white samite that covered the back of it, it remained what it was: the hand of a woman who lives out of doors, and who handles sharpened steel.

"My responsibility," she repeated. "Even if it's only for today, then the ultimate responsibility is *mine*."

Ash stared. After a moment, both de la Marche and Bishop John bowed their heads.

"Just as well you got a surgeon," Floria added, sardonically. "I've had to take responsibility for men dying long before this. All right. Send out your killers."

For all her certainty, there was a dazed numbness in her expression that Ash recognized.

"Having someone die when you're digging an arquebus ball out of their stomach isn't the same as ordering a death. Florian, I was going to order it anyway."

"She is either Duchess or she is not," Philippe Ternant said, speaking without opening his fragile closed eyelids. "Demoiselle Ash, you must act with her permission."

Ash bit down on a raucous remark. *Florian doesn't need that right now.*

Florian rubbed her fingers one against the other. "Ash, I have never had the least desire to be Duchess. If I had any taste for Burgundian politics, I would have come to court, here, when I was a girl."

Ash glimpsed momentary dismay on several faces.

Still decisively, Floria announced, "I'll come into the palace daily, but I can't run the company hospital at a distance. Baldina isn't good enough unsupervised. I'm staying at the company tower. I'll be talking to the abbots about additional hospices for the civilian wounded. Ash, I'll be taking over the ground floor, too. The men can sleep in the cellars."

That isn't the way to do this! These guys want you here: you're their Duchess . . .

Holding back a desire to yell at her surgeon, Ash said, "You wouldn't rather put the wounded in the cellars, given the bombardment?"

Floria nodded, sharply.

"Okay, I'll get that sorted."

A distant roar sounded outside. Ash paced over to one window, then the next, peering through the gaps between shutter and frame. One gave her the glimpse of dragon-tail fire, arcing through the sky.

"Isn't that nice. The Nones bombardment. You could set the town clock by that crew down at the south bridge. Angeli, you got a point about this tower. No need to make it *easy* for them."

The atmosphere relaxed a little at that. *But I don't want to be mending fences all the time . . .* Meeting Floria's green gaze, she saw the raw edge of panic that underlay her determination.

"Okay, guys. That's given us a framework to work in. Ten minutes stand-down, for beer and bitching." She grinned. "Then back here, and we'll start working things out in detail."

Hidden under the noise of their chairs scraping back from the table, Florian said shakily, "I need Margaret's army soon. Don't I?"

The council went on past the early November sunset, and into evening. Servants brought in sweet-smelling pure wax candles, and Ash sighed, in the middle of a discussion, suddenly breaking off to think *This is luxury!*, remembering the noxious tallow tapers that are all the company's stores now hold.

Rank has its privileges. A cynical smile pulled up one side of her mouth, and she caught Romont's unwary, amazed look, and went back to thumping the table and shuffling gold plate on the tablecloth into the disposition of Burgundian companies around Dijon's walls.

"Half his men are merchants' sons!" one of the *centeniers*, Saint-Seigne, thundered. "I will not put my knights at the same gate as Loyecte's men!"

Barely withholding the words, Ash sighed internally. *Oh for fuck's sake!*

"This is a council of weariness," Olivier de la Marche said tactfully. He turned to Florian. "Your Grace, none of us has slept. There is much to do, to make certain we are as fully prepared as we can be. Half of us will sleep through the day, now, half through the night."

"Except the Maid of Burgundy, who'll be up until Matins, and rise at Lauds . . ." Robert Anselm whispered to Ash.

"Ah, bugger off, *rosbif*!"

He gave a happy, rumbling chuckle.

"Christ, you *do* need sleep!" Ash elbowed him. "Florian—"

"Don't go anywhere yet," the surgeon said bluntly, over the noise of men rising, bowing, and withdrawing themselves from the ducal chamber.

The verdant-robed Bishop of Cambrai rose from his chair, as the rest did. Instead of moving toward the chamber door, Bishop John walked back down the table toward the surgeon-Duchess Floria.

"Bishop John." Florian stabbed a long, white finger toward Ash. "About tomorrow night—this is the witness I want at my investiture."

He beamed. "*Madame cher duchesse*, of course."

Aware that Anselm and Angelotti were waiting for her, talking urgently to the readmitted escort, Ash protested, "I haven't got time to spare to go through another damn hours-long public ceremony, Florian!"

The Bishop startled. "Public? The people don't need to see this. They know who the *Duchesse* is. They recognize her in the streets. Taking the ducal coronet is between her and God."

"Another good reason why you don't need me," Ash said dryly.

"The *Duchesse* wishes you to stand private vigil with her, and myself, and the other two witnesses, through the night. The following morning's mass gives her the crown, but nothing men can do can make her less, or more, than she already is."

"I'm busy! I've got a fu—a company to run! No, an army! I've got to look through all the duty rolls of the Burgundian companies—"

Florian's hand closed over her arm, with all the strength of surgeon's fingers. "Ash. I want a friend there. You don't have to tell me you think it's a load of cock."

Startled, Ash rapped out, "You don't have to tell me you think exactly the same thing!"

Floria smiled painfully, ignoring the churchman's expression. "That isn't the point. Remember when you talked to Charles? You want to know 'why Burgundy.' So do I. I'm Duchess, Ash. I want to know, why Burgundy—and, why me?"

Ash blinked. Sleeplessness shuddered through her. She put the weakness to the dark back of her mind where she loses such things. "Will this 'vigil' of yours tell us 'why Burgundy'?"

Florian switched her gaze from Ash to the Burgundian Bishop. "It better had."

vii

SHE SLEPT AN hour in one company's guard-house, down by the south gate; another hour in the armory, while clerks sorted out inventories. The rest of the night and the following morning saw her among hackbutters, archers, squires to knightly men-at-arms, judging their morale, hearing their officers' reports, but most of all, letting them see her.

"A Pucelle?" one noseless veteran of Duke Philip's campaigns remarked. "Quite right, too—God sent one to the French, the least He could do was send one to us!"

His spoiled speech gave her the option of appearing not to understand. She merely grinned at the billman. "Granddad, *you're* just surprised to find there's still a virgin in Dijon."

That was being repeated, with embellishments, before she left that barracks, and it followed her all the way to the Viscount-Mayor's hall, where it was received with less delight and more shock. By that stage—talking all the time to two, three, four men simultaneously—she was past caring what civilians thought.

At noon, back at the tower, stripped to her shirt by her pages, she sat down suddenly on her pallet, dizzy enough that she tipped over slowly and sprawled face forward, asleep before she was conscious of touching the straw-filled linen.

She slept through the short light hours of the afternoon, waking once at the noise of her pages, three nine-year-old boys huddled around the great hearth, polishing the rust-spotted plates of her armor: cuirass, cannons, vambrace, pauldrons. . . . The smell of neat's-foot oil being worked into the leather straps roused her enough to lift her head off the bed, blinking.

Across from her, on the other side of the hearth's heat, Robert Anselm lay slumped asleep on a truckle bed, one huge, immobile, silent lump. She hitched one elbow in, to get her arm under her and push herself up.

"Boss." Rickard squatted down beside her palliasse. "Message from Captain Angelotti—'you're not indispensable, the company is managing perfectly well without you: go back to sleep!' "

Ash grunted an indistinguishable protest; was flat face-down and asleep again before she could properly voice it. When she woke for the second time, one of the pages was cutting bread by the hearth-fire and nibbling crusts, and Angelotti was sprawled on the truckle bed—asleep on his back, with a face like an angel, and snoring like a hog in a wallow.

Rickard looked up at her from where he knelt, scouring her sallet-visor with the finest white sand.

"Boss, message from Captain Anselm and Messire de la Marche—'you're not indispensable; the *army's* managing perfectly well—' "

"Ah, bollocks!" she said thickly.

She did not dream: there was no hint of the scent of boar, or the chill taste of snow; nothing but deep unconsciousness. Godfrey, if he is a presence, is at too deep a level to touch her conscious soul.

When sleep finally let her go, she rolled over in a tangle of warm linen shirt, blankets, and furs; and the slanting light from one slit-window put sunset's red gold across her face.

"The doc—the *Duchess* sent word," Rickard said, as soon as he saw she was awake. "She wants you at the chapel."

She arrived in the bathhouse of the palace's Mithraic chapel as Floria del Guiz stepped up out of the wooden tub, and servants swathed her in pure white linen. Water dampened the cloth. The steam that filled the air began to dissipate quickly in the chill.

"This is what you call immediate, is it?" Florian called.

Ash handed her cloak and hat to her page and turned back to find the surgeon-duchess temporarily wrapped in a vast fur-trimmed blue velvet robe. Ash walked across the flagstones toward her.

"I had stuff to do. I needed to talk with Jonvelle and Jussey and the rest of Olivier's *centeniers*." Ash yawned, stifling it with her fist. She looked at Florian, eyes bright, as the woman waved her attendants away. "*And* the refugee French and German knights, and their men. Very nice, everyone's being. We'll see what happens when it comes to me giving them orders . . ."

"Next time, get here when I ask."

Floria spoke harshly. Ash opened her mouth to snap back. The woman added, "I'm *supposed* to be a Duchess. You're showing me up in front of these people. If I *do* have any authority—I don't need it undermined."

"Uh." Ash stared at her. Finally, she shrugged, put her hand through her cropped silver hair, and said, "Yeah. Okay. Fair enough."

They stared at each other for a few seconds.

"I understand," Ash protested.

"Boss's vanity is hurt."

"You're—" Ash stopped: rephrased *you're not really a Duchess*! "You know, whatever it is you do with the Wild Machines—you're not a Duchess to me or the company."

A little wistful, the older woman said, "I'm glad to hear it."

"But I still don't have time to waste on this. If it is a waste. Have you spoken to that Bishop yet?"

"He won't say anything until I go through this vigil."

"Ah, fuck it. Let's do it, then. Who needs sleep anyway!"

The Duchess's attendants emerged again from behind the long hessian curtains that separated each of the great baths—one with wine, and two others with towels and fresh clothing. Ash stood absentmindedly watching as they unwrapped and dried the gold-haired woman, her mind running through roster lists.

Floria turned her head, opened her mouth as if to say something, flushed, and turned away. Pinkness flooded the skin of her throat and bare breasts. Ash—expecting a caustic remark, rather than embarrassment—abruptly felt herself color and turned her back on the group of women.

Does she feel like I used to feel when Fernando watched *me*?

It is five months since she touched him, in bed; her fingers still remember the smooth silk heat of his cock, the velvet electricity of his skin; the flex and thrust of his bare buttocks under her hands as he pushes inside her. Fernando: who may be dead, now, in the Carthage earthquake—or, if he isn't, has likely divorced her by now. Too dangerous for a renegade German now in a Visigoth household to have a Frankish wife. . . .

And to be the brother of a Burgundian Duchess? Ash suddenly thought. *Hmm. I wonder if he's in even more trouble, if he's still alive?*

"Let's get going." Florian appeared at her shoulder. She eyed Ash's start with curiosity, but did not say anything. A faint pinkness remained to her skin, but it might have come from the rough toweling, and nothing more.

"How long is this going to take?"

"Until Prime tomorrow."

"All night? Fuck . . ."

They had dressed Florian in a plain white linen overgown, and under it a gown of white lambswool, also with no decoration. A linen coif covered her short gold hair. As the women withdrew, she looked over her shoulder, snapped her fingers, and beckoned; and the youngest girl came back with the fur-lined blue velvet robe.

Ash watched Florian struggling into the voluminous garment. Turning to signal her own page to bring back her hat and campaigning cloak—the stone walls' chill soaking the air already, even so soon after nightfall—she smiled, mildly. "Who needs a vigil? You ain't having any trouble taking to behaving like a Duchess . . ."

Florian stopped pushing her arm through the slit of a hanging sleeve, and stared back over her shoulder at the departing attendants. "That's not fair!"

Ash reached out, twitched the sleeve down over Florian's shoulder, and turned toward the curtain that masked the tunnel leading to the chapel. Leaving her page and escort behind, she stepped forward and held back the coarse cloth.

"Duchess takes precedence, I believe . . ."

Florian did not laugh.

Torches in cressets lit the low passage, their smoke making the air acrid. Ash found her fingers automatically going to her belt and her dagger. The relief of being in civilian clothes and out of armor for an hour made her body blissful, but chilled; and she swung her cloak around her shoulders as she walked into the tunnel after Florian.

Florian came to a dead halt in front of her. Without turning, she said, "I had someone ordered out of the council room this afternoon."

Ash let the hessian curtain fall behind her. It cut off sound, left them isolated under the low granite roof. She stepped around the motionless woman.

"And they went." Florian raised her head. "If I'd wanted to, I could have had men throw them out."

"If you wanted, you could have more than that."

Ash glanced up ahead: the farther curtain did not stir. No priests yet.

"That's the problem." Floria's voice fell flat and muffled, deadened by the ancient stone.

"Ah, you wait," Ash said reflectively, linking her arm through the surgeon's, beginning to pace toward the far end of the corridor. "You wait till you want someone thrown out *real* bad. Then, you start cutting corners . . ."

"You mean, I make some illegitimate use of this power I've been stuck with?" Under the demand, Florian's voice had a tone of panic.

"Everybody does it at least once. Every lance leader, every *centenier*. Every nobleman."

"And yours was?" Floria snapped.

"Mine?" Ash shrugged, letting her arm drop out of the crook of the woman's elbow, maintaining her easy pace toward the far curtains. "Oh, that's got to be . . . the first time I got six of my men to cripple the living shite out of somebody. Back in—I don't remember—some northern French town."

She was conscious of Florian's face in profile as they walked, the glowing torches casting red light on her cheekbones. A tightly controlled shiver went through the older woman.

"What happened?"

"Some civilian said 'Hey, girlie, you can wear hose, and you can wave a sword around, but you're still a cunt who has to squat down to piss'—he thought that was very funny. I thought, okay, I have six hefty guys here, wearing mail that I paid for, and my livery. . . . They kicked the crap out of him, smashed his face and both knees."

The face Florian turned was desperate. As if she searched for an excuse, she asked, "And how long would your authority have lasted, if you'd allowed him to say that without reprisal?"

"Oh, about five minutes." Ash raised a brow. "But then, I didn't have to have them cripple him. And I didn't have to go into town that afternoon looking for trouble."

She was unaware of her own expression: part hooligan-enjoyment, part shame and regret. "I was pretty young. Fourteen, maybe. Florian, you're going to get this. The first time five hundred guys stand there and cheer you to the echo, and then go piling into combat because *you* say so . . . you start feeling you can do *anything*. And sometimes you will."

"I don't want to find out if I will."

Ash put out her hand to draw aside the second curtain.

"Tell me that if we're still here in six months. Once you taste it, you can't go back. But it isn't worth chucking your weight about." She tugged at the heavy cloth. "After a while, if you do too much of it, people stop listening to you. You're not in charge. You're just out in front. . . ."

Florian huddled her gown more tightly over her white robes. "Don't you find it terrifying? You're in charge of an *army*?"

Ash flashed her a quick grin. "Don't for fuck's sake ask Baldina about my laundry."

Florian, her expression fixed, glanced away without responding.

She needs a serious answer, and I'm too scared to give it.

Ash raised her voice. "Hey, come on! Aren't there any fucking priests *in* this chapel? Where's your bloody bishop?"

A disapproving older female voice said, "He's consecrating the chapel, young demoiselle. Do *you* want to tell him to hurry up?"

Ash stepped into the antechamber expecting, for a second, to see Jeanne Châlon, but the woman facing her looked nothing like the surgeon's noble aunt. Only the voices were similar. Torches smoked in the cold air, and Ash squinted at the fat, round-faced woman in wimple and looped-up kirtles, and at the man behind her, whose face seemed naggingly familiar.

"Demoiselle," the elderly man pulled off his coif. His scalp shone pink in the torchlight. "You won't remember me, I daresay. You might remember Jombert here. He's a fine dog. This is my wife, Margaret. I'm Culariac; Duke's huntsman." He turned watery eyes to Floria del Guiz. "Duchess's huntsman, I should say; pardon me, Your Grace."

A cold nose pressed against Ash's fingers. She reached down and scratched behind the ears of a white lymer sniffing at the fur-trimmed skirts of her demi-gown under her cloak.

" 'Jombert'!" she said. "I remember. It was you that came out to the Visigoth camp at the truce, to ask if the hunt could ride."

The man's face broke into a smile at her recognition. His wife continued to scowl. After a few seconds, Ash recognized the look. *Well, I'm not learning to fight in skirts to please her.*

"We're here as your witnesses, Your Grace," the old man added, with another bow. What self-importance there might have been in his expression vanished as the lymer abandoned Ash, gave a quick sniff to the surgeon-Duchess, and padded back to nose at his master's thigh. Culariac gazed down in pure affection.

Which is he more proud of, Ash wondered, *his hound, or his position here? He'll be drinking on the strength of both, tomorrow night. If the town isn't taken by then.*

" 'Witnesses'?" she belatedly queried.

"Just to see Her Grace does stay in there, all night." The woman jerked her thumb at the farther side of the anteroom, where a curtain masked another doorway. Woven in green-and-gold thread, it shimmered heavily in the dull light.

"We'll stay out here," the woman Margaret said. "No, don't you worry, Your Grace; I've brought some sewing with me; Culariac will wake me if I sleep, and I'll wake him."

"Oh." Florian looked blank. "Right."

A faint, almost imperceptible vibration ran through the stone floor. Ash identified it as a trebuchet strike, not far from the palace itself. The old woman touched her breast, making the sign of the Horns.

Falling in beside Florian as she walked toward the far doorway, Ash murmured, "Where the fuck did they find *her*?"

"Chosen by lot." Florian kept her voice equally low.

"God give me strength!"

"That, too."

"Your damn bishop had better give us some answers."

"Yes."

"You picked a real worldly priest there."

"Why would I want a devout one?"

Jolted by the answer, Ash shoved aside the curtain embroidered with oak leaves. The granite facing of the walls and ceiling gave way to natural limestone. The floor of the passage dipped, so that they walked down a long series of very wide and shallow steps. Ash saw that the torch-holders spiked now into undressed, gray-white stone, the marks of chisels still plain in the walls. Smoke wavered in the draft from air vents carved into living rock.

"Won't be so cold if we're underground," she remarked pragmatically.

Florian hauled up the train of her gown, where it scraped along the limestone floor, and bundled the cloth up in her arms in front of her as she walked. "My father had his knighthood vigil here. I remember him telling me about this, when I was very young. It's almost all I can remember of him." She glanced up at the vaulted ceiling, as if she could see through stone to the ancient palace above. "He was a favorite of Duke Philip. Before he changed his loyalties to the Emperor Frederick."

"Hell. I knew Fernando had to get it from somewhere."

"My father was married in Cologne cathedral." Florian turned her head, smiled briefly at Ash's evident shock. "We got the news, in the end, from Constanza. Another good reason for me not to have come to your wedding."

Ash caught her shoe on the uneven stone, stumbling over the threshold in Floria's wake, and for a second she did not see the smoky, tiny chamber that they entered, but the soaring pillars and gothic arches of the cathedral, the shafts of light, and Fernando reaching out to touch her and say *I smell piss . . .*

Worse than a whore! she thought fiercely. *He wouldn't have laughed at a whore.*

Ash made the sign of the Horns automatically, aware that Florian was standing stock-still in front of her now, her head raised, staring. The chapel's terra-cotta tiles felt uneven, worn by centuries of men walking to the iron grille to celebrate the blood-mass. Ash shivered, in a room barely twenty feet square: claustrophobia not eased by the torchlight falling from above, through the ceiling grating.

"My feet are cold," Florian whispered.

"If we're in here all night, more than your feet will get cold!" Ash kept her voice low with an effort. As her vision adjusted, and filled with dully glittering luminescence, she added, "Green Christ!"

Every free square foot of the walls was covered in mosaic, each square of the mosaic not glass, but precious gem; cut to glow in the shifting torchlight.

"Look at that. A king's ransom. More than a king's ransom!" Florian muttered. "No wonder Louis's jealous."

"King's ransom be buggered, you could equip a dozen legions if this lot's real . . ." Ash leaned in close, peering at a mosaic of the birth of the Green Christ—his imperial Jewish mother sprawled under the oak, half-dead from bringing forth her son; the Baby suckling at the Sow; the Eagle, in the oak's branches, lifting up his head, depicted about to take wing on the flight that will—in three days—bring Augustus and his legions to the right spot in the wild German forest. And in the next panel, Christus Viridianus heals his mother, with the leaves of the oak.

"Might be rubies." Ash winced at the wax running from the candlestick over the back of her hand. She held the light closer to the wall, studying the neat squares that delineate a puddle of birth-blood. She felt a sudden nausea. With an effort, she added, "Might just be garnets."

Florian walked a quick circuit of the walls, glancing at each panel briefly—Viridianus and his legion in Judea, gone native after the Persian wars; Viridianus speaking with the Jewish elders; Viridianus and his officers worshiping Mithras. Then Augustus's funeral, the coronation of his true son, and, in the background, the adopted son Tiberius and the conspirators, the desire for the oak tree upon which they will hang Viridianus—bones broken, no blood shed—already plain on their faces.

One circuit of the room, back to where Ash stands by the birth; and the last panel is Constantine, three centuries later, converting the Empire to the religion of Viridianus, whom the Jews still consider nothing more than a Jewish prophet, but whom the followers of Mithras have long and faithfully known to be the Son of the Unconquered Sun.

"Doesn't look like anyone's held mass yet," Ash said doubtfully.

In the center of the room, two stone blocks are set, to chain the bulls. Between them, an iron grate is let into the floor, stiff with old black debris of sacrifices. Featureless darkness shows beneath. The iron bars are not wet.

Ash tried the iron gates that closed off the shallow passage leading up toward the air. The heavy chains hardly rattled. She stared, for a moment, at the ridged stone slope, down which the bull is led into this boxlike room.

When she turned back, she saw a glimmer in Florian's eye—recognizably laughter. Half-frowning, half on the verge of a giggle, Ash muttered, "What? *What?*"

"They bring a bull for the Mass," the older woman said, and snuffled, sounding all herself again. "Wonder what they'd make of a couple of old cows?"

"Florian!"

Without any hesitation, the surgeon crossed to the remaining exit: a small wooden door set into the corner of the room. She opened it. The dark stairwell beyond flared with torchlight stirred up by the draft of the door's opening. One glance over her shoulder, and Florian hauled up her gown and demi-gown clear of her feet, and sidled through the door. Ash stared for a long minute, watching her coifed head sink lower, walking down the cramped spiral of the stair.

"Wait up, damn it!"

The narrow stair, set into the thick wall, turned back so swiftly on itself that she could never have come down it successfully in armor. The chill granite left damp marks on her furred demi-gown. Florian blocked the light from below. Ash groped in her wake, feeling the wood of a doorjamb, and then came out suddenly into an open space with a vast drop in front of her.

"Shiiit . . ."

"This is old. Monks' work." Florian, beside Ash, also stared out into the brick-lined shaft. "Maybe God's grace kept them from falling off!"

Torchlight came down from above through the iron sacrificial grille. It barely stirred the shadows on the walls of the shaft. Far below, more lights glowed—the steadier, less smoky glow of many candles.

The door that Ash had come out of opened all but sheer

onto the shaft. Now her eyes adjusted to the dimness, she saw that a stair ran down, deosil,[30] along the side of the wall. Descending . . .

"Let's go." She touched Florian's arm, and slid herself along the tiny platform to put one foot on the first step.

A knee-high wall, studded with mosaic, was the only barrier between the stair and the drop—by no means high enough to be reassuring: one slip, and a body would pivot straight over the stonework.

"Bugger this!" Florian muttered. Glancing back, Ash saw her face shiny with sweat. Her own breath caught in her throat.

"Hang on to my belt."

"No. I'll manage."

"Sooner we're down, the better."

Inhaling the scent of pitch and beeswax, and the dampness of stone and brick, Ash took a breath, set herself a mental pace, and began to walk down the stairs with as much ease as if they were defender's stairs in any castle. The steps were shallow, worn away in the middle with the tread of countless years. At the corner of the shaft, the stairway made a sharp right angle, continued on down. Her eyes adjusting more now to the light from below, she could see the sketched lines on the far walls: the glitter of mosaic; the stair that they would have to descend. She kept her gaze away from the dark void on her right-hand side. Down and turn. Down and turn. Down, turn.

"There has to be another way in!" Florian snapped, behind her.

"Maybe not. Who's going to come down here but the priests?" Another turn. Pulling off her glove and letting her hand stray out to brush the wall, she kept her orientation, counteracting the pull of the drop. "There's your qualification for the Duke's chaplain, Florian—doesn't suffer from vertigo!"

Another snuffling giggle from behind. " 'Duchess's chaplain'!"

---

[30]Clockwise.

I wish it was that easy.

The yellow glow of candles encompassed them. Feeling their heat, Ash glanced up, realizing that their light now blocked out the view of the Mithras grating above. She was no more than fifteen or twenty feet above floor level now. Above tiles marbled red and black—no: terra-cotta, but with the traces of every day's mass still spilling down from the plain stone block that is the altar.

The last corner, the last steps, the little wall ending; and she stepped out onto the bottom of the shaft, into the chapel, the skin on the pads of her fingers worn rough. Pulling her glove on, Ash said, "Thank God for that!"

Florian jostled her, coming off the stairway in haste. She reached up and wiped her sweating face. Her fair hair glowed in the light of dozens of candles.

"Thank God indeed," a voice said, from the shadows beyond the altar, "but with more devoutness, possibly, demoiselle?"

"Bishop John!"

"Your Grace," he acknowledged Floria del Guiz.

Surprised to find her knees a little weak, Ash took a few determined steps about the chapel that stood at the bottom of the sacrificial shaft. Now, in the candlelight, she could see that it was wider than the shaft itself to east and west: continuing on under a low brick barrel vault either end, one vault containing church plate, the other a painted shrine.

How long before we can ask him why Burgundy? *And how long before he'll answer?*

A novice in a green-and-white cassock bowed his way past his bishop, carrying a lit wax taper, vanishing up the narrow stairs that clung to the walls. Ash smelled the sweetness of beeswax candles. Within a minute, every inch of this lower end of the shaft glittered. Masons had squared off the limestone, craftsmen had laid mosaics of the Tree, the Bull, the Boar, and—around the marble altar slab, dark with congealed blood—a square of floor taken up by an oval-eyed Green Christ.

With almost simultaneous movement, Florian reached up and dragged the linen coif from her head, and Ash pushed back her hood and took off her hat. She stifled a grin—*both of us have been dressing as men for too long!*—and felt her chilled body relax in the growing heat from the candles.

Beside her, Floria looked questioningly at the Burgundian bishop. "Do we celebrate a mass now?"

"No."

The little round-faced man's voice fell flatly in the small box of a room.

"We don't?" Ash realized that she could hear the footsteps of other priests or novices, the sound coming from above, through the grating; but neither the smell nor the sound of a bull-calf.

"I may be accused of trying to repopulate Burgundy on my own," the Bishop of Cambrai said, small black eyes gleaming with something that might have been amusement, "and of loving the fair flesh far too much, but one thing I am not, *Madame cher duchesse* Floria, is a hypocrite. I had the opportunity to observe not just your captain here, but yourself, during our meeting in the Tour Philippe. I need not repeat what you said. You're so far estranged from your faith that I think it will take more than one night to bring you in charity with God again."

"Surely not, Your Grace?" Ash said smoothly. "The surgeon—the Duchess—here has always taken field mass with us, and she works with deacons in our hospital—"

"I'm not the inquisition." Bishop John shifted his gaze to her. "I know a heretic when I see one, and I know a good woman driven from God by the cruelty of what circumstances have caused her to do. That's Floria, daughter, and it's you, too. If you ever had any faith, I think you lost it in Carthage."

Ash's lips pressed together for a second. "Long before *that*."

"Yes?" His soft black brows went up. "But you've come back from Carthage talking of machines and devices, a woman bred like one of Mithras's bulls—and nothing at all of the hand of God in this. 'Maid of Burgundy.' "

Ash shifted, under her cloak, rubbing one fist absently across her belly under the demi-gown.

Bishop John turned back to Florian. "I can't withhold communion if you ask for it, but I can strongly advise that you don't ask."

Beside Ash, Floria del Guiz huffed an exasperated breath, folding her arms across her body. The cloth of her full gown fell down in sculptured folds about her, trailing on the uneven terra-cotta tiles. The warm light of the candles put a deeper gold into her hair, which fell to her shoulders now it was unconfined by her linen coif, limned her profile, but did little, even warming her skin tone, to hide the gauntness of her face now.

"So what *do* we do?" Floria asked acidly. "Sit around down here for the night? If that's all, I could be much more use to your duchy if I had some sleep."

Bishop John watched her with a brilliant gaze. "Your Grace, I'm a man of the Church, with a very large family of hopeful bastards; and more to come, I should think, flesh being what it is. How should I cast the first stone at *you*? Even without a mass, this is still your vigil."

"Which means?"

"You'll know that, by the end of it." The Bishop of Cambrai reached out, touching the altar as if for reassurance. "So will all of us. Pardon me if I tell you that Messire de la Marche is as anxious as I am to know what you make of this."

"Bet he is," Ash murmured. "Okay, so no mass; what *does* she do, Your Grace?"

The flames of the candles flared and dipped, shadows racing across the mosaic walls. The acrid smoke caught in the back of Ash's throat, and she stifled a cough.

"She takes up the ducal crown, if God wills it. I advise some time be spent in meditation." Bishop John bowed his head slightly to Floria.

Ash gave way and cleared her throat with a hacking cough. Wiping at her streaming eyes, she said, "I expected this all to be planned out, Your Grace. You're saying Florian can do what she likes?"

"My brother Charles spent his night in prayer here, in full armor, fourteen hours without a break. That told me, at least, what Duke we were getting. I remember my father told me *he* brought wine, and roasted the Bull's flesh." The bishop's small pursed mouth curved in a smile. "He never said, but I suspect some woman kept him company. A night in a cold chapel is a long time to be alone."

Ash found herself grinning appreciatively at Charles's half brother, Philip's son.

"You," he added, to Floria, "bring a woman with you, one who dresses like a man."

Ash's smile faded.

"As you've guessed," Bishop John of Cambrai said, "your aunt Jeanne Châlon has spoken to me."

"And what did she say?"

A quite genuine distress showed on the churchman's face at Florian's sharp demand. Ash—who has enough experience of men like this, in positions of power like this—thought *What's that old cow been saying to him? Two minutes ago it was* Madame cher duchesse*!*

The bishop spoke directly, and with distaste. "Is it true that you have had a female lover?"

"Ah." There was a smile on Florian's face, but it had very little to do with humor. "Now let me guess. There is a noblewoman and a spinster—her niece is made Duchess—but there's a terrible scandal in the family. She comes to tell you before it all gets out as rumor. Tells you she *has* to confess all this, it's her duty."

"Cover your ass," Ash rumbled, startled to find herself sounding very like Robert Anselm. She added, "Jesus, that cow! You didn't hit her hard enough!"

Floria did not take her eyes off the Bishop.

"More or less," John admitted. "Should she have preferred family loyalty to warning me that as well as dressing like a man, you act like a man in other ways?"

A few seconds of silence went by. Floria continued to stare at the Bishop. "The technical charge was that she was Jewish, treating Christian patients."

" 'She'?"

"Esther. My wife." Florian smiled very wryly, and very wearily. "My female lover. You can find it all out in the records of the Empty Chair."

"Rome's under darkness, and you'd never make the journey," Ash cut in. "Don't say anything you don't want to say."

"Oh, I want to say it." Florian's eyes were fiery. "Let the bishop here know what he's getting. Because I *am* Duchess."

Ash thought the Bishop of Cambrai flinched at that one.

"Esther and I became lovers when I finished studying medicine at Padua." Floria folded her arms, the cloth of her robe bundled up to her body. "She never, not for one instant, thought I was a man. When we were arrested in Rome, she'd just had a baby. We weren't getting on too well. Because of that."

"She had a *baby*—?" Ash stopped and blushed.

"Just some man she fucked one night," the surgeon said contemptuously. "He wasn't her lover. We had fights about that. We had more fights about Joseph—the baby. I was jealous, I suppose. She gave so much time to him. We were in the cells for two months. Joseph died, of pneumonia. Neither of us could cure him. The day after that, they took Esther out and chained her up and burned her. The day after *that*, I had a message that Tante Jeanne had paid my ransom: *I* was free to go. So long as I left Rome. The abbot there said they'd have to burn male sodomites, but what did it matter what a woman did? So long as I didn't practice medicine again."

Floria's words dropped into the cold air of the chapel, delivered with a numb bravado that Ash recognized. *We do that, all of us. After a field of battle.*

"My aunt's been creeping round me since I got back," Florian said. "Bishop, did she tell you that the last thing I did when I was here in August was punch her? I laid her out in the public street. I'm not surprised she's gone behind my back to you. But did she tell you?—she could have paid Esther's ransom, too. She just chose not to."

"Perhaps . . ." John of Cambrai was evidently struggling; he stared away at the mosaics. "Perhaps there was too little money for her to do anything but rescue family?"

"*Esther* was 'family'!" Florian's tone lowered. "My father wasn't dead then. She could have written to him, if she wanted money."

"And the Abbot of Rome," John went on, "would have been looking to burn Jews—if I remember the time right, there were bread riots; blaming it all on a Jewish woman would have been an acceptable crowd-pleaser. He would have been more wary of burning a Burgundian woman who had been born noble, and who evidently had noble family still alive. No matter how she was behaving at the time."

Seeing his face, how he simultaneously seemed to want to hold out his hands to Floria, and to back away, Ash understood.

He's a man who chases women. But he can't chase Florian: Florian's not interested in men. I'm not sure it's a Church thing at all with His Grace of Cambrai.

As if to confirm it, John of Cambrai gave her a conspiratorial glance. It lasted no more than a second, but it was gravely and heterosexually flirtatious, invited complicity, said, without words, *you and I are not like this woman. We're normal.*

Momentarily intimidated by green robes and rich embroidery, Ash looked away.

Godfrey would never have said any of that. Robes don't make a priest.

She shrugged one arm out from under her cloak, and put it around Florian's shoulders. "That poisonous old cow's been mischief-making, but so what? I was there: Florian made the hart. She's Duchess. If Jeanne Châlon doesn't like it, that's just tough shit."

"If she spreads it around," Floria started.

"So what if she does?"

"In the company, last summer—"

"That's soldiers. And they're all right with you now." Ash brought her other arm out from under her cloak and put it on Florian's other shoulder, turning the woman to face her. She spoke with great intensity, driving her point home. "Understand this. Olivier de la Marche will do what you say. So will his captains. And there's an army outside Dijon. Internal dissent would be suicidal right now, but the chances are that it won't happen. People have got other things to worry about. And if there are some people who still want to make trouble—

then you put them in jail, or you hang them off the city walls. This isn't about them approving of you. This is about you being their Duchess. That means keeping everybody rounded up and pointed in the same direction. Okay?"

Whether it was Ash's intensity, or the sheer confusion on the bishop's face, Florian started nervously to smile.

"The Burgundian army has provosts," Ash added, "and the Viscount-Mayor has constables. Neither of them has them for the fun of it. *Use* them. If it comes to it, the Bishop here can be 'retired' under house arrest to the monastery up in the northeast *quartier*."

Bishop John approached. "Understand me."

Ash, not sure how much of his change of tone was a response to the thought of military power, backed off.

He reached out and took Floria's hands. "*Madame cher duchesse*, if I'm aware of your—spiritual difficulties—then equally I'm aware that I have . . . difficulties of my own. Whatever you are, I am your father in the Church, and your servant in the duchy."

The rich colors of the mosaics behind him glinted in the shifting light. Now that he stood next to her, Ash realized that Bishop John stood an inch or two shorter than Floria.

"What you are is our Duchess." He shook both her hands in his grip, for emphasis. "God save us, Floria del Guiz, you're my brother's successor. If God lets you take the ducal crown, it isn't for any of us to disobey His will."

"Crown? The *crown* doesn't matter. What does a piece of carved horn matter!" Florian freed her hands and took a step forward. She made a fist, thumped it against her chest. "I know what I am, but I don't know *why* I am, or how! Suppose you tell me? You expect me to come back to a city I haven't seen since I was a child, and do this? You expect me to come back to strangers, and do this? You tell me what's going on!"

Her breathless voice fell flat against the walls, the mosaics deadening the acoustics. A whisper of sound went up the brick-lined shaft, toward the grating and the air. As if they stood in the bottom of a dull, soundless well.

When John of Cambrai did not answer, the surgeon became icy.

"I haven't taken communion since I left the Empty Chair. I don't intend to start now. There's not going to be a mass tonight; you can tell the acolytes to go home and get some sleep." Florian shrugged. "If you want a vigil, tell me why the Dukes of Burgundy are like they are. Tell me what I've been stuck with. Otherwise, I'll just curl up in the corner and sleep. I've slept worse places on campaign; Ash will tell you."

"Yeah, but you were drunk then," Ash said, before she thought.

"Madame Duchesse!" the bishop protested.

Florian said something to him. Ash took no notice. The shifting light on the shrine caught her eye under the far barrel vault, and her vision finally adjusted enough to let her make out the dim, painted carvings.

She turned away from the Bishop and surgeon, walked straight past the plain altar, to the shrine. Marble, painted and gilded, glowed in the light of thigh-thick beeswax candles.

"Christus Viridianus!" she blurted out. And then, as both of them looked at her, startled, she pointed. "That's the Prophet Gundobad!"

"Yes." Bishop John's demure features showed no expression that might not be a trick of the shifting light. "It is."

Florian stared. "Why do you have a shrine to a heretic?"

"The shrine is not Gundobad's," the bishop said, moving forward. He pointed to one of the minor figures. "The shrine is Heito's. Sieur Heito was Duke Charles's ancestor. And will have been yours, Your Grace, it now becomes apparent."

"I didn't expect to find him here." Ash reached up and touched the cold carved marble of Gundobad's sandal and foot. "Florian, the Duke was going to tell me before he died. I suggest you ask the Bishop, now . . . '*why Burgundy*'?"

Turning, she caught an expression on Bishop John's world-weary face—something approaching excitement. Mildly, he said, "The Duchess brought you, demoiselle, but it is her decision as to how she spends her vigil. Remember that, and show due respect."

"Oh, I respect Florian." Ash put her fists on her hips, mentally closing ranks without a second thought. "I've watched her puke her guts out, outside the surgeon's tent, and come back in and take a longbow arrow out of a man's lung—"

Of course, it would be better if she hadn't got drunk in the first place.

"—I don't need a gang of Burgundians to tell me about Florian!"

"Quiet," Florian said, with something of the blurred chill in her eyes that she had, covered in hart's blood, at the end of the hunt. "Bishop—you told me what Charles of Valois brought here. You told me what Duke Philip brought. You didn't ask me what *I've* brought."

"Questions," Bishop John said. "You come with questions."

"So do I," Ash muttered, and when the bastard son of Philippe le Bon looked at her, she jerked her thumb at the shrine. "Do you know what you've got there?"

"That is Gundobad, prophet of the Carthaginians, at the moment of his death."

"Gundobad the Wonder-Worker," Ash said steadily. "I know about Gundobad. I know a lot about Gundobad, since I went south. Leofric and the Wild Machines, between them—I know what really happened, seven hundred years ago. Gundobad made the land around Carthage into a *desert*. He dried up the rivers. How the hell . . ." Ash's voice slowed. "How the hell did the Pope's soldiers manage to burn him alive?"

She ignored Florian's quick shudder: it might have been the older woman feeling the cold.

"You have a point," the surgeon said, her voice steady.

"He was the *Wonder-Worker*," Ash said again. "If he could do that to Carthage, to the Wild Machines, he shouldn't have died just because some priest ordered it!"

With a glance at Floria del Guiz, Bishop John demurred, "He cursed Pope Leo[31] and brought about the Empty Chair."

There are side panels in the chapel, one of which is the

---

[31]Is this a reference to Pope Leo III? This would put Gundobad's death on or before AD 816.

death of Leo—blinded, hunted, torn into scraps of flesh—but she knows that story too well to look.

"Any man who could turn half of North Africa into a desert," Ash said steadily, "shouldn't have died at the hands of the Bishop of Rome. Not unless there's something we don't know about Pope Leo! *No*—" she corrected herself abruptly. "Not Leo. Is it?" And she turned back to the stonework. "Who is this Heito?"

There was a silence broken by nothing but the odd drip of condensation.

Florian's voice sounded harsh and sudden. "I expected to pray tonight. I prayed when I was a girl. I was . . . devout. And if there were going to be answers, I expected them to be about Burgundy, about what *happened* to me out there, on the hunt."

Floria sighed.

"When I left Carthage, I thought we'd left the desert demons behind. But here they are." She pointed to a detail in the back of the shrine: the heretic Gundobad, preaching from a rock in a verdant southern landscape, and in the background, the tiny distant shapes of pyramids.

"Florian . . ."

"I thought we'd come where they couldn't reach you." Florian's eyes were dark holes, in the candles' shadows. "I saw you walk away, remember? I saw them *make* you do it!"

"They couldn't do it when I spoke to them two days ago. This isn't about me," Ash said. "I didn't hunt the hart. You did. Now I want to know, why Burgundy? And the answer's Gundobad. Isn't it?"

Bishop John, as she turned on him, continued to look not at Ash but at Florian. At Florian's small nod, he spoke.

"This is the square of St. Peter," he said, touching key points on the painted stonework. "Here, at the cathedral door, is where great Charlemagne was crowned. He had been dead a year when his sons, and Pope Leo, put on trial the Carthaginian prophet Gundobad, for the Arian heresy. Here is Gundobad, in the papal cells, with his wife Galsuinda, and his daughter Ingundis."

"He *married*?" Ash blurted. "Shit. I never thought about that. What happened to them?"

"Galsuinda and Ingundis? They were made slaves; they were shipped back to Carthage before the trial—I believe Leo used them to carry a message to the then King-Caliph." Bishop John steepled his fingers. "Although I believe the King-Caliph of that time was not sorry to be relieved of such a prophet, darkness and desert having come to his lands all in one year."

"But it wasn't! It wasn't one year!" Ash hears in her head the voice of the *machina rei militaris*, when she was prisoner in Carthage: impassive, impersonal, retelling an undeniable history. "The darkness didn't come until the 'Rabbi's Curse,' four centuries later. That's when the Wild Machines drew down the sun, to feed them the strength to speak through the Stone Golem. Gundobad was long before that!"

"Is it so?" Bishop John nodded. "We tell it differently. Stories of ages past become confused. The memory of man is short."

The memory of the Wild Machines is longer. And a damn sight more accurate.

"Nevertheless," he added, "it was in that year that the lands about Carthage ceased to be a garden, and became a desert, and Gundobad fled north to preach his heresy in the Italian states."

"How much of this is true?" Florian demanded. "How much is old records and guesswork?"

"We know that Leo died the year that Gundobad cursed him. We know that no pope thereafter lived more than three days in Peter's Chair. And the great empire of Charlemagne was overthrown among his quarreling sons that year, or not long after.[32] Christendom became nothing but quarreling Dukes and Counts, no Emperor."

"And this Heito?"

"My 'ancestor'?" Florian said dryly, on the heels of Ash's question. "Clearly, if he was alive in Pope Leo's day, he's probably the ancestor of half of Burgundy by now!"

---

[32]This fixes the date! If these are accurate references, the year is AD 816, two years after Charlemagne's death. (Although dissolution began the year after Leo's death, some do not date the fall of Charlemagne's empire until AD 846 and the Treaty of Verdun.)

"Yes."

John of Valois looked as if that simple acknowledgment was some significant piece of knowledge.

"And that's why everybody rides with the hunt," Ash filled in, with a sense of cold inevitability: fact fitting into fact. "Everybody you can get *with Burgundian blood* . . . Florian, it's another bloodline. Only it isn't Gundobad's child. It's this Heito's descendants. Heito's children." She turned on the bishop. "Aren't I right?"

"Who for the last four generations have been the legitimate sons of the Valois," the bishop confirmed, "but we have always known, breeding horses and cattle as we do, how characteristics skip a generation, or turn up in a cadet line. When we were the Kingdom of Arles, it was no great matter for a peasant to become king, if he hunted the Hart. We have become complacent, since my great-grandfather's time. God reminds us to be humble, Your Grace."

"Not *that* fucking humble!" Ash snorted, at the same time as Floria del Guiz objected loudly: "My parents were noble, both of them!"

"My apologies, Your Grace."

"Oh, screw your apologies!" Florian's voice dropped half an octave, took on the volume that presaged, in camp, a rapid readjustment of the surgeon's tent. "I have *no* idea what's going on. Suppose you tell me!"

"Heito." John laid his hand against the carved figure's mailed foot, looking up at him. "He was a minor knight in Charlemagne's retinue; one of Charlemagne's sons took him into service after Charles's death. He was appointed guard over Gundobad, after the trial. He was there when Gundobad cursed the Holy Father. And he was there when Gundobad sought to extinguish, by a miracle, the flames of his pyre."

The bishop flicked a glance at Ash.

"He'd heard the news from North Africa," he added, more conversationally. "It wasn't hard for him to realize that Gundobad wanted far more than a mere miraculous escape—that he was desirous of giving us a desert where Christendom now stands. And Gundobad would have, if not for Heito the Blessed."

"Who did what?" Florian persisted.

"He prayed."

Ash, staring up at the bas-relief carving, wondered if Heito's face had had that expression of stilted piety—*whether, in fact,* she reflected, *he wasn't filling his braies and praying out of sheer terror. But it worked: something worked . . . because Gundobad* died.

"Heito prayed," the bishop said. "All men have in them some small part of the grace of God. We who are priests are born with a very little more—a very, very little, sufficient only, if God grants it to us, to perform very minor miracles."

A sudden memory of Godfrey's face made Ash wince. She could not bring herself to speak to the *machina rei militaris*, to ask—as she suddenly wanted to—*what do you think of God's grace* now*?*

"Heito had the grace of God in abundance, although as a humble knight he had no reason to know this until he met his test."

They stood in silence, surveying the bas-relief shrine.

"Heito told his sons that, when the fire was lit at Gundobad's pyre, he heard the heretic praying for escape, and for vengeance on all whom he called 'Peter's heretics,' throughout Europe. The story comes down that, when Gundobad prayed, the flames *did* die. Heito was moved to prayer. He begged God's grace to avert the devastation of Christendom, and to help in kindling the fire again. Heito's story to his sons is that he *felt* God's grace work within him."

Florian's hands strayed to her mouth. It was difficult to see, in the candlelight, but her skin seemed pale.

"Heito relit the pyre. Gundobad died. Christendom was not laid waste . . . Heito witnessed the death of the Holy Father, not long after; and the death of his appointed successor. He prayed that the Curse of the Empty Chair would be lifted—but, as his son Carlobad tells us, in his *Histoire*, Heito felt a lack of strength within himself. He had not the grace to do it. Nor his son after him, though Heito married his son to the most devout of women."

"And then?" Ash prompted sardonically. She reached out,

tucking Florian's arm within her own, feeling how the surgeon was swaying very slightly. "No, I can guess. They married holy women, didn't they? All of Heito's sons . . ."

"His grandson, Airmanareiks, was the first who hunted the hart. You must understand, at that time Burgundy was as full of miracles, and appearances of the Heraldic Beasts, as any other land in Christendom. It was not until later that . . . as they say: God lays his heaviest burden on his most faithful servant. We had gained grace enough to have our prayers answered. Without some burden, we might have forgot our debt to Him."

" 'Burden' be damned," Ash said cynically. "You can't pick and choose. If you stop miracles, you stop miracles. End of story. No wonder Father Paston and Father Faversham have been desperate since we crossed the border! And didn't you have trouble with the wounded the first time we came here, after Basle?"

Florian nodded absently. "I thought it was fever, from low-lying water meadows . . ."

"We had hoped to grow strong enough, one day, to remove the curse and see another Holy Father ascend to Peter's Chair. That has not been granted to us. We have, though, done what Heito set out to do. Neither Burgundy nor Christendom has been corrupted into a wasteland," Bishop John said. "We have been ruled by the Franks, and the Germans, and by our own Dukes; but always we took the holiest of women as brides, and always the Lord of Burgundy was the one who hunted the Hart. Christendom has been safe. We have paid our price for it."

Ash, ignoring the last of what he said, caught Florian's hand in hers and swung the woman around to face her.

"That's it. That's *it*!" She took in a breath. "Heito knew what Gundobad had done to Carthage. He knew Gundobad had living children. *That's* what he was afraid of. Burgundy being made into a wasteland!"

"And he bred for a bloodline that doesn't do miracles—that keeps miracles from being done." Florian's hands shut tight around Ash's gloved fingers, almost cutting off the circulation. "They didn't know about the Wild Machines. They were just afraid of another Gundobad."

"Well, she's out there, right enough!" Ash jerked her head in a random direction, understood to mean *beyond these city walls*. "Our Faris. Another Gundobad. Anytime the Wild Machines want to make her act . . ."

"Except that she can't. Because of me."

"First Charles, then you." Ash couldn't stop a smile. "Jeez, I thought *I* was good at finding trouble and jumping into the middle of it!"

"*I didn't ask for this!*"

Her voice echoed back from the walls of the shaft. Dull, booming reverberations faded away. The wind from above shifted the candlelight, and brought a scent familiar from slaughterhouses: old blood, old urine, and dung. Fear, and death, and sacrifice.

The silence deepened. No knowing, now, how much of the night is gone, or whether across the city, in the cathedral, they are waking to sing Lauds, or Matins, or Prime.

"It was Duke Charles's dream," the bishop said, "to regain the middle kingdom of Europe—to become, in time, another Charlemagne, another Emperor over all. How else to stop us wasting our time in quarrels and wars, and unite Christendom against our enemies? A Charlemagne with Heito's grace. My brother was a man who might have been that . . . but it was not given to him. If he had turned his eyes south, we might not be in such desperate trouble now. God rest him. But you are Duchess now."

"Oh, I know that," Florian said absently. She reached up and rapped her knuckles on Heito's stone shin. "Now you tell me something. Tell me, why is there sunlight over Burgundy?"

viii

"WHAT?" ASH LOOKED around, confused, at the shadowed chapel.

"Outside. Daytime. Why is it light? Why isn't it *dark*?"

"I don't get it."

Florian hit one hand into the other. "You told me. The Wild Machines draw down the sun. That's *real*. So—why isn't it dark here? Why is there sun in Burgundy? It's dark in the lands all around us."

Ash opened her mouth to refute the argument. She closed it again. Bishop John's frown showed pure bewilderment. The wind from the sacrificial shaft brought the smell of cold stone and corruption, deep here in the earth.

"Does it—feel—real?" Ash asked. "The sunlight?"

"Would I know?"

"You knew about the Hart!"

Florian frowned. "Whatever's in my blood, I used it for the first time, on the hunt. I did something. But after that . . . no. I'm not *doing* anything."

"After the hunt, there is nothing for you to do," Bishop John said. "It is not what you do, it is what you are. You have only to live, and you are our guardian."

"I can't tell," Floria said. "I can't feel anything."

Sweat sprang out in Ash's palm. *What else don't we know?*

"Maybe it's people here praying for light. The Bishop here says all men have grace . . ." She began to pace on the terracotta tiles, stopped in the small space, and swung around. "No, *that* doesn't work, because I guarantee men have been praying as hard as shit in France and the Cantons, too! And it was black as the ace of spades when we came through there. If God's grace was going to do a miracle through prayer, we'd have seen the sun over Marseilles and Avignon!"

"I'm no longer devout." Florian smiled painfully. "While I was in the sacred baths, I was thinking. I know what I do—I preserve the mundane. So did Duke Charles. I wondered why things were so bad in the infirmary. I've had men dying on me since I got here. Men I'd expect to see live. Charles's praying priests didn't do him any good, either! This is the real world, here."

The bishop murmured, " 'God lays His heaviest burden on His most faithful servants.' We can't have His gift without His penalty."

Florian hit her hand into her fist again. "So why is it *light* here?" She looked down at her tumbled robes, and her bare hands. "And why was there a miracle at Auxonne?"

For a second, Ash is back on the field, among rain-sodden mud, with jets of jellied flame searing across men's burned-black faces. She absently wipes her hand across her mouth. The stench is still clear in her memory.

Ash remembers priests on their knees, the snow coming down as the wind changed. "I asked de Vere to ask the Duke to let his priests pray—for snow, so the enemy would have no visibility; for the wind in our favor, so their shafts would drop short."

Floria, eyes bright, gripped Ash's arm. "At first I thought the Duke must have been injured. Weakened. But de la Marche told me it happened before he was wounded." Bewildered, Floria turned to the bishop. "Shouldn't those priests have been praying for nothing? Or is there—I don't know—a weakness in the bloodline?"

"We are only men," Bishop John said mildly. "We have nurtured the line of ducal blood, century upon century, but we are only men. Imperfect men. These things must happen, only once or twice in a generation. If we could reject *all* grace, how could God send us a Hart to be made flesh?"

"The Hart," Florian said. "Of course: the Hart."

"Florian won't be perfect," Ash said abruptly. "She *can't* be. I've been in Carthage. Two hundred years of incest." The expression on the bishop's face almost made her laugh. "That's what it took the Wild Machines to get a Faris. Two hundred years of scientific, calculated human stock-breeding. Incest! And what have you been doing in Burgundy?"

"Not incest!" Bishop John gasped. "That's against the laws of God and man!"

A raw, coarse laugh burst out before Ash could stop it. She grinned at the bishop's pallid face, there being nothing else to do now but laugh, scarified by irony. All mercenary now, she snorted out, "That's what you get for following God's law! You said it to me, at the hunt. *Burgundy has a bloodline*. Well, Burgundy should have done it properly! Dynastic marriages, chivalric love, and a bit of adultery at best—shit. That's no way to breed *stock*. You guys needed a Leofric here!"

A little ironically, Florian said, "Remember, I succeeded. I made the Hart real." Her voice contrastingly quiet, her gaze abstracted, she walked back toward the shrine of St. Heito. With her back to Ash, she said, "If the Dukes need to prove themselves—I have. If I hadn't, the Wild Machines would have made their miracle at the hunt."

"Oh. Yeah." A little embarrassed at her outburst, Ash coughed. "Well . . . yeah, there's that."

". . . Until I die." Barely a whisper. Florian turned to face them. "I still don't understand. I'm alive. What the *Ferae Natura Machinae* do when they draw down the sun is real—"

"Oh, it must be." Ash sounded sardonic. "The Wild Machines don't do miracles—if they did, they wouldn't need the Faris! And Burgundy would have been charred and smoking six hundred years ago."

Florian gave a loose-limbed shrug that did not belong on anyone wearing court dress. "We're right about that, or we'd be dead. But, Ash—we shouldn't be seeing the sun."

A brief burst of novices' voices came from above as the iron-studded door opened, then shut. Bishop John of Cambrai called to them to leave, up a shaft that echoed now.

Puddled wax alone remained of the smaller candles, the fatter ones still burning down, beginning to enclose their flames like yellow lanterns. A stray cold draft blew across the back of Ash's neck. She reached up to scratch under the fur collar of her demi-gown with one finger.

"It's no use me trying to—I won't take them by surprise again."

"No. I know that." Florian gathered up her robes again, hugging them against herself, as if for comfort. "But I'm right. Aren't I? Bishop, you can't answer this one. There's still something we don't know!"

"This must be taken to your *grand conseil*," John of Cambrai said. "Or the *petit conseil* first, perhaps, Your Grace. There may be those who can answer this. If not, then we conclude, I think, that God may do His will as He wills it, and if He chooses to bless us so, then all we may rightly do is give thanks for His light."

Ash, alienated by his expression of shaky piety, remarked, "Godfrey says that God doesn't cheat."

Florian turned away from the bishop's hand, and Ash saw her face, her eyes prominent, dark-circled, stressed. Catching Ash's gaze, the woman said, "I didn't want to know that there's *still* something I don't know!"

The Bishop of Cambrai stepped back toward the altar. His soft, black eyes reflected the candlelight. He moved with gravitas. When he turned back, he held in his hands a circlet carefully cut, glued, and shaped from horn. The ducal crown.

"You had questions. They have been answered," he said. "This is your vigil. Will you take the crown?"

Ash saw her panic. The glittering walls pressed in, in the candle's yellow gloom; the brick vaults above sweating niter, and the tiles underfoot smelling of old blood. There is nothing here to remind her of the filigree stone of the palace above, all white light and air. This place is a fist of earth, ready to close around them.

Florian said finally, "Why do I have to? I don't need it, to do what I do. This whole thing—*I don't need this!*"

She backed a step away from the Bishop of Cambrai.

"You didn't need this," Ash said grimly. "*I* didn't need this. But you understand something, Florian—*make your mind up*. Are you running away from this, or are you Duchess? You commit yourself to one or the other, or I'll kick your sorry ass so hard you're going to wonder what fell on you!"

"What's it to you?" Florian said, almost sulkily. It was not a tone Ash was used to hearing from her, although she suspected Jeanne Châlon might have heard it a lot, fifteen years ago.

Ash said, "None of us owe Burgundy anything. You could be what you are in London or Kiev, if we could *get* there. But I'm telling you now, if you're staying here, you'd better be committed to being Duchess. Because there's no way I'm putting people's lives on the line as army commander if you don't mean it."

Bishop John said, half under his breath, "Now we see why God brought you here, demoiselle."

Ash ignored him.

Florian muttered, "We've—the Lion's agreed to defend Dijon."

"Ah, for fuck's *sake*! If I find us a way out—fuck knows how!—they'll go if I say go. I've been talking to people. They don't give a flying toss about the glories of Burgundy, and they really, really don't give a shit about fighting alongside Messire de la Marche. Some of us have died here, but they don't have any *loyalty* to this place—"

"Shouldn't I have? If I'm going to be crowned?"

"And do you?"

"I do."

Ash stared at Floria's face. There was very little to go on, in her expression. Then, in a flood, everything there: doubt, dread, fear at having committed herself, fear at having said, not what is true, but what is required. Tears filled up her eyes and ran over her lids, streaking her cheeks with silver.

"I don't want to do this! I don't want to be this!"

"Yeah, tell me about it."

A flicker of the old Florian: sardonic bleakness: "You and the Maid of Burgundy."

"Our guys won't fight for some Duchess," Ash said, "but they'll fight for you, because we don't leave our own. You're the surgeon, you went to Carthage; they'll fight like shit to keep you alive, the same as they'd fight to hang on to me or Roberto or each other. But we really don't care if it's fighting ragheads to keep the Duchess alive, or fighting Burgundians to get you out of here. The *Burgundians* need to know you're Duchess: now do you *get that*?"

"What do you want to do?"

Refusing the distraction, Ash said rapidly, "Me? I'll do whatever I have to do. Be their banner. Right now, I need to know what *you're* going to do. They'll know if you don't mean it!"

Florian moved away, stepping on the chill flagstones of the chapel as if they were hot, all her body fidgeting with indecisiveness.

"This is a place for confessing sins," she said abruptly.

The bishop, from the shadowed altar, said, "Well, yes—but in private—"

"Depends. On who you need to confess to."

She walked back and took Ash's hands. Ash was astonished at the coldness of the older woman's skin—*almost in shock*, she thought—and then she made herself concentrate on what Florian was saying:

"I'm a coward, when it matters. I can pull people out of the line-fight. I can hurt them when I need to. Cut them wide open. Don't ask me to commit to anything else."

Ash began to speak, to say *Everyone's afraid; fight the fear*, and Florian interrupted:

"Let me tell you something."

About to answer with a casual *sure!*, Ash stopped and looked at her. *She wants to tell me something I don't want to hear*, she realized, and paused, and then nodded in assent. "Tell me."

"This is hard."

Bishop John coughed, artificially, drawing attention to his presence. Ash saw Florian's gaze flick to him, and away; unclear whether she was giving tacit consent to the man's presence, or merely so far past caring that she couldn't be bothered to acknowledge him.

"I'm ashamed of one thing in my life," Florian said. "You."

"Me?" Ash realized her mouth was dry.

"I fell in love with you, oh . . . three years back?"

Into silence, Ash said:

"That's what you call cowardice? Not telling me?"

"That? No." A glimmer in the light: more welling tears wet on Florian's cheek. She took no notice of her own weeping. Her voice didn't change. "First I wanted you. Then I knew I could love you. Real love; the sort that hurts. And I killed it."

"What?"

"Oh, you can do that." Florian's eyes glittered, in the shifting light. "I couldn't *know* that you didn't want me. Esther said she didn't want me. And then she did. So you might . . . but I watched you. Watched your life. You were going to *die*. Sooner or later. You were going to come back from a field on a hurdle, with your face chopped off, or your head blown in, and what was I going to do then? *Again?*"

The bishop's long fingers wrapped around his Briar Cross, pale in the torchlight. Ash saw how the skin over his knuckles strained white.

"So I killed the love and made you into a friend, because I'm a coward, Ash. You were trouble. I don't want to take on trouble. Not anymore. I can't take it. I've had enough."

Dispassionately, Ash asked, "Can you kill love?"

"*You're* asking *me* that?" Florian shook her head violently. Her voice exploded in the catacomb-darkness. "I didn't just want a fuck! I knew I was capable of falling in love with you. I strangled it. Not just because you're going to die young. Because you don't let anyone *touch* you. Your body, maybe. Not *you*. You pretend. You're untouchable. I couldn't find the courage to let it grow, not when I knew that!"

Watching, Ash sees—past her own gauche embarrassment, and a sneaking wish not to have been told any of this—how much damage the woman has done to herself.

"Florian . . ."

And she sees that what looks back at her, from Florian's whitened face, is not only shame and anger.

"So how come you keep telling me about it?" Ash demanded quietly. "How come you keep teasing me with it? And then telling me it's okay, you don't want me, you'll back off again. And then you tell me again. How come you can't leave me alone?"

"Because I can't leave you alone," Floria echoed.

Conscious of dust, damp, the glitter of candles on old mosaics, Ash would give anything to run out of this place—weighed down by history as it is—into daylight. Leave all of this, leave everything.

Am I that detached? Is that bad?

"Why do we hope?" Floria said. "I could never understand that."

Careful to say and look nothing that could be construed as acceptance, Ash only shook her head.

"It wouldn't have been any good," she said. "If you'd told me three years ago, I would have kicked you out—probably screamed for a priest. Now, I think I'd give anything if I could want you. But half of that is guilt because I never gave Godfrey what he needed. And I still want Fernando more than either of you."

She looked up, not aware until then that her head had drooped, and that her field of vision held only the floor mosaic of the Great Bull of Mithras, bleeding to death from a dozen mortal wounds.

"You know . . ." Sweat stood out on Florian's skin, making her forehead shiny. With one swift movement, she wiped her palm across her face, smearing wet hair back. "You certainly know how to finish something off. Shit. Don't you? That was . . ."

Brutal.

"That was *me*," Ash said. "I'm *not* going to make thirty; I *don't* want to fuck you; I love you as much as I can love anybody; I don't want you hurt. But right now I need to know what you're going to do, because I have to give the fucking orders around here, so will you please fucking *help* me?"

Florian lifted her hand and touched Ash's cheek with her fingers. Brief, light, and the expression on her face just shy of that square-mouthed uninhibited bawl that children have when they burst out crying in pain. She shuddered.

"I don't like not having answers!"

"Yeah, me either."

"At least you know how to run an army. I don't know how to run a government."

"I can't help you there."

Florian lowered her hand to her side.

"Don't look for some dramatic decision." Floria shivered. "I was brought up here. I know I *ought* to commit myself. I'm going to do everything I can—but you know what? I'm one of your fucking company, too, remember! Don't treat me like I'm not! The only people I care about is us. If there's a safe way out of here for all of us, *I'll take it*. I'm different now. I ought to stay. I know I don't understand everything about the Wild Machines. That's the best you'll get."

Ash reached for the ties of her cloak, slipped the knot, swung off the heavy wool, and swathed it around the older woman.

Florian looked into her face. "I can only do what I can do. I can't be your lover. And—I can't be your boss, either."

Ash blinked, jolted. After a minute, she nodded acknowledgment. "Shit, you don't give me any rope. . . . Guess we'll have to manage, won't we?"

Ash put her hand out and gave Florian's shoulder a little shove. The woman smiled, still wet-faced, mimed avoiding a blow. Ash squinted up at the invisible darkness of the night outside.

Bishop John of Cambrai cleared his throat. "Madame, the crown?"

The tall woman reached and took the horn circlet out of his grasp, dangling it carelessly in her long fingers.

"Sod waiting till dawn. And screw the witnesses," Ash said, "Bishop John, you just tell them to keep their mouths shut, or show us whatever back way there is out of here. If you want me and Florian tonight, we'll be in the tower with Roberto and Angeli and the guys."

The message arrived four days later.

Black shadows leaped up on the flint-embedded walls of the garderobe,[33] sank, then grew again as the candle flame was all

[33]Lavatory.

but extinguished by the draft from below. The wind rustled the hanging gowns either side of her. Ash, hitching the back of her demi-gown and shirt up around her with numbed fingers, swore.

Beyond the heavy curtain, Rickard's voice asked, "Boss, you busy?"

"Christ Viridianus!"

The wax- and wine-stained demi-gown slid out of her frozen fingers, down her hips, onto the wooden plank. A chilling wind from the night below struck up Ash's back. Her flesh felt red-hot by comparison. She yelled, "No, I'm not *busy*. Whatever gave you that idea? I'm just sitting here with my arse hanging out, taking a dump; why not invite the whole fucking Burgundian *council* in? Jesus Christ up a Tree, here I am *wasting time*—are you sure you can't find something *else* for me to do while I'm in here!"

There was a noise which, had she bothered to decipher it, rather than attend to the necessities of her toilet, she might have deciphered as an adolescent male having alternately bass and soprano giggles.

"The doc—the Duchess—Florian wants you, boss."

"Then you can tell her lady high-and-mightiness the Duchess she can come and wipe my—" Ash broke off, grabbing at the candlestick that her elbow had just knocked. A great black shadow jolted up the walls, and the wick flared and smoked. Hot wax spilled over the back of Ash's hand.

"Bitch!" she muttered; "Got you, you little bastard!" and set the candle upright again. She peered at it. The heavy beeswax candle had melted past the next mark, before she spilled it: past Matins, an hour short of Lauds.[34]

"Rickard, do you know what fucking *time* it is!"

"The doc says a message came in. They want her up at the palace. She wants you, too."

"I expect she bloody does," Ash muttered under her breath. She reached out to the box of fresh linen scraps.

---

[34]Matins: midnight; Lauds: 3 A.M.; the time referred to is therefore 2 A.M.

"It's Messire de la Marche who has the message."

"Son of a whore-fucking, cocksucking, arse-buggering *bitch*!"

"You all right, boss?"

"I think I just lost my Lion livery badge. It fell off my demi-gown." Ash, hauling her split hose up her legs, peered down below the hem of her shirt, through the hole in the plank, at a black and empty void. She stood up with the care that a knowledge of a two-hundred-foot drop below one brings. Two hundred feet of excrement-stained tower wall, invisible in the night outside, but nothing to want to bounce down on your way to the caltrop-strewn no-man's-land at the foot of Dijon's walls. . . .

"Come and do these damn points up!" Ash said, and the swing of the curtain as the boy pushed it back made the candle flame swing again, yellow light illuminating the boy still wearing his mail shirt, for God's sake, and an archer's sallet with a rather sorry yellow plume in it.

"Going somewhere?" she inquired of the back of his head, where he bent over tying points with practiced skill. The visible part of his neck grew red.

"I was just showing Margie some shooting techniques . . ."

In the dark? and *I bet that's not all you were showing her!* became the two foremost remarks in Ash's mind. With Anselm or Angelotti—except for the extreme unlikelihood of Angelotti showing anything to anyone called Margie—she would have said just that.

Given his embarrassment, she murmured, " 'Margie'?"

"Margaret Schmidt. Margaret the crossbow-woman. The one that was a soeur, up at the convent."

His eyes shone, and his face was still visibly pink in the candlelight. Ash signaled him to buckle the sword belt around her waist, as she held the candle up to give him the light. *So she's still in the company? I wonder if Florian knows?*

"Can you write up the reports now, before morning council?"

"I've done most of it, boss."

"Bet you're sorry the monks taught you to read and write!"

she observed absently, giving him the candle to hold and settling the belt, purse, and sword more comfortably about her waist and hips. "Okay, do the reports, bring them to me at the Tour Philippe le Bon. It'll be quicker."

She hesitated for a moment, hearing an unidentifiable noise, and realized that it was rain, beginning to beat on the walls below her. The ammoniac stench of the stone room grew stronger. That did not so much offend her as pass her by entirely. A gust of rain-laden wind spurted up, chilling the stone walls, and shifting the heavy garments hanging around her.

"Oh, great. Next time it's a wet arse, as well." Ash sighed. "Rickard, get one of the pages; I need my pattens,[35] and a heavy cloak. I take it Florian's in the infirmary? Right. So tell whoever's on guard to get their asses in gear, I need six guys to go as escort to the palace with us." She hesitated, hearing a scrabble and whine from the room beyond the curtain. "And get the mastiff-handler—I'll take Brifault and Bonniau with me."

"You're expecting to be attacked in the streets?" Rickard, shielding the candle's flame with his hand, looked wide-eyed for a second.

"No. The girls just haven't had their walk yet." Ash grinned at him. "Get scribbling, boy. And, just think—if Father Faversham's right, after a life like this, you'll hardly spend any time in Purgatory at all!"

"*Thanks*, boss . . ."

She all but trod on his heels, stepping out of the garderobe, so as not to lose the light of the candle. The main fireplace shed some light, still, into the company tower's upper story, by which she saw the curled blanket-strewn forms of pages asleep around the meager warmth. Rickard took the candle to his pallet to work with, kicking one of the pages as he went; and she stretched, in the dim light, feeling the bones of her shoulders crack and shift.

Viridianus! When did I last sleep through a night? Just one

---

[35]Raised wooden platforms that strap on over shoes, for walking through mud.

night without fucking Greek Fire missiles and army paperwork, that's all I want. . . .

Blanket-wrapped forms unrolled: two pages coming to dress her for the pitch-black, rain-blasted ride through the muddy streets to the ducal palace, the mastiffs Brifault and Bonniau padding silently up, surefooted, to her side.

Ash found Florian down on the second floor, in the aisle that ran around the hall in the thickness of the walls, seeing to a patient in smoky taper light. The man sat with his hose slung around his neck, naked from the waist down. A smell of old urine hung about the stonework and flesh.

"So, de la Marche wants you?" Ash peered over the surgeon's shoulder.

"I'm just finishing up." Florian's long, dirty fingers pulled at a gash that started above the man-at-arms's knee. He gasped. Blood, black in the light, and a glint of something shiny in the depths—bone?

"Hold him," Florian said, over the man's shoulder to a second mercenary, kneeling there. The second man wrapped his arms tightly around the injured man, pinning his arms down. Ash sat down on her heels as Florian washed out the gaping hole again with wine.

"De la Marche—" the surgeon peered into the wound; swilled it out again "— will have to wait. I'll be done soon."

The man-at-arms's face shone in the light of tapers, beads of sweat swelling up out of his skin. He swore continuously, muttering *Bitch! Bitch! Bitch!* on ale-heated breath, and then grinned, finally, at the surgeon.

"Thanks, doc."

"Oh—anytime!" Florian stood up and wiped her hands down her doublet. Glancing down at Baldina and two junior deacons, she added, "Leave the wound uncovered. Make sure nothing gets into it. *Don't* suture it. I don't give a shit about Galen's 'laudable pus.'[36] The uncovered wounds I saw in

---

[36] *'Pus bonum et laudible'*; a misunderstanding of Galen's actual writings that must have cost hundreds of thousands of lives in Europe, between the decline of Roman military medicine, and the Renaissance.

Alexandria didn't stink and go rotten like Frankish wounds. I'll bandage it in four days' time. Okay? Okay: let's go."

The leaded glass window of the *Tour Philippe le Bon* was proof against the rain, but freezing drafts found their way in around the frame and chilled Ash's face as she peered through her reflection, out into blackness.

"Can't see a fucking thing," she reported. "No, wait—they've got Greek Fire lights all along the east bank of the Ouche. Activity. That's odd."

She stepped back, blinking against the apparent brilliance of two dozen candles, as the chamber door opened to admit Olivier de la Marche.

Florian demanded, "What is it?"

"News, Your Grace." The big man came to a halt, in a clatter of plate. His face was not clearly visible under his raised visor, but Ash thought his expression peculiarly rigid.

"More digging?"

"No, Your Grace." De la Marche clasped his hands over the pommel of his sword. "There's news, from the north—from Antwerp."

At the same moment that Ash exclaimed, "Reinforcements!" Florian demanded, "How?"

"Yeah." Ash flushed. "Not thinking. That's a damn good question. How did news get in through *that*, messire? Spies?"

The Burgundian commander shook his head slightly. The torchlight glanced from his polished armor, dazzling Ash. Through black afterimages, she heard de la Marche say, "No. Not a spy. This news has been allowed through. There was a Visigoth herald; he escorted our messenger in."

Florian looked puzzled. Ash felt her stomach turn over.

"Better hear him, then, hadn't we?" Ash said. As an afterthought, she glanced at Florian for acknowledgment. The surgeon-Duchess nodded.

"It isn't going to be good news. Is it?" Florian said suddenly.

"Nah: they wouldn't let *good* news through. The only question is, how bad is it?"

At de la Marche's shout, two Burgundian men-at-arms brought in a third man, and backed out of the ducal chamber again. Ash could not read their expressions as they went. She found her hand clenching into a fist.

The man blinked at Floria del Guiz. He held his arms wrapped across his body, a cloak or some kind of bundle gripped close to himself.

De la Marche walked behind the messenger and rested a hand on his shoulder. No armor, Ash noted: a torn livery tabard and tunic, stained with blood and human vomit and let dry. Nothing recognizable in the heraldry except the St. Andrew's cross of Burgundy.

"Give your message," Olivier de la Marche said.

The man stayed silent. He had fine sallow skin and dark hair. Exhaustion or hunger, or both, had made his features gaunt.

"The Visigoths brought you here?" Florian prompted. She waited a moment. In the night's silence, she walked to the dais, and sat on the ducal throne. "What's your name?"

Ash let Olivier de la Marche say, "Answer the Duchess, boy."

Only a boy in comparison to de la Marche's fifty or so, she realized; and the man lifted his head and looked first at the woman on the ducal throne, and then at the woman in armor; all without the slightest sign of interest.

Shit! Ash thought. Oh *shit* . . .

"Do I have to, messire? I don't want this. No one should be asked to do this. They *sent* me back, I didn't *ask*—" His voice sounded coarse: a Flemish townsman, by his accent.

"What did they tell you to say?" Florian leaned forward on the arm of the throne.

"I was at the battle?" His tone ended on a question. "Days ago, maybe two weeks?"

His anguished look at de la Marche was not, Ash saw, because he did not want to tell his news to women. He was beyond that.

"They're all dead," he said, flatly. "I don't know what happened on the field. We lost. I saw Gaucelm and Arnaud die.

All my lance died. We routed in the dark, but they didn't kill us; they rounded us up as soon as it was dawn—there was a cordon . . ."

Seeing Florian about to speak, Ash held up a restraining hand.

The Burgundian man-at-arms hugged his bundled cloak closer to him—not even wool: hessian, Ash saw—and looked around at the clean walls of the Tour Philippe, and the mud that his boots had tracked across the clean oak boards. There was wine on the table, but although he swallowed, he did not appear otherwise to see it.

"It's all fucked!" he said. "The army in the north. They rounded us all up—baggage train, soldiers, commanders. They marched us into Antwerp—"

Ash grimaced. "The Goths have got Antwerp? Shit!"

Florian waved her to silence. She leaned forward, looking at the man. "And?"

"—they put us all on ships."

Silence in the high tower room. Puzzled, Ash looked across at de la Marche.

In a high whine, the man said, "Nobody knew what was going to happen. They hauled me out of there—I was so fucking scared—" he hesitated. After a second, he went on: "I saw them herding everyone else up, pushing them with spears. They made everybody go on board the ships that were at the dock. I mean everybody—soldiers, whores, cooks, the fucking commanders—everybody. I didn't know why it was happening; I didn't know why they'd held me back."

"To come here," Ash said, almost to herself, but he gave her a look of complete disgust. It startled her for a moment. Evidently not seeing the Maid of Burgundy.

"What would *you* fucking know!" He shook his head. "Some fucking woman done up like a soldier." He glanced back at de la Marche. "Is this other one really the Duchess?"

De la Marche nodded, without reproach.

The man said, "They cast the ships off. No crew, just let 'em drift out into Antwerp harbor. Then there was one almighty fucking *whoosh*!" He gestured. "And the nearest ship just burst into fire. It wouldn't go out. They just kept shooting Greek Fire at the ships, and when our men started trying to swim, they used them for crossbow practice. There was all torches along the quay. Nobody got out. All the water was burning. That stuff just floated. Bodies, floating. Burning."

De la Marche wiped his hand across his face.

"Most of us died outside Antwerp." The man went on: "I don't know how many of us there was left after the field. Enough of us to fill six or seven ships, packed in tight. And now there's nobody. They sent me with this."

He held out the cloth bundle. As dark and stiff as the rest of his clothes, it was nevertheless not, Ash saw, his cloak. Hessian sacks.

"Show me." Florian spoke loudly.

The man squatted down, cut and filthy fingers plucking at the tied necks of the sacks. De la Marche reached over him, dagger out, and cut the twine with his blade. The man took two corner edges of one sack and lifted. A large heavy object rolled out onto the oak boards.

"*Fuck.*" Florian stared.

Ash swallowed at the stench. *Damn, I should have recognized that. Decay.* She looked questioningly at de la Marche.

The refugee man-at-arms reached out and lifted the matted, white-and-blue object, seating it down facing the surgeon.

His voice sounded completely calm. "This is Messire Anthony de la Roche's head."

The severed head's eyes were filmed over and sunken, Ash saw, like the eyes of rotting fish; and the dark beard and hair might have been any color before blood soaked them.

"Is it?" she asked de la Marche.

He nodded. "Yes. I know him. Know him very well. Demoiselle Florian, if you need to be spared the others—"

"I'm a surgeon. Get on with it."

The man-at-arms removed a second, then a third, severed head from his sacks; handling these two with a kind of bewildered delicacy, as if they could still feel his touch. Both were women, both had been fair-haired. It was not clear whether the marks were bruises or decomposition. Long hair, matted with blood and mud and semen, fell lank onto the floorboards.

Ash stared at the waxy skin. Despite death, the head of the older of the women was recognizable. *The last time I saw her was in court here, in August.*

So much hanging on this: Ash can feel herself trying to see a different woman, a noblewoman, or a peasant, sent in to spread false fear. The features are too recognizable. For all the sunken, colourless eyes, this is the same woman that she saw shrewishly berating John de Vere, Earl of Oxford; this is Charles's wife, the pious Queen of Bruges.

The man-at-arms said, "*Mère-Duchesse* Margaret. And her daughter, Marie."

Ash could recognize nothing about the second head, except that the woman had been younger. Looking up, she saw Olivier de la Marche's face streaked with tears. *Mary of Burgundy, then.*

The man said, "I saw them killed on the quay at Antwerp. They raped them first. I could hear the *Mère-Duchesse* praying. She called on Christ, and the saints, but the saints had no pity. They let her survive long enough to see the girl die."

A silence, in the cold room. The sweet smell of decay permeated the air. A whisper of rain beat against the closed shutters.

"They've been dead less than a week," Ash said, straightening up, surprised to find that her voice cracked when she spoke. "That'll put the field when, about the same time that Duke Charles died? A day or so before?"

Florian merely sat shaking her head, not in negation. She abruptly sat straight. "You don't want people talking to this man," she said to Olivier de la Marche. "He's coming to my hospice in the company tower. He needs cleaning up, and rest. God knows what else."

Ash said dryly, "I shouldn't worry about rumor. The Lion will know anything you don't want known, anyway. You can't hide this for long."

"We can't," de la Marche agreed. "Your Grace, I don't know if you realize—"

"I can hear!" Florian said. "I'm not stupid. There's no army in the north now. There's no one alive to raise another force outside Dijon. Isn't that right?"

Ash turned her back on the crouching man, the Burgundian commander, the surgeon-Duchess. She let her gaze go to the shutters, visualizing the night air, and the rejoicing Visigoth camp beyond the walls.

She said, "That's right. We got no army of the north coming here. We're on our own now."

[original e-mail documents found inserted, folded, in British Library copy of 3rd edition, *Ash: The Lost History of Burgundy*, (2001) — possibly in chronological order of editing original typescript?]

Message: #377 (Anna Longman)
Subject: Ash
Date: 16/12/00 at 06.11 a.m.
From: Ngrant@

format address deleted
other details encrypted by
non-discoverable personal key

Anna--

So many seismographic ears listening, so many satellites overhead—post-Cold War technology—and the political instability in the Middle East—I doubt a sparrow falls without it being logged by the appropriate authorities!

Certainly nothing that affects the Mediterranean seabed would go unnoticed; therefore, if there are no records.

sorry, wait, Isobel needs this.

Too deep in the translation to say more, I MUST get it FINISHED.

--Pierce

Message: #378 (Anna Longman)
Subject: Ash
Date: 16/12/00 at 06.28 a.m.
From: Ngrant@

format address deleted
other details encrypted by
non-discoverable personal key

Previous message missing?

Anna--

No, you're right. After a while, I have to take a break. My mind seizes up; all I translate becomes gibberish.

I am still haunted by the knowledge that when I come to do a second draft, there will exist a completely possible potential second version of the translation—a story different in all its particulars, but equally valid as a transcription of the Latin.

I suppose I am saying that I have to make decisions of interpretation here, and I am not always happy they are the correct decisions. I wish we had more time before publication.

I will send you the next section of manuscript as soon as I have a rough draft. I must *complete* this, in sequence—there are whole sections at the end that could easily bear any one of several interpretations! Which one I decide upon will be determined by what goes before.

For that, and other, reasons, I won't show the translation to anybody here except Isobel. However, I have been talking in general terms to James Howlett. Really, I don't know what to make of him. He talks blithely about "reality disjunctures" and "quantum bubbles"—he *seized* on my mention of the sunlight in Burgundy, but if he has an explanation, I don't understand it! I had no idea that, as a historian, I should need to be a mathematician, or that a grounding in quantum mechanics would be necessary!

Think about it, Anna—I'm coming to realise that we will publish first, but that is only the *beginning* of the work that other specialists will do with this material.

--Pierce

PART TWO

15 December AD 1476–25 December AD 1476

"TESMOIGN MON SANG MANUEL CY MIS"[37]

[37]"Witness my hand's blood here placed"—French. Variant on the more usual "witness my *seing manuel* [signature] here placed" on contracts and other documents?

i

THE CONSTANT HOWLING of wolves echoes across the river valley.

"Bold enough to come down in daytime, now," the big Welshman, Geraint ab Morgan remarked, his breath huffing white as he strode through the cold, dry street beside Ash. "Little furry bastards."

"Rickard's got three wolf pelts now." Ash's smile faded. *And he's killed more than wolves with that sling.*

Three weeks, and the huge open-air fires in the Visigoth camp burn constantly, day and night; the Burgundians can look down from their walls and watch the warmth—watch the legionaries visibly thriving. Three weeks after the news from Antwerp: the fifteenth of December, now, and the fucking Visigoths can *afford* to let wolves scavenge in their camp.

And I made myself commander in chief of this. Captain-General; Maid of Burgundy; Sword of the Duchess.

Duchess Florian. God help her.

"I must be a fucking *lunatic*!" Ash said under her breath. Geraint glanced down at her. She said, "They still bringing supply trains up the river, out there?"

The edge to the wind made both of them sniffle back mucus. It's cold enough that snot freezes.

"Oh yeah, boss. Rag'ead sledges, on the ice. The Lion gunners have taken out a few with those mangonels, though."

Barred doors faced her, under the overhanging upper stories of the houses. No one yelled warnings and emptied bedchamber pots; no children played in the mud. Yesterday and today, there have been reports of wells freezing.

Some part of her has been frozen, too, since she held Margaret of Burgundy's severed head. *They are not coming, no one's coming, there are no men in Burgundy under arms now except here!*

And I'm supposed to be in charge of them.

That knowledge makes even the palace, which still has hearth-fires, an unbearable succession of meetings, briefings and muster-rolls. A stolen hour off duty with Lion Azure company business has a welcome familiarity, even if there is little else pleasant about this particular incident.

"Your punishment list's getting far too long," Ash said, her voice falling flat in the freezing air.

"They were carrying off doors for firewood. Stupid buggers," Geraint remarked, without anger. "I told them to take it from abandoned buildings, but they can't be arsed to go up to the northeast gate. Took it from here."

Behind them both, Rickard's sling whipped out; and the young man swore. "Missed it!"

"Rat?" Ash queried.

"Cat." Rickard coiled the leather strip up, his bare fingers purple with cold. "There's good eating on a cat."

The rhythmic hammer of a Visigoth siege machine began to pound again from the direction of Dijon's northwest gate.

"That won't do 'em no good." Showers of rock will harass, rather than harm; make people stay within doors. Which they do in any case, lacking candles, now, and lacking food: the remaining rations going to the soldiers.

The diet everywhere is horseflesh and water.

A black object flashed in the corner of her vision. Both she and Geraint simultaneously and automatically flinched. The distant boom of siege guns alerts you; Greek Fire roars as it arcs through the air; trebuchet shot drops, silently, with no warning before the street explodes in front of you.

Rickard ran forward from the provost's escort and stooped over something small on the cobbles. He stood, cupping it in his hands.

"Sparrow," he called.

Better than another damn spy or herald coming back in pieces.

Rickard rejoined them. Ash touched the small, feathered body—cold as the stones of Dijon palace—and glanced up.

There was no mark on the bird. It had evidently fallen, frozen dead, out of the air.

"Won't make lunch, even for you," she said; and he grinned. She signaled the escort, moving forward. Her boots skidded on the icy cobbles with every step—far too dangerous to ride, here—and she wiped tears out of her eyes every time a street corner brought them face-to-face with the wind again.

The desultory Visigoth bombardment continued. Sound carries in this weather: she could be up the northwest quarter of the city, instead of here, close by the south bridge.

"They're not assaulting the gates," Geraint said.

"They don't need to." *They can just let us watch their camp—always warm, always with enough to eat. If it isn't a bluff. They're flourishing.*

Icicles clung to eaves, dropping old, glassy fangs toward the street. There is frost here that hasn't melted in all fifteen days of this freezing weather. And the ice snaps the ropes of mangonels and trebuchets.

They're not attacking. But they're not falling apart, either. Or mutinying. I suppose— Ash quickened her step, careful to keep all expression off her face. *—I suppose that means the Faris has got her nerve back. So . . .*

So what will she do? What will anyone else do? What can I *do?*

Masonry walls radiate cold. Her eyes scanned, automatically, as she walked, ready to send ab Morgan's men to investigate bodies—every night, now, brought two or three people found frozen to death in the streets. On the walls, men-at-arms freeze to their watch points. One man was found frozen to his horse. The earth is like marble: these dead can't be buried.

"Boss," Geraint ab Morgan said.

"Is this the place?" Ash was already stepping forward, between the ripped lath-and-plaster walls that had held a door a short time ago. The seasoned oak posts and lintel had been removed, along with the door and part of one support beam. The front of the house was taking on a sag.

On the floor inside, on filthy rushes, six women and five children sat huddled together. Four adult men stood up, shivering, and approached the gaping hole, facing Ash. The tallest one, speechless, stared at her livery, his scowl fading to incomprehension rather than recognition.

"The men who did this have been punished," Ash said, and stopped. The light from the door let her see the long-cold hearth. It was no warmer here than in the winter street. "I'll send you firewood."

"Food." One of the women cuddling a child looked up. The light from the door shone on eyes big in their sockets, hard cheekbones, and cold-whitened skin. "Send us food, you posh cow!"

Another woman grabbed frantically at her arm. The first woman shook the hand off, glaring at Ash over her child's head.

"You fucking soldiers get all the food. I've got my cousin Ranulf here from Auxonne, and the girls, and the baby—how can I feed them!" She lost all her violence in a second, shrinking away from the provost men-at-arms as they came to stand around Ash. She put her arm over the child. "I didn't mean anything! What can I do? They're starving here, after I offered them a home. How can I look him in the face? My husband's dead, he died fighting for you!"

For you, Ash thought. *But this isn't the time to say so.*

If I was still boss of mercenaries, I'd be looking to sell this place out about now. Hell: about three weeks ago. . . .

"I'll send food." Ash turned abruptly enough to collide with Geraint ab Morgan, pushed her way past him back into the open air, and strode back up the street, heels ringing on the frozen mud.

"Where *from*, boss? Men won't like it." Geraint scratched under the gown bundled over his armor. "We're on half rations now, and down to the horses? We can't feed every refugee family here?" And, plainly frustrated at her silence: "Why d'you think the raghead bitch won't let civilians leave this city, boss! They know how much pressure it puts on us!"

"Henri Brant tells me the horse meat is nearly finished." Ash did not look back at Geraint or Rickard as she spoke. "So, now we can't afford to feed the guard dogs, either. When my mastiffs are slaughtered, send one to that house back there."

"But, Brifault, Bonniau—!" Rickard protested.

Ash overrode him: "There's good eating on a dog."

It's come on her, over the last few weeks: she has wept for the men being injured and killed on the walls of Dijon, in the bombardment. To her surprise, de la Marche and Anselm, and even Geraint ab Morgan, have understood it, thought it no damage to her authority. Now, walking in the cold street, she feels the icy track of one tear sliding down her cheek, and shakes her head, snorting with a bitter amusement at herself. Who weeps for an animal?

Under her breath, as always, she murmured, "Godfrey, have you heard her?"

—Nothing. Still nothing. Not even to ask if you speak to me—to the machina rei militaris.

Anything he knows, they know. I can't even ask Godfrey how I can cope with being Captain-General.

"Put double guard on the stores," she said as Geraint lumbered up beside her. "Any man you catch taking bribes, take the skin off his back."

There are things she knows, as Captain-General of Burgundy, that she would rather not know. *We've got food now for what, three weeks? Two? Somehow—somehow we have to take an initiative!*

But I don't know how.

"Maybe," she said, too quietly for Geraint, or Rickard, or her voices, "maybe I shouldn't be doing this job."

Unmelted frost crunched under her boots, coming into an open square. Wind brought tears leaking from her eyes. The frozen fountain in the middle of the square bulged with ice.

"We'll go up to the mills," she announced. "I want to check the guard on the millraces, now they're frozen. Animals have been getting in that way; I don't want men doing it. Geraint, you and the provosts see to my orders; Rickard, you come with me and Petro."

Giovanni Petro's archers, on rota for escort again, muttered under their breaths; she knew them to be comparing the exposed southwest wall of Dijon with the provosts' warm guardroom back at the company tower. A small grin moved the frozen muscles of her face.

As she strode into the maze of alleys leading off the square, she heard Petro's "Furl that bloody banner before we get to the wall!" behind her, and glimpsed a man-at-arms lowering the identifying Lion Affronté with its rapidly sewn-on Cross of St. Andrew.

She crossed the open end of an alley, to her left.

A flicker of movement punched her across the street.

Jogging footsteps jolted her. Men holding her under the arms, under the crook of her knees: carrying her. Her armor clattered. The world swung dizzily about her.

"What—?"

"She's not dead!"

"Get her to safety! Go, go, go!"

A swelling pain hit her. Her sagging, steel-clad body jarred in their grip. She cannot feel where she hurts. A gasp, another gasp—trying to wrench air into her winded lungs.

"Put her down!"

"I'm okay—" She coughed. Hardly heard her own voice. Was aware of herself supported, of a stench of excrement, of dim light, stairs, flaring torches, and then a room in natural light.

"I'm *alive*. Just—winded—"

She coughed again, banged her arm defenses against her cuirass, trying to put her arm around her chest, and looked up from where she leaned, supported between Petro and Rickard, and found herself looking at Robert Anselm, at Olivier de la Marche.

"*Fuck* me." She tried to wrench herself upright. Pain shot through her body. "I'm *fine*. Anybody see me fall? Roberto?"

"There's rumors starting—"

She cut him off: "You and Olivier, get back out there! They'll know there's nothing much wrong with me if you're out there and visible."

"Yes, Pucelle." De la Marche nodded, turning away, with a group of Burgundian knights. Faint ice-bright light leaked in through round-arched windows, showing her concerned faces. The second floor of the company tower. Florian's hospital.

"What 'appened?" Anselm demanded.

"Fucked if I know—Petro? Who's down?"

"Just you, boss." The sergeant of archers shifted his grip, easing her upright as she found her body able to move again. Something stung. She looked down at her left hand. The linen glove inside her gauntlet dripped, soaked through with red blood. The cold let her feel no pain.

"Didn't you hear it, boss?" Giovanni Petro asked. At her blank look, he added, "Trebuchet strike. Took out the west wing of the Viscount-Mayor's palace, off the Square of Flowers—shrapnel come flying down the alleys, you copped it."

"Trebuchet—"

"Bloody big chunk of limestone."

"Fucking Christ!" Ash swore.

Someone, behind her, shoved as she tried to regain her feet, and she found herself standing, swaying. A sharp pain went through her body. She put her bloodied fingers to her cuirass. The pages removed her sallet; she turned her head and saw Florian.

Half Duchess, half surgeon, Ash thought dizzily. Florian wore a cloth-of-gold kirtle, with a vair-lined gown thrown over it, belted up any old how with a dagger and herb sack hanging from her waist. The rich garments trailed, dirt-draggled, black for eighteen inches up from the hem. Under her kirtle, Ash could see she was still wearing doublet and hose.

She wore neither coif nor begemmed headdress, but she was not bareheaded. Carved and shining, the white oval of a crown enclosed her brows.

It was neither gold, nor silver, nor regular. White-brown spikes jutted up in a rough coronet. Skilled hands had carved white antler into a circlet, fastening the polished pieces with gold fittings, forming the horns of the hart into an oval crown. It pressed down on her straw gold hair.

"Let's get the armor off you." Businesslike and brusque, Floria del Guiz took a firm grip under Ash's left arm and nodded to Rickard. The young man, with two of the pages helping, rapidly cut the points, unbuckled the straps, and lifted her pauldrons off her shoulders. She looked dizzily down at his bowed head as he unbuckled the straps down the right-hand side of her breastplate, plackart, and tassets, undid the waist strap, and let one tasset swing as he unbuckled the fauld.

"Okay—" He popped the cuirass open, hinging open and removing the metal shell all in one go, steel plates clattering. She swayed again, struck by the freezing air, feeling naked in nothing but arming doublet and hose, leg and arm defenses. Her teeth chattered.

"*Fucking* hell!"

Still holding the armor, he demanded, "Are you all right, boss? Boss, are you all right?"

His adolescent voice squeaked, going high for the first time in weeks.

"Shit—I'm fine. Fine!" Ash held her arms out from her sides. Her hands shook. The little brush-haired page slit the points of her arming doublet. "Where'd it get me?"

Rickard laid the body armor down in a clatter of steel, staring at it. "Right in the chest, boss."

Florian blocked her view, reaching down to her arming doublet, and carefully pulling the sweaty, filthy garment open.

"Rickard, I'm fine; the rest of you, I'm okay. Now fuck off, will you? Florian, what's the damage?"

Robert Anselm still hovered in the doorway. "Boss . . ."

"What part of 'fuck off' didn't you understand?" Ash inquired acidly; and when the Englishman had vanished, yelped under her breath: "Shit, that *hurts*!"

Floria knotted her fists in Ash's arming doublet again, yanked it wide open, got her hand in to the ribs on Ash's left-hand side, and felt with remarkably gentle fingers under her breast. Ash had not been wearing a shirt under the arming doublet, and her flesh shrank from the bitingly cold air, from Floria's chill flesh, and from the prodding fingers on her bruised skin.

"Easy!" Ash winced again, grinned shakily. "Hey. It's not like they were aiming at me!"

"It's not like that will matter," Floria mimicked, sardonically. She peered at Ash's side, face all but inside the open arming doublet. Her breath steamed in the cold air. Ash felt it shivery-warm against her skin, and momentarily stiffened.

"Haven't you got something better to do than mess about in hospitals, Duchess?"

There were women with Florian who were not from the company, she realized as she said it. The Duchess's maids and Jeanne Châlon sniffed, and looked much as if they agreed with Ash.

"No. I've got patients here. I've got patients up at St. Stephen's, and in the two other abbey hospices . . ." Florian grinned. "I'd left Blanche in charge here; you're lucky to have me."

"Oh, sure I—fuck! Don't *do* that!"

"I'm checking your ribs."

Peering down, Ash could see her open doublet, bare breast, and a raised, reddened area of skin perhaps the size of a dinner plate below her left breast. She shifted a little, feeling now the separate aches from hipbone, armpit, pectoral muscle, and—now she realized it—the base of her throat.

"That's going to go all sorts of pretty colors," she observed.

Floria straightened up and sat down on the medical chest that was doing duty for a bench (tables and chairs long since gone for firewood), and tapped her dirty finger thoughtfully against her teeth. "Your lung's okay. You might have sprung a rib."

"No wonder, boss!" Rickard straightened up, still bundled in jack, livery jacket, and fur-lined demi-gown; his hood barely pushed back from his face even inside the tower and close to the remaining hearth-fire. "Look at this."

He held up Ash's cuirass by the shoulders, fauld and tassets still attached. The plackart, unstrapped from the upper breastplate, caught the light in a glinting craze.

"Fuck me." Ash reached out and slid her gloved fingers across the case-hardened steel. The curve of the plackart was shattered, like ice when a rock hits it. At her gesture, he turned the body armor around. On the back of the breastplate, over the place where her left ribs would be, the softer iron bulged back.

Her fingers went without volition to her bare torso, touching the swelling skin.

"It bloody *cracked* it. My plackart! And the breastplate, too. Two layers of steel, and it fucking *cracked* it!"

The light from the winter blue sky outside the window flashed from the steel. She slowly removed her gauntlets and fumbled to pull the edges of her doublet together. Florian took her left hand, probing for stone splinters. Her breath hissed as she stared at the Milanese breastplate in Rickard's hands. "The armorer can't hammer *that* out. Sweet Green Christ up a Tree, that's *my* luck for this siege! Holy Saint George!"

"Never mind the soldier saints," Floria remarked under her breath, with asperity, "try Saint Jude![38] Tilde, I'll need a witch hazel and Saint-John's-Wort poultice. Wash this hand in wine. It doesn't need bandages."

The maid-in-waiting curtsied, to Floria's obvious amusement.

Jeanne Châlon caught Ash's eye and sniffed again, disapprovingly.

"Niece-Duchess," she said pointedly, "remember you are called to the council, at Nones."[39]

"Actually, aunt, I think you'll find that *I* called *them*."

Jeanne Châlon flushed. "Of course, my lady."

" 'Of course, my lady,' " Rickard muttered under his breath, in mincing mockery.

Floria caught his eye and scowled. "You need to get the rest of this metalware off her. Tilde, where's that poultice?"

A man sat up on a pallet closer to the hearth. Ash saw it was Euen Huw. Dirty beyond belief, and gaunt, with the fine catgut of Floria's stitches poking up out of his shaven hair, the wiry Welshman still managed to grin woozily at her.

"Hey. Don't you let her prod you around, boss. Heavy-handed, she is. Working for the rag'eads, I swear it!"

"You lie down, Euen, or I'll put some more stitches in that thick Welsh head of yours!"

He smiled at Florian. As he half fell back onto his pallet, he murmured, "Got a cushy number, now, haven't we? Comes of having a smart boss, see. Gets our surgeon crowned Duchess.

---

[38]Patron saint of lost causes.

[39]3 P.M.

Boss in charge of the army. Even the damn rag'eads give up when they hear that."

I wish! Ash thought. She saw it mirrored on Florian's face.

She held out her arms to Rickard and the pages, who stripped her of couters, vambraces, cannons. Shucking the arming doublet painfully down to her waist, she flinched as Florian prodded at her back.

The woman surgeon straightened up. "Whatever you hit when you landed, the armor saved you. Have you got a shirt I can tear up? I'm going to bind those ribs tight. You'll be stiff; it'll hurt; you'll live."

"Thanks for your sympathy . . ." Ash gritted her teeth at the touch of the poultice. "Rickard, you take my kit across to the armory. Tell 'em Boss needs a new breastplate and plackart. They can pull anything they need out of the army stores. But I need it done yesterday!"

"Yes, boss!"

The light here came from one set of opened shutters. Farther into the hall, the shutters were closed. Fire-heated bricks, placed under blankets, took a very little of the freezing chill off the air. Men on pallets moved, uneasily, someone groaning continuously, another man muttering to himself. Some had purple-bruised, stitched flesh left uncovered; other men had bloodied bandages. Only a few men sat playing dice, or cleaning their kit, or arguing. Most huddled down.

Ash's eyes narrowed against the dull light. "You've got twice the number of sick here since yesterday. We haven't had an attack on the walls. Is it the bombardments?"

Florian looked up briefly. "Let's see. I've got twenty-four men wounded here. Three men are going to die because I can't do anything about the shock and bleeding; one man from a stinking wound, the other from a poisoned wound. The broken shoulder bones, ribs, and broken wrists should mend. I don't know about the stove-in breastbone. Baldina took an arrow out of one of Loyecte's men; I haven't wanted to move him out of here. There are ten burn cases, that's Greek Fire. They'll survive."

She spoke without reference to the parchment notes stuffed in the corner of the medicine chest.

"There's more than twenty-four men in here."

"Twenty men down with campaign fever," Florian stated. Her expression, studying Ash's half-bare body, was clinical in the extreme. She ignored the hiss of breath as the poultice touched Ash's skin.

"Dysentery," she elucidated, whipping bandages with a sure hand. "Ash, I tell them to bury bodies away from the wells. The ground's rock-hard. I tell them to make sure there are slit-trenches dug, on the waste ground back of the forge.[40] They shit anywhere they please. I've got civilian cases of dysentery in the abbeys. More than there were yesterday. And that's more than there was the day before. Once it gets a hold. . . ."

"What about stores?"

"No fresh herbs. Even with the civilian abbeys, we're low on Self-Heal, goldenrod, Lady's Mantle, Solomon's Seal. Baldina and the girls can give them camomile, to calm them down. Marjoram, on sprains. That's it." Her gaze flicked to Ash's face. "I'm out of everything else. We bandage. We sew." She smiled wryly. "My people are washing out wounds with Burgundy's finest wines. Best use for them."

Ash shrugged herself painfully back into her doublet. Rickard held out a brigandine, brought by one of the pages, and began to buckle her into it.

"I got to go. In case they think I *am* dead. Morale."

Florian glanced at the pallets, her attention on a man with a chopping cut across the side of his jaw. "I hadn't finished my rounds. I'll see you at the palace. Dusk."

"Yes *sir* . . ." Smiling, Ash essayed a few steps, a little shaky, but mostly balanced.

Back on the ground floor, she found the stench of Cuckoo-Pint starch and billowing steam filling the entire hall. Damp warmth hit her. Women with sore hands, kirtles caught up into their belts, banged around the tubs, through the wet, shouting orders and lewd comments. She found herself behind Blanche

[40]In post-Roman Western Europe, the practise of burying the dead at a distance from the living, and of organising army latrines, dates from the beginning of the fifteenth century.

and Baldina at the foot of the stairs as Antonio Angelotti appeared, holding out a yellowed linen shirt and complaining in rapid-fire Milanese.

"Madonna," he broke off to greet her. His expression changed, seeing her bandaged left hand. "Jussey wants you at the mills."

"Yeah, I was on my way there. You come with me—"

"Boss," a female voice said.

Ash halted, as Blanche put her arm around her daughter's shoulders, the dyed-blond heads together. Baldina's kirtle as she turned to face Ash was laced only loosely at the front.

Under it, the belly of a woman great with child showed as a sharp curve. *Not visible before Auxonne. But she must have been carrying it from spring: at Neuss, say?*

"You should be eating better," Ash said automatically. "Ask Hildegarde: tell her I said so."

Baldina put her hands on her belly in an immemorial gesture. Winter sunlight shot through the steam, illuminating her in a glaze of light; and Angelotti's icon-face and yellow ringlets beside her made Ash think caustically *Haven't I seen you guys in a church fresco somewhere?*

"Have you got a father for it?" Ash added.

Baldina grinned wryly. "Now what do you think, boss?"

"Well, draw on company funds: an extra third-share."

Not that that amounts to much, now.

The younger woman nodded. Her mother, a little awkwardly, said, "Put your hand on it, boss. For luck."

"For—" Ash's silver brows went up. She put her unbandaged hand palm-flat on Baldina's belly, feeling the heat of the woman's body though kirtle and shirt and gauntlet glove.

In Ash's memory, a woman-physician of the Carthaginians says, *The gate of the womb is spoiled; she will never carry to term.* A pang, that might have been for anything—lost chances, perhaps—went through her, stinging her eyes.

"Here's luck, then. When do you drop?"

"Near Our Lord's mass. We're naming it for Saint Godfrey, if it's a boy." Baldina turned her head as someone else yelled. "All *right*! Coming! Thanks, boss."

Ash smiled, saw the escort gathering ahead of her at the

door, and walked away from the stairs, on across the great hall, Angelotti falling into step beside her.

"Well, there's one thing I'm sure of," she said, in a rasping attempt at humor: "It isn't yours!"

Angelotti gave a calm smile, at odds with his vulgar Italian: "Not until pretty bum-boys give birth."

Almost at the door of the hall, with cold wind swirling the steam into towers of whiteness, he touched her arm. "Don't think of us as friends, madonna. We're not your friends. We're men and women who obey you. Burgundy's men, too. That is not what friends do."

She gave him a startled look. The relief of that detached view sank in. She nodded absently.

He added, "Even if what I say is half-true, it is not wholly false. Men who have given you the responsibility of leading them are not your friends; they expect more of you. 'Lioness.' "

"So: is this a warning?" A little cynically, she said, "Gun captains go anywhere. The Visigoths would give you a job with their siege machines—they wouldn't send your gun crews against these walls. You're too expensive to kill off. Shall I expect to be told when you're going, or shall I wake up in the next few days and find you and Jussey's lads gone?"

His oval eyelids shut, briefly, allowing her one look at the smooth perfection of his face. He opened his eyes. "Nothing like so easy, madonna. Fever has a grip, famine is here. Sooner, rather than later, now, you'll commit us to an attack—and we'll do it."

Four days later, in the company armory, she looks down at herself. At a new breastplate and plackart buckled into her body armor; only the brightness of the buff leather, and therefore the newness of the straps, giving away that this mirror-finish steel is not her original Milanese-made harness.

"Shit-hot job . . ." She brought her arms together, let her body follow the lines of someone moving a weapon in precise arcs. Nothing caught, or pulled.

"Not *my* job, boss." Jean Bertran, something over six feet tall, forge-blackened like a pageant-devil, gave her a look equal parts diffidence and cynicism. "I roughed it out like Master Dickon taught me. Took it to the old Duke's royal armorers for the rest. The lads here did the buckles."

"Tell 'em fucking brilliant—"

"Boss!" a voice bawled. "Boss! Come quick!"

She winced, turning, catching her bruised flesh painfully. Willem Verhaecht's second-in-Command, Adriaen Campin, stumbled across the ice-rutted paving stones and into the forge.

"Boss, you'd better come!"

"Is it an assault?" Ash was already staring around wildly. "Rickard, my sword! Where are they coming this time?"

The big Fleming shook his head, red-faced under his war-hat. "The northeast gate, boss. I don't know *what* it is! Maybe not an attack. Someone's coming in!"

"In?" Ash stared.

"In!"

"Fucking *hell*!"

Rickard thumped back from the recesses of the armory, the sword and belt slung over his shoulder, her livery jacket in his hands. In a frantic few seconds, Ash found herself attempting simultaneously to answer questions from the lance leaders crowding in after Campin, and answer Robert Anselm—and Duchess Florian—as they came in on the men-at-arms' heels.

"Son of a *bitch*!" she bellowed.

Silence fell in the armory, apart from the subdued hiss of the coals in the forge.

"Double the wall guard," she ordered rapidly. "This could be a diversion. Roberto, you and twenty men, with me, to the northeast gate. Florian—"

The surgeon shoved her herb sack at Baldina. "I'm with you."

"No, you're damn well not! The goddamn Visigoths would like nothing better than a shot at the Burgundian Duchess. I'll get you an escort back to the palace."

"What part of 'fuck off' didn't you understand?" Floria del Guiz murmured, her eyes bright. She grinned at Ash. "There is such a thing as morale. As you keep telling me. If I'm Duchess, then I'm not afraid to walk the city wall here!"

"But you're not the normal type of Duchess—oh shit, there isn't time!"

Rickard held her livery surcoat up high, by its shoulders. Ash fisted her gauntlets, ducked under, and dived up, attempting to shove her fists and remaining arm defenses through the wide sleeves. Two moments' breathless tugging and panic got it down over her head. Rickard slung the sword belt around her waist, buckled and tugged; and she settled the hilt of the single-handed blade to where she wanted it, grabbed her cloak from him, pulled her hood up, and strode out of the room.

Too cold again to ride without danger to the horses. The hurried half run to the northeastern side of Dijon took them perhaps half an hour. In that time, they saw no one but soldiers up on the walls, and Burgundian men-at-arms on street patrol. Not a dog barked, not a cow lowed; the bright, eggshell blue sky shone, birdless, no doves in the dovecotes now. The winter wind brought tears into her eyes, snatched the breath out of her throat.

Panting from the climb up to the top of the gatehouse, she joined Olivier de la Marche and twenty or more Burgundian nobles on the wall. The big Burgundian was shading his eyes with his gauntlet, peering northeast.

"Well?" Ash demanded.

Willem Verhaecht ran from the battlements to her side. He pointed. "There, boss."

A squabble broke out behind her—de la Marche noting Floria's presence, the surgeon-Duchess refusing to listen to his explosive, protective complaints—but Ash ignored it.

"What the *fuck* is that?" she asked.

Rickard elbowed his way through the Lion men-at-arms to her side. He carried her second-best sallet under his arm. She took it, thoughtfully, standing bareheaded in the icy wind, a woman with scars, and feathery silver hair now grown long enough to cover the lobes of her ears.

Ash glanced at her nearest captain of archers and covertly back at Floria. "How far's crossbow range from here?"

Ludmilla Rostovnaya smiled with a face still taut from healing burns. "About four hundred yards, boss."

"How far away are their lines from this wall?"

"About four hundred and one yards!"

"Fine. Anything comes a yard closer to us, I want it skewered. Instantly. And watch those bloody siege engines."

"Yes, boss!"

The Visigoth tents shone white under a winter-clear sky. Spirals of smoke rose straight up from their turf-roofed huts, surrounding this quarter of the city. A neighing came from their horse-lines. She strained her gaze to see siege machinery, could see none within range. A scurry of people ran, five hundred yards away, ranks parting; and something else moved, between the tents, northeast along the road that ran by the river. Horses? Pennants? Armed or unarmed men?

Rickard squinted, rubbing his watering eyes. "Can't tell the livery, boss."

"No—*yes*. Yes, I can." Ash grabbed the arm of Robert Anselm, standing next to her; and the broad-shouldered man, bundled up against the bitter cold, grinned from under his visor. "Sweet Christ, Robert, is that what I think it is?"

Sounding lighthearted for the first time in weeks, her second-in-command said, "Getting old, girl? Getting shortsighted?"

"That's a fucking red crescent!" Ash spoke loudly. The noise from the Burgundian knights cut off. She pointed. "That's the *Turks*!"

"Motherfuckers!" Floria del Guiz exclaimed, fortunately in the broad patois of the mercenary camp. Jeanne Châlon pursed her lips, disapproving the vehemence; Olivier de la Marche choked.

A neat column of cavalry horses trotted out from between the Visigoth ranks. At this distance, in winter's haze, all Ash could make out were white pennants with red crescents, and riders in fawn robes and white helms. No spearpoints silhouetted against the sky: therefore, not lancers. The column wound out of the Visigoth camp into the deserted land between it and the city walls: horses picking their way across churned mud vitrified by black frosts. A hundred, two hundred, five hundred men . . .

"What are they *doing*? I don't believe it!" Ash swore again. She threw her arms around the shoulders of Ludmilla Rostovnaya and Willem Verhaecht, embracing them. "Well spotted! What the *hell* are they doing?"

"If they plan to attack us, it is foolish," Olivier de la Marche said. He made an obvious effort and turned to Floria del Guiz. "You see we have guns on the walls, my lady."

Floria wore her *I do know one end of an arquebus from the other* expression; Ash has seen a lot of it in the past month.

"Don't fire," Floria said.

It was unmistakably an order. After a moment, de la Marche said, "No, my lady."

Ash grinned to herself. She murmured quietly, "And to think I thought you'd have trouble being a Duchess . . ."

"I'm a doctor. I'm used to telling people what to do." Floria rested her hands on the battlements, staring out at the approaching armed horsemen. "Even when I don't know what's best."

"Especially then."

Ash put her helmet on, and when she glanced up from buckling the strap, the Turkish riders were close enough that she could see they carried round shields and recurved bows; and their helmets were not white, but were covered by a white felt sleeve that hung down over the backs of their necks.

"They are indeed Turks," Olivier de la Marche said, his voice loud in the icy silence. "I know them. They are the Sultan's crack troops, his Janissaries."

The mingled respect and awe on the faces of both her men and the Burgundians was enough to let Ash know they shared de la Marche's opinion.

"Fine. So they're shit-hot. What are they doing *here*? Why are they heading for this city?" Ash leaned out from one of the embrasures, frustrated. A great number of troops—Legio VI Leptis Parva, by the eagle—milled about on the edges of their earthworks, but otherwise made no move. Watching.

"If they're intending to come inside the city . . ." De la Marche's voice trailed off.

Ash found herself watching the Janissaries' cavalry mounts and thinking not of military use, but only of food on the hoof. There were no Turkish packhorses visible. "If they're intending to come inside the city, then why aren't the Visigoths slaughtering them?"

"Yes, Demoiselle-Captain, exactly."

"They're never going to let five hundred Turks in here to reinforce the siege. What the fuck is going on!"

Robert Anselm snuffled.

Ash looked sharply at him. The big man wiped his wrist across his nose, stifling another snuffling laugh, caught her eye, and broke out into a loud guffaw.

"That's what's going on. Take a look at that, girl! It's fucking mad—so who's behind it?"

Now the head of the column was within a hundred yards of Dijon's east gate, it was possible to discern European riders among the Turkish cavalry. Not many of them, Ash saw: not above fifty men. She wiped her streaming eyes again, staring into the wind.

A great red-and-yellow standard flew above the few Europeans; and a personal banner. The wind blew the cloth toward them, among Turkish pennants, and it was a second before a gust unrolled the silk on the air so that all could see it. A ripple of exclamations went along the wall. Up and down the battlements, a great ragged cheer went up, on and on.

Ash blinked at the yellow banner. A tusked blue boar, flanked by white five-pointed stars.

"Holy *shit*!"

It was not necessary, the man's name was being shouted from one end of the walls to the other, but Robert Anselm said it anyway.

"John de Vere," he said, "thirteenth Earl of Oxford."

ii

A BRIEF SHOUTED confrontation between the Burgundians and Oxford: the gates of Dijon opened just long enough for five hundred men to ride through: Ash pelted down the stairs, off the wall.

Her men crowded her on the steps, scabbards tangling; she found herself barely ahead of Robert Anselm, Olivier de la Marche treading on her armored heels.

"An Oxford!" Robert Anselm bellowed the de Vere battle cry happily. *"An Oxford!"*

The crowd poured off the walls at the same time as the great city gates clashed shut. Iron bars slammed noisily back into place. A weight cannoned into Ash's back, she skidded on cobblestones, and grabbed the person who had fallen into her—Floria, feet tangled in her jeweled skirts, cursing.

"Is it him? It *is* him! The man's a lunatic!" Floria exclaimed.

"Tell me something I don't know!"

A great orderly mass of Ottoman Turks—five hundred at least—formed their horses up into a square in the market space behind the gate. The icy wind whipped the mounts' tails. Mares, mostly, she saw at a glance, tough fawn-colored mares, and their armed riders sitting their dyed-leather saddles in complete stillness, no shouting, no calling out, no dismounting.

A rawboned gray gelding galloped out of the mass of Turks, three or more horses with it. The yellow-and-blue banner streamed out, carried by the lead rider.

The armored banner-bearer, riding without a helmet, curly fair hair flying and a great smile on his face, was Viscount Beaumont. De Vere's three brothers rode at his heels; behind Dickon and Tom and George, on the gray, came John de Vere himself.

The Earl of Oxford flung himself out of the saddle, throwing the warhorse's reins to any who might get them—Thomas Rochester, Ash saw. His battle-harsh voice bellowed, "Madam captain Ash!"

"My lord Oxford—oof!"

The English Earl threw his arms around her in a crushing embrace. Ash had a split second to reflect that she was far better off wearing plate than she would have been wearing mail. Her ribs stabbed pain into her side. She gasped. John de Vere, still holding her in a bear hug, burst into tears. "Madam, God save you, do I find you well?"

"Wonderful," she whispered. "Now—let—go—"

The Englishmen were all, she saw, either in tears or waving their hands around and talking excitedly—Beaumont wringing Olivier de la Marche by the hand; Dickon de Vere embracing Robert Anselm; Thomas and George loud among the throng of Burgundian nobles. The rows of mounted Janissaries gazed down from their horses at this spectacle, seeming mildly interested, if impassive.

John de Vere wiped his face unself-consciously. His skin had become pale in the months since she had seen him last. Winter mud covered him to the knee. For the rest—she looked him up and down, fists on her hips—the English Earl stood in battle-worn harness, faded blue eyes watering in the wind, so little different that it made her heart lurch.

"My God," she said, "am I glad to see you!"

"Madam, your expression alone is worth gold!"

The Earl clapped his hands together, partly in satisfaction, partly against the cold. His eyes traveled across the crowd. Ash followed the direction of his gaze. She saw it take him noticeable seconds to realize who he stared at.

"God's ballocks! It's true, then? Your physician is Charles's heir? Your Florian is Duchess of Burgundy now?"

"True as I'm standing here." Ash's face ached with the smile she couldn't keep off it. She added, thoughtfully, "My lord."

"Give me your hand," he said, "and not your 'my lord.' "

Ash stripped off her gauntlet and clasped his hand, moved almost to tears of her own. "If it comes to that, I guess you have the distinction of being the only Englishman ever to employ the reigning prince of Burgundy—since she's still on my books, and I'm still on yours."

"The more reason for you to have trusted me to return."

Floria del Guiz appeared through the crowd that parted to let the Duchess of Burgundy pass. The Earl of Oxford sank gracefully down on one knee. His brothers joined him, and Viscount Beaumont, kneeling before her, and the Burgundian nobles.

"God be with you, madam doctor," John de Vere said, not appearing at all incommoded to be kneeling. "You have been given a harder task than any man would wish."

Ash opened her mouth to speak, hesitated, and shut it again. She put her hands behind her back, forcing herself to wait for Floria to speak first. *Duchess Florian*, she reminded herself uncomfortably.

Floria's sudden smile dazzled. "We have to talk, my lord Oxford. Is this all your men? Are there more?"

"These are all," de Vere said, getting to his feet. Ash saw him glance back automatically at the Turkish troops in their neat, disciplined rows.

"Regrettably, Mistress Florian, I speak little of their language." The Earl of Oxford pointed to a moustached soldier in mail hauberk and peaked helm. "My sole interpreter. He's from Wallachia; a Voynik auxiliary. Do you have anyone here who speaks Turkish?"

Ash, glancing at Floria before she answered, said, "Not me, my lord. But I wouldn't be at all surprised. Robert"—she signaled Anselm over—"do we have anyone who speaks Turkish?"

"I do." Anselm made an awkward bow to the Earl, and pointed over at the Italian gunner, who had joined Ludmilla Rostovnaya and the missile troops. "Angelotti does. We fought in the Morea[41] in sixty-seven and sixty-eight. Maybe as late as seventy. Some damn Florentine shot me in the leg; I hauled Angelotti out of the Adriatic. Never been to sea since."

---

[41] A Greek theatre of war in which the Turks fought the Venetians.

He took a breath, still unsteadily gazing at the Earl of Oxford. "Yeah. I speak the language."

"Good," de Vere approved absently. "I do not wish to be dependent on one man who may be killed."

His eyes stayed fixed on Floria del Guiz, in her female clothing. Ash saw him shake his head in wonderment.

Losing patience, Ash demanded, "Are you going to tell us what's going on here, my lord?"

"It is Burgundy's Duchess that I should tell." De Vere's face creased with humor. "I daresay she'll let you listen, madam."

Floria del Guiz, surrounded by maids, Burgundian nobles, and Thomas Rochester's lance in their self-imposed duty as bodyguard, grinned broadly at Ash. "No chance!"

"Oh, she might. She might." Ash beamed at John de Vere. She spread her hands a little. "Meet the Captain-General of Burgundy's armies, my lord—the Maid of Dijon."

The Earl of Oxford gazed at her beatifically for several seconds. His head went back in a great bark of laughter. Beaumont and the de Vere brothers joined in. What Ash saw in de Vere's expression, as he registered the bristling disapproval of de la Marche and the Burgundian knights, was sheer delight.

He walloped her solidly on the arm. "So. This is how you hold to your *condotta* with me, madam?"

"I'm at your command now you're back, my lord."

"Of course you are." His faded blue eyes glowed with humor. "Of course. As an Englishman, madam, I'm more than happy to leave Holy Virgins to foreigners. Much safer." More soberly, he added, "What news have you had of late from outside the walls?"

Floria said grimly, "For about the last three weeks, nothing."

Robert Anselm added, "The Visigoths aren't taking the walls, but they've got this place shut up tighter than a duck's arse, my lord."

"You have had no intelligence at all?"

Ash blinked against the low brilliance of the winter noon. "They tied us up solid, about the same time they stopped pressing the assaults on the walls. We haven't got any spies out or messengers of our own in, since."

At the mention of assaults, she saw de Vere's face change, but he said nothing.

Robert Anselm said cynically, "We stopped sending people out when they started coming back in by trebuchet, in two separate sacks. Last one was that French guy, Armand de Lannoy." He shook his head. "He's been feeding the crows for a week now. Don't know why he thought it was so damn important to get out."

"I can answer that question, Master Anselm," the Earl of Oxford said. As the last of his exuberance died down, Ash noted the strain underneath. "Madam Duchess, better to say it to you and your advisors all at the same time."

Ash overrode what the surgeon might have been about to say. "How the *fuck*—my lord—did you get in here?" She found that she was waving her own hands, in much the same way as the English, and put them down by her side. "Did you sail from Carthage to Constantinople? Have you seen the Sultan? Is this all your troops? What's happened?"

"All in time, madam. And in the Lady Duchess's hearing." John de Vere glanced momentarily from the surgeon in her filthy jeweled gown to the white sun in the winter sky.

"Plainly," he said, "you are Burgundy's Duchess, as Charles was the late Duke. Tell me, madam, are you—you *must* be what Duke Charles was. Or we would not have a sun in the sky above us."

Floria's dirty, stained hands went to her breast. A white pectoral Briar Cross hung from a golden chain, itself not rich, but carved from the same horn of the Hart as her ducal crown. Her knuckles whitened: she did not, for a second, meet the eyes of any of the Burgundian nobles surrounding her.

"She's Charles's successor," Olivier de la Marche said in the tone of a man who hears a law of nature—the tide, perhaps, or the return of the moon—questioned.

"Oh, she's the Duchess, all right." Ash, conscious of her bruised ribs, and the weight of her armor, shifted from foot to foot in the cold wind. *She is what the Wild Machines need to destroy, now.* "I'll tell you something I *do* know, my lord Oxford. The Faris knows that. She's sitting out there in that camp—she's been sitting out there for five weeks now—and she knows that Florian is the person she needs to kill. And she isn't doing a damn thing about it."

With raised fair eyebrows, John de Vere gazed around at the battered buildings and deserted streets of Dijon.

Ash shrugged. "Oh, she's letting hunger and disease do her work for her, but she's almost stopped the assaults. I'd give half the company war chest to know what her officers are saying. And the other half to know what she's thinking, right now."

The Earl of Oxford said, "I believe that I can tell you that also, Captain Ash."

The sound of distant siege-engine fire echoed through the air from the west of the city. Faint vibrations shook the earth under her feet.

"Get your Turks away from the walls. We'll take council of war," Floria said briefly. "*In*doors."

As the court entered the private chambers of the Duchess, the Earl of Oxford and his brothers were again swept up into a crush of more of the lords of Burgundy, greetings being exchanged, questions shouted. The Janissary captains followed in Oxford's wake with expressions of polite bewilderment.

Each of the dismounted Turks wore the same thing, Ash noted in astonishment: a fawn-colored robe with hanging sleeves, over a mail hauberk; a curved sword belted at the waist; bow and shield; and a helmet with a sleeve of white cloth hanging down behind. The uniformity of their clothing and their bearded faces made her feel that she was in the chamber with one man twenty times over, and not with twenty men. The contrast with her own escort, Thomas Rochester's lance—war-hats buckled down over their cowls, wearing a selection of mail, leather, and stolen plate armor, each man in his own chosen color of filthy hose gone through at the knee—was marked.

"We'll never feed them," Floria said flatly, walking in at Ash's side. She caught Ash's glance. "Henri Brant's been advising me. As well as the castellan of Dijon. We can't feed the people we've got."

"Try thinking of it this way. Five hundred cavalry mounts is two hundred and fifty tons of meat."

"Good God, girl! Will they wear it?"

"The Turks? Not for a second, I shouldn't think. Let's not borrow trouble," Ash said thoughtfully. "Find out why he's brought them here, first."

The glassed windows in the ducal chamber kept out much of the freezing wind, but it whined in the chimneys, a hollow sound under the raucous voices. Here, silk hangings still decorated the bed, and there were chairs as well as chests, and a great fire burning in the hearth.

Floria fixed Jeanne Châlon with a challenging eye. "Spiced wine, Tante."

"Yes, Niece-Duchess, of course. At once! If the kitchens have any left."

"If that lot of thieving bastards don't have a cask squirreled away somewhere," the Duchess of Burgundy remarked, "then we might as well surrender to the Visigoths right now. . . ."

Ash snorted. Floria left her side, walking forward into the chamber, and the men drew aside for her without thinking about it. Ash bit her lip. She shook her head, amused at herself, and followed the surgeon toward the fire.

Floria called to her pages. "Pull the chairs around the hearth. No need to freeze while we talk."

Breath whitened the air. Despite the fire, it was cold enough to make Ash's teeth ache. She moved forward, among the general rearrangements, and stood with her back to one side of the carved stone hearth, below a Christ-figure with intricate foliage curling around Him.

Floria seated herself on the carved-oak chair that it had taken two pages to shift closer to the warmth. The Burgundian knights and lords and bishops turned toward her, falling silent, watching their bedraggled, bright-eyed, and completely confident Duchess.

The Earl of Oxford said, "May I suggest, madam, that you clear the chamber somewhat? We shall do our business more speedily if we are not burdened with overmuch debate."

Floria rattled out a handful of names. Within minutes, all

but a dozen of the court dispersed—in remarkable good temper, and anticipation, Ash realized—and the mulled wine came in; and the Duchess looked at the English Earl over the rim of her gold goblet.

"Talk," she said.

"All of it, madam? It has been three months and more since we stood on the beach at Carthage."

Floria rapped out, *"God give me strength and, failing that, patience!"*

John de Vere bellowed with laughter. He sank down, not asking ducal permission, onto a chair close to the burning logs. A scent of sweat and horse emanated from him, with the rising heat. Ash, watching him and his brothers and Beaumont, had a sharp flash of how it had been with the sun of August on Dijon's fields, when they had dined together. Despite the presence of Olivier de la Marche and the Turkish commander, she felt a strong and welcome familiarity.

"Start with him, Master de Vere." Floria del Guiz tilted the cup slightly toward the remaining Janissary officer.

"Start with why you're in here, not out there, and not dead," Ash clarified. "That's a whole battalion you just brought in here!"

The Earl of Oxford stretched out his boots to the flames. "You would have me begin at the end. Very well. I am here and alive, because I have this man and his cavalry with me. Plainly, five hundred men are no match for six thousand encamped Visigoths. However—I informed the Faris, in all truth and honor, that if his men die here, the Osmanli[42] Sultan Mehmet, second of that name, will consider himself to be instantly at war with the Visigoth Empire."

A moment's silence, in which nothing could be heard but the fire crackling and the wind in the chimney.

John de Vere added, "She knew it to be true. Her spies must have informed her by now of the troop buildup on the western border of the Sultan's empire."

---

[42]Europeanised as 'Ottoman'. From Osman Bey, founder of the Turkish empire.

Ash softly whistled. "Yeah, well, he can afford to make threats like that."[43]

"This is no threat."

"Thank Christ and all His sweet saints for that." Ash shifted, pain jabbing her ribs under the cuirass. "So, let me get this right, you just rode across from Dalmatia or wherever—"

"Five hundred men are a big enough troop not to be bothered," the Earl of Oxford said mildly, "while being no threat to the King-Caliph's army."

"—and then you rode up to Dijon, and you said, 'let me inside the besieged city with fresh troops,' and they said, 'oh, okay'—"

Dickon de Vere flushed, and said hotly, "We risk our lives, and what do you do but carp and jeer!"

"Be quiet, boy." The Earl of Oxford spoke firmly. He smiled at Ash. "You have not stood siege for so long. Let Captain-General Ash ask her questions after her own fashion."

Impetus gone and slightly deflated, Ash said, "They're not fresh troops, these Turks. They're hostages."

The Ottoman commander said in halting German,[44] "I do not know this word."

Ash looked at him, startled. He was, under the felt cap and beard, fair in coloring—probably a Christian by birth.

"It means, if they attack us, if you die; then those men out there—" She indicated the window. "—the Visigoths, they

[43]Mehmet II (ruled 1451–81) was, in fact, Sultan of the Osmanli or Ottoman Empire at the time of their conquest of Constantinople; and was thus the man known to be responsible for the fall of Byzantium, the eastern Christian empire.

[44]The Sible Hedingham text here reflects the horrendous variety of languages being used. The Burgundian court habitually spoke French when in the south, and Flemish when they went north. Ash's company would speak English (in several varieties), Italian, German, French (of two varieties); their own *patois*; and probably a smattering of Greek, Latin, and 'Gothic'. I suspect that the Turkish officer uses a few words of German simply because that is the farthest west he has travelled up to this point.

I have attempted to imply interpretation, rather than spell it out each time as the Sible Hedingham ms. does.

die, too. All the while you're in Dijon, an attack on the city is an attack on the Sultan."

His beard split to disclose a smile. "Woman Bey know![45] Yes. We are the New Troops.[46] We are come to protect, in Mehmet and Gundobad his name. Our lives are your shield."

"This is the Başi Bajezet," Dickon de Vere blurted. "He commands their *orta*."[47]

"Tell Colonel Bajezet he's very welcome," Ash murmured. The Voynik behind the Ottoman commander translated quietly into his ear. The bearded man smiled.

Floria said abruptly, "Will it work?"

"For now, yes, Mistress Florian. Duchess: your pardon." John de Vere straightened up in his chair. A tang of singed leather came from the boots he withdrew from the hearth. He reached out for the wine goblet a page handed him and drank. It was not apparent how many days he had been in the saddle or how many hundreds of leagues he might have ridden.

"Why?" Floria said.

"By your leave, madam." The Earl of Oxford beckoned his Voynik interpreter, said something in his ear, and the Voynik auxiliary and his commander bowed and retreated from the chamber.

John de Vere said abruptly, "It is dark now as far as Hagia Sophia and the Golden Horn."

"The sun?" Floria turned her head toward the window, the winter sun beyond the glass illuminating the lines around her eyes.

"No sun, madam. Constantinople is as dark as Cologne and Milan." The Earl rubbed his face. "Luckily for me. After I left you, we sailed to Istanbul,[48] then traveled overland to Edirne.

---

[45]Bey: 'commander'.

[46]*Yeni çeri*: 'Janissaries' literally 'new troops'.

[47]Regiment. The text is inaccurate here, as an orta would be commanded by a higher-ranking officer than a mere *başi*; a *çorbaşi*, or colonel, perhaps. (Literally, 'chief soup-maker'.)

[48]Literally, 'the city'; post-conquest term for Constantinople.

I was admitted to the Sultan's presence within weeks. I told him, through an interpreter, what I had seen and heard in Carthage. I told him that Burgundy is, sweet Christ knows why, all that stands between us and the dark; for proof of that, he should witness how the sun still shines on Burgundy."

George de Vere said taciturnly, "His spies confirmed it."

Oxford nodded. He leaned forward, toward the Duchess in her chair. "Sultan Mehmet has two whips driving him, Mistress Florian. He fears this darkness spreading from Africa, and he desires to conquer the Visigoth Empire and its subject nations of Christendom as he did Byzantium. I have told him Burgundy must stand. I do not know if he believes me, but he is willing to make this much effort. If the Visigoths do prove too strong to be challenged now, he has lost but a regiment of Janissaries proving it."

Floria looked as though she had a sour taste in her mouth. "And if the Visigoths *don't* take Dijon—I get a Turkish army on my doorstep, going hammer and tongs at them?"

A month ago she would have said we *not* I. Ash sipped her wine: bottom-of-cask stuff not much improved by the scrapings of a palace kitchen spice drawer.

"How long has he given you?" she asked John de Vere.

"Two months. Then he withdraws Colonel Bajezet." The Earl looked consideringly into the fire. "If I were at a Lancastrian English King's court, say, and a mad Osmanli Earl came and asked me for troops, I do not know that I should lend him so many or for so long!"

Ash drank, watching the light on the surface of the wine. The ducal chamber smelled of man's sweat and of wood ash. She did not know whether it would hurt her ribs more to sit or to continue standing. A hand touched her shoulder. She winced, aware that the top of her breastplate had been driven into her flesh, too, that she had bruises in those muscles.

Floria del Guiz said, "Ash, have we got two months?"

She raised her eyes, not even aware of the woman having moved. Floria's face under the hart's-horn crown was the same as ever—lined, now, from unwelcome responsibilities. Unknown capabilities. Herself and Floria: the irresistible force rattling off the immovable object. The Duchess's grip loosened.

"If the siege isn't pressed? I doubt it." Ash walked away from her, across the room to one of the windows. Beyond the glass, the skies of Burgundy shone a hard pale blue. Too cold even to snow. Ash touched the freezing glass.

"But the siege isn't the point, not now. Except for the fact that it keeps you here—I've prayed for snow," she said. "Sleet, snow, fog; even rain. Anything to limit visibility! I'd have you and half a dozen of the lads over the wall and away. But it stays clear. Even the fucking moonlight . . . And anybody we send out is killed, or doesn't come back."

She turned to face them: de la Marche, severe; Oxford frowning; Floria anxious.

"It isn't about that army out there! It isn't about the Turks—sorry, my lord de Vere. It's about the Duchess of Burgundy and the fact that we can't get out of here, can't get you away somewhere safe. Keeping you alive, Florian. You and what you do. That's all it's about now, and I'd open up Dijon right now for the Visigoths to plunder—happily!—if I thought I could get you away in the confusion. I can't risk it. One stray arrow could finish everything."

What the Earl of Oxford heard in that, she knew, was not what Floria del Guiz was hearing—or what Oxford would hear, once appraised of the hunting of the hart. Olivier de la Marche bit at his lip. The surgeon scowled.

"Have we got two months?" Floria repeated. "Not just food. Before the Faris—"

"I don't know! I don't know if we have two days, or two hours!"

The Earl of Oxford looked from one woman to the other: the mercenary in plate, cropped hair shining; and the surgeon-turned-Duchess awkward in her woman's clothing. He reached up and scrubbed his hand through his sand-colored hair.

"There is something I don't understand here," he confessed. "Before you explain yourself, madam, let me finish my tale. You in the city have had no word at all of what goes on in the Faris's camp?"

"We'll have to brief you." Ash relaxed her clenched fists. She strode back toward the warmth of the hearth-fire. "As for intelligence—we've heard nothing. I can guess. She'll have been getting frantic messages from Carthage saying *why the fuck have you stopped the war, you can't do this, get on with it*. Am I right? And it'll have to have been couriers. If *I'm* too scared, now—" Ash grinned mercilessly. "She won't talk to the Stone Golem. She knows what else hears her when she does." She snorted. "And I bet there's been messages going back to Carthage from her officers, too! They must think she's gone nuts."

"Are you sure she hasn't?"

"Frankly? No." Ash turned to the Earl of Oxford. "This is speculation. What do you *know*?"

"I know," the Earl said, "that my men and I are a week in front of two Visigoth legions traveling north to Dijon."

"Shit!" Ash stared at him. "Fresh troops from Africa? He hasn't got any! Has he pulled them out of Egypt—or Carthage itself?"

"Sultan Mehmet has an extensive spy network." John de Vere placed his goblet carefully on the floor. "I trust his information. The Sinai fortresses are still manned. As for Carthage . . . Riding with these legions, on his way here to take personal command of his armies and send the Faris home to Carthage, is the King-Caliph Gelimer."

Stunned, Ash said, "Gelimer's coming *here*?"

"He has to make his example of Burgundy."

"But, *Gelimer*?"

The Earl of Oxford leaned forward in his chair, stabbing a finger emphatically in the air between them. "And not alone, madam. According to the Sultan's spies, he has representatives of two of his subject nations with him. One is Frederick of Hapsburg, lately Holy Roman Emperor. This I know for truth; we came across his lands, riding here. The other is said to be an envoy of Louis of France."

The travel-stained English Earl paused. Olivier de la Marche, nodding furiously, bent to hear what Chamberlain-Councelor Ternant whispered in his ear.

"King-Caliph Gelimer must take Dijon," John de Vere announced flatly. "And—pardon me, madam Florian—he must kill the Duke or Duchess. You are the heart of resistance to him, and Burgundy is the last land that stands against him in conquered Europe. That's why, if his female general won't do it for him—the man must come here and do it himself."

Olivier de la Marche glanced at Floria for permission, and spoke. "If he fails, Lord Oxford?"

John de Vere's gaze sharpened, the lines creasing in the corners of his eyes. It was, Ash saw, a smile that lacked all kindness: a pure wolfish expression.

"France has a peace treaty with the King-Caliph." De Vere displayed an open hand to Ash. "Your French knight who was so anxious to escape Dijon? He would have been trying to reach Louis with news of the failing siege. France has been all but untouched by this war. I give you the dark, but Maine, Anjou, Aquitaine, Normandy—all of them could mobilize, now, if they thought Gelimer weak."

"And the north Germanies—!" Ash ignored de la Marche's sharp look, lost in battle calculations of her own that momentarily ignored Burgundian troops and Duchess and Wild Machines. "Frederick surrendered so fast this summer, half his armies never got into battle! Sweet Christ, the Visigoths are out on a limb!"

John de Vere's gaze stayed on Floria. "Madam, there are villagers and villeins from France and the Germanies flocking over the borders into Burgundy. Outside of your lands there is nothing but howling darkness, cold, and a winter such as men have never known. That is all Louis or Frederick would need as an excuse to come in now and attack the King-Caliph, that their own people have taken protection with you."

"Refugees." Floria winced, wrapping her fur-lined gown more tightly around her. "Out in that. Good God. What's it like beyond the border, if this is better? But I don't know about these refugees."

"You don't need to know, madam, for the Spider to make that his excuse."

"And then there's the Sultan." Ash ignored her surgeon's outrage, looked at de Vere with growing fierce exultation. "The waiting armies of the Turk . . . Gelimer *has* to take Burgundy. If he doesn't win here, and quickly, France and the Germanies will carve up Europe between them and the Turks will be in Carthage in a month."

"Sweet Christ, Ash!" Floria stood up. "Don't sound so bloody *pleased* about it!"

"Maybe England will come in, too—" Ash broke off. She looked down at her hands, and then back up at Floria. "I enjoy the thought of that son of a bitch in trouble."

"*He's* in trouble? What about *us*!"

Ash guffawed, not able to stop herself even for the look of sheer outrage on Philippe Ternant's face. Floria laughed out loud. She sat down again in the ducal chair with her legs apart under her skirts, as a man wearing hose sits; and her bright eyes and thick gold brows were still the same under the horn crown.

"No harvest," Floria said. "No cattle. No shelter. Those bastards have made it a wasteland out there. If people are coming *into* these lands, it must be hell outside . . ."

Excitement died. *And we don't even know* why *we have the sun—by rights, we* shouldn't *have*!

Floria's expression was taut, ambiguous—also gnawing at that unspoken question?

Olivier de la Marche lifted his hand, catching de Vere's attention. "It's dark as far as Constantinople now, you say, my lord? The King-Caliph can't have intended that. Not such a deliberate provocation to the Turk."

Philippe Ternant added, "If it is the lands which they conquer that fall under the Penance with them, then Constantinople would still be bright. Not Visigoths, then. My lord of Oxford, our Duchess's knowledge of the Great Devils must be shared with you."

"I know something of this matter already." De Vere's face was still; Ash thought him remembering a sea strand outside

Carthage, and a silver glow in the south. "Only, I am uncertain as to the lady's place in this."

"The Duchess will tell you later." Ash caught Floria's eye, and surprised herself by waiting for the surgeon's nod before going on: "My lords, it seems to me that Gelimer's caught in his own trap. I stood in Carthage three months ago, when he took the crown, and I heard him promise the Visigoth lords and everyone else that he'd smash Burgundy as an example—he *has* to do it now. He's got his own *amirs* on his heels, Louis and Frederick closing in, and the Sultan waiting to see if now's the time to come in from the east." A brief smile moved her mouth. "When he started to get reports of the Faris soft-pedaling the siege here and his conquests grinding to a halt, I'll bet money that he shat himself."

Floria sat up in her chair. "Ash, what you mean is, he has to kill us. Me. As quickly as possible."

Clear through the frost-bitten air, not muffled by the expensive glass, a lone bell tolled. Potter's Field, Ash realized: more bodies stacked for a thaw that would enable burial. The impact of rocks and artillery boomed from the south of the city. The roofs and walls between this palace and the army outside the city did not seem much of a barrier.

Ash slowly nodded.

"Christ up a Tree!" Floria exclaimed, oblivious to the shock of her Burgundians. "And you act like this is *good* news!"

Her head whipped round at John de Vere's burst of laughter. The English Earl met her questioning stare, shook his head, and held out an inviting hand to Ash:

"Madam, you have it, I think?"

"It *is* good news!" Ash walked across the bare boards to Floria, taking the woman's hands between her own. Fiercely intense, joyous, she said, "It's the best news we could have. Florian, *the Duchess of Burgundy has to stay alive*. You know that's all that matters, whether you like it or not. I've spent five weeks trying to find a safe way out of Dijon, to get you away to somewhere else—France, maybe; England, who cares? Anywhere, as long as it's not here, at risk from any damn Visigoth peasant with an arquebus. And every time I've got someone over the walls, they've come back dead."

De Vere nodded approval; some of the Burgundians looked grim.

"I haven't been able to break us out of here," Ash said, still holding Floria's gaze. "There's been nothing we can do. That's what's demoralizing. Doing nothing except wait for the Faris to make up her mind to attack or not. Well—now someone else is making it up for her."

"Someone who's not going to sit outside the walls waiting," the surgeon-Duchess observed. The grip of her fingers tightened on Ash's hands. "Christ, Ash! What happens when Gelimer gets here and they really start trying!"

"We hold out."

She spoke so closely on the heels of Floria's words that she eradicated them. De la Marche and Ternant began to look up with cautious enthusiasm.

"We hold out," Ash said again. "Because the longer we can do it—the longer Dijon stands—then the weaker Gelimer looks. Day by day by day. *He's made us a* public *test of his strength.* The weaker he looks, the more chance of Louis or Frederick breaking their treaties and attacking him without warning. The more chance of the Sultan deciding to invade, without warning. Once that happens—once it does turn into a three-cornered fight—then we've got options again. We can get you out of here. We can hide you."

"Get you to a foreign court," the Earl of Oxford put in.

Ash let go of Floria's hands. She reached out and picked the horn cross from the woman's breast, the antler chill under her fingers.

"If it comes to it," she said softly, "and they kill you outside of Dijon, but they're occupied with a full-on war, then the Burgundians can hold another Hunt. It doesn't matter who's Duke or Duchess, so long as somebody's there. Someone who can stop the Faris."

Ash could see on Olivier de la Marche's face that he took it for a hard piece of military realism. Florian snorted.

"You always did have odd priorities! *I* want to stay alive.

But you're right, they could hunt," she said, "and there would be someone to stop the Wild Machines."

I would sooner have you alive.

It caught under her breastbone, a pain as sharp as sheared ribs. Ash stared at the woman—disheveled, insouciant, not one word in five weeks of refusal to take on the appalling responsibility of the Duchy. *And in five weeks I haven't seen you drink.*

Ash said quietly, "We've got a *chance*. Other enemies for the Visigoths mean other allies for us. The Faris can die on a field of battle just as easily as Jack Peasant can. If the Visigoth army is defeated by someone else, we fight back, go south, destroy Carthage, destroy the *machina rei militaris*—destroy the Wild Machines."

"Blow them up!" Floria said. "If it takes all the powder in Christendom!"

"All we have to do, now, is hold Dijon." Ash grinned at her, at them all. Cynicism, black humor, desperation, and excitement: all clear on her scarred face.

"Hold Dijon," she repeated. "Just a little bit longer. Against Gelimer and all his legions. It's a war of nerves. All we have to do is hold out long enough."

iii

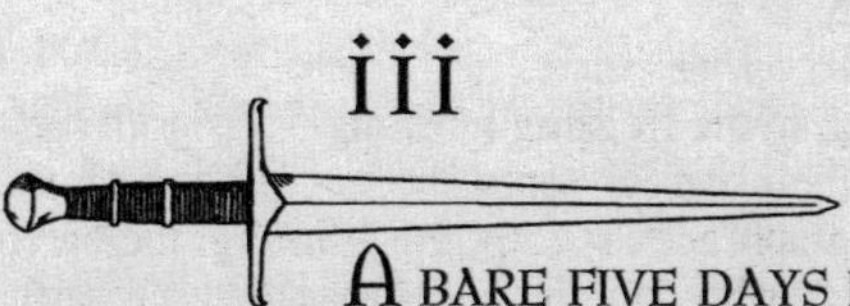

A BARE FIVE DAYS later, the legions of the King-Caliph marched up from the south to Dijon.

The torches and campfires of the Visigoth armies surrounded the city with an unbroken rim of flame. Ash, on the battlements of the company's tower, peered out into a frost-bitter and utterly clear night. The moon, three days past the full, illuminated every bare yard of earth out to the enemy trenches and barricades, every tent peak and eagle and standard in their camp—

Where they sleep, warm and fed. Or fed, anyway.

—and every patrolling guard squad.

She went down, snatching an hour's sleep between briefings with her Burgundian command group, was back up on the roof at false dawn.

Rickard came up, bringing her nettles brewed into small beer—Henri's current substitute for wine—and sat with her, bundled into Robert Anselm's great cloak, trying not to show how much his teeth chattered.

"Let 'em come, right, boss?"

Ash hauled her coney-fur lined gown tighter over her mail. Hunger was a dull ache in her gut. "You got it. Let 'em make the worst mistake they've ever made."

With dawn, a killing frost fell. A lone bell rang out for the hour of Terce.[49]

"There." Rickard freed an arm from the thick woolen cloak to point.

Breath misted the air in front of her face. The skin of her face was numb. Ash peered off the tower into the clear, freezing light that fell from the east, let her gaze swing around over the Visigoth camp: the movement of men around the tents, turf huts, fire pits, and trenches, until she saw where Rickard pointed.

"They're early," she commented. "My lord of Oxford underestimated them."

Pray God that's his only mistake.

Men were running, in the freezing morning—Visigoth serf-troops piling out of their barrack-tents, the sun glinting off the scale armor of the cataphracts, spearpoints glinting; the harsh bellow of horns and clarions ringing out across the chill earth. She shaded her eyes from the fierce rising white sun, wondering if somewhere in that moving mass the Faris woke, walked, gave orders, sat alone.

Within a very few minutes the Visigoth troops were formed

---

[49] 9 A.M.

up in legionary squares, the eagles of the XIV Utica and VI Leptis Parva going up way beyond bow and cannon range of the walls of Dijon, all along the road. The wind brought distant horns. Ash watched as the road up from the south filled with men marching, black standards and eagles catching the light, and below the flags the helmets of hundreds of soldiers, and ahead of them all the ceremonial bronze-armored war chariot of the King-Caliph.

Ash nodded to herself, watching a banner with a silver portcullis on a black field come into sight. Carthage's twilight walls pressured her memory. Her bowels churned uncomfortably.

"There you go, Rickard. That's the King-Caliph's household guard. And the Legio III Caralis . . . can't see the other one . . ." Ash put her arm around the boy's cloaked shoulder. "And that's Gelimer's personal banner, there—and there's the Faris's. Right. Now we wait, while the pot comes to the boil."

Two hours later, Ash fell asleep sitting upright in the main hall.

One oak chest remained, tucked into the side of the big hearth against the wall. She sat on it, in full armor, hearing the Burgundian *centeniers*, each in turn; and then her own lance-leaders and their men. Willem Verhaecht and Thomas Rochester, Euen Huw and Henri Brant, Ludmilla Rostovnaya and Blanche and Baldina. Processing problems. Where exhaustion slowed her mind, instinct and experience took over.

She fell asleep leaning into the hearth corner, upright, in full armor, in the middle of a briefing. Dimly, she heard the plates of her harness scrape against stone; it was not enough to wake her. The banked fire glowed, giving warmth to one side of her face.

She was still aware, as from a long way away, of the laconic voices of exhausted men, dropping kit on their palliasses and slumping down, hoping for sleep to do away with hunger. And of Anselm's voice bellowing up from the courtyard: holding close-quarter weapons drill. Some part of her still ran through

Angelotti's and Jussey's calculations of remaining ammunition: bolts, arrows, arquebus- and cannonballs.

Even held by the paralysis of sleep, some part of her still remained on guard.

She had a moment to realize, *It's because I don't want to dream. I don't want to hear Godfrey, it's too hard when I can't talk to him. Because the Visigoths can ask the Stone Golem what I say. Because the Wild Machines will hear, even if they don't speak . . .* Then she fell into sleep as if down a dark well, and a heartbeat later hands were shaking her by the pauldrons and she moved a sleep-sticky mouth and looked up into the face of Robert Anselm.

"Wha—?"

"I said, you should have seen it!"

The line of sun from the arrow-slit windows lay much farther across the floorboards. Ash blinked, said grittily, "Give me a *report*, Robert," and reached out as Rickard handed her a costrel of water.

"We've had a parley come out from the raghead camp." Robert Anselm squatted down in front of the chest she sat on. "You should have seen it! Six fucking golem-messengers, each with a banner. A fucking dwarf *drummer*. And one poor sod with a white flag walking up to the northwest gate between them, praying our grunts weren't trigger-happy, and shouting for a parley."

"Who was it?"

"Mister Expendable," Robert Anselm said, with a smile at once wolfish and sympathetic. "What did you think, girl, Gelimer himself? No way. They sent Agnes."

Caught by surprise, Ash snickered. "Yeah, I can see Lamb wetting himself with that one. Remind me to make that man an offer if the situation changes. Tell him if he hires on with Florian, I won't give him all the shitty jobs! When was this? Why do they want a parley? What's the result?"

"About an hour ago." Robert Anselm's hazel eyes gleamed under arming cap and sallet. "The result is, Doc Florian wants to go out and talk to them."

"You're out of your fucking mind!"

The Burgundian knights and nobles in Floria's chamber

glared at Ash; she ignored both them and Olivier de la Marche's covert, relieved look of approval.

"Someone has to tell her," the Duchess's deputy murmured.

"If you set one foot outside the walls, I don't care if you've got Mehmet's five hundred Turks up your arsehole, you are a *dead woman.* Don't you understand me?"

Floria del Guiz held her crown between her hands, turning it, fingers stroking the contours of the carved white horn. She raised her eyes to Ash.

"Get a grip," she advised.

" 'Get a grip'? *You* get a fucking grip!" Ash clenched her fists. "You listen to me, Florian. The Wild Machines have to kill you, and they know it. If Gelimer's still taking the Stone Golem's tactical advice, that's what it'll be telling him. If he isn't, he *still* has to kill you—you're Burgundy: if he kills you, the war in the north fizzles out, the rest of Christendom starts saying 'yes, boss,' again, and the Turks look for a peace treaty!"

In the background she was aware of de la Marche and the council nodding agreement, John de Vere exchanging a quiet comment with one of his brothers.

"You know what I'd do if I were Gelimer," Ash continued softly. "Once I had you in the open outside these walls, I'd open up with the guns and siege machines and wipe you off the map. You and anybody else at the parley. I wouldn't care if it meant wiping my own guys out, too. Then I'd apologize to the Sultan for killing his Turks—an 'unfortunate accident.' Because with you *gone*, and Europe solid, there's a two-to-one chance Mehmet will decide it's not the time for a war just yet. I'm telling you, you go out there and you're dead. And then there's nothing to stop the Wild Machines, nothing at all!"

The overcast sky glimmered pale gray through the glass. Shifting cloud disclosed a white disc of sun, no stronger than the full moon. Floria del Guiz continued to turn the horn crown between her strong, dirty fingers. Exhaustion marked her, as if two thumbs of candle-black had been smeared under her eyes.

"Now you listen," she said. "I've spoken to this council, and to my lord Oxford, and now I'll tell you. We have no food. We've got sickness: dysentery, maybe plague. We've got a city full of starving people. I'm going to hold a parley with the Visigoths. I'm going to negotiate their release."

Ash jerked a thumb at the world beyond the window. "So they can starve out there with the other refugees?"

"I'm not a Duchess, I'm a doctor!" Floria snapped. "I didn't ask for this crown, but I've got it. So I have to do something. The hospices are full; the abbot of St. Stephen's was here in tears two hours ago. There aren't enough priests to pray for the sick. I took an oath, Ash! First of all, *do no harm*. I'm going to get the civilians out of this siege before we have an epidemic."

"I doubt it. Gelimer's going to be happy enough if we die of disease."

"Shit!" Floria swore, swung around, and began to pace up and down the chamber, kicking the hem of her gown out of the way: a tall, dirty scarecrow of a woman, noticeably thinner now than when they had ridden in the wildwood. She scowled, gold brows lowering. "You're right. Of course you're right. Ash, there *has* to be some way we can do this. If there's a parley, at least they're not attacking us. It gains time. Therefore, we have to agree to it."

"We might. You don't. You hunted the hart, remember?"

Glancing around the chamber, Ash noted Richard Faversham among her own men, the English deacon's face shrunken under his black beard. His eyes burned. He was nodding.

Floria said, "But Gelimer specifies, if I'm not present, there's to be no parley."

John de Vere said, into the silence, "Hold a parley, madam, but make sure King-Caliph Gelimer himself is present at it as well as yourself. They then cannot use their siege engines or guns."

"I wouldn't count on it. If I were him, I'd get there, then leg it, and let the artillery take care of it." Ash slid her hand down to the scabbard of her sword, for comfort. "Florian's right about one thing. We *do* need the delay. Once they start any serious assault, it's going to show up how low we are on ammunition and men. Okay . . ."

Floria shrugged. "I'll find a way to do this, Ash. Never mind the hart. Where can we hold a parley?"

"On a bridge?" John de Vere offered. "Are all the bridges down? That would be neutral territory."

"No!" Olivier de la Marche growled, "No!"

"Madness, my lord!" Philippe Ternant cried. "We know what treachery bridges can bring. The late Duke's grandfather, Duke John, was treacherously slain on a bridge during a truce, by the whoreson French.[50] They cut off his right hand! It was most vile!"

"Ah." De Vere's pale brows went up. He said mildly, "Not a bridge, then."

Ash converted a laugh into a cough. "Where, then? Not in the open. Even if Gelimer was there, it would still be too easy to load up one of their Greek Fire throwers, and get us before we could get back inside the city walls."

A silence: in which the knots in the firewood cracked as the fire burned down. A cold draft breathed down through the chimney, despite the fire.

Robert Anselm laughed. Ash looked across at him.

"Spit it out. You got something?"

Anselm looked first at her, then at de Vere, and rose to his feet. Standing, stubbled head gleaming, he said, "You want somewhere that isn't in the open, boss, don't you."

Colonel Bajezet said something to the interpreter. Before the Voynik could translate, Robert Anselm was nodding.

"Yeah, your lads did that in the Morea a couple of times. Built a tiny fort out in no-man's-land and had both sides meet inside. If anyone started a fight, everyone got killed." Anselm hunched his shoulders. "Won't work, Başi. They could still get us on the way there, or the way back."

The Turk raised his hands. "Plan, what?"

"Meet 'em underground. In a sap."

---

[50]John the Fearless, d. 1419.

"In a—" Ash stopped. Robert Anselm looked her straight in the eye. He did not smell of wine, or the fermented rubbish Henri Brant's cooks had concocted from pig garbage. He stood with his head up.

Ash thought, *Is that de Vere, his old Lancastrian boss? Or has he finally decided to get his finger out on my behalf? Either way, if he has, do I care?*

Yes. I care. I'd rather he'd done it for me. It's me that's putting other people's lives in his hands.

"A sap," she repeated. "You think we should meet the Visigoths in a tunnel."

This time it was de Vere who laughed, and his brother Dickon with him. Viscount Beaumont said cheerfully, in English, "And I suppose we ask them to hold the negotiations until we have dug one, Master Anselm?"

Anselm put his hand back on his sword pommel. He glanced at Ash. She nodded.

"Gelimer wouldn't risk artillery. Collapse a tunnel—" Anselm smacked his palm down flat for illustration. "Everybody's dead. Start a fight in one, and you got a bloodbath. Same thing. Everybody dies; no one can be sure they'd survive—that includes Gelimer. Take the Colonel's Turks down with us, and I reckon that'd swing it."

There was a buzz of discussion. Ash watched Robert Anselm, without speaking. He watched her, and not John de Vere. She slowly nodded.

"But not Florian. Me, de la Marche, anyone; not Florian. Or—" she brightened. "Not the first time. That's what we tell Gelimer. It's what, now, the twenty-third? We can spin this out for three or four days, past Christ's Mass. That's more time; it's all more time . . . if we make him think Florian will come out if we can get negotiations started . . ."

Florian interrupted her thinking aloud. "If it were you out there, you'd attack. To hurry the parley up."

"Gelimer will do that anyway. We're going to lose people." Ash's grim expression faded to amazement as she looked back at Anselm. "A sap. It *won't* work, Roberto, we don't have time to send a mine out from the walls."

"Don't need to. I know where there's one of theirs, that we countermined. Under the White Tower. You remember, girl. It's the one Angelotti's lads cleared out with a bear."

De la Marche looked aghast; the Earl of Oxford spluttered his watered wine back into his cup; Floria whooped. "You never told me this! A *bear*?"

"It was two or three days after the hunt." Ash grimaced. "Before we would have thought of bear steak. There was a bear left in Charles's menagerie."

Robert Anselm took it up. "Angelotti's lads heard the Visigoths mining toward the wall. The ragheads were tunneling under the wall, propping it up with wood. They were going to set fire to the props and bring the city wall down when they collapsed. Angelotti's engineers dug a countermine, and we opened it into their tunnel one day, and the following night, when they were in it, the gunners got the bear out of the menagerie."

Ash frowned, trying to remember. "It wasn't just a bear, was it . . . ?"

"They got a couple of beehives out of the abbot's gardens as well. They put the bear down into the tunnel," Robert Anselm said, "and they dropped the beehives down after, and shut the end of the countermine up fucking quick."

Floria's face contorted, obviously visualizing men, darkness, bees, an animal maddened by stings. "Christ!"

Her exclamation was drowned out by laughter from the men-at-arms.

"We did see 'em come up out of the other end pretty damn fast!" Anselm confessed. "*And* the bear. *And* the bees. They closed their end up, but they ain't been down there since! We could open that up. Clear out the bodies."

There was a raw, black edge to the laughter in the room. Ash saw Floria's face, appalled at the cruelty. She stopped laughing.

Florian looked down at the horn crown in her hands.

"It's worth trying. We have to keep them talking. I don't want to see another assault on the walls. We have to put some bait in this. We'll tell them the Duchess *will* be there—*no*."

Floria, completely inflexible, repeated, "No. This is my decision. Tell Agnes Dei, yes, I'll meet with Gelimer."

Forty-eight hours later, on the very day of Christ's Mass, the Duchess of Burgundy and the English Earl of Oxford, together with the Captain-General, the Janissaries of the Turk, and the Duchess's mercenary bodyguard, met in parley with King-Caliph Gelimer and his officers and allies of the Visigoth Empire.

The tunnel stank of old sweat, and blood, and dank earth and urine: so strong that the lanterns guttered and burned low.

Ash walked with her hand on the war-hammer shaft stuck through her belt. No room for bill-shafts, for spears; only close-quarter weapons here. She shot a glance at the sides of the sap—widened out in a desperate hurry in the last two days, fresh planks shoring up the walls and the roof a bare eighteen inches above her head.

Angelotti, standing with one of the Visigoth engineers and Jussey, nodded confirmation to her. "It's a go, boss."

"Anything drops on my head, it's your ass'll suffer for it . . ." Ash spoke absently; gesturing for Robert Anselm to hold up his lantern, hearing voices from the far end of this widened underground mine. Cold still air walked shivers up her spine, under her backplate.

I suppose at least, with Florian with us, we don't have to worry about tiny miracles.

Shit. They don't need their priests. All they need to do is send one of their golem-diggers in; this roof will come down with a thousand tons of earth—

She bit her lip, literally and deliberately. The words were in her mouth: *Position of Visigoth troops, location of Visigoth command?*

But it won't know. Couriers from here to Carthage are out of date. If the Faris isn't reporting to the Stone Golem, it can't give tactical advice about their camp here. It won't do me any good to speak to Godfrey.

I just want to.

"Is he there?" Robert Anselm said quietly.

The gravel that covered the floor of the sap crunched underfoot as she walked forward. She squinted in the poor light. The voices ahead of her died down.

A pale, cold blue light began to glow. Visigoth slaves uncovered globes of Greek Fire, no larger than Ash's fist. She saw first their thistledown white hair and familiar faces, where they knelt either side of the passageway. Then, between the two lines of them, she saw men in mail and rich robes, and one in the midst of them, in a great fur-lined cloak, his beard braided with golden beads, the King-Caliph, Gelimer. He looked strained, but alert.

"Confirm," she said. "Move the rest up. He's here."

No banners—the low roof didn't allow it—but all the armed men wore liveries, stark in the cold light. Gelimer's portcullis. The Faris's brazen head. A notched white wheel on a black ground. A two-headed black eagle upon a field of gold. The lilies of France quartered with blue-and-white bars.

Black double eagle. She searched the mass of faces in front, and found herself looking at Frederick of Hapsburg.

The Holy Roman Emperor had only one man with him that she could see, a large German knight in mail, carrying a mace. A small, dry smile crossed Frederick's lips as he saw her. Conquest and surrender notwithstanding, he looked much the same as he had in the camp outside Neuss.

"In person? Son of a bitch . . ." She stepped to one side as men came up behind her, de Vere's Turks. The Janissaries lined the walls and stood three ranks deep in front as Floria del Guiz walked forward, surrounded by twenty men of the Lion Azure, in mail hauberks and open-faced sallets. Burgundian troops flanked them to either side.

Elbow to elbow with Floria on one side, Colonel Bajezet and his interpreter on the other, and with John de Vere crowded close in behind her, Ash has a sudden visceral memory of Duke Charles, downed by a Visigoth flying wedge at Auxonne, his armor leaking blood between the exquisitely articulated plates. She felt herself start to sweat. Her palms tingled.

She did the familiar thing, alchemized emotion into excitement: let her vision go flat in the unnatural light and take in, without effort, which men were armed with swords (which they might have difficulty drawing in a scuffle), which with maces and picks and hammers; which of Gelimer's lord-*amirs* were armored and helmeted—all—and which were the obvious targets.

One of the Burgundian knights behind her said something foul under his breath. She looked questioningly at him as the group halted.

"That is Charles D'Amboise,"[51] the Burgundian, Lacombe, said, indicating the French liveries, "Governor of Champagne, and that whoreson arselicker beside him is the man who betrayed the friendship of Duke Charles. Philippe de Commines."

Much more, and the towering, fair-haired Burgundian would have spit on the earth. Ash, as she might with one of the company, nodded acknowledgment, and said, "Watch him—if he moves, tell me."

Ash stepped ahead of Floria, among the spotless silent Janissaries.

"We're here for a parley with the King-Caliph." Her voice fell flat in the enclosed space. "Not with half the lords of France and Germany! This isn't what we agreed to. We're pulling out."

It's too much to hope for that I might get away with this—spin out the negotiations about negotiations to another few days. . . .

The French knight bowed, where he stood cramped in beside the little dark man that Ash recognized as de Commines from his previous visit to Charles's court. He said smoothly, "I am D'Amboise. My master Louis sends me to serve the King-Caliph. I am here to acquaint Her Ladyship the Duchess with the benefits of the *Pax Carthaginiensis*. As is my lord of Hapsburg, the noble Frederick."

---

[51]A trusted servant of Louis XI, reportedly sent in the autumn of 1476 to abduct Duchess Yolande of Savoy on behalf of the King of France, for political reasons.

Charles D'Amboise continued to look at Ash with a perfectly open and amiable expression. Ash grinned at him.

"You're here as Louis's *spy*," she said. "And, like 'my lord of Hapsburg,' you're here to see Burgundy stand against the King-Caliph. In which case, if I were King-Caliph, I'd watch my back . . ."

Her grin did not waver at D'Amboise's evident unease. *Any dissent we can spread is good!*

Six of the Turks had positions in front of Ash and Floria. There was not space enough in the mine for more than that. Ash looked past the mail and hanging sleeves of the Janissaries—men consenting to use their bodies as a human shield—and saw Gelimer's bearded face, in the light of the Greek Fire globes.

He was showing no emotion. Certainly no anger, or uncertainty. He seemed both older and more military than when she had last seen him, in Carthage, lines drawn in the skin around his mouth, and a long mail hauberk and coat of plates under his cloak.

Harsh illumination, cold darkness beyond: the mine is not so different from the dark palace at Carthage, with the great Mouth of God above her and the tiles about to crack and shiver apart in an earthquake. Seeing the man again shocked her. No picture in her memory of Gelimer running from his throne—instead she had a sudden physical recall of the dead flesh of Godfrey Maximillian. A long shudder went down her spine under her armor.

"Where is the Duchess of Burgundy?" Gelimer's light tenor also flattened, under the low, boarded tunnel roof.

Over Ash's shoulder, Floria said dryly, "You're looking at her."

The King-Caliph's eyes remained on Ash for a long moment. He shifted his gaze to regard the cloaked woman wearing the bone crown. "The fortune of war means I must have you killed. I am not a cruel man. Surrender Burgundy to me, and I will spare your peasants and your townsmen. Only you will die, Duchess. For your people."

Floria laughed. Ash saw Gelimer startle. It was not a

demure laugh; it was one she had heard often in the surgeon's tent, with Floria outside of two or three flagons of wine—a loud, pleasant, raucous contralto.

"*Surrender?* After we've resisted? Get out of here," Floria said cheerfully. "I'm a mercenary company's surgeon. I've seen what happens to towns under siege when enemy troops sack the place. The people I've got in here are safer staying in here, unless we sign a peace."

Gelimer shifted his gaze from Ash, again, past her to the Burgundian lords. "And this—*woman*—is what you would have lead you?"

There was no answer. Not, Ash saw as she quickly glanced back, from uncertainty or doubt. Obdurate faces regarded the King-Caliph with contempt.

"She is most wise and most valiant," John de Vere said, with stinging courtesy. "Sirs, what is your business with the Duchess?"

Ash appointed herself discourteous mercenary Captain-General to his noble foreign Earl, and said loudly, "If that's his best offer, they ain't *got* any business with the Duchess! This ain't serious. Let's fuck off."

De Vere let her see his brief amusement.

"Call your She-Lion off," the Visigoth King-Caliph said contemptuously to de Vere. She saw his eyes flick from the English Earl to the noble Burgundians behind him, skimming over herself and the Turkish commander and Floria del Guiz.

He's looking for the man in command, Ash realized.

He's thinking: Not the Englishman, not in Burgundy. The Burgundian lords? Which one? Or Olivier de la Marche, back in the city?

And then she saw Gelimer's small-eyed gaze flick to D'Amboise and Commines, and from the Frenchmen to Frederick of Hapsburg. Only a split second of loss of control.

God bless you, John de Vere! Everything you said is right. He's here because he has to have Burgundy, and because he thinks he has to look as though he's not afraid of us in front of them.

Ash smiled to herself and glanced back to grin reassuringly

at Florian. She whispered in the woman's ear, her lips touching the soft hair under the hart's-horn crown:

"Gelimer would have done better to just pile in, never mind a parley—and he hasn't done it, and they're watching him now, like a hawk, to see what he does next."

"Can we keep him talking?"

Looking at Gelimer, and his closed expression under the gold-rimmed helmet he wore, brought memory vividly into her mind: the man riding in driving snow in the desert, with his son—his son—the boy's name was gone from her. *Is it still snowing in Carthage?*

She formed a fast and brutal judgment. "He'd be all right if this was armies. Maybe all he did three months ago was talk himself into a job he can't hold down—but if it was just a matter of telling his generals and his legions what to do, he could win this one. But it's the dark, and the cold. I don't know how much he knows. He'll hesitate if we give him half a chance."

"Keep talking," Floria murmured. "Let's spin this out as long as we can."

The Visigoth King-Caliph turned to listen to a man speaking at his shoulder, appearing not to hear what Ash said. He nodded, once. The air, growing warm with the number of bodies crowding the mine, caught at the back of Ash's throat. The kneeling slaves holding the Greek Fire globes in their padded iron cages appeared bleached by light: fair brows and lashes air-brushed from weather-beaten faces.

The mass of armed men parted, with difficulty letting others through from the back of the King-Caliph's party. Ash could not at first make out faces among the blaze of heraldry, the glint of mail and sword hilts and helmets.

Greek Fire reflected back from a river fall of hair the color of pale ashes, robbed of all silver in this light. Ash found herself looking again into the Faris's face.

"Faris." Ash nodded a greeting.

The woman made no reply. Her dark eyes, in her flawless bright face, regarded Ash as if she were not present. Her flat gaze brought a momentary frown to Ash's face. About to comment, Ash realized that King-Caliph Gelimer was—while apparently listening to his advisor—watching her with a complete and total avidity.

Disturbed, she contented herself with another nod, which the Faris again ignored. The Visigoth woman, armored and in black livery, had a dagger at her belt; Ash could not see a sword hilt, in among the crush of bodies.

Why is Gelimer watching me? *He should be watching the Duchess.*

Is this some kind of diversion, so he can try to have Florian killed?

She inhaled, surreptitiously, trying to catch the scent of slow match on the air, to discover if there were arquebuses hidden in the mass of Gelimer's men. Movement caught her eye, brought her sword hand across her body. She stopped.

Two Visigoth priests came pushing through the crowd in the Faris's wake. They held the elbows of a tall, thin, bareheaded *amir*, a man with unruly white hair and the expression of a startled owl. Behind the *amir* stumbled a pudgy Italian physician—she recognized Annibale Valzacchi. *And the* amir *is Leofric.*

"Green Christ . . . !" Ash became aware that she had closed her hand around Floria's arm only when the woman winced.

"That's the lord-*amir* that had you prisoner? The one who owns the Stone Golem?"

"Yeah: you never saw Leofric in Carthage, did you? That's him." Ash did not take her eyes from Leofric's face, watching the elderly man across the space of perhaps five yards. "That's him."

Not just my sister, but this.

A pain came deep in the pit of her stomach. Stairways, cells, blood; the intrusive painful stab of examination: all sharp-edged in her mind. She rode the ache out, not letting it show on her face.

Leofric wore the rich furred gown of a Visigoth lord, over mail. He appeared unaware of the priests' grip on his arms, and frowned at Ash with a puzzled expression.

"Greetings, my lord." Her mouth sounded dry even to her.

John de Vere whispered encouragingly in her ear, "Madam, yes, talk. It is all time gained."

Two slaves stood with the Lord-*Amir* Leofric behind the front row of Visigoth troops, one a child, and one a fat woman. Ash could see neither clearly. The child cradled something in the front of her stained linen robe and shivered. The adult woman drooled.

In the fierce, flat white light, Leofric's eyes focused on Ash. His face crumpled. Into the silence, he wailed, "Devils! Great Devils! Great Devils will kill us all!"

IV

THE JANISSARIES IN front of Ash did not move, their alert surveillance intense. Florian looked taken aback; de Vere, although he did not show it, no less so. Ash shifted her gaze from Leofric to the King-Caliph. No surprise showed on the Visigoth ruler's face.

"The head of House Leofric is unwell," Gelimer said. "If he were himself, he would apologize for such a discourtesy."

"Ask her!" Leofric swung round imploringly toward Gelimer, the two priests gripping his arms even more firmly. "My lord Caliph, I am not mad! Ask her. Ash hears them, too. She is another daughter of mine, Ash hears them as this one does—"

"No." The Faris's voice cut him off. "I cannot hear the *machina rei militaris* any longer. I am deaf to it."

Ash stared.

The Visigoth woman avoided her gaze.

With complete certainty, Ash thought, *She's lying!*

"You said she wasn't talking to the Stone Golem . . ." Floria whispered, her tone one of rueful admission.

"Not because she can't." Ash watched Gelimer wince and glance at the foreign envoys.

Frederick of Hapsburg was smiling a little, with the haughty and calculating smile she remembered from the summer at Neuss; and he caught her eye and lifted a brow slightly.

"To our business, lords." Gelimer fixed his gaze on Floria. "Witch-woman of Burgundy—"

The Lord-*Amir* Leofric interrupted obliviously. "Where did I go wrong?"

Floria, who looked as if she had been about to make some dignified ducal response, stopped before she started. The surgeon-Duchess put her fists on her hips with difficulty in the crowded space, and stared at the Visigoth lord. " 'Go wrong'?"

Ash peered down the mine, between the shoulders of the Turkish Janissaries, the blue-white blaze of the Greek Fire making it paradoxically harder to focus on Leofric's face. Something about the shape of his mouth made her shudder: adult men in their right minds do not have such an expression. She remembered Carthage, was overwhelmed suddenly between contradictory revulsion, hate, and pity.

He's not right. Something's happened to him, since I was there. He's not right at all. . . .

She cut the emotions away from herself, concentrating only on the tunnel, the armed men, the sounds of voices, the shifting of feet and hands.

Leofric gazed down at the child-slave in front of him. He drew one arm from the priests' grip, reached down, and plucked a white-and-liver-colored patched rat out of the child's arms. He held it up and stared into its ruby eyes. "I keep asking myself, *where did I go wrong?*"

The child—recognizably Violante; taller, thinner—lifted up her hands for the animal. Ash recognized the rat when it wriggled in midair, thrashed its tail from side to side, and dipped its furry head down to lick the girl's fingers.

She felt eyes on her, switched her glance to see Gelimer watching her again with avid, analytical care.

"Oh, fuck . . ." Ash breathed.

Gelimer signaled. The two priests closed around Leofric again. Valzacchi pulled the *amir*'s hand down, shrinking from the animal.

The white-haired man looked vague, and relinquished the rat absentmindedly to his slave girl. "Lord Caliph, the danger—"

"You put on this madness as an excuse for treachery!" the King-Caliph said, in a rapid Carthaginian Latin that Ash thought only she and de Vere, apart from Gelimer's Visigoth followers, understood. "If I have to kill you to silence you, I will."

"I am not mad." Leofric answered in the same language. Ash saw Frederick of Hapsburg look puzzled, and D'Amboise, too; the other Frenchman, Commines, smiled quietly.

Ash glanced at de Vere. The English Earl nodded. She waited until she was sure he was watching the French and German delegations, and then reached up and unbuckled her helmet. *Time to stir the pot.* She took the sallet off and shook out her short hair, facing the Visigoths under the harsh light.

"My God, but they are *twins*!" Charles D'Amboise exclaimed. "A Burgundian mercenary and a Visigoth general? Their voices, their faces—what is this?"

"Sisters, I hear," de Commines put in sharply, staring at the Visigoth King-Caliph. "Lord Gelimer, His Grace the King of France will ask, also, why you have your generals fighting both sides of this war! If it *is* a war, and not some conspiracy against France!"

"The woman Ash is a renegade," Gelimer said dismissively.

"Is she?" Charles D'Amboise's shout made the young slave girl in front of him flinch, and huddle the piebald rat to her chest. He bellowed at the King-Caliph: "*Is* she? What shall I tell my master Louis? That you and Burgundy conspire together, and this sham of a war is fought on both sides by you! That Burgundy is France's ancient enemy, and has you for an ally! And, worse than *all* this"—the French nobleman flung out his hand, pointing at John de Vere, Earl of Oxford—*"the English are involved!"*

Ash whooped. It was drowned out in the guffaws, catcalls,

and congratulatory comments to de Vere that echoed from Thomas Rochester's lance. Rochester himself wiped streaming eyes.

Gelimer's hand stroked his beaded beard.

When the applause, boos, and cries of "God rot the French wanker!" died down, the King-Caliph said in a measured tone, "We do not bring our legions to raze the city of an ally, Master Amboise."

Plainly alerted by the sound of Gelimer's voice, the Lord-*Amir* Leofric suddenly bellowed out loud, his voice blaring in the low-roofed tunnel: "You must ask her! Ash! Ash!"

A dribble of earth fell down between planks, touching his face, and he winced and wrenched himself back with a cry. Panting, he fixed his gaze on Ash.

"Tell my lord the King-Caliph! *Tell him*. The stone of the desert has souls! Great voices speak, speak through my Stone Golem, and *she* has heard them, and *you* have heard them—" Leofric's voice lost depth. His face saddened. "How can you let this petty war keep you from speaking of such danger?"

"I—" Ash stopped. Floria's shoulder was pressing against hers, hard against her backplate; de Vere had one thoughtful hand to his mace's grip.

"Tell him!" Leofric yelled. "My daughter betrays me, I am asking you—begging *you*—" He wrenched both arms free of the priests, stood for one second, then raised his head and stared straight at Ash. "The Empire is betrayed, we're all to die soon, every man of us, every woman, Visigoth or Burgundian—*tell my lord Caliph what you hear*."

Ash became aware again of Gelimer's intense stare. She looked away from Leofric, took in all the Visigoth group, the foreign envoys, stood for a moment in a complete state of indecision.

The faintest hiss came from the Greek Fire globes. Violante, cuddling her rat, looked up from under her chopped-off hair at Ash, her expression unreadable. The adult woman slave began to pick at the girl's tunic, dribbling without wiping her wide lips, and whining like a hound.

"Okay." Ash rested her hands on her belt, a few inches from

sword and dagger. With a sense of immense relief, she said, "He might be mad, but he isn't crazy. Listen to him. He's telling the truth."

Gelimer frowned.

"There are—" Ash hesitated, choosing words with care. "There are great pyramid-golem in the desert, south of Carthage. You saw them when we rode there, Lord Caliph."

Gelimer's lips twitched, red in the nest of his beard, and he stroked his hand across his mouth. "They are monuments to our holy dead. God blesses them now with a cold Fire."

"You saw them. They're made of the river silt and stone. Stone. Like the Stone Golem."

He shook his head. "Nonsense."

"No, not nonsense. Your *amir* Leofric's right. I've heard them. It's their voices that have spoken to you through the Stone Golem. It's their advice that has brought you here. And believe me, they don't care about your Empire!" With a curious sense of release, she nodded toward the white-haired Visigoth lord. "*Amir* Leofric isn't crazy. There are devils out there—as far as we're concerned, they're devils. And they won't rest until the whole world is as cold and dead as the lands beyond Burgundy."

She had little hope of convincing him. She saw from his face that she probably had not. Nonetheless, she felt the release in herself: simply to be able to speak of it aloud. From behind the ranks of Janissaries, she watched Gelimer, and he could not look away from her.

"Which is the more likely?" he said. "That this talk of devils is true, when we so plainly have God's visible mark of favor? Or that House Leofric has some factional plot against the throne? Which his slave-general joined, at his command. And now you. Captain Ash, you should have died in my court, dissected for the knowledge you would bring us. That is how you will die, when I have taken Dijon."

" 'When,' " Ash remarked dryly.

Florian, at Ash's side, interjected, "Lord-Caliph, she's telling you the truth. There are golem in the desert. And you've been fooled by them."

"No. Not I. I have not been the fool."

Gelimer signaled again. The larger of the two priests holding Leofric let go of him and pushed his way through the press of men to the woman slave standing beside Violante. The woman flinched away from him and began to cry in great unrestrained sobs and gawks and chokes. The priest hauled her forward by the iron collar around her wattle-skinned neck.

"My lords of France and the Holy Roman Empire," the King-Caliph said. "You have seen that my lord Leofric is ill. You see his slave-daughter, our General, is also not in health. And now you hear from this mercenary Captain-General of Burgundy the ramblings of a lunatic. This is why, gentlemen. This woman. I brought her for you to see, and judge. This is Adelize. She is the mother of both these young women."

The priest punched the slave woman. She stopped roaring. A complete silence fell. Ash heard only a hissing sound in her ears. Thomas Rochester, beside her, gripped her shoulder.

"If this is the dam," Gelimer said, "what wonder if the pups are mad?"

Ash stared at the idiot woman. Under the rolls of fat, the outline of her face could be similar to that of the Faris, standing impassively beside her; it had a gut-wrenching familiarity that Ash did not let herself feel. An old woman, fifty or sixty. The woman's pale hair was by now gray, no trace of color left.

Ash opened her mouth to speak, and could say nothing, her voice lost.

"With such a dam, what can you expect of the cubs?" Gelimer repeated rhetorically. "Nonsense such as this talk of great devils."

"Your Faris, your commander in the field, she also suffers this lunacy?" De Commines said sharply.

"The crusades of our Empire have never been dependent on one commander." The King-Caliph sounded serene.

John de Vere stirred, fair brows dipping, obviously doubting that serenity. "Madam, he thinks it worth discrediting the commander who has won him Europe, to discredit Leofric and you."

Ash said nothing. She stared at Adelize, at the woman who wept now without sound, wet tears blubbering her cheeks.

Two hundred years of incest. Sweet Christ and all the Saints. Is this what I *am going to be—*

The Faris reached out and rested her hand on the woman's hair. Her hand moved softly, stroking. Her face remained impassive.

"With that disposed of," King-Caliph Gelimer said briskly, "we turn to our business with Burgundy."

Ash missed what Floria said. She turned her head aside, choked up the searing hot vomit in her throat, spat it into her hand, and let it fall to the floor. Her eyes ran: she blinked back the water in case anyone should think she wept.

"—an envoy," the King-Caliph was saying.

"Envoy?"

"He says he wants to send one in to us," Floria whispered. Her face, intent, promised compassion and analysis later; in this second, she was all alertness, all Duchess. "I'm going to let him. The man's probably a spy, but it's all delay." She spoke up. "If he's acceptable, we'll take him."

Gelimer's hand stroked his beaded beard again, the gold flashing. He said mildly, "You will find him acceptable, Duchess of Burgundy. He is your brother."

Ash did not take it in. There was a stir in the group of armed men in front of her, someone pushing their way through. Her gaze went past the man. She looked back, suddenly thinking *I know that face!*, wondering which of Gelimer's Franks he might be—a mercenary she'd met in Italy, maybe, or some Iberian merchant? And in a split second, the light fell full on his face, and she saw that it was Fernando del Guiz with his hair cropped, and that he wore a priest's high-collared robe.

A *priest*?

How can he be a priest: he's my husband!

Last seen, he had been a young man with blond hair falling shaggy to his shoulders, dressed in the mail and furred robes of a Visigoth knight. Now, unarmed—not even a dagger!—he wore a dark priestly robe buttoned from chin to floor-length hem, and tightly belted at the waist. It only showed off the breadth of his shoulders and chest the more. Something about his scrubbed cleanliness and shining yellow hair made her long to walk over to him and bury her face in his neck, smell the male scent of him.

The shifting light of the golems' torches cast shadows enough to hide her expression. Amazed, she felt her cheeks heating up.

"Fernando," she said aloud.

Abruptly conscious of her hacked-off short hair and general siege-induced grubbiness, she shifted her gaze away as he looked at her. There was no pectoral cross on the chain around his neck, but a pendant of a man's face carved with leaves tendriling from his open mouth. *Arian priest, then. Christus Viridianus! What on earth—?*

Angry with herself, she raised her eyes again. Someone had expertly shaved his hair back above his ears in a novice's tonsure. He looked faintly amused.

"Abbot Muthari *must* be hard up," Ash remarked, in a voice with more gravel in it than she liked. "But I might have known you'd get into skirts as soon as you could."

There was an appreciative rumble from the soldiers. Ash overheard Robert Anselm translating her remark for Bajezet's men; their laughter came in a few seconds late.

There I go: motor-mouth, she thought, still staring at Fernando. Knowing that whatever she said, automatically, was nothing more than a time-filler while she stared up at him, thinking, *Has he really taken vows as a priest?* and *Are the Arian priests celibate?*

A warmth ran down her skin, loosening the muscles of her thighs, and she knew that the pupils of her eyes must be wide.

"This is my ambassador," the King-Caliph said.

Fernando del Guiz bowed.

Ash stared.

"Shit," she said. "Well. Shit. Merry fucking Christmas."

Gelimer ignored Ash. He spoke to Floria, his gaze shifting between her and the other Burgundians. "You can see beyond your walls; you are not blind. I have three full legions outside Dijon. It is obvious you cannot hold out. Surrender Dijon. By the courtesies of war, I give you this chance, but nothing more. Send me your answer, by my envoy—tomorrow, on the feast of St. Stephen."

V

"GET THAT BLOODY sap blocked up again!" Ash ordered. "Barrels of rocks first, and then earth. I don't want anyone assaulting in through there. Move it!"

"Yes, Captain!" One of the Burgundian commanders strode back to his men, where they sat or crouched under shattered houses, directing them with brief, efficient shouts.

Floria said, "One of you—Thomas Rochester—tell de la Marche I'll be with Ash. Call the council."

"I'll go," John de Vere forestalled her. "Madam, I am anxious to discuss the Caliph's words with Master de la Marche; shall I bring him to you?"

At Floria's nod, the English Earl gave an order to his interpreter and marched off rapidly at the head of the Janissaries.

The rumbling of rubble-filled barrels across the cobbles drowned out the noise of their passing. The streets smelled of burning. The freezing wind blew, not the woodsmoke of cooking fires, but Greek Fire's metallic tang. Ash glanced from the men in jacks and war-hats, slinging meal sacks full of dirt in a chain toward the entrance to the countermine, to Florian, the woman pulling off the horn crown and running her fingers through her man-short gold hair. Hair as short as her brother's.

"Let's go," Ash said. "Shame if a long shot from a mangonel sprayed you all over the pavement, now."

"You don't think they'll keep this truce?"

"Not if we present them with an opportunity!" Ash looked away from Floria to Fernando del Guiz. He stood in the middle of John de Vere's Turks. Recognizable as a renegade to anyone who knew his face from Neuss, or Genoa, or Basle.

"Get him covered up." Ash spoke to one of Rochester's sergeants. "Give him your hood and cloak."

She watched the sergeant put the cloak on Fernando del Guiz, knot the ties, tug the caped hood over his bare head, and pull the hood forward. A pang moved her: wanting, herself, to be the one to do it. *He's my husband. I've lain with this man. I could have had his child.*

But I stopped wanting him before I left Carthage. He's a weak man. There's nothing to him but good looks!

"Bring him along with us," Ash said. "Florian's going to be in the hospice at the tower, anyway."

There was an imperceptible relaxation in the mercenaries standing around Fernando del Guiz. It wouldn't have been there if he had still been in knight's armor, she thought. She could read on their faces the thought *It's only a priest.*

"For those of you who don't know," she said, raising her voice a little, "this man used to be a knight in Holy Roman Emperor Frederick's court. Don't assume you can let him anywhere near a sword. Okay: let's move out."

With undertones of self-satisfaction in his voice, Fernando protested, "I'm an envoy, and a Christian priest. You don't have to be afraid of me, Ash."

"*Afraid* of you?"

She stared at him for a moment, snorted, and turned away.

Floria murmured, "Gelimer doesn't know me very well. Does he? Blood's much thinner than water in this respect."

Ash made an effort and achieved cynicism. "Fernando probably told Gelimer you were his loving sister and he could persuade you to turn cartwheels naked through Dijon's north gate while signing a surrender . . ."

"Or that he was your loving husband. Let's go," the surgeon-Duchess invited.

Stepping out into the wrecked territory behind the city gates, Ash couldn't prevent the automatic upward glance. Of the party, only Fernando looked bewilderedly at the soldiers, up at the sky, and back down at Ash again.

"Oh, I trust Gelimer to keep the truce . . ." Ash remarked, with a raucous sarcasm.

Ash moved off in the familiar position: surrounded by a group of armed men. Between banner and escort, and keeping her footing on the paths raked clear of masonry and oak beams, there was little of her attention she could spare for the German ex-knight. Little of her mind that she could give over to the thought *That's my husband!*

She felt glad of it. Cold bit deep. The sap below the earth had felt warmer than these chill, exposed streets of Dijon and the empty winter sky. Ash beat her hands together as she walked, the plates of the gauntlets chinking. Shadows streamed north from the roofs, and the abbey bell rang for Terce. A quick glance up assured her of the Burgundian and the Lion presence on the city walls, keeping the besiegers under surveillance.

As they reached the streets in the south of the city, Florian gave her a curious look and signaled the guards to move up as she quickened her pace. It left Ash and Fernando walking side by side, him overtopping her by a head, a slight degree of privacy ensured by respect for commander in chief and Duchess.

Let 'em listen, Ash thought.

"Well," she said, "at least you're still the Duchess's brother. I suppose you've divorced *me*."

It came out entirely as sardonic as she had intended it. There was no shake in her voice.

Fernando del Guiz looked down at her with stone green eyes. Close up, she was very conscious of the power of his body, striding beside her, knew equally that most of the attraction stemmed from him not knowing it, from his unconsciousness—still!—that it was anything special to be well fed and clean and strong.

I thought I got over this! In Carthage! Oh shit . . .

"It wasn't a divorce, in the end." He sounded faintly apologetic, dropping his voice and looking around at the escorting mercenaries. "Abbot Muthari's learned doctors decreed it wasn't a valid marriage, not between a freeman of the nobility and a bondswoman. They annulled it."

"Ah. Isn't that convenient. Doesn't keep you out of the priesthood." She couldn't stop some of the astounded curiosity she felt leaking into her tone. What she felt about an annulment was not available to her yet. *I'll think about that later, when I've got time to spare.*

Fernando del Guiz said nothing, only glancing down at her and away again.

"Jesus, Fernando, what *is* this!"

"This?"

She reached across and prodded his chest, just below the oak pendant of Christ on the Tree; thought *That was a mistake, I still want to touch him, how damn obvious can I get!*, and grunted, " 'This.' This priest's getup you're in. You're not seriously telling me you've taken vows!"

"I am." Fernando looked down at her. "I took my first vows in Carthage. Abbot Muthari let me take the second vows when he reconsecrated the cathedral in Marseilles. God accepted me, Ash."

"The Arian God."

Fernando shrugged. "All the same thing, isn't it? Doesn't matter which name you call it."

"Sheesh!" Impressed by the careless dismissal of eleven centuries of schism, Ash couldn't help smiling. "*Why*, Fernando? Don't tell me God called you, either. He's really scraping the bottom of the barrel if He did!"

When she looked up to meet Fernando's gaze, he looked both embarrassed and determined.

"I had the idea after you talked to me in Carthage. You were right. I was still taking the King-Caliph's arms and armor: why would he listen to me say we shouldn't be fighting this war? So I thought of this. This is the only way I can give up the sword and still have men *listen* to me."

She kept looking at him, long enough for her concentration to miss a beat, and for her foot to catch a fragment of broken brick. Recovering with a sword-fighter's balance from the stumble, she said, half-stifled, "You entered the church for *that*?"

His mouth set, mulishly, making him look momentarily no more than a boy. "I don't need to be ignored like a peasant or a woman! If I'm not knightly, then I have to be *something* they'll respect. I'm still del Guiz. I'm still noble! I've just taken my vows to be a *peregrinatus christi*."

Tears swelled the lower lids of her eyes. Ash looked into the wind and blinked, sharply. She was momentarily in Carthage's palace, hearing a *nazir* say *Let him through, it's only the* peregrinatus christi, and seeing Godfrey's lined, bearded face in the mass of foreign soldiers.

I need him here, now, not as a voice in my head!

"You'll never be a priest," she said harshly. "You're a fucking hypocrite."

"No."

The escort clattered under the gateway and into the courtyard in front of the company tower. A blaze of cold wind whipped in through the open gates, spooking the remaining horses. Anselm bellowed orders to the men, over the noise from the forge. Florian immediately found herself intercepted by a dozen courtiers.

"So you're not a hypocrite." Ash wiped wind tears out of her eyes. "Yeah. Right."

"I never bothered much about praying, it was priest's work. I'm a knight." The tall, golden-haired man stopped. He spoke under the noise the men made. "I *was* one. I'm a priest now. Maybe God made me see how fucking crazy this fighting is! All I know is, one day I was a traitor Frankish knight, with no patron, and nobody listening to me—and now I'm not killing anyone, and I might just get some of Gelimer's nobles to listen when I say this war's wrong. If you call that hypocrisy—fine."

"Ah, shit."

Something in her tone obviously puzzled him. He shot a glance at her.

"Nothing," Ash snapped. She felt resentful, bad-tempered.

I might not have liked the separation, but at least it was settled. I might not have liked you being a weaseling, lying little shitbag—but at least I knew where I was with you.

I resent you making me think about this again. Feel *again.*

"Nothing," Ash repeated, under her breath.

If he had had a glib response, she would have walked away from him. Fernando del Guiz looked down at the flagstones in adolescent male embarrassment, kicking his bootheel against the ground, under the hem of his robe.

Ash sighed. "Why did you have to come back doing something I can respect?"

A mass of people blocked the company tower's steps. She heard Florian's raw voice raised. One glance found her Anselm; without more prompting, he began to give brisk orders. Men in company livery began to shift Burgundian courtiers out of the arched doorway.

Without looking at Fernando, she said, "You're wrong, you know. About war. And if there was a better way than going to war, we're *long* past the point where it was an issue. But I suppose you've had the guts to put your balls on the line . . ."

He coughed, or laughed, she was not sure which. "This is the Arian priesthood, not Our Lady of the Bloody Crescent!"

One of the escorting Turkish soldiers glanced across at that, nudged his mate, and said something under his breath. Ash stifled her grin.

"The goddess Astarte's very popular round here right now, so let's keep the religious dissent to a minimum, shall we?"

Fernando's smile was warm. "And you call me a hypocrite."

"I'm not a hypocrite," Ash said, turning to go into the tower as the crowd cleared. "I'm an equal-opportunities heretic—I think you're *all* talking through your arses . . ."

"This from the woman who was marked by the Lion?" He made a movement, reaching up to brush her scarred cheek with his gloved hand. She had let him touch her skin before she realized she was not going to move.

"That was then," she said. "This is now."

She heard, ahead, a roar of male laughter, loped up the steps to the door and walked in, in the midst of her escort, into chaos in the lower hall.

"Boss!" Henri Brant gave her a smile that showed the gap between his missing front teeth. He slapped the shoulder of a man shouting into the crowded hall: Richard Faversham, in green robes, his black beard untrimmed, his face flushed.

Momentarily forgetting the others with her, Ash stared at the tower's ground-floor hall. A fierce fire burned in the hearth, surrounded by off-duty Lion Azure mercenaries in various states of dishevelment, ladling some liquid out of a cauldron. The beams were draped and hung with long strands of ivy. Baldina banged a tabor; blind and lame Carracci sat with her, fingering out notes on a recorder in duet with Antonio Angelotti. There were no trestle tables covered in yellowing linen, but men sat with their wooden bowls and cups where tables would have been ranked against either wall. She smelled cooking.

"Merry Mass of Christ!" Henri Brant exclaimed, his warm breath hitting her in the face. Whatever they were drinking—not having the swine to feed now, it was probably fermented turnip-peelings—it had a kick to it.

"God bless you!" Richard Faversham leaned down and gave her the kiss of peace. "Christ be with you!"

"And with you," Ash growled. She ignored Florian's chuckle. After a second, surveying the hall and her men, she grinned at Henri Brant. "I take it you're doing two servings, so the lads on duty can come back here?"

"Either that, or find my balls boiling in the pot!" The steward pushed his coif back on his sheepswool-curly white hair, sweating from the heat of close-packed bodies if not from the fire. "We couldn't hoard much. Master Anselm thought, as I did, better to eat now and starve the sooner, rather than let the Christ-Mass pass without celebration. So did Master Faversham!"

Ash studied the large black-bearded Englishman for a moment.

"Well done!" She clasped both men's hands warmly. "God knows we need something to keep our minds off this shithole we're in!"

Unguarded, she looked around and met the gaze of Fernando del Guiz inside his concealing hood. He was watching the soldiers and their sparse revelry with a strange expression. *Not contempt*, she guessed. *Compassion? No. Not Fernando.*

"We're holding council. The Burgundians will be along any minute. I'll come down for mass. Henri, can you send Roberto to me? And Angeli. I'll be up in the solar."

The tower's top floor had been dressed in her absence. Green ivy hung stark over the round arches, bright against the sand-and-ocher colors of the walls. A hoarded single Green candle burned, scenting the room. Rickard turned from supervising the pages as she entered: obviously proud of the evergreen, the hearth-fire, the food in preparation—and stopped, his face freezing, recognizing Fernando del Guiz under the hood.

"The Duchess will have this hall to speak with her brother," Ash said formally. "Rickard, we're expecting de la Marche, can you clear that with the guys on the door, and get these kids out of here?"

"Boss." Rickard looked twice at the robes under the cloak, then stalked past Fernando del Guiz, flared brows dipping, hand resting down on his sword hilt. She noted, as he walked out with the pages, that the boy was as tall as the German ex-knight now. Not a boy. A squire, a young man, all this in the last half year.

"Good grief!" Floria shook her head, saying nothing more. She moved closer to the hearth, let her cloak fall open, and extended her hands to the blaze. Ash saw she was wearing a fur-lined demi-gown over male doublet and hose again.

Fernando del Guiz reached up and put his hood back. He looked quizzically at the surgeon-Duchess. "Sister. You make a strange Duchess."

"Oh, you think so?" Her gaze warmed. "And you don't make a strange priest?"

Ash blurted, "Why the hell pick *you* to come in here? Because priests are sacrosanct? De la Marche would love a traitor to hang up on the walls—cheer everybody up, that would!"

Fernando still spoke to Floria. "I had no choice. I came up with the Abbot Muthari, from Carthage. The King-Caliph dragged me into court as soon as he heard who the Duchess of Burgundy was. They interrogated me—not that there's much I could tell him, is there, Floria?"

"No." Floria turned to watch the fire. "I remember seeing you once, when I was about ten. The only time I ever stayed on my father's German estates. You would have been born that year."

"Mother used to have Tante Jeanne to stay—is she still alive?—and they'd talk about you in whispers."

His face creased under his rumpled hair. Ash thought she

saw something relaxed, despite the circumstances, in his humor. As if he were comfortable with himself.

He added, "I thought you'd run off with a man. I didn't know you'd run off to *be* a man!"

"I 'ran off' to be a doctor!" Floria snapped.

"And now you're Burgundy's Duchess." He looked at Ash. "Then it came out that you were made captain of the Burgundian armies here, and I was doubly useful."

Ash snapped, "That must have made a pleasant change."

"Except that I could tell him even less about you—'she's a soldier; I married her; she doesn't trust me.' I could tell him how good a soldier you are. And I'm not, you see. But by now, they know that."

His wry expression confused her. Ash looked away. She had an impulse to provide him with food, with drink. An impulse to touch the faint blond stubble on his cheek.

Deliberately brutal, she said, "No. You're not. The ragheads still letting you keep Guizburg?"

"Priests have no lands. I've lost most of what I had. I'm still useful, by virtue of being Floria's brother. While I'm useful, I can talk—this is a hopeless war, for both sides—"

"Christ up a Tree, I need a drink!" Ash turned and began to pace the floorboards, beating her hands together for circulation. "And where the hell is de la Marche? Let's get this 'envoy' crap over with!"

There were no pages to serve out rations: all the baggage-train brats down in the hall below, by the sound of it—shrieks and yells echoed up the spiral stairwell, not subdued by the ragged hangings blocking the doorway. Cold wind found its way between the window shutters.

Tension kept Ash pacing. Florian squatted by the fire with her cloak held out open around her, to trap the heat, a campaigner's trick remembered from half a dozen winters with the company. Fernando del Guiz folded his arms and stood watching both women, smiling wryly.

Ash strode to the stairwell, and yelled, "Rickard!"

A longer space of time elapsed than she was used to before he called up, panting, "Yes, boss?"

"Where the fuck's de la Marche and Oxford and the civilians?"

"Don't know, boss. No messenger!"

"What are you doing?"

Rickard's flushed face appeared in the dim light of the stairwell, a dozen steps below. "We're going to do the mumming, boss. I'm in it! Are you coming down?"

"There's no word from Oxford?"

"Captain Anselm sent another man up to the palace just now."

"Hell. What are they *doing*?" Ash glanced back over her shoulder. "It's a damn sight warmer down there than up here, isn't it? And there's food. Okay: we'll wait for my lords of England and Burgundy downstairs! And get me a drink before you start pratting around."

"Yes, boss!"

A great burst of sound came as she stepped off the bottom stair and into the main hall: nothing to do with her or, as she first thought, the presence of Fernando del Guiz, but a carol being bellowed by two hundred lusty male throats:

> *"The Boar's Head in hand bear I,*
> *With garlands gay and rosemary,*
> *I pray you all sing merrily,*
> *Caput apri defero,*
> *Reddens laudes domino.*
> *Qui estis in convivio—"*

Floria took a place beside Ash against the wall, in the small stir of men-at-arms and archers acknowledging their commander's presence. Ash signaled them back to their singing. Floria murmured under her breath, "We could do with a boar's head . . ."

"I don't think we've even got the rosemary to cook with it!" Ash felt a wooden bowl and horn spoon shoved into her hand, yelled thanks to one of the pages, and realized that she had settled back against the stone wall shoulder to shoulder with Fernando del Guiz.

She had to look up to meet his eyes.

The shrill sound of Carracci's recorder rose above the voices of men and women. She heard Angelotti playing descant. It was not possible to speak over the volume of sound.

I'd forgotten he's so tall. And so young.

There being no tables on which to set the trenchers, the woman doing the cooking and the other baggage women were rushing about the hall, from group to group, ladling out pottage. Ash held out her bowl, caught for a second in the rush of conviviality, and spooned the hot broth into her mouth. The carol thundered to a close.

"The mummers!" someone yelled. "Bring on the mummers!"

A roof-shaking cheer.

Beside her, Fernando del Guiz, his hood still raised, studied the contents of his bowl and tentatively began to eat. What could be seen of him was anonymous, priestly; he drew no glances from armed men. Ash kept her eyes on the men shoving a space clear in the center of the hall.

There was no Christmas kissing-bush hanging from the rafters: someone had strung up a pair of old hose—being at least green in color, she supposed—and John Burren and Adriaen Campin were drunkenly pretending to kiss each other underneath it. She attended analytically to the cheers and catcalls—a little shrill, not all the men joining in. She glanced toward the guards on the great door. No runners; no messages yet.

What is keeping them?

Fernando del Guiz chewed at some unrelenting piece of gristle and swallowed. On the other side of Ash, Floria had stopped eating to talk enthusiastically to Baldina. The men-at-arms around them were watching the center of the hall.

There was a certain amount of relief on the young man's face as he turned his head to gaze down at her. He nodded, as if to himself. "Can we speak privately?"

"If I take you into a corner somewhere, everyone will be watching. Let's talk here."

To her own surprise, there was no malice in her tone.

Fernando took another spoonful of the pottage, frowned, put back the spoon, tapped the shoulder of the man in front, and handed the bowl forward. When he looked back at Ash, his face in the hood's shadow was drawn, wry, and uncertain. "I came to make a peace with you."

She stared at him for a long moment. "I didn't even bother to find out if you were alive or dead. After Carthage. I suppose it was easier to think I had other matters to worry about."

He studied her face. "Maybe."

About to question that, Ash was interrupted by a loud and ringing cheer. The mummers' procession wound around the center of the hall, between men and women packed back to the walls. A rhythmic clapping bounced off the walls, together with inebriated yells.

"What's this?" Fernando shouted.

Two large men-at-arms in mail hauberks, in front of him, turned around and shushed Fernando.

"It's the mumming," Ash said, only loud enough for him to hear.

The head of the procession walked into the central clear space. It was Adriaen Campin, she realized, the big Fleming wrapped in a horse blanket and wearing a bridle over his head. Rags of cloth, for ribbons, fluttered at his knees and ankles. Campin, his blanket sliding down, put his fists on his hips and bawled:

> *"I am the hobby horse, with St. George I ride,*
> *It's fucking cold out, so we've come inside!*
> *Give us room to act our play,*
> *Then by God's Grace we'll go away!"*

Ash put her hands over her face as the men-at-arms cheered and the hobbyhorse began to dance. Beside her, she heard Floria whimper. On her other side, Fernando del Guiz quaked; she felt his arm, pressed against her in the crowd, shaking with amusement.

"Not used to seeing this one at Christ's Mass," he said. "We always did it at Epiphany Feast, at Guizburg . . . do I take it you think this city won't hold out until Twelfth Night?"

"That what you're going to tell Gelimer?"

He grinned boyishly. "Gelimer will hate this. The King-

Caliph hopes you're all cutting your own throats, not making merry."

Ash looked away from Campin's high-kicking horse-dance. She thought one or two of the men around her caught the King-Caliph's name. She shook her head warningly at Fernando. The warmth of the hall brought the smell of his body to her: male sweat, and the own particular smell that was just his.

Obscene, brutal, and blackly humorous comments drifted her way. Ash caught the eye of those of her men who obviously did recognize the fair-haired priest as the German knight who had briefly been their feudal lord. The comment moved to where she would not hear it.

Why am I sparing his *feelings?*

"You're going to have to tell me," she said, surrendering to the impulse. "Fernando, how did you get to be a priest!"

For answer, he extended his arm, pulling his sleeve up a little. A comparatively new scar was still red and swollen across his right wrist, although to a professional eye mostly healed.

"Hauling Abbot Muthari out of the palace when it collapsed," he explained.

"I'd have left him!"

"*I* was looking for a patron," Fernando remarked sourly. "I'd just spoken up for you, remember? In the palace? I knew Gelimer was going to dump me faster than a dog can shit. I would have hauled anyone with jewelry or fine clothes out of the wreckage—it happened to be Muthari."

"And he was dumb enough to let you take vows?"

"You don't know what it was like in Carthage then." The man frowned, his expression distant. "At first, they thought the King-Caliph was dead, and the Empire going to dissolve in factions—then word came down that he was alive and it was a miracle. Then those spooky lights showed up in the desert—where we rode out? With those tombs? And *that* was supposed to be a curse. . . ."

Seeing him so far away in his mind, Ash said nothing to disturb his chain of memories.

"I still think it is," Fernando said, after a second. "I rode out there when we recovered Lord Leofric. There were serfs and sheep and goats out there that had . . . they were dead. They were melted, like wax, they were *in* the gates of the tombs—half in and half out of the bronze metal. And the light—curtains of light, in the sky. Now they're calling it the Fire of God's Blessing."[52]

Seeing it with his eyes, the painted walls of pyramids where she had ridden out into the silence imposed by the Wild Machines, Ash felt the cold hairs prickle at the nape of her neck.

Fernando shrugged, in the tight-sleeved robe, one hand reaching up to close around his oak pendant. "*I* call it djinn."

"It isn't djinni, or devils. It's the Wild Machines." She pointed at the sky beyond the round stone arch of the window. "They're sucking the light out of the world. I don't want to think what that's like when you're right up close to them."

"I'm not *going* to think about it." Fernando shrugged.

"Ah, that's my husband . . . *ex*-husband," she corrected herself.

Whether Adriaen Campin had finished his dance or whether the hobbyhorse had merely fallen over was unclear. Half a dozen men dragged him off. Baldina and several more women threw clean rushes down onto the floor, and Ash saw Henri Brant walking out over them into the empty space. He wore a full-length looted velvet robe that had been red, before grease spattered it mostly black. A metal circlet sat on his white curls, spikes jutting up from it, cold-hammered from the forge. More horse harness had been cannibalized to make a neck chain out of bits.

Anselm's done good, Ash reflected, trying to spot her second-in-command in the hall and failing. *We needed this.*

Henri Brant, with a great deal of authority, held up his hands for quiet and declaimed:

> *"I'm England's true king*
> *And I boldly appear,*

---

[52]This description is tantalisingly similar to some of the rumoured results of military experiments with extreme electro-magnetic force. The 'curtains of light' are presumably charged particles, like the *aurora borealis*.

Seeking my son for whom I fear—
Is Prince George here?"

One of the English archers bellowed, "You a *Lancastrian* or a *Yorkist* English King?"

Henri Brant jerked his thumb over his shoulder at the mummer playing St. George. "What d'*you* think!"

"It's Anselm!" Floria exclaimed, straining up on her toes to see. She turned a shining face to Ash. "It's Roberto!"

"Guess that'll be a Lancastrian King, then . . ."

There was a great deal of noise from those company men who did not come from England, but were entirely happy to wind up those who did. Ash was caught between chuckling at them, and the sheer contentment of watching their high spirits, and the intent expression on Fernando's face.

"I half expect you to offer me a contract with the Caliph," she said.

"No. I'm not that stupid." After a second Fernando del Guiz touched her arm and pointed at the mummers, face alight with momentary unguarded enjoyment. Her gut thumped. She was struck by the lean grace of him, and his wide shoulders, and the thought that—if war had not come to trouble him—he might have continued winning tournaments and gambling, might have married some Bavarian heiress and sired babies and never dipped deeper into himself than necessary, certainly never found himself taking religious vows.

"What *do* you want with me?" she said.

A cheer drowned out whatever he said. She looked and saw Robert Anselm, lance in hand, stomp into the cleared space between the company men-at-arms and baggage women.

"My God. You won't see armor like that again!" Floria yelled.

Her brother gaped. "God willing, no, we won't!"

More pauldrons, spalders, guard-braces, and rere-braces had been buckled and pinned onto Anselm's wide shoulders than it seemed possible for any man to support. He rattled as he walked. The leg harness was his own, but the German cuirass had plainly been made for a much larger man—Ash suspected Roberto had borrowed it off one of the Burgundian commanders. The fluted breastplate caught the light from the slit-windows and shimmered, silver, where it was not covered by an old tawny livery jacket with a white mullet device. The lance he carried bore a drooping white flag—a woman's chemise—with a red rose scrawled on it.

Anselm shoved the visor of his sallet up, displaying his grinning, stubbled face. He rapped the lance shaft on the flagstones, and threw out his free arm in a wide gesture.

"I am Prince George, a worthy knight,
I'll spend my blood in England's right!"

He punched his fist in the air, mimed awaiting a cheer, and when it came, cupped his hand to where his ear would have been, if he hadn't been wearing a helmet. "I can't *hear* you! Louder!"

Sound slammed back from the tower's stone walls. Ash felt it through her chest as well as her ears. Anselm went on:

"There is no knight as brave as me—
I'll kick your arse if you don't agree!"

Fernando del Guiz groaned, delicately. "I don't remember mumming being like this at Frederick's court!"

"You have to be with mercenaries to see real class . . ."

There was something still boyish in his face when he laughed; it vanished when he stopped. Strain had etched lines that had not been there in Carthage. *Three months*, she thought. *Only that. The sun in Virgo then, the sun just into Capricorn now. So short a time*.

She saw him stiffen as a raucous jeer greeted the entrance of another of the mummers.

Euen Huw strode unsteadily forward in a mail hauberk with a woman's square-necked chemise worn over it. The yellow linen flapped around his knees. The men-at-arms and archers cheered; one of the woman—Blanche, Ash thought—gave a shrill whistle. Ash frowned, not able to stop herself laughing, still puzzled. Not until the Welshman, wincing at his scalp-stitches, put on a looted Visigoth helm with a black rag tied around it, did she recognize the parody of robes over mail.

Euen Huw mimed sneaking into the open space, clutching a looted Carthaginian spear. He declaimed:

> *"I am the Saracen champion, see,*
> *Come from Carthage to Burgundy.*
> *I'll slay Prince George and when he's gone*
> *I'll kill all you others, one by one."*

"Take you a fucking long time!" someone shouted.

"I can do it," Euen Huw protested. "Watch me."

"Watch you shag a sheep, more like!"

"I 'eard that, Burren!"

Ash did not meet Fernando's eye. On her other side, Floria del Guiz made a loud, rude noise, and began to wheeze. Ash clamped her arms across her breastplate, aching under the ribs, and attempted to look suitably commander-like and unimpressed.

"You'll have to forgive them being topical," she said, keeping her face straight with an immense effort.

Euen Huw snatched a wooden cup of drink from one of the archers, drained it, and swung back to face Robert Anselm.

> *"I challenge you, Prince George the brave,*
> *I say you are an arrant knave.*
> *I can stand by my every word—*
> *Because you wear a wooden sword!"*

"And besides, you're English crap," the Welsh lance leader added.

Robert Anselm shoved his lance and makeshift banner aloft and struck an attitude:

> *"By my right hand, and by this blade,*
> *I'll send you to your earthly grave—"*

"Ouch," Floria said gravely.

Antonio Angelotti appeared at her side, and murmured, "I did tell him. *Terza rima*, I offered . . ."

Ash saw the fair-haired gunner clasp Floria's arm, as he might have done with any man, or the company surgeon, but not the Duchess of Burgundy. Ash smiled, and, as she glanced back, caught something like wistfulness on Fernando's face.

Anselm lowered his lance and pointed it at Euen Huw's breast, the Welshman taking an automatic step back. Anselm proclaimed:

"I'll send your soul to God on high,
So prepare yourself to fly or die!"

Ash saw the lance and spear tossed aside, both men drawing whalebone practice swords from their belts. The shouts, cheers, and jeering rose to a pitch as the fight began, half the English archers near her chanting, "Come on, St. George!" and banging their feet on the stone floor.

"Look at that." Ash pointed. "They couldn't resist it, could they!"

Out in the center of the hall, Robert Anselm and Euen Huw had abandoned their exaggerated and pantomime blows and were circling each other on the rushes. As she spoke, Anselm darted a blow forward, the Welshman whipped it round in a parry and struck; Anselm blocked—

"They had to make a genuine fight of it." Florian sighed. She was smiling. The noise of the men-at-arms rose even higher, seeing a contest of skills beginning. "I suppose they'll get back to the mumming eventually . . . come on, Euen! Show them how well I sewed you up!"

Under the noise of cheering and the thwack of whalebone on plate and mail, Fernando del Guiz said, "Is it peace between us, Ash?"

She looked up at him, standing beside her, hood drawn forward, in a hall full of his enemies, apparently unmoved. *But I know him, now. He's afraid.*

"It's been a long time since Neuss," she said. "Married, and separated, and attaindered, and annulled. And a long way from Carthage. Why *did* you speak up for me? In the coronation—why?"

Apparently at random, Fernando del Guiz murmured, "You'd think I would have remembered your face. I didn't. I forgot it for seven years. It didn't occur to me that if there was a woman in armor at Neuss, it might be the one I'd—seen—at Genoa."

"Is that an answer? Is that an *apology*?"

The light slanting down from the arrow-slit windows cast a silver light on the heads of the crowd. It flashed back from Anselm and Euen Huw, leaping on the rushes in a mad duel, the cheering shaking the ivy hanging from the rafters. The cold sank into her bones, and she looked down at her white, bloodless hands.

"*Is* it an apology?" she repeated.

"Yes."

In the center of the hall, Robert Anselm drove Euen Huw back across the rushes with a savage, perfectly executed series of blows, as hard and rapid as a man chopping wood. Whalebone spanged off metal. The English archers hoarsely cheered.

"Fernando, why *did* you come here?"

"There has to be a truce. Then peace." Fernando del Guiz looked down at his empty hands, and then back up at her. "Too many people are dying here, Ash. Dijon's going to be wiped out. So are you."

Two contradictory feelings flooded her. *He's so young!* she thought; and at the same time: *He's right. Military logic isn't any different for me than it is for anyone else. Unless Gelimer's more frightened of the Turks than I think he is, this siege is going to end in a complete massacre. And soon.*

"Christ on a rock!" he exclaimed. "Give in, for once in your life! Gelimer's promised me he'll keep you alive, out of *Amir* Leofric's hands. He'll just throw you in prison for a few years—"

His voice rose. Ash was aware of Floria and Angelotti looking across her, toward the German knight.

"That's supposed to impress me?" she said.

Robert Anselm feinted and slashed the whalebone blade clear out of Euen Huw's hands. A massive cry of "Saint George!" shook the rafters, thundering back from the stone walls of the tower, drowning anything she might have said.

Disarmed, the weaponless Saracen knight suddenly stared past Robert Anselm's left shoulder and bellowed, "It's behind you!"

Anselm unwarily glanced over his shoulder. Euen Huw brought his boot up smartly between Anselm's legs.

"Christ!" Fernando yelped in sympathy.

Euen Huw stood out of the way as Anselm fell forward, picked up Anselm's sword, and thumped a hefty blow down on his helmet. He straightened, panting and red-faced, and wheezed, "Got you, you English bastard!"

Ash bit her lip, saw Robert Anselm writhing dramatically on the floor, realized *his color's okay; he can move*—and that Euen had kicked him on the inside of the thigh, and that the two of them had planned it. She began to applaud. Either side of her, Fernando and his sister were clapping, Angelotti laughing with tears streaming down his face.

"Ruined!" Henri Brant shouted, rushing forward with his king's robes swirling, and his iron crown skewed. "Ruined!

"Is there no doctor to save my son,
And heal Prince George's deadly wound?"

A hum of expectation came from the crowd. Ash, checking by eye, saw no one of her men-at-arms and archers and gunners not either eating or drinking, or cheering on the mummers. She did not look at Fernando. The pause lengthened. In the group of mummers at the hearth, an altercation appeared to be going on.

"*No*—" Rickard shook the other mummers off and walked forward. Ash realized from the overlong gown that all but drowned him, and his sack of smithy tools, that he must be supposed to play the part; but the young man didn't stop, walking forward into the crowd toward her, and the men gave way in front of him.

He reached them, bowed with adolescent awkwardness to her and then to the surgeon-Duchess.

"I don't have the wisdom to play the Noble Doctor," he stuttered, "but there is one in this house who does. Messire Florian, please!"

"What?" Floria looked bewildered.

"Play the Noble Doctor in the mumming!" Rickard repeated. "Please!"

"Do it!" one of the men-at-arms yelled.

"Yeah, come on, Doc!" A shout from John Burren, and the archers standing with him.

Robert Anselm, flat and dead on the rushes, lifted up his head with a scrape of armor. "Prince George is dying over here! Some bastard had better be the doctor!"

"Messire Florian, you better had," Angelotti said, beaming.

"I don't know any lines!"

"You do," Ash protested. She snuffled back laughter. "Your face! Florian, everybody knows mumming lines. You must have done this before, some Twelfth Night. Get on out there! Boss's orders!"

"Yes, *sir*, boss," Floria del Guiz said darkly. The scarecrow-tall woman hesitated, then rapidly unbuttoned her demi-gown and—with the squire's help—began to struggle into the Noble Doctor's overlong garment. Shaking it down on her shoulders, hair disheveled, eyes bright, she said under her breath, "Ash, I'll get you for this!" and strode forward.

Rickard slung her the clanking bag of tools and she caught it, pulling one out by the handle as she walked forward into the open space at the center of the hall. She put her foot thoughtfully on Robert Anselm's supine chest, and leaned her arm on her knee.

"Oof!"

"I am the Doctor . . .

Fuck," Floria said. "Let me think: hang on—"

"My *God*, she's like Father!" Fernando surveyed his half sister, then smiled down at Ash. "Shame the old bastard's dead. He'd have liked to have known he had two sons."

"Fuck you too, Fernando," Ash said amiably. "You know I'm going to keep her alive, don't you? You can tell Gelimer *that*."

In the center of the hall, Floria was using a pair of bolt cutters to push back the fauld of Anselm's armor. She prodded the bolt cutters tentatively into his groin. "This man's dead!"

"Has been for years!" Baldina shouted.

"Dead as a doornail," the surgeon-Duchess repeated. "Oh shit—no, don't tell me—I'll get it in a minute—"

Ash linked her arm through Fernando's, under his cloak. She felt his robe; and then the shift of his body weight as he leaned toward her, and put his hand over hers. His warmth brought another warmth to her body. She tightened her grip on his arm.

Out in the hall, Floria moved her foot from Robert Anselm's breastplate to his codpiece. Jeers, catcalls, and shouts of sympathy shook the tower. She declaimed:

> *"The Doctor am I, I cure all diseases,*
> *The pox, and the clap, and the sniffles and sneezes!*
> *I'll bind up your bones,*
> *I'll bind up your head,*
> *I can raise up a man even though he be dead."*

"I'll bet you can!" Willem Verhaecht yelled, on a note of distinct admiration.

Floria rested the bolt cutters back across her shoulder. "Don't know why you're worrying, Willem, yours dropped off years ago!"

"Damn, I knew I'd left *something* in Ghent!"

Ash, grinning, shook her head. Over by the hearth, the last of the cauldrons had been scraped clean, and the pots drunk dry; the women were wiping their hands on their aprons and standing with bare arms, sweating and applauding.

That was less than half rations. And this was Robert's Christ-Mass overindulgence. We are *in the shit.*

Fernando said suddenly, "Gelimer's going to make you an offer. He told me to say this: even *I* don't believe it. If Dijon surrenders, he'll let the townspeople go, although he'll have to hang the garrison. And as for my sister—the King-Caliph will take the Duchess of Burgundy to wife."

"You *what*?"

Antonio Angelotti, unashamedly listening in, said, "Christus! that's neat, madonna. There'll be immediate pressure on us to surrender from the merchants and guildsmen. It's tense between us and them as it is."

"To *wife*?" Ash said.

"It's his mistake." Fernando bristled a little at the Italian master gunner, and spoke to Ash: "Frederick's men already say Gelimer must be weak, or he'd just walk in here. Nothing will come of the offer, but"—a shrug—"it's what I was told to say."

"Oh, Christ. I'll look forward to telling de la Marche *that* one." Reminded, Ash glanced toward the doors again. Nothing there but the guards—and they had turned their heads, watching the surgeon-Duchess and St. George.

Floria's voice rang out:

"By my right and my command,
Dead Saint George now up shall stand.
By my wit and for your gain,
I will make him live again.
Now in front of all men's eyes
Lift your head: arise, arise!"

Robert Anselm sprang to his feet and bowed with a flourish. One of his pauldrons fell off and clattered to the flagstones. Euen Huw, Henri Brant, and Adriaen Campin ran forward; the Saracen Knight, the King, and the Hobby Horse holding hands.

Floria del Guiz seized Anselm's hand, and Euen's, and called Rickard forward. Ash saw her whisper in the squire's ear. Rickard nodded, took a deep breath, and shouted:

"Prince George lives again,
This Christmas Twelfth Night.
Now pay us our fee
And we'll bid you good night!"

Amid raucous applause, a shower of small coins and old boots bounced off the hall's flagstones around the mummers. They bowed.

The company's men-at-arms crowded in close to clap Floria and the others on the back. Someone hauled some of the ivy creepers down, and the spiraling greenery got wound around the company's doctor, steward, second captain, lance leader, and squire. Ash, her eyes on Floria's face, felt suddenly bereft. *Even if we can make it through this, everything's different now.*

Someone cheered; Florian's shining fair hair appeared over the heads of the crowd, hoisted up between Euen Huw and Robert Anselm. She waited, not going forward yet to give her own congratulations. She looked up at Fernando del Guiz. He seemed to be more nervous than a few minutes before.

"A *priest* . . ." She shook her head, smiling less caustically than she might have expected. "Done any good miracles yet?"

"No. I'm only in first vows, celibacy vows; I won't know if I can do that sort of thing until it shows up if I have grace." After an infinitesimal pause, he added, "Ash . . . It's a different priesthood. If you don't need to be celibate for grace, you don't have to be. When you reach high rank you can marry. Muthari has. I've seen her: she's Nubian."

"Nice for him," Ash said ironically. She noted, with a distanced surprise, that her mouth had gone dry. A curdle of apprehension made her stomach cold. *What's he trying to tell me?*

"What are you trying to tell me, Fernando?"

A smile moved the corner of his mouth. It was apparent to her that he had been holding it back, that something was taking his mind away from being in a besieged city as a none-too-trusted envoy, and not allowing him to worry about bombardment or truce-breaking or any of the other things that had been weighing her down for three months now.

"There is something I ought to tell you," he said.

"Yeah?"

He said nothing for several seconds. Ash studied his face. She wanted, again, to touch his lips and his jaw and the ridge of his heavy, fair brows, not just for the flush it was bringing to her body to think about it, but from a feeling almost of tenderness.

"Go on," she prompted.

"Okay. I just never expected . . ." He looked away, into the crowded, raucous hall, and then back at her. There was a suppressed energy, a brightness, about him.

"I didn't expect to fall in love," he said gravely, his voice almost cracking like a much younger man's. "Or if I did, I expected it to be with some nobleman's daughter with a dowry, that my mother had picked out for me, or an earl's wife, maybe. . . . I didn't expect it to be with someone who's a soldier, Ash—someone who has silver hair and brown eyes and doesn't wear gowns, just armor . . ."

The breath stopped in her throat. Aware that her chest hurt, she stared up into his eyes. His face was transfigured; no mistaking the genuineness of it.

"I . . ." Her own voice croaked.

"I won't get my estates back now. I'll just be a priest dependent on alms. Even if I could marry, later . . . She'll never look at me, will she? A woman like that?"

"She might." Ash met his gaze. Her fingers were prickling; her hands sweating. She felt a weakness in her muscles, a soaring surprise, could think only *Why didn't I realize I wanted this?*

"She might," Ash repeated. She dared not reach out and take his hand. "I don't know what to say to you, Fernando. You didn't want to marry me, you were forced to. I wanted to have you, but I didn't want *you.* But, I don't know, you've come back doing this"—she waved her hand at the priest's robe—"and I can respect it, even if I don't think you stand a chance in hell of convincing anybody."

I can respect it, she repeated silently to herself. A feeling of lightness went through her body.

"Fernando, the minute I looked at you, back there, I thought you were different. I don't know. Even if Arian priests can marry, I'm still not legally able to. But . . . if you want to try again . . . yes. I will."

The surge of excitement at committing herself made her dizzy. It was several seconds before she realized that Fernando was staring at her with an expression of shock.

"What? *What?*"

"Oh shit!" he said miserably. "I've done this all wrong, haven't I?"

"What do you mean?"

Staring at him, utterly lost, she could only watch him shift his feet, stare up at the rafters, let out an explosive breath.

"Oh God, I've explained this all wrong! I didn't mean you."

"What do you mean, you didn't mean me?"

"I said 'silver hair,' I said 'brown eyes' . . ." His hand fisted; he smacked it into his other palm. "Oh, shit, I'm *sorry*."

Totally calm, Ash said, "You don't mean me. You mean her."

He nodded, mutely.

A wave of heat went through her. She flattened her hands against the stone wall behind her, keeping her balance. Her cheeks flushed bright red. Searing embarrassment wiped out everything, even the stabbing pain under her breastbone. Her muscles tensed to take her stamping off, out of the hall, up the stairs—*to where? To throw myself off the roof?*

"Oh, Jesus!" Fernando del Guiz said, his voice agonized. "I wasn't thinking. I mean her—the Faris. I wanted to tell you about it. Ash, I never meant you to think—"

"No."

"Ash—"

"Take no notice," she said savagely. "Take no fucking notice. Shit!" Unconsciously, her hand had become a fist, that pressed up against her solar plexus. "Oh, shit, Fernando! What is it about *her*? She's not one of your proper women, she's a soldier, too! We're mirror images!"

She broke off, remembering hacked-off hair, and the old, pale scars on her face. She couldn't look at Fernando. One snatched glance told her he was as red as she must be.

"We're the same!"

"No, you're not. I don't know what the difference is," he muttered, doggedly. "There's a difference."

"Oh, you don't know?" Her voice rose. "Don't you. Really. Oh, I'll tell you what the difference is, Fernando. She never had her face cut up. She's never been poor. She's been adopted by a Lord-*Amir*. She was never a whore who had to fuck men when she was ten years old! That's the difference. She isn't spoiled, is she!"

She stared into his eyes for a long minute.

"I could have loved you," she said quietly. "I don't think I knew that until now. And I wish I'd never let you know it."

"Ash, I'm so sorry."

Recovering herself into arrogance, keeping the tears out of her voice, Ash said, "So: have you fucked her yet?"

A deeper red rose up his white neck, where the high collar of his cassock and his hood did not hide it.

"No?"

"She rode out to escort the King-Caliph to Dijon. She called on me to act as her confessor on the way back." He swallowed, Adam's apple bobbing. "She wanted to know why I was a priest now, instead of a knight—"

"But did you fuck her?"

"No." He looked momentarily angry, then besotted, then apologetic, and ran his gloved hand through his hair, mussing it. "How can I? If I get to a rank in the church where I can marry—"

"You're in a fucking dream-world!"

"I love her!"

"You just love a dream," Ash spit out. "What do you think she is? Some woman on a white horse, who leads men into battle and doesn't kill? Do you think she's as good as she is beautiful?"

"Ash—"

"She's one of us, Fernando. She's one of the people who organizes killing people. That's what I am, that's what you've been, that's what she is. Christus! can't you think with anything else but your cock!"

"I'm sorry." In an extreme of embarrassment, he spread his hands. "I did it all wrong. I didn't know you'd think I meant you. I thought you knew I—"

Ash let the silence between them grow.

"Thought I knew you wouldn't touch me again if your life depended on it?" she said.

"No! I mean . . ." Fernando looked down helplessly at the floor. "I can't explain it. I've seen you. I'd seen her before. This time it was . . . different."

"Ahh—fuck off!"

Hot and cold with humiliation, she stared away, not seeing the celebrating men in front of her, not seeing the chipped edges of the window embrasures or the dark, cold sky beyond.

Now I know what people mean when they say they wish the ground would open and swallow them up.

Fernando's voice sounded beside her, quiet, but with authority.

"It's nothing to do with you. There's nothing *wrong* with you. I hated you—but then I listened to you—Ash, I wouldn't be a priest if it wasn't for you! I didn't know it until just now, when I found out I *am* sorry I hurt you. I love her. I feel like you're my, I don't know, my sister, maybe. Or my friend."

Sardonic, tears in her voice, Ash said, "Stick to 'friend'—leave sisters out of it. Your sister wants to touch me a whole lot more than you do!"

He blinked.

"Never mind," Ash said. "Forget it. Forget this whole thing. I don't want to hear about it again."

"Okay."

After a second, Ash said, "Does she know?"

"No."

"So you're worshiping from afar, just like the troubadours say."

He colored again, at her sarcasm. "Might be just as well. I'm bad at this. I just wanted to apologize to you, and then tell you how I feel about her. Ash, I never meant to hurt you."

"You've done it better than when you did mean to."

"I know. What can I say?"

"What can anybody say?" She sighed. "Just one of those things, isn't that what they call it? If you want to do something, Fernando, just don't say anything to me. Okay?"

"Okay."

She turned away from him, watching her men. A welcome numbness pushed her hurt and anger and pride away, leaving only relief in its place; *it hurts too much to think about* being superseded by *it's not worth getting worked up about*.

After a few moments, her jaw tightened with the effort of pushing away the urge to weep.

"It isn't as easy as it used to be," she said

"What?"

"Doesn't matter."

Before she could do anything to get her voice under control, there was a disturbance at the main door.

Ash looked across into bright daylight as the doors opened. A blast of cold air sliced through the hall's sweaty warmth. She heard boots and weapons clash, put up her hand to shadow her eyes.

De Vere, his brother Dickon, twenty Turks, Olivier de la Marche, and some of the Burgundian army commanders walked in. Jonvelle stopped dead and stared at her, his face whitening.

"I told you!" John de Vere roared.

Ash found them all staring at her: Oxford's brother with wide eyes. Even the Janissaries appeared mildly interested. She put one fist on her hip, scrabbling for composure, for raw humor.

"What's the matter, did I forget to dress?"

The Burgundian *centenier*, Jonvelle, swallowed. "*He Dieux*![53] It *is* her. It *is* the Captain-General."

Ash fixed him and the English Earl with an authoritative eye. "Someone is going to tell me what's going on here . . ."

The Burgundian stared, as if he were taking in every detail—a woman at home in plate leg harness and arm defenses, in a polished Milanese cuirass, with dirty white hair cut short to her ears, and wood-fire smuts on her scarred cheeks. Still flushing a dull red.

"You're here," Jonvelle repeated.

Ash turned her back on Fernando del Guiz, and folded her

[53]"By God!"

arms. "That's what I've been sending bloody messages to tell you! Okay . . . Where *ought* I to be?"

"You may well ask," John de Vere said. "You should excuse Master Jonvelle. He sees Captain-General Ash here—and so do we all. But, it seems, one hour ago, Captain-General Ash was given a slave escort back from the Visigoth camp and admitted to Dijon through the northeast gate. She is there now."

Ash stared at the English Earl. "She damn well isn't!"

"We left her at the gatehouse not ten minutes since," John de Vere said. "Madam—it is your sister. The Faris. She says she is surrendering herself to you."

[original e-mail documents found inserted, folded, in British Library copy of 3rd edition, Ash: The Lost History of Burgundy, (2001) — possibly in chronological order of editing original typescript?]

Message: #381 (Anna Longman)
Subject: Ash
Date: 16/12/00 at 07.47 a.m.
From: Ngrant@

format address deleted
other details encrypted by
non-discoverable personal key

Anna--

Such a change, to be writing in English! I'll attach a file with the next section of the Sible Hedingham text that I've translated.

I'm taking a break from the translation tomorrow. Correction: this morning.

I've finally been comparing the two metallurgy reports on the 'messenger-golem' found at the land site. One of Isobel's graduates has been giving me a hand over breakfast. Now, it's just possible that these are reports on two *different* archaeological remains that got confused in the lab. If they're two reports on the same specimens of cast bronze, then they contradict each other in almost every reading, from plant material content to implied background radiation.

Either the department got one or other of the analyses wrong—which, I grant you, is the conclusion of any sane, rational person—or, these reports are tracing *a process in the artefact itself* which could have been going on between the first report in November and the second one two weeks later.

How can an artefact appear "new" (post 1945) in November, and in December, "old" (4–500 years)?

Anna, if there is a process at work here, of any kind, no matter that I may have details or premises wrong—then *what else are we going to see?*

I have persuaded Isobel to contact her Colonel ████ and beg the use of a military helicopter. She has just told me he's given his authorisation. An ex-Russian Mil-8 will be waiting for me at Tunis airfield, just before dawn, in two hours' time. And Isobel is lending me one of her graduate students.

The helicopter pilot is prepared to overfly the area to the south of Tunis, as far as the Atlas Mountains. We have video equipment.

In archaeology, aerial surveys can be crucial. With low-angle light, the smallest disturbances in the ground cast shadows, and the shapes, the 'floor plans', of long-disused settlements can appear plainly evident.

Although a previous, brief, geophysical survey of the areas I am interested in shows nothing definite, I think that it may be different for us. If only because Isobel and I, using the 'Fraxinus' manuscript, have some idea of where we should be looking.

If there is any remnant left—if there is any remnant that is *now* there—that is part of the pyramid-structures that 'Fraxinus' calls 'Wild Machines'; then I want the evidence catalogued.

Either by accident or design, we have become what we are. But since history has no Visigoth 'empire', in the sense that these texts describe it, either in the mediaeval period or at any other time, then I am left to conclude that—well, to conclude what? That *both* sides in that conflict were changed; eradicated? And that this post-fracture history of ours contains a few remnants, a palimpsest version, of what was before?

And yet, and yet. The Sible Hedingham ms. could have lain undiscovered, in Hedingham Castle as your William Davies suggested. The messenger-golem could be an undiscovered artefact, excavated. But *what* am I to make of the site on the seabed, where even the present depth-readings and geological features contradict Admiralty and satellite surveys?

If we have found Carthage, what else might we find, in the barren land to the south?

I will contact you again immediately after the helicopter flight.

--Pierce

Message: #211 (Pierce Ratcliff)
Subject: Ash
Date: 16/12/00 at 08.58 a.m.
From: Longman@

format address deleted
other details encrypted and
non-recoverably deleted

Pierce--

You people are taking this seriously.

Let me talk to Dr Isobel.

--Anna

Message: #216 (Pierce Ratcliff)
Subject: Ash
Date: 16/12/00 at 09.50 a.m.
From: Longman@

format address deleted
other details encrypted and
non-recoverably deleted

Pierce--

Sorry, impatient—what's happened on the flight?? Are you back?

Just heard from Jonathan: although they are unaware of the full extent of your discoveries, the independent film company want to start shooting with you, on-site, as soon as they can—before the Christmas break, if possible. What will Dr Isobel say to this?

HAVE YOU FOUND ANYTHING IN THE DESERT?

--Anna

Message: #383 (Anna Longman)
Subject: Ash
Date: 16/12/00 at 10.20 a.m.
From: Ngrant@

format address deleted
other details encrypted by
non-discoverable personal key

Ms Longman--

I hope you will not mind if I add something at this juncture.

I think it inadvisable for outside filming to begin here yet. Perhaps after Christmas and the New Year? I am keeping the expedition's own video records up to date, however.

Please, call me Isobel.

--I. Napier-Grant

Message: #218
Subject: Ash
Date: 16/12/00 at 10.32 a.m.
From: Longman@

format address deleted
other details encrypted and
non-recoverably deleted

Dear Isobel--

Has Pierce told you that the editor of the Second Edition of ASH, Vaughan Davies, has reappeared after being missing, thought dead, for almost sixty years?

Can you confirm what Pierce has told me about the status of your archaeological seabed site off the coast of Tunisia?

Does that have any connection with your reluctance to allow outside film teams in?

Or, is Pierce under a lot of stress?

--Anna

Message: #385 (Anna Longman)
Subject: Ash
Date: 16/12/00 at 11.03 a.m.
From: Ngrant@

format address deleted
other details encrypted by
non-discoverable personal key

Anna--

From a cursory glance at the files, I do not disagree substantially with anything that Pierce has written to you.

This will perhaps answer your last question.

As for myself . . . I am stunned. Didn't Pierce make a joke that one day he and I would send you the Ratcliff-Napier-Grant theory of Scientific Miracles? What Tami Inoshishi and Jamie Howlett are speculating, now, is not so far from that, perhaps.

If my theoretical physicist colleagues are right, it is deep consciousness, at the level of the species-mind, that in a sense _creates_ the universe. Imagine a constant process by which the wave-front of Possibility (random unordered chaos) is, moment by moment, collapsed from all the states in which it _might_ exist into the one in which it _does_ exist. In short, a process by which the Possible is constantly becoming the Real. That is time: that is how we experience the universe. And, Tami states with amazing self-confidence, the cause of the wave-front's collapse into a stable 'present' at the moment we experience as 'now' is the _perception_ of it, by the consciousness of a species (that perception being an active, not a passive perception).

And with Pierce's translated manuscripts in mind, I mentioned jokingly, to both Tami and James this morning, that this possible ability to collapse the wave-front would have to be genetic ability. Tami, seriously, said that it would not even be difficult to see how this could arise. It would be one of the greater evolutionary advances possible, to have a universe which is stable, in which effect follows cause, in which what you did yesterday stands a good chance of being valid today.

Not a conscious ability, she said. It would take place on a subatomic level; on a level as instinctive as photosynthesis in a plant, or the heartbeat in a human being.

I wish Pierce were here on the ship, but I shall have to wait until the helicopter returns to ask him—I wonder if one can speculate that reality, before the human species became intelligent, was more flexible, less able to confine itself to one possibility out of the infinite number of states in which the universe can exist. I should like to ask him if this might not account for why every human culture has a mythic pre-history, a legendary past, before 'history' itself begins?

For all that I know—and this is why I am reluctant to confine these discoveries to a book or film documentary; I am seriously thinking of throwing this site open to interdisciplinary investigation: shipping in theorists from _every_ field—for all I know, all life has a certain limited ability to collapse random possibility into predictable reality. Plants, dolphins, birds: each tries to affect its environment favourably. The most basic form of this _must_ be the perception of the subatomic 'building blocks' of reality, at the moment of 'now', as neither unstable nor random, but as order and pattern and sequence.

I am an archaeologist, not a physicist; and I watch and listen to Tami and James with open-mouthed astonishment. Before he left this morning, Pierce said to me that they do sound like a Ratcliff-Napier-Grant Theory of Scientific Miracles. You have only to say that there could exist a genetic ability to _consciously_ collapse the possible states of the universe into the Real—would not that be a 'miracle'? Posit that such an ability could carry sufficient genetic defects that it hardly ever survives conception and birth. And then I look at Pierce's translations and find myself thinking, there you have the Rabbi, and Ildico, and the Faris, and (one supposes) the Visigothic 'Prophet Gundobad', who is unidentified in this history because it is not this history in which he existed.

I have spent most of my adult life aware of how very little solid evidence of our past there is left, and how very _careful_ one must be in interpreting what does exist and can be discovered. Were you not in London—were you here, just off the coast of North Africa, with an _impossible_ site a thousand metres below your feet—then you might understand why I don't dismiss these speculations of a 'fracture' in history.

I do not say that I give credence to them, either.

And then, of course, there are the practical consequences. I had hoped to get past Christmas before a public statement became necessary, but I can see that I may have to revise my opinion.

--I. Napier-Grant

Message: #219
Subject: Ash
Date: 16/12/00 at 11.36 a.m.
From: Longman@

format address deleted
other details encrypted and
non-recoverably deleted

Isobel--

You loaned Pierce an assistant, and got him a helicopter. You must give credence to something.

--Anna

Message: #388 (Anna Longman)
Subject: Ash
Date: 16/12/00 at 03.15 p.m.
From: Ngrant@

format address deleted
other details encrypted by
non-discoverable personal key

Pierce has radioed in. Transcript of relevant part of message.

I. Napier-Grant

>Everything's grounded.
>It was bad enough getting off the ship.
>We are back in Tunis. If I can't hire a jeep, or buy a bloody camel, I
>am prepared to WALK into the desert.
>Low-angled sunset light is as good as dawn.

Message: #390 (Anna Longman)
Subject: Ash
Date: 16/12/00 at 06.15 p.m.
From: Ngrant@

format address deleted
other details encrypted by
non-discoverable personal key

Anna--

Nothing.

--Pierce

Message: #221 (Pierce Ratcliff)
Subject: Ash
Date: 16/12/00 at 06.36 p.m.
From: Longman@

format address deleted
other details encrypted and
non-recoverably deleted

Pierce--

What do you mean, NOTHING?

--Anna

- -

Message: #391 (Anna Longman)
Subject: Ash
Date: 16/12/00 at 07.59 p.m.
From: Ngrant@

format address deleted
other details encrypted by
non-discoverable personal key

Anna--

I mean the quotidian, I suppose. The everyday, the mundane. Nothing to get worked up about. No, there is nothing in the desert south of here. Isobel's worn out her welcome with my use of military helicopters, trailing—once flight restrictions were finally lifted—through the airspace between here and the Atlas Mountains.

There may be something buried under residential areas, or under industrial plants; who knows? Certainly there were no archaeological teams on hand when some of these places were built. If there were remains, they're gone, obliterated. Or, more likely, there was nothing; the manuscript 'evidence' is mere symbolism, the metallurgy reports simple human error.

What did you expect me to find you, Anna? A glowing pyramid?

Sorry.

I must confess, I had hoped for SOMETHING. A few ridges in the earth, visible at sunset or dawn. It wouldn't be much to ask, would it, that a shadow in the ground should 'come back'? Just to let us know the 'Wild Machines' were not what they plainly are: a mediaeval literary conceit. A mere device.

Isobel's team are keeping the survey material, but naturally, the land area isn't their priority right now. Underwater remains, 'Gothic Carthage', that's the priority.

Your book-and-film deal is on course, don't worry.

--Pierce

Message: #222 (Pierce Ratcliff)
Subject: Ash
Date: 16/12/00 at 08.45 p.m.
From: Longman@

format address deleted
other details encrypted and
non-recoverably deleted

Pierce--

Damn the 'book- and-film deal'. What about you? Are you all right?

I know I've done very little, but I've talked to the Davies family, in person; I've got drawn into this too.

I can't imagine how you and Dr Isobel are feeling right now, but this isn't just another book as far as I'm concerned. If there's anything I can do to help, I will. You know I mean it.

--Anna

Message: #392 (Anna Longman)
Subject: Ash
Date: 16/12/00 at 08.57 p.m.
From: Ngrant@

format address deleted
other details encrypted by
non-discoverable personal key

Anna--

I know. Thank you.

Yes, I suppose it is difficult to see Tami Inoshishi and James Howlett knee-deep in the image files of this project; talking at machine-gun speed to everybody on the team. I confess that, yes, no one has much time for a mere historian at this point, and yes, my nose is out of joint. I suppose my time will come with the textual evidence.

None of that really matters, I suppose, beside the crashing disappointment. I was so CERTAIN that we were going to find remnants of the 'Wild Machines', or at the very least, the site where they existed. The 'machina rei militaris', when we get it free for examination—and I imagine that's going to take months, if not years—will answer some questions. But, like Isobel's golem, I fear it will be dumb about how and why it moved.

E pur si muove: Nevertheless, it moves. As Galileo said, in rather different circumstances!

Scholarly jests aside, I feel very bitter. I was so sure. You see, once the basic premise is accepted, none of it is unreasonable. My first draft of the 'Afterword' says as much, and I am going to let you see it. This was based on 'Fraxinus', and the discovery of the 'clay walker', before we found the Sible Hedingham document, so it is unrevised:—

> AFTERWORD to the 3rd edition: Ash: The Lost History of Burgundy
>
> (Excerpt:) (iii) THEOLOGY AND TECHNOLOGY: THE IMPLICATIONS OF 'FRAXINUS ME FECIT'
>
> . . . the mediaeval mind behind the 'Fraxinus' manuscript couches its description of the various Carthaginian machines in quasi-religious, quasi-mythological terms, where, for example, it speaks of the 'soul' of Fr. Godfrey Maximillian becoming 'trapped in the Stone Golem'. We, with the benefit of a vocabulary belonging to twentieth century artificial intelligence, would more properly refer to this in terms of the neural pattern of his personality becoming uploaded into, or imprinted on, the *machina rei militaris* at a moment of great physical and mental trauma. One might speculate that the proximity of Ash at the moment of Godfrey Maximillian's death, herself a genetic conduit to the *machina rei militaris,* might have some as-yet-undetermined causal link with this unique event.
>
> Similarly, the autonomous 'Wild Machines' are described in spiritual and religious terms. However, it is possible to make another translation, different from the dramatised one I have used in the body of the text, translating 'Fraxinus' literally, but with a vocabulary not yet available in 1476. This is an amended excerpt from Ash's 'download' at Carthage:
>
>> The Wild Machines do not know their own origin, it is lost in their primitive memories. They suspect it was humans, building religious structures ten thousand years ago, who accidentally 'put rocks in order'—constructed ordered, [pyramid-]shaped edifices of *silt-bricks and stone* [silicon].

Large enough structures [of silicon] to absorb *spirit-force* [electro-magnetic energy] from the sun. From that initial order and structure came *spontaneous mind* [self-aware intelligence]. The first primitive sparks of [electro-magnetic] force began to organise [in solid-state networks], creating the *Ferae Natura Machinae* [silicon-based 'machine' intelligences].

Five thousand years ago, those *primitive minds* [proto-intelligences] became conscious. After that, they could begin to evolve themselves deliberately. The Wild Machines *manipulated the energies of the spirit-world* [drew upon solar electro-magnetic energy], to the point where [visible-spectrum] light began to be blocked out in the immediate region around them. As they became more structured, organised, and powerful, so their ability to *draw power from the nearest and greatest source in the heavens* [extract and store this form of solar energy] became more efficient: the darkness spread. This [North African coast] became a land of stone and *twilight* [solar-energy 'shadow']: vast monuments and pyramids under an eternally-starry sky.

[The machine intelligences] knew that humanity and animals existed; they registered their *weak little souls* [neuro-electric fields]. They were unable to establish direct communication until the advent of the Prophet Gundobad. After Gundobad's death, it was not until Leofric's family developed the *Stone Golem* [solid-state tactical computer] that the Wild Machines had a reliable channel by which they could communicate with humanity, and not just its *wonder-workers* [human minds capable of consciously collapsing the local quantum state]. They hid behind the voice of the [tactical computer], easing their suggestions [into the data], manipulating Leofric's ancestors into beginning a breeding programme.

The Visigoth saint, Prophet Gundobad, whose *relics* [surviving DNA material] were used in the *machina rei militaris* and whose bloodline eventually produced the Faris and Ash, was one of those very, very few people (like Our Lord the Green Christ) [first history] who have the power to *perform miracles* [individually alter the basic fabric of reality]. What the *secret breeding* [genetic engineering] was designed to produce was not someone who could *speak at a distance to the Stone Golem* [perform an at-a-distance neuro-electric or neuro-chemical? download from the tactical computer]—although it was necessary they be able to [communicate through the computer], since that is the only link between the Wild Machines and humanity. What the Wild Machines were trying to breed was another *miracle-worker* [human capable of consciously affecting the quantum foam]. A Gundobad. One that would be under their control, and subject to the *command* [immense electro-magnetic pulse] they planned [to emit] to trigger their *evil miracle* [consciously-guided alteration of the basic fabric of probable reality].

Also from the AFTERWORD:—

(Excerpt:) (vi) GENETICS AND THE MIRACULOUS: BREEDING SCHRODINGER'S CAT

(Revised passage, after discovery of the Sible Hedingham ms.:)

. . . In this past history which we have lost, the ability to consciously, deliberately collapse the wave-front could arise spontaneously. In that first history, despite the catastrophic genetic links, it is just possible that a tiny conscious talent could be bred, to be strong enough to be effective—hence the priests' genuine small miracles; hence the bloodline that House Leofric produced among its slaves and the Faris.

Conversely, the ability to prevent the 'miraculous' happening, to prevent the wave-front being collapsed into anything but the most probable quotidian reality, might also conceivably arise as a spontaneous genetic mutation: hence the nature of the ducal bloodlines in Burgundy.

But, what happened _after_ everything changed? . . .

I am not sure, now, why I was so certain that some trace of the Wild Machines must remain, after such a fracture in the universe's history as we seem to see the traces of, here. Purely, I suppose, this question—

If there had been no 'black miracle', we should not be seeing these traces of a fracture in history. But, if the Wild Machines precipitated the Faris into causing the fracture and altering the fabric of the universe, then why is there no trace of their having survived it?

If you want to wipe the human race out of history, presumably you want to be around afterwards to take advantage!

What HAPPENED?

--Pierce

Message: #223 (Pierce Ratcliff)
Subject: Ash
Date: 17/12/00 at 03.10 a.m.
From: Longman@

format address deleted
other details encrypted and
non-recoverably deleted

Pierce--

Sorry, shouldn't be posting in the early hours, can't think straight, _but_—

If the Carthage site and the messenger-golem are what you say they are, you don't mean

>>What HAPPENED?

You mean: what IS STILL HAPPENING?

What will happen if you fly over the desert *again,* in, say, a month's time? What will you see *then?*

--Anna

PART THREE

25 December AD 1476–26 December AD 1476

"EX AFRICA SEMPER ALIQUID NOVI"[54]

[54]"Always something new out of Africa." (The more common rendering of Pliny the Elder's *'Semper aliquid novi Africam adfere'*.) The Sible Hedingham mss.,#4

i

ASH FELT THE wind from the company tower's door, blowing in past the group of knights: keen, and with a bitter, damp edge to it. Bewilderment gave way to clarity with a speed that surprised her. *Kill her and the Wild Machines do nothing. For the next twenty years. Minimum.*

She said, "We have to execute her, right now."

The Earl of Oxford nodded soberly. "Yes, madam. We do."

She saw Jonvelle's gaze go past her, and turned her head.

Floria walked toward them, stripping ivy leaves from her shoulders, Robert Anselm close behind. Jonvelle bowed to his Duchess.

"What's this?" Floria demanded.

Ash quickly looked to see where Fernando del Guiz was—a bare yard away, stark amazement on his face. Angelotti stood at the German priest's side, one hand on the bollock dagger at his belt.

"The Faris is here," Ash said flatly.

"Here?"

"You got it."

"Here in *Dijon*?"

"Yes!" There was an audience, Ash saw, but nothing to be done about it. The company's archers and men-at-arms formed a tight-packed circle, avidly listening. Euen Huw, stripping off ivy creeper and his "Saracen" chemise, pushed in beside Angelotti, Rickard, openmouthed, beside Ash herself.

"Tell her, my lord," Ash appealed to de Vere.

"Madam Duchess, report says that while we were convening with the King-Caliph, a party of unarmed Visigoth slaves approached the northeast gate. The guards did not fire on them, and were even less likely to do so when they saw, as they thought, Captain-General Ash coming back in under their escort." Oxford nodded to Ash. "The Visigoth woman has chopped off her hair and dirtied her face. It will have been enough to get her in. All but a half dozen of the slaves went back to the Visigoth camp; the woman then sits herself down and demands to speak to the Duchess of Burgundy, and to Ash, to whom—she says—she surrenders."

"She's out of her mind." Floria blinked. "Is this true?"

"I see no reason to doubt Jonvelle's men. I have, besides, seen her now. It is the Visigoth general."

"She has to be killed," Ash said. "Somebody get my ax: let's get up to the northeast gate."

"Ash—"

Amazed, Ash heard something close to hesitation in Floria's voice. Jonvelle drew himself up, plainly ready to take orders from his Duchess.

"This isn't a matter for *argument*. We don't mess around here," Ash said gently. "Fucking hell, girl. You hunted the hart. She's my blood relative, but I know that we have to kill her, *now*. She's what the Wild Machines will use, to make an evil miracle. The second you're killed, that's what happens: they act through her—and we're dead. All of us. As if we'd never been." Ash watched Floria's face. "Like it is beyond these borders. Nothing but cold and dark."

"I came only to be sure it was not you, Captain Ash," John de Vere said briskly. "Otherwise, I am not sure but I should have done the task myself."

Jonvelle coughed. "No, sieur, you would not have. You would not have been obeyed by my men. We are at the command of Burgundy, not England. Her Grace must give the word."

"Well, God's grace grant that we do it now!" De Vere was already turning, giving orders to the Janissaries, when Floria interrupted:

"Wait."

"Christ, Florian!" Ash shouted, appalled. "What do you mean, 'wait'?"

"I'm not ordering any execution! I took an oath to do no

harm! I've spent most of my adult life putting people back together, not killing them!" Floria gripped Ash's arm firmly. "Just wait. Think. *Think* about this. Yes: I hunted the hart: she's no danger while there's a Duchess of Burgundy."

The Earl of Oxford said, "Madam Florian, this is a hard truth, but men and women are dying in the streets of this city from siege-weapon fire, and if by the same accident we were to lose you, with the Faris yet living, we lose everything."

"You were in Carthage with me," Ash urged. "You saw the Wild Machines. You saw what they could do to me there. Florian, in Christ's name, have I ever lied to you about anything important? You *know* what's at stake here!"

"I won't do it!"

"You should have thought of that when you killed the hart," Ash said wryly. "An execution isn't easy. It's vile, messy, and unjust, usually. But there isn't a choice here. If it makes it easier—if you don't want the blood on your hands—then me and my lord the Earl and Colonel Bajezet's five hundred Turks will go up to the northeast gate and do it now, whatever anyone says."

Floria's fist clenched. "No. Too easy."

What there might be of an ache inside—for Floria; for the Faris; for herself, even—Ash put away, in the same way as she forced tears back from her prickling eyes. Ash put her hand over Floria's, the woman still in the Noble Doctor's long gown, fragments of palmate green leaves caught in her hair, her cheeks red with the heat of the hall.

"Florian," she said, "I'm not going to waste any time."

Robert Anselm was nodding; it was apparent from the faces of the company's lance leaders that there was no disagreement. They might look with all sympathy at the doctor; but in terms of action, Ash judged, that was irrelevant.

Angelotti said quietly to Floria, "It's never easy, *dottore*. After battle, there are some men who cannot be saved."

"Sweet *Christ* but I hate soldiers!"

Hard on Floria's agonized, appalled exclamation, a soldier in Jonvelle's livery tumbled through the door between the company's guards. Ash narrowed her eyes to better see his sweating, distraught face under the brim of his war-hat. She immediately beckoned the man forward, then signaled her deference to Jonvelle himself.

"Yes, Sergeant?" Jonvelle demanded.

"There's a Visigoth herald at the northeast gate! Under flag of parley," the man gasped. He dashed the edge of his cloak across his streaming nose and heaved in another breath. "From the King-Caliph. He says you have his general here, and he demands that you release her. He's got about six hundred of our refugees rounded up in the ground between the lines. He says, if you don't let her go, they'll kill every last man, woman, and child of them."

The refugees and their escort stood in the excoriated no-man's-land under Dijon's walls, between the northeastern gate and the east river.

Ash wore no identifying livery, had her bevor strapped on, and her visor cocked barely high enough above it to give her a field of view between the two pieces of armor. She rested her shoulder against the battlements of the gatehouse, knowing herself barely visible to any outsider, and stared down.

Behind her, an abbey bell rang for Sext. The midday sun cast a pale, slanting southern light. The crowd of men and women standing aimlessly on the cold earth seemed small, truncated by perspective. One man beat his hands together against the bitter wind. No one else moved. Breath went up in mist white puffs. Most of them stood together, in ruined clothes, huddling for warmth; most looked to be barefoot.

"Dear God," Jonvelle said, beside Ash. He pointed. "I know that man. That's Messire Huguet. He owns all the mills between here and Auxonne; or he did. And his family: his wife and child. And there's Soeur Irmengard, from our hospice in St. Herlaine's."

"You're better off not thinking about it," Ash advised.

It was not the dirt that moved her, or the other evidences of their living rough, but their faces. Under the blank expressions that long experience of pain gives, there was still a bewilderment, an inability to understand how and why this destitution should have happened at all, never mind happened to them.

"Is the King-Caliph serious, Captain?" Jonvelle said.

"I see no reason why he shouldn't be. Roberto told me they crucified several hundred refugees in sight of your walls here, back in October, when they were trying to force a quick surrender."

Jonvelle's face assumed a blank severity. "I was in the hospice," he confessed, "after Auxonne. There were stories of massacres. Knights act sometimes without honor, in war."

"Yeah . . . tell me about it, Jonvelle." She squinted northeast, at the trenches and fortifications of the Visigoth camp, saw the wooden shielding that would shelter mangonels and arbalests. "They won't even need engines. Longbows and crossbows will do it at this range."

"Christ defend us."

"Oh, *we're* fine," Ash muttered, absently trying to count heads. The estimate of six hundred would not be far off: it might even be a few more. "It's them you want to worry about . . . Captain Jonvelle, let's have as many hackbutters and crossbowmen up here as we can manage. Make it look like we're concentrating our forces here. Then get some units by the postern gate."

"You will get a very small number of hunger-weakened women and children to that gate," the Burgundian said. "Never mind through it."

"If it comes to it, that's what we'll do. Meanwhile . . ." Ash moved back from the crenellations, walked a few yards down the wall to her own herald's white pennant, and leaned out over the hoarding. "Below there!"

Two of the stone messenger-golems stood a little way out from the foot of the wall. In front of them, under his gold- and black-embroidered white banner, Agnus Dei stared upward. A dozen of his own mercenaries were with him, and a few more under a red livery that Ash did not recall until she saw Onorata Rodiani standing beside the Italian condottiere.

"Hey, Lamb."

"Hey, Ash."

"Mistress Rodiani."

"Captain-General Ash."

"They still dealing you out the shitty jobs, then?"

Onorata Rodiani's face was unreadable at the distance. Her voice sounded taut. "Boss Gelimer was going to send your own men, Mynheer Joscelyn van Mander's men, to do this. I persuaded him it might not be in his best interests. Do we have a deal here?"

"I don't know. I'm still checking it with my boss." Ash leaned her plate-clad arms on the stonework. "Your man serious, is he?"

Agnus Dei tilted his armet's visor up, a straggling coil of black hair escaping. His red mouth made a mobile space in his beard, far below, his voice coming up clearly to Ash:

"The King-Caliph gave us orders to demonstrate his commitment here. These golem will go over and tear one of those peasant women or children apart, at the word of command. Madonna Ash, I wish we might deem that to have been done, I have no great wish to do it. But we stand where my master sees us."

The dull light flashed off the flutings of his German gauntlet as he raised his hand.

The sandstone-colored figure of the golem trod toward the refugees. Even from the walls, Ash could see the depth of its footmarks in the churned earth, could guess at the weight of each limb. Women screamed, pressing back against the Visigoth spearmen, hauling their children as far back into the press of people as they could; one or two men made as if to move forward, most fought to get away.

The golem reached forward with a smooth precision, bronze gears glimmering. Its metal-and-stone hand went past one spearman's shoulder—Ash couldn't see if the soldier reacted—and closed on something. The arm pulled smoothly back. A woman of about fifty kicked and clawed and screeched, hauled forward by the grip on her biceps. Two small children were pulled through the spear-line, clinging to her thighs.

A sharp *snap*! bit through the winter air.

The woman drooped and hung awkwardly from the golem's hand, her arm and shoulder the wrong shape. Shaken loose, the two children raised square-mouthed squalls. One of the spearmen kicked them back into the refugee crowd. Ash found herself muttering "thank you!," knowing that it was, for once, a gesture toward safety.

She leaned forward between the merlons and bellowed: "You don't have to—"

The golem did not lift its head. Alone in some solipsistic world, in which flesh is no more significant than any other fabric, it dragged the semiconscious woman with the broken shoulder around until she faced the northeast gate. Her ankles, under her long kirtle, were brown with mud, yellow with shit.

Gears of bronze slid and glinted. As she scratched and clawed at stone arms with the ripped fingers of one hand, the golem reached down and closed his huge hand around both her thighs. A sharp screech shattered the morning. Ash saw stone fingers buried to the second knuckle in flesh.

The golem lifted the woman up between its two hands. It grasped her at neck and thigh, front and back.

It wrung her body, like washing.

All noise stopped. Pink intestines slid and steamed in the chill air. The golem released the twisted flesh. In her own mind, Ash tabulated broken back, broken pelvis, split body-cavity, broken neck—*don't be stupid: you* can't *smell it from up here!*

She blinked and looked away.

As far as she could see, in the cold air that made her eyes run, Agnus Dei's gaze was fixed on the gray frost haze over the Ouze River.

"Christ." Ash let out a long breath. "Shit. How long have I got to come back with an answer?"

Onorata Rodiani, apparently unaffected, called up, "You've got as long as you like. *They*"—she pointed with one steel-clad, flashing arm at the refugees—"have got until Boss Gelimer loses patience. You have the woman who, until today, was his Empire's first general and commanded his troops in Christendom. How long? Your guess is as good as mine, Captain-General Ash; probably better."

"Okay." Ash drew herself up, resting her palms flat on the battlements. "I'm on my way. You can tell your man, we've got the message."

* * *

Floria del Guiz said, "If I kill her, six hundred people die."

Ash followed the Duchess of Burgundy through the cloisters of St. Stephen's Abbey—six streets back from the north-east gate—which Jonvelle's men had judged a safe place for keeping the Faris under guard.

"If you don't kill her, *everybody* dies."

"I'm not dead yet," Florian snarled, as the large group of armed men entered the main buildings. "If I *do* get killed, it may be under circumstances where the Burgundians can hunt again—I'm thinking about six hundred people out there. They're the ones I'll have to watch die."

"No reason for you to *watch* it," Ash observed pragmatically. She caught the look on Florian's face, sighed, her pace slowing. "But you will. Because the first time this happens, everybody thinks they have to. Trust me, you're better off staying away from the walls."

At Ash's shoulder, Jonvelle said, "And this from you, Captain-General, who are planning to sally out of the postern gate and rescue who you can of them?"

Momentarily embarrassed, Ash glanced back to check that her own men, as well as the Burgundians, were following her toward the refectory.

"It's worth a try," she muttered. "You ask those poor bastards outside."

The cloisters behind her rang to the boots of soldiers, on flagstones striped white with frost. Even at noon, frost still lay where each shadow of a pillar was cast. Inside, entering the great whitewashed refectory, there was at least the heat from the kitchens. Ash ignored the monks, scurrying in the background, and the sounds from the dormitories, taken over for nursing the sick.

"Look, Florian, I'll put it this way—do you want to order the Faris's execution now, so the Burgundians are happy with it, or do you want to watch me and my lord Oxford and the company get killed by the army, trying to reach her?"

Florian made a spitting sound, gave Ash a look of frustrated, contemptuous anger. "You mean that, don't you."

The exiled English Earl gave her a quizzical look, but what he said was, "Madam, I also agree."

A woman stood up in the crowded refectory.

Winter sunlight bounced back from the white walls. It illuminated motes of dust, the woman's hacked-off silver hair. A woman, standing up between Visigoth slaves in short tunics; a woman wearing European doublet and hose that were plainly not made for her, were far too big. The chopped-off hair threw her cheeks into sharp relief. No smeared dirt could give the impression of scars. She looked very young. She wore neither armor nor sword.

Across the few remaining wooden benches and tables, Ash found herself facing the Faris.

The child-slave at the Faris's left was Violante, shivering in the cold. A gray-haired fat woman sat on the floor, half-hiding under the long table: Adelize.

Floria del Guiz walked past Ash and put herself between them.

"Have some sense," she said. "We have to send her back, to save lives. Right now! She's no danger while I'm alive."

Ash glared at the woman blocking her way. She thumbed her sword loose from the scabbard's tension. "You might not have noticed, but there's a fucking war on. While you're alive, yes; but that might not be for long!"

Floria made a wry mouth, and flapped her hand as if pushing the gesture with the sword away. When she spoke, it was not a plea, but irritable scorn:

"For Christ's sake, Ash! If you won't save the people out there, here's another reason to keep her alive for a few hours—think about this, if nothing else: *up until today, she's been the Visigoth army commander*."

"Shit." Ash looked away from the Faris, to Floria. "You *have* been paying attention while you've been company doctor."

The surgeon-Duchess, disheveled and oddly dignified, repeated, "Visigoth army commander. Think how much she knows about this siege. She knows what's happened *after* she stopped reporting through the Stone Golem! That's *weeks*! She can tell us what it's like out there *now*!"

"But the *Wild Machines*—"

"Ash, you're going to have to talk to her. Debrief her. Then we send her out again, to Gelimer. And we pray," Floria said, "that he doesn't start a massacre out there before we do it."

The immediate rush of people into the room behind them slowed. Ash became aware of men-at-arms spreading out: her units, and Burgundian army units, and Jonvelle talking urgently to the just-arrived Olivier de la Marche. She caught the eye of Robert Anselm, held up a warning hand. *No action yet.*

"Do you know what you're risking?"

Floria's brows went up. She looked momentarily very like her younger half brother. "I know I'm risking six hundred people's lives out there, if King-Caliph Gelimer decides to start killing them in the next few minutes and not the next few hours."

"That's not what I meant."

"No, but it's true, too."

"Shit." Ash gazed around.

She registered Angelotti's presence at the refectory door: the master gunner talking excitedly to Colonel Bajezet. Apart from the Burgundian troops surrounding the Visigoths, there was a woman in green there—Soeur Maîtresse Simeon—obliviously and waspishly trying to coax Adelize out from under the table.

The fat, drooling, white-haired woman wept and flapped her hands, slapping the nun's hands away.

At Ash's side, Fernando del Guiz tried to conceal an expression of disgust. She looked away from him, feeling heat, knowing her cheeks were reddening.

"Fucking Christ!" she exclaimed bitterly, fists on hips. "We're going to have the whole bloody *town* in here. Roberto! Seal this room off!"

Anselm did not look to the surgeon-Duchess for permission. Jonvelle moved to intercept him, and only stepped back at Floria's acerbic order: "No one else in here—unless it's the abbot!"

"This is a Michaelmas Fair," John de Vere sighed. "Captain, an enemy commander in one's hands is not to be despised; this might turn the siege. And though the matter concerns more men than there are in Dijon, we have men here whom we command, whose lives should not be spent needlessly."

Fernando del Guiz folded his arms, regarding the monastery room with bewildered confusion. He shook his head, laughed with an expression that plainly said *What else can one do?* "If I could see the King-Caliph's face, now—!"

Ash gave an order. Two of Jonvelle's men came to escort him outside. He went with no protest.

Ash turned back to face the Faris.

"*Why?*" she said.

The light from the refectory windows fell clearly onto the Faris's face. With this second look, Ash saw at once how drawn she was: her skin a bad color, her eyes red-rimmed. Her left hand kept feeling for something at her thigh. The mirror image of Ash's own gesture: hand resting down on her sword. When she finally spoke, it was quietly, to Ash, in the version of Carthaginian that one hears most often in the military camps:

"Don't forget that I permitted the hunt."

"What?" Floria moved to stand at Ash's side, staring at the Visigoth woman. "I didn't catch that."

"She's reminding me that she let the hunt go ahead. And that, if not for her, there wouldn't be a Duchess now."

Catching Florian's eye, Ash had no need to speak to confirm that they were sharing a moment of grim amusement.

"It's true," Ash said, "she did."

The Faris swallowed. Her voice came out taut. "Tell your Burgundian woman that. She owes this to me."

" 'This'?"

The Visigoth woman switched to the language of southern Burgundy, speaking with a perceptible accent. "Refuge. Sanctuary. I gave the orders, I held my commanders back so that you could ride out into the wildwood."

The Faris stood awkwardly in the European dress she wore, plainly not used to hose, or the short skirts of the doublet that she unconsciously kept pulling down. In the five weeks since they had met across the table in the Visigoth camp, she seemed to have grown thinner; or perhaps, Ash surmised, it was that she wore no armor, had no soldiers with her, seemed a much younger woman altogether.

"That was more than a month ago," Ash said grimly. "In that time you could have traveled back to Carthage and destroyed the *machina rei militaris*. Now *that* would have been useful."

A flick of fear on the Visigoth woman's face.

"Would *you* go back to Carthage? Would *you* go so close to the Wild Machines again?" She met Ash's eyes, her own red and puffy with long sleeplessness, and Ash had time to think *Is this how* I *look?* before the Faris added, "I would have gone. I could not. Not go so close, not when they're here—" She touched her temple. "Not when they can . . . use me, without my consent. You are hearing them, too."

"No."

"I don't believe you!" Her voice cracked on a shout.

Adelize began to whoop and roar.

The Faris broke off, reaching down, and stroked the woman's hair with tentative fingers. Violante gave her a look of contempt and knelt and took the woman into her thin arms, straining to reach around her shoulders.

"Not to be afraid," Violante said in the slaves' Carthaginian that Ash hardly understood. "Adelize, not to be afraid."

The woman Adelize gently pushed Violante back, stroking the front of the girl's tunic—no, not the tunic, Ash saw. Stroking the bulge of a body, small and moving, that wriggled itself up to Violante's neckline.

Ash watched as the gray-and-white rat licked her mother's fingers.

Adelize stroked it. She spluttered, "Poor, poor! Not to mind. Easy, easy. Not to be afraid."

"I talked with my father Leofric." The Faris's hand did not stop stroking Adelize's hair.

"He can talk?" Ash asked sardonically.

"He and I, we have tried to persuade the lord Caliph Gelimer that the Stone Golem must be destroyed. He will not do it. Gelimer believes nothing my father says. All this 'conspiracy' of the Wild Machines is, he says, a political trick of House Leofric's, nothing that he will act upon."

"Fucking hell!" Ash said, overriding both Florian and John de Vere. "You've got two legions out there, what was stopping you killing Gelimer, going back to Carthage, and hammering the Stone Golem into gravel? *What?*"

Her anger faded with the bewildered look on the woman's face.

She's heard the Stone Golem for twenty years, had it as her advisor in combat for as long as she remembers, and everything she's done in her life has been for the King-Caliph: no, going home at the head of an armed rebellion is something she wouldn't contemplate—

"I know that we have been betrayed," the Faris said, "and my men about to die, whether they win or not. I have been trying to save their lives. First, by leaving the siege to engines, not assault; second, by letting the Duchess of Burgundy live, to stand in the path of the southern demons. You would have done the same thing, sister."

"I'm not your bloody sister, for Christ's sake! We hardly know each other."

"You are my sister. We are both warriors." The Faris's fingers ceased stroking Adelize's head. "If nothing else, remember this is our mother."

Ash threw up her hands. She turned on Floria. "*You* talk to her!"

Ash saw Robert Anselm's gaze on her, realized that he and Angelotti were—quite unconsciously—staring from her to the Faris, and from the Faris back to her. John de Vere murmured something to Bajezet, the Turk also pointing to the Faris.

The surgeon-Duchess asked, "Why are you here in Dijon?"

"For sanctuary," the Visigoth woman repeated.

"Why now?"

Olivier de la Marche strode forward, with Jonvelle behind him, to take up a place defending their Duchess. Jonvelle spoke, answering Floria's question. "Your Grace, to infiltrate the city and assassinate you, one would suppose. I am with our Maid, Ash, on this. She will give you no useful information. Have her executed without further talk."

The Faris, with the first hint of an acerbic humor akin to

Ash's, said, "*Amir*-Duchess, since you ask it, I am here now because now is the hour at which the King-Caliph issued a warrant for my arrest and execution."

"Ah." Ash nodded with satisfaction.

"He has put Sancho Lebrija in my place as commander," the Faris said.

Ash remembered the humorless, brutal cousin of Asturio Lebrija, a man to do nothing else but take orders from his King-Caliph. "When did Lebrija take over?"

"Now. An hour since." The Faris shrugged. "*Amir* Gelimer made it plain at the parley that he considered me spoiled and lunatic. After that, said before his allies, how could he continue to use me as a commander? He has considered me part of what he sees as House Leofric's plotting; this was a way to dispose of me."

"Of *course*," Ash said.

"I knew then that I would be executed within the hour. I left the meeting a little ahead of the others, called my slaves, changed my clothes to these captured garments, and ordered the slaves to escort 'Ash' to the gate of Dijon. And they let me in."

The Faris's hand went up to her newly cut hair. At two yards' distance, the dirt marking her face did not conceal the fact that she had no scars.

"*Amir* Gelimer has ordered my father to kill and dissect all the slaves of our bloodline—Adelize, Violante, these others here, myself. I believe my father Leofric will do it. If he thinks it will convince the King-Caliph of the truth of what he says about the Wild Machines, he will do it without hesitation. He will do it . . ."

Ash could not hear it, but she knew the other men standing in this bright refectory of Dijon's abbey heard the Visigoth woman speak in her voice, Ash's voice, with only the accent to differentiate them. She stared at the face of her twin, everything else—hostages, the war, the Wild Machines—forgotten in that strange recognition.

"You trusted me," the Faris said. Her identical voice urged: "You trusted me enough to tell me that Duke Charles was dying—when you came to my camp for parley, before the hunt? There was that trust between us, when, by your reasoning, you should have killed me. I have little hope you won't kill me now. But with Gelimer, there is no hope."

She sighed, shifting her head as if the river-fall of hair were still there, her hand going up to her loss. Her glance shifted to the surgeon-Duchess of Burgundy.

"I am foolish," the Faris said. "There is no hope here, either. For you to be safe, you need me to die."

Floria, frowning, bit at the skin at the edge of her fingernail. "Wild Machines or not, Gelimer needs to kill me for quite different reasons. This war isn't going to stop now. He doesn't know the consequence of his actions. That's irrelevant. If you were dead—"

"If *I* were dead," the Faris said softly, "it would be the end of the Wild Machines' influence for a generation and more. Before another could be bred like me. Longer, perhaps. It will take time and another King-Caliph before the Stone Golem is trusted again."

"But it will be," Floria said.

Olivier de la Marche said flatly, coming forward, "Demoiselle Duchess, that is for our sons and grandsons to finish. And for that reason, consider: Burgundy must survive now. We *must*! Or else, when that day comes, there will be no one to stand against the demons of the south. They may do their pleasure, with no Duke or Duchess to prevent them. If Burgundy is gone, they may make what black miracle they will, and then all is as if we had never lived and striven against them."

Ash stared at the weather-beaten face of the tournament champion and Captain of the Guard. The Burgundian soldier nodded, sharply.

"I know the powers of Burgundy's Duke, Demoiselle-Captain. What should these southern demons care that we kill this miracle-worker of theirs now? They can breed another, whether it is twenty years or two hundred. If Burgundy has been destroyed, then in twenty years or two hundred, there is nothing to stand in their way. And winter *will* cover all the world."

A stir at the door made Floria turn her head. Ash saw the

Abbot of St Stephen's enter with a clutch of monks. Olivier de la Marche intercepted him, soothing his stifled imprecations. The refectory's monks sidled out of sight.

"How long?" Floria demanded.

"A quarter hour since I was on the wall." Ash squinted at the sun's light through the ogee windows. "Maybe more."

Floria put her hands together, linking her fingers and resting them against her lips. She stared at the Faris. Abruptly, she dropped her hands and stated, "If I keep you alive now, there are six hundred people standing in the mud outside the walls who are going to die. But if I hand you back to Gelimer, thousands more people are going to die in the war."

Ash saw John de Vere nodding, and Olivier de la Marche.

Floria, remorseless, continued: "If I kill you, the Wild Machines can't use you for their wonder-working—but that won't stop the war. Or the deaths. The war's going to go on whether you're alive or dead. We're losing. On the other hand, if I keep you alive, your knowledge as commander of their armies means that we can keep on fighting. And Burgundy has to survive, or there's nothing to stop the Wild Machines the *next* time they succeed in breeding a child of Gundobad's line. Ash, have I got this right?"

The surgeon-Duchess's voice was acerbic. Ash almost smiled, aching for the woman. "You didn't miss anything that I can see."

"And these are my choices."

"And mine."

"No. No, not this time." Floria's gaze took in Anselm and Angelotti and the company men, moved to Olivier de la Marche and Jonvelle and the gathering of Burgundian nobles and commanders.

"You said it yourself. I hunted the hart. It's my decision."

"Not if I decide differently."

It was out before she could retract it. Ash shook her head, disgusted with herself. *Yes, it's true, but this wasn't the time to remind her of it.*

Oh, shit.

At a loss to avoid the crevasse opening up at her feet, Ash protested, into the silence, "You can talk about twenty or two hundred years all you like. You're forgetting today. One stray arrow, one rock from a mangonel, one spy or assassin that Gelimer manages to get into this city—and then we've got the Wild Machines' 'miracle' happening at that instant. I don't care what my sister—" Ash spoke the words very deliberately, "—*what* my sister knows about Visigoth troop dispositions and war plans."

Her gaze locked with Floria's, ignoring the whole room: Anselm murmuring something concerned to Angelotti, the Turks impassive, the Burgundians in their war-worn armor still splendid beyond all other countries of Christendom.

"Florian, for Christ's sake, can't you see it? I don't want to cause a split. But handing her back to Gelimer is just ridiculous." Ash grimaced. "And letting her live, here, is too great a risk to you."

"No risk from me," the Faris interrupted quietly, again with a flash of the same humor that Ash recognised as her own. "The risk is not from me. You forget something, sister. When the Duchess of Burgundy dies, then I—lose myself, to the Wild Machines. When I become a . . . a channel, for their power . . ." The Visigoth woman visibly sought words: "I think I will be—swept away. *Jund* Ash, I want her to live even more than you do!"

It carried weight with the Burgundians; Ash saw it in their expressions. She shivered, in the stone refectory, the memory of ancient voices in her mind: that sensation of being swept away, like a leaf in a river current, swept away and drowned.

"I'm not saying you're about to assassinate her," Ash remarked dryly. "Sweet Green Christ up a Tree, you'd have been a damn sight less trouble if you'd stayed outside Dijon with your army!"

She heard the plaintive note in her voice without being able to do anything about it. A ripple of laughter went around the room.

"I hear the clock striking the half," Robert Anselm said, his tone relieved even while he was looking over his shoulder at the door, as if anticipating one of Jonvelle's men-at-arms arriving from the wall. "Need a decision."

Floria linked her dirty fingers again, knuckles strained.

"I've made enough hard decisions in the infirmary, when I was with the company."

Now would be the time, while she still thinks she has time to decide.

Ash kept her hand off her sword grip. She read a flash of apprehension on Angelotti's face, realized she had moved—body balanced, feet slightly apart—into what any mercenary would see as a combat stance. *Any mercenary except Florian,* she amended. The gold-haired woman stood frowning.

Enough of de la Marche's men-at-arms between me and the Faris that I won't get through for certain. But I'm their commander now, so—

Robert Anselm strolled across the flagstones to her side. Ash did not shift her attention: aware of all the room, of men talking, of the Burgundians glancing between their Duchess and her Captain-General.

"Don't fuck her over," he rumbled. "If you push it, they'll follow her, not you."

"If I take *her* out—" Names attract their owners' attention; Ash did not say *the Faris*: "—it doesn't matter, it's done."

Robert Anselm managed to keep a level expression, watching the Duchess and the Burgundian men-at-arms, the Visigoth woman and the silver-haired slaves with her. He said, "You try and kill her, and you'll start a civil war here."

Ash glared at him: a broad-shouldered man still in someone else's borrowed, overlarge German breastplate. He watched her from unflinching hazel eyes.

"Then the doc's fucked," he said. "Burgundy's fucked, too. Start a civil war inside Dijon, and Burgundy finishes right here, girl. The ragheads make catsmeat of us: thank you and good night. And those bloody things breed another monster in twenty years, and there's nothing to stop them."

His words wrenched her mind away from the Faris: she saw what she had been refusing to see and thought simply *No, nothing left: no bloodline of Burgundy. There'll be a massacre, like at Antwerp and Auxonne. Then the Wild Machines will automatically succeed, whenever they try, because there will be nothing capable of stopping them.*

"Oh, son of a *bitch* . . ." Ash breathed.

She rubbed her eyes, aching in the white light from the windows. Her muscles flooded with what she recognized, startled, as a release of tension. She scowled. *What am I so happy about?*

The answer was present in her mind immediately:

I don't have to take this decision.

Self-disgust filled her. She shook her head, wryly. The disgust was not as powerful as the relief. Her mind yammered at her, finding no flaw in Robert Anselm's reasoning, telling her, *You can't make this decision, it has to be Florian, and you can't argue with her without losing everything—*

"Oh, shut up!" Ash said, under her breath. She looked at the startled face of Robert Anselm. "Not you. Yes. You're right. I wish you weren't."

And I wish I knew if I meant that.

Ash gestured across to Florian. "It's your call."

The woman's dark gold brows came down, her expression so clearly reading Ash's moral cowardice that Ash looked away.

She found herself watching her twin. The Faris still stood by the refectory table. One finger ceaselessly traced the raised grain of the scrubbed wood. She made no other movement. She did not look at the surgeon-Duchess.

Could I have come here, the way she has?

Ash did not let herself look at Violante or Adelize.

Floria wiped her face with her hand, in a gesture familiar to Ash from a hundred occasions in the hospital-tents. She sighed heavily. She did not look to anyone around her for assistance, confirmation, or support.

"I've got patients at the infirmary here," Floria said. "I'll be with them." She beckoned Olivier de la Marche forward. "You and Ash question the Faris. We'll convene again at Nones,[55] and discuss what you've learned."

A sigh of release. Ash could not judge which of the men—John de Vere, Bajezet, de la Marche, Anselm—it came from.

The Faris sat down hard on the wooden bench beside Violante. Her skin paled to the point where she might have

---

[55] 3 P.M.

been taken for a woman with a terminal illness: her eyes large and dark in hollowed sockets.

"If I'm not in the infirmary, I'll be in the almonry; they wanted to talk to me about food stocks," Floria del Guiz said unemphatically. "When there's news from the wall, come and find me."

ii

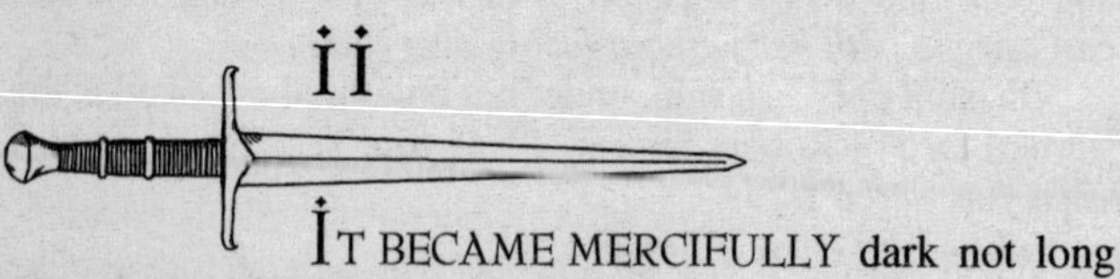

IT BECAME MERCIFULLY dark not long after the abbey bells rang for Nones.

The short winter day died to dusk. Ash stretched her leg as she leaned back against the hearth-surround in the company's tower. Green ivy still hung on the stonework. Burned flesh stabbed pain into the back of her thigh. *It is still the day of Christ's birth*, she thought, dazed.

The Christ's Mass massacre.

Blanche, her yellow hair matted under a filthy coif, wiped her now-thin hands on her kirtle. "We've run out of goose grease in the infirmary. Too many Greek Fire burns."

Ash clenched her fists behind her back. Under the bandage, raw flesh yelled pain at her. Peeling the plate and cloth from her injured thigh had made her bite deep teeth marks into the wooden grip of her dagger.

"How many incapacitated?"

"You know men." Blanche snapped. "All of them say they'll fight tomorrow. I'd say six of them will still be in bed next week. If the walls are standing!"

The woman's asperity, Ash saw, was not directed at her. Part of it was plain concern and an evident affection for the injured. The rest was self-blame, even in the face of lack of materials.

Ash wanted to say something comforting, could think of

nothing that was not condescending. "Any that can walk, send them down here. I'll be talking to the lads."

Blanche limped away. Ash noted a respect in the way that archers and billmen stood aside for her: a middle-aged woman with bad teeth, growing gaunt from starvation, who in easier times they might each have paid a small coin to fuck. With a sense of sadness, she thought, *I should have seen that in her before. Not left it to Florian to find.*

Angelotti, approaching the fire as Blanche left it, said, "How many civilians did we save?"

"We never got out of the dead ground in front of the postern gate. They saturated the area with Greek Fire from the engines. You were up on the walls: what happened?"

The gunner, his astonishingly beautiful face powder-blackened, shrugged lithe shoulders. "The golems tore people apart. They began a little way beyond our gate and went through them like herd dogs. Those men and women that ran as far as their camp lines were shot down with bows. We shattered one golem with cannon fire, since it obliged us by walking straight toward the wall for the space of five minutes; but for the rest we shot with bow and arquebus, with no success . . ."

"The burns are bad," Ash said, into his silence. "Digorie and Richard Faversham are upstairs praying, not to much answer, I think. No tiny miracles, Angeli. No loaves and fishes, no healing. Being on Burgundy's side has its problems."

The Italian touched his St. Barbara medal. "It would have taken more than a small miracle. The intercession of all the saints, perhaps; there are six hundred dead out there."

Six hundred men, women, and children, jointed like the fowls Henri Brant cooks in the cauldrons in the kitchens, and lying on the cold, black earth between the city walls and the besieging camp.

And what will Gelimer do *now*?

"De la Marche is still debriefing the Faris. I left them to it." Ash flinched again, putting weight on her burned leg. "Let's get everybody in here, Angeli. I'm going to talk to them, before I talk to the *centeniers*. Make sure they understand what's going on. Then I'll tell them what we're going to do now."

From one corner of the hall, Carracci's recorder ran through a sequence of notes, halted, ran through them again. One of the pages touched him on the arm and he fell silent. The stink of tallow-dip tapers rose up. With the slit-windows shuttered, and the faint lights, Ash could not see as far as the back of the hall. Men filed in, sitting down on the heaps of belongings on the flagstones, exchanging quiet words. Men-at-arms; men, women, and children from the baggage train; some faces—Euen Huw, Geraint ab Morgan, Ludmilla Rostovnaya—still greasily smoke-stained from the abortive rescue sally.

The lances of the company filed in, sat down, watching her, and the talk died down to a waiting silence.

"What we have to think about," Ash said, "is a long-term solution."

She did not speak loudly. There was no need. Other than her voice, the only noise came from a few drops of melted ice falling down the throat of the chimney behind her and hissing into the fire. Their faces watched her, with intent attention.

"We've been thinking too close to home, and too short-term." Ash shifted her shoulder off the wall and began to walk between the groups of seated men. Heads turned, following her in the smoky hall. She folded her arms, walking with a deliberateness that concealed the pain of the burn wound. "Hardly surprising—we've been having our asses kicked from here to breakfast. We've had to fight our own battles before we could do much thinking ahead. But I think now is the time. If only because, as far as Gelimer is concerned, we don't know if we've still got a truce."

She became aware of Robert Anselm and Dickon de Vere by the door, nodded acknowledgment but didn't speak, not breaking her train of reasoning. She continued to walk, a woman in armor, among men sitting with their arms around their knees, lifting their heads as she passed.

"We've been concentrating on keeping a Duke or Duchess of Burgundy alive. Because Burgundy is what stands against the great demons in the southern desert, Burgundy is what stops them using their miracle-worker to wipe out the world. And now we have their miracle-worker right here, in Dijon."

There was no overt dramatization in the way she spoke: she could have been in her own command tent, thinking aloud. A baby cried, and was hushed. She touched Carracci briefly on the shoulder as she walked past him.

"So it ought to be simple. We kill the Faris. Then it doesn't matter if Burgundy falls, because she's dead, and the Wild Machines have lost their—channel," Ash said, choosing the Visigoth woman's own word: "Their channel for what they're going to do: put out the sun and make the world as if we had never been. Except that it's *not* simple."

"Because she's your sister?" Margaret Schmidt spoke up.

"She's not my sister. Except by blood." Ash grinned, altered her tone, and said, "The only close relatives I have are you lot, God help me!"

There was an appreciative chuckle at that.

"It's not simple." Ash cut off the noise. "We're not thinking ahead. If the Faris is dead, but the war here is still lost, then the Visigoths will raze Burgundy from sea to sea—they have to. If for no other reason, then because they don't want Sultan Mehmet in Carthage with the army that took down Byzantium."

"Fucking right," Robert Anselm rumbled.

"And if Burgundy's gone, if the blood of the Dukes of Burgundy no longer exists, then it won't matter if the Wild Machines take a thousand years to breed another Faris—as soon as they do it, the world is gone. Wiped out, changed, the moment they succeed. And everything we've done here will be gone—as if we had never been born."

Plainly, those men who had been present in the abbey had been talking; there was little surprise at what she said.

"And so we have to win this war," Ash added.

She couldn't stop a smile. It was answered here and there: Geraint ab Morgan; Pieter Tyrrell.

"Sounds simple, doesn't it?"

"Piece of piss!" an anonymous voice remarked, from the ill-lit gloom.

"You think only the Burgundians care about the war here?"

Ash turned in the direction of the voice, and picked out John Burren. "You have a stake. You all have countries; all mercenaries do. You're English, Welsh, Italian, German. Well, the Visigoths have fucked most of those lands, John Burren, and they'll get across the Channel yet."

Dickon de Vere opened his mouth to say something, and Robert Anselm's elbow landed heavily in the boy's ribs. The youngest de Vere shut up with surprising good grace.

"If Burgundy gets wiped out, every one of us who's died in this campaign has died for no reason. This is what we're going to do." Ash reached the middle of the hall again, still cupping her elbows in her hands. She looked around at the men. "We're going to fight back. When I left de la Marche, he had five separate scribes there to keep up with everything the Faris is telling him. We're going to take the war to the Visigoths. And we have to do it *first*—before that lot out there roll right over us!"

She glanced up into the smoke-blackened rafters, paused, went on:

"We know what their weak points are, now. So. First, we need to raise the siege—I grant you that's the difficult part. We need to get our Duchess Florian out of Dijon, and away." Ash smiled at the low noises of approval. "Then, we're going to fight beside the allies that we'll have. And we will have allies, because Gelimer is looking weaker every hour. We'll have the Turks and the French, minimum."

There were nods of agreement. She tapped her fist in her palm, went on concisely:

"We can kill the Faris, but that's just a precaution—in time, there'll be more where she came from. We can't reach the Stone Golem—they won't let us raid Carthage like that twice! So what we have to do—the only thing we can do—is take the war to the Wild Machines. Win here, and take the war to Africa. Give the Visigoth Empire to the Sultan, if we have to! We have to take the war south, and we have to destroy the Wild Machines themselves."

She paused for a moment, to let it sink in. She picked Angelotti and the other gunners out of the gloom and nodded toward them:

"Once we get through the people around them, the Wild Machines can't *fight*. They're *rocks*. They can't do anything except speak to the Faris and the Stone Golem. I dare say Master Angelotti, and as many dozen powder ships and bombards as we can muster, can reduce them to a lot of confused gravel in very short order." Ash nodded, acknowledging Angelotti's bright, sudden grin. "So that's where we're aiming—North Africa. And we aim to be there by the spring."

Those that had been in Carthage would have talked to those men who remained in Dijon. Ash looked keenly around in the gloom, watching faces, seeing determination, apprehension, confidence.

"There's no other way to do this," Ash said. "It won't be easy, even with what we know. If, once we've raised this siege, some of you want to go back to England, or travel farther north out of the darkness, I won't stop you: you can leave with your pay. What we're doing is dangerous; trying to fight back and get to North Africa will get a lot of us killed."

She lifted her hand, cutting off what several people began to say.

"I'm not appealing to your pride. Forget it. I'm saying this is as dangerous as any other war we've fought in, and like every other time, those who are going to quit should do it now."

She could already identify some who might: a few of the Italian gunners, maybe Geraint ab Morgan. She nodded thoughtfully to herself, hearing a black joke or an ironic comment made in an undertone; three hundred and fifty able-bodied soldiers regarding her with the blank, bland faces of men who are at once afraid and practical.

"So when are we going to kick three legions' asses?" The English crossbowman, John Burren, jerked a thumb at the masonry walls, plainly intending to indicate the Visigoth legions encamped around Dijon.

Before she answered him, Ash nodded a general dismissal: "Okay. Lads, get your kit sorted. Talk to your officers. I want an officer meeting first thing tomorrow morning."

She turned back to the English crossbowman.

" 'When'?" she repeated, and grinned at John Burren.

"Hopefully, before Gelimer decides we haven't got a truce anymore, and all three legions come right over these fucking walls!"

She visited the quarters of the Burgundian commanders, going from house to barracks to palace, holding much the same conversation everywhere in the dark winter afternoon of Christmas Day. Where possible, she spoke with the Burgundian men who would be fighting. She covered miles on the cobbled streets of Dijon, changing her escort every hour.

The light cloud cover cleared, stars came out; all that did not change was the crowd in front of the almonry, holding at a steady thousand strong all through the night, waiting for the tiny dole of dark bread and nettle beer.

The seven stars in the sky shone bright in the frost: the Plough clearly visible over the spires of the abbey of St. Stephen's.

Ash left her escort outside the two-story red-tiled building in the abbey grounds that did duty as the abbot's house, entering and passing through guards and monks alike with unquestioned authority.

The sound of a Carthaginian flute echoed down the cramped stairs. She unbuckled her helm and shook out her short hair. Her eyes, that had been blurred with thought, with attention to others' words, sharpened. She scratched through her hair with bitten-nailed fingers, and gave a kind of shrug that settled her shoulders in her armor. That done, she bent her head and walked up the narrow, low-ceilinged stairs to the upper room.

"Madam—Captain," a tall, lean monk corrected himself. "You have missed the abbot. He was just here, praying with the mad foreign woman."

"The abbot's a charitable man." Ash didn't break step on her way to the door. "There's no need for you to come in. I'll only be a few minutes."

She ducked her head under the thick oak lintel, entering the farther room, ignoring the monk's very halfhearted protest. The floor of the house was uneven under her boots, warped boards creaking. As she straightened, she took in pale beams gold in a lantern's light, white plaster between them, no scrap of furniture, and a heap of blankets beside the diamond-paned window.

Violante and the Faris sat together on the floor by the lantern. Ash saw their heads turning as she came in.

The blankets moved as the boards shrieked underfoot. Sweat-darkened gray hair became visible: Adelize sitting up and rubbing at her eyes with a chubby fist.

"I didn't know you were here." Ash stared at the Faris.

"Your abbot has put the male slaves in another room. I am here with the women."

The sound of the flute came again as the Faris spoke, plainly from somewhere else in the abbot's house. Ash moved her gaze to Violante, to Adelize, back to the woman who now—hair cropped short, and in someone's overlarge Swiss doublet and hose—seemed even more her twin.

"There's a family resemblance," Ash said, her mouth drying.

She could not take her eyes off the idiot woman. Adelize sat wrapped in many woolen blankets, rocking and humming to herself. She began to bang her fist on her knee. It was a second before Ash realized that she was keeping time with the flute music.

"Shit," Ash said. "She's why they killed so many of us, isn't it? They thought we'd end up like that. Shit. You ever wonder if that's what you've got to look forward to?"

The child Violante said something rapid.

"She doesn't understand you, but she doesn't like the tone of your voice," the Faris explained.

As if disturbed by the voices, Adelize stopped rocking and clutched at her stomach. She began to whimper and mew. She said a word. Ash barely understood the slaves' Carthaginian; made it out at last: "Pain! Pain!"

"What's the matter with her? Has she been injured?"

Violante spoke again. The Faris nodded.

"She says, Adelize is hungry. She says, Adelize has never known hunger before. She was cared for, in the birthing rooms. She doesn't understand the pain of an empty gut."

Ash stepped forward. The rattle of her armor, which she no

longer much heard, sounded loud in the enclosed space. The middle-aged woman scrambled up onto her feet and backed away, shedding blankets.

"Wait—" Ash stopped moving. She said, in a deliberately soothing tone, "I'm not here to hurt you. Adelize. Adelize, I'm not here to hurt."

"Not like!" Violante began rearranging the blankets around the woman. Adelize absently lifted the cloth up, picking at her sagging belly under her tunic, and scratching at gray pubic hair. A great web of white lines and stretch marks seamed her thighs, belly, and breasts. Violante pulled the blankets down, adding something in rapid Carthaginian.

"She says, Adelize is frightened of people in numbers, and in war gear." The Faris at last got to her feet. "The child is correct. Adelize will have seen few men other than those my father Leofric bred to her, and few people in number at all."

Ash stared at Adelize in the poor light. *Do I look like her?* The woman was heavy around the jaw, and her eyes were sunk in puffy flesh; she might have been anywhere between forty and sixty. Or even older: there was something naive about the unlined softness of her cheeks.

A wrenching pity moved her, overlain by disgust.

"Christ!" Ash said again. "She's retarded.[56] She really is."

Adelize's blankets moved. In the lantern light, Ash caught a brief glimpse of something wriggling back into the folds; and the faint smell in the room made sense to her. Rat. Violante spoke, unintelligibly.

"What?"

The Faris bent to pick up a blanket and wrap it around her own shoulders. Her breath huffed white in the air. "She says, show respect for her mother."

"*Her* mother?"

"Violante is your full sister. And niece," the Faris added, with a quiet smile on her face at Ash's disturbance. "My father Leofric bred our brother back to our mother. Violante is one of the children. I brought two of the boys away with me."

---

[56]In the original text, 'one of God's touched,' and 'God's fool'.

"Oh, for Christ's sake! *Why?*" Ash burst out.

The woman ignored that. Ash had a moment to muse, *You would think, when she has my face, that it would be easy for me to read it*; then the Faris said, "Why are you here?"

"What?"

"Why have you come here?" the Faris demanded. At some time in the past few hours, she had washed her hands and face; the skin was pale in the guttering lamp's light. Dark-eyed, clear-skinned; and now with hair that barely covered her ears. She spoke in a voice hoarse with long explanations. "Why? Am I to be executed now? Or do I have as long as to tomorrow? Have you come here to tell me what your Duchess Florian decrees?"

"No," Ash said, shaking her head absently, ignoring the hard edge to the Faris's tone, "I came to see my mother."

It was not what she intended to say. Certainly it was not what she intended to say in front of other people. Her hands chilled with shock. She stripped off her gauntlets, rebuckled the straps, and hung them off the grip of her sword. Crossing the floor, she squatted down in front of Adelize. Her scabbard's chape scraped the floorboards.

"She doesn't know who I am," she said.

"She does not know me, either," the Faris said. "Did you expect her to recognize you as a daughter?"

Ash did not answer the Faris immediately. She squatted close enough to Adelize to smell the old-urine-and-milk stench from her skin. An unguarded, wild lurch of the idiot-woman's arm had her up on her feet, automatically, combat reflexes triggered, hand gripping her dagger.

Adelize reached out. She stroked the muddy leather of Ash's boot. She looked up. "Not to be afraid. *Not* to be afraid."

"Oh, Jesu." Ash wiped her bare hand across her face. It came away wet.

One of the rats, a curly-pelted white one, ran up to Adelize. Delighted, the woman forgot everything else in petting it with heavy fingers. The animal licked her.

"Yes." Ash looked away, bewildered. She stepped back, finding herself standing beside the Faris. "Yes, I thought she'd know me. If I'm her daughter, she *ought* to know me. I ought to feel she's my mother."

Very tentatively, the Faris put her hand into Ash's and gripped it, clasping her with cold, identical fingers.

"How many children has she had?"

"I looked in our records." The Faris did not remove her hand. "She littered every year for the first fifteen years; then three more litters after that."

"Christ! It almost makes me glad I'm barren." A flick of her gaze to the Faris, Ash's sight blurring. "Almost."

Another of the rats—patched fur dim in this light, but she was almost sure it was Lickfinger—ran up Adelize's arm to her shoulder. The woman cocked her head, chuckling as the rat's whiskers tickled her face. She paid no attention to Ash.

"Does she even *know* she's had babies?"

The Faris looked affronted. "She knows. She misses them. She likes small, warm things. What I believe she does not know is that babies grow. Since hers were taken away at birth to wet nurses, she does not know they change to become men and women."

Blankly, Ash said, "Wet nurses?"

"If she nursed, it would hinder conception. She has given birth eighteen times," the Faris said. "Violante was her next-to-last. Violante does not hear the Stone Golem."

"You do," Ash said sharply.

"I do. Still." The Visigoth woman sighed. "None other of Adelize's children were—successful, except for me. And for you, of course." She frowned, and Ash thought *Do I look like that? Older, when I frown?* The Faris went on, "Our father Leofric wonders now, how many others he culled too young. He has kept all of Leovigild's siring, now, and all of Adelize's children born this spring. We have two living brothers, and another sister."

Ash became aware that she was gripping the Faris's hand tightly enough to hurt. Embarrassed, she stared down at the crooked floorboards. Her breath came short, her chest burned.

"Fucking hell, I can't take it in." She lifted her gaze to the Faris's face, at her side; thought *She's nineteen or twenty, the same as I am*, and wondered why the Visigoth woman should suddenly appear so young.

"It need not be twenty years before there's another Faris," Ash speculated, voice flat in the cold room. "If Leofric weren't mad as a March hare now, and if Gelimer believed even half his intelligence about the Wild Machines . . . Maybe, if they looked at what they've got, there'd be another one of you in a few months: next spring or summer."

The Faris said, "I will tell you what my lord Caliph Gelimer would do, if he credited what we say of the Wild Machines. He would think them a superior kind of Stone Golem. He would think them wise voices of war, advising him how to spread the empire to all civilized lands. And he would be seeking a way to build more Stone Golems, and breed more of me, so that he could have not one general and not one *machina rei militaris* but dozens."

"Sweet Christ."

The Faris's hand was warm and slick in her own. Ash loosened her grip. She said, her eyes still on Adelize, "*Could* House Leofric build another Stone Golem?"

"It is not *impossible*. In time." The Faris shrugged. "If my father Leofric lives."

"Oh, Jesu," Ash said, aware of the chill air freezing her fingertips, of the stars outside the window, of the smell of unwashed bodies subdued by the cold. "The Turk won't like that. Nor will anyone else. A machine for talking to the great war-demons of the south—they wouldn't rest until they had one, too. Nor would the French, the English, the Rus . . ."

The Faris, watching Adelize, said absently, "Or if our knowledge were lost, and Leofric dead, and the House destroyed, so that there were still only the one Stone Golem—they will not let us keep it."

"They wouldn't rest until they'd taken Africa, taken Carthage, destroyed it utterly."

"But Gelimer does not credit it. He thinks it all some political plot of House Leofric." The Faris shivered under her blanket. She said thickly, "And I have nothing more to do with the fortune of the Visigoth Empire, do I? Nothing more to do, myself, than sit here and wonder if I am to be killed, come morning."

"Shouldn't think so. What you're telling de la Marche is far too useful."

It rang false as she said it. Ash took her eyes off Adelize and finally let herself realize, *I am standing in the same room as this woman, she is unarmed, I have a sword, I have a dagger; if her death were a* fait accompli, *Florian would just have to wear it. There probably* wouldn't *be a civil war.*

She expected agonizing indecisiveness.

Kill her. In front of her mother, her sister? My sister? She is my sister. This, for all of what it is, is still my blood.

What she felt was a warm relaxation of tension.

Ash said with rough humor, "Sweet Green Christ! Haven't you got enough troubles without worrying if your sister's going to kill you? Faris, I won't. Right now, I can't. But I know I should."

She rested her hand across her face again, briefly; and then looked up at the Visigoth woman.

"It's Florian. You see. The danger to Florian. I can't let that carry on." The words stuck on her tongue, sheer weariness tripping her up. She found herself waving her arms as excitedly as an Englishman. *"Can you keep them out?"*

"The Wild Machines?"

"Keep them out. Not listen."

The expression on the Faris's face, dimly visible now in the lamplight, shifted between fear and confusion. "I—*feel*—them. I told the King-Caliph I did not hear the Stone Golem, and I do not; I have spoken no word to it in five weeks. But I feel it. And through it, the *Machinae Ferae* . . . there is a sensation—"

"Pressure," Ash said. "As if someone were forcing you."

"You could not withstand them, when they spoke through the Stone Golem to you, in Carthage," the Faris said softly. "And their power is growing, their darkness spreading; they will reach me, here, use me to change—"

"If Florian dies." Ash squatted again. She reached out, carefully, and touched Adelize's greasy gray-white hair. The woman stiffened. Ash began small stroking movements. "It's Florian. I can't let you go on being a danger to her. If you live, and the Wild Machines use you . . ."

"While we besieged you, I tried to break the link with the *machina rei militaris*," the Faris said. "I used a slave-priest, so he could tell no one and be believed. He prayed, but the voice of the machine stayed with me."

"So did I." Ash stopped stroking Adelize's matted hair. "So did I! And it didn't work for me either!"

Astonished laughter: she found herself grabbing the Faris's hands, the two of them laughing, and Adelize looked around, gazing from one to the other, from Ash to the Faris, and back again.

"Same!" she crowed triumphantly. She pointed from face to face. "Same!"

Ash bit her tongue. It was quite accidental; it stung; she tasted blood in her mouth. She thought, *Please say you know me.*

The fat woman reached up and stroked the Faris's face. She moved her fingers toward Ash. Ash's stomach twisted. The soft, plump fingers touched her skin, stroked her cheek, hesitated at the scars, retreated.

"Same?" Adelize said questioningly.

Ash's eyes filled. No water spilled down her cheek. She touched Adelize's hand gently, and stood up.

"There may well be more bred the same as you," Ash said, "but if you'd gone back and destroyed the Stone Golem—there's only one *machina rei militaris*. That would have cut you off from the Wild Machines. And it would have cut *them* off. They'd have to wait for another Gundobad or another Radonic, to build them another machine. Harder than breeding brats."

"Some men would have followed me. The ones I led in Iberia, who've known me many years. Most would not. And Carthage is well prepared against its victorious generals returning to overthrow a King-Caliph."

"You might have tried!" Ash grinned at herself, then, and shook her head ruefully. "Okay. I take your point. But if you'd destroyed the Stone Golem, I wouldn't be worrying about whether I should kill my sister now."

"Not kill!" Adelize said fiercely.

Ash glanced down, startled. Violante knelt at Adelize's side, obviously whispering a translation; the retarded woman glared up, pointing her finger at Ash, and then at the Faris. "Not kill!" she repeated.

A physical pain hurt her. *There is something wrong with my heart*, Ash thought. Her clenched fist pressed against her armor, over her breast, as if that could relieve her. The sharp, hollow pain hurt her again.

She reached out and ruffled Violante's hair. The child flinched away from her. She touched Adelize's hand. Stumbling, she turned and walked out of the room, ducking the lintel, striding past the thin monk, saying nothing when she picked up her escort outside the abbot's house, nothing until she reached the palace, and the Duchess's quarters.

"I'm here to see Florian."

The bead-bright eyes of Jeanne Châlon peered around the carved oaken door. "She is not well. You cannot see her."

"I can." Ash leaned one plate-covered arm up against the wood. "Are you going to try and stop me?"

One of the waiting women, Tilde, peered around Jeanne's shoulder. "She is not well, Demoiselle-Captain. We've had to ask my lord de la Marche to come back tomorrow."

"Not well?" Ash's mind sharpened, came into focus. She demanded curtly, "*What's wrong with her?*"

Tilde glanced at Jeanne Châlon, embarrassed. "Captain-General . . ."

"I said, what's wrong with her? What's her illness?—never mind." Ash shoved her way past them. She ignored the other servants and waiting-women, shouldering her way through them, leaving them to quarrel with her escort. She crossed to the ducal bed and threw back the hangings.

A stench of spirits made her cough.

The Duchess Florian, fully dressed in man's doublet, shirt, and hose, lay sprawled facedown on the bedding. Her mouth was open, dribbling copiously on the sheet. She breathed out a stink of alcohol. As Ash stood gazing down, Florian began stertorously to snore.

"She was up on the wall this afternoon, wasn't she?"

Jeanne Châlon's white face appeared at Ash's side. "I told her not to. I told her it was not befitting a woman, that she should watch what God Himself turns His face away from. But she wouldn't heed me. Floria has never heeded me."

"I'm glad to hear it." Ash bent down and pulled wolf furs gently over Florian's legs. "Except in this case. How long was she drinking herself into insensibility?"

"Since sunset."

Since the hostage massacre.

"Well, she won't do this again." Ash's lips quirked. "We haven't got the drink. Okay. If she wakes, send for me. If she doesn't—don't disturb her."

She was thoughtful on the way out of the palace, conscious of Ludmilla Rostovnaya's escort chatting among themselves, and conscious that her legs ached, and that her burned thigh muscle was throbbing. A haze of weariness floated her along. Not until she stepped out into the bitter, freezing night did she wake to full alertness.

The Plough had sunk around the pole of the sky. A few hours now and the day of Christ's Mass would be over, the feast day of Stephen dawning.

A fierce blue light illuminated the night sky, traveling at high speed.

"Incoming!"

A bolt of Greek Fire hissed in an arc and fell to earth in the square, splashing an inferno across the stone cobbles. A man ran out in the spirit blue light and raked thatch down from a corner of an outbuilding.

Shit! is this it? Gelimer's lost his General, and he's tired of holding to the truce—?

Another bolt shot high, vanished outside the walls of Dijon on its downward arc.

"Take cover!" Ash ordered, stepping smartly back into the palace's gatehouse. Another shot—stone, not fire; an impact that jarred up from the flagstones through her feet.

"Motherfuckers!" Rostovnaya murmured something caustic about Visigothic marksmanship: her men growled agreement. "At Christ's Mass, too! Boss, I thought we had a truce until Lord Fernando goes back to them tomorrow?"

Straining her hearing, praying for sounds to carry in the frozen night air, Ash hears nothing now—no shot dropping on other quarters of the city.

Visigoth siege engines, placement and ammunition loads; orders of infantry assault troops! Ash formulated the thought in her mind, not speaking it out loud, and shook her head.

Even if I could speak to the Stone Golem, it wouldn't be any use my asking. Its reports from here are dependent on courier; it must be two or three weeks out-of-date.

At least that means Gelimer can't use it for tactical advice against us. Even if the Wild Machines can use it, he can't. And Godfrey would hear him. Small mercies—

She stopped, stunned.

"Captain?" Ludmilla Rostovnaya said, in the tone of someone who has said the words before.

"What?"

Ash registered dimly that she heard no more bombardment: that these desultory shots are not the opening barrage before an assault—only some bored gun crew, probably Gelimer's Frankish mercenaries. Her realization blocked out any thankfulness that the truce remains unbroken.

"Do we go back to the tower?" The Rus woman peered through the night and the gatehouse's gloom, illuminated by guttering Greek Fire. No other impact shook the ground. "Captain? What is it?"

Ash spoke numbly.

"I've . . . just realized something. I can't think why I didn't see it before."

iii

THE STRIPED BOARLET nosed at the snow, whip-thin tail wagging furiously. Ash watched its nose strip up the ice crust from the soft white beneath. A flurry of black leaf mold went up. The animal grunted, in deep content, troweling up acorns.

A man with an acorn-colored beard put back his hood and turned to look at her.

—Ash.

"Godfrey."

Exhaustion carried her along the edge of sleep. It was no great difficulty to be simultaneously aware that she lay on her straw palliasse beside the tower's hearth, the noise of squires' and pages' voices fading in and out as sleep claimed her, and to know that she spoke aloud to the voice in her head.

The dream brought her his image, clear and precise: a big man, broad in the chest, his gnarled feet bare under the hem of his green robes. Some of the grizzled hairs of his beard were white, and there were lines deeply cut at the side of his mouth and around his eyes. A face beaten by weather; eyes that have squinted against the outdoor light in winter and summer.

"When I met you first, you were no older than I am now," Ash said quietly. "Christ Jesu. I feel a hundred."

—And you look it, too, I'll lay money on it.

Ash snuffled a laugh. "Godfrey, you ain't got no respect."

—For a mangy mongrel mercenary? Of course not.

The dream-Godfrey squatted in the snow, seeming to ignore the ice caking his robe's hem, and put one hand wrist-deep into snow to support himself. His breath whitened the air. She watched Godfrey tilt his head over—shoulders down, bottom up, until he seemed about to fall—to peer between the legs of the rootling three-week-old boar.

"Godfrey, what the *fuck* are you doing?"

The dream figure said, "Attempting to see if this is a boar or a sow. The sows have better temper."

"Godfrey, I can't believe you spent your childhood in the Black Forest trying to look up a boar's arse!"

"She is a sow." The snow shifted, and the boar's head came up, as he shuffled closer.

Ash saw her gold-brown eyes surveying the world suspiciously from under straw-pale lashes of incredible length. The dream-Godfrey talked quietly to her, for a lost amount of time, Ash drifted. She saw him finally reach out a cautious, steady hand.

The sow turned back to rootling. The man's hand began to scratch her in the place behind her ear where the thick, coarse winter coat is absent, and only soft hairs cover the gray skin. Her nose came up. She snorted: an amazing small, high squeak. He exerted more pressure, digging into the hot skin.

With a soft thump, the female piglet fell over on her side in the snow. She grunted in contentment as the man continued to scratch, her tail wagging.

"Godfrey, you'll have me believing you were suckled like Our Lord, by a boar!"

Without taking his hand away from the boarlet, Godfrey Maximillian looked back toward her. "Bless you, child, I have been rescuing God's wild beasts all my life."

White showed in his priest-cropped hair, as well as his beard. He reached for his Briar Cross with his free hand: large, capable, and scarred. A workman's hand. His eyes were dark as the sow's, and each detail of his face was clear to her, as if she had not seen him for months and now he was suddenly before her.

"You think you'll always remember the face," Ash whispered, "but it's the first thing to go."

—*You think there will always be time.*

"You try to fix it in your mind . . ." Ash stirred, on the mattress. Like water sinking through sand, the clear dream of Godfrey Maximillian in the snow sank away. She tried to hold it; felt it sliding from her mind.

—Ash?

"Godfrey?"

—I cannot tell how long it is since last we spoke.

"A few days." Ash shifted over onto her back, her forearm across her eyes. She heard Rickard's voice, breaking in mid-sentence for the first time in weeks, telling someone that the Captain-General could not see them at this hour: wait but an hour more.

"It's the evening of Christ's Mass," she said, "or the early hours of St. Stephen's day; I haven't heard the bells ring for Matins. I've been afraid to speak with you in case the Wild Machines—" she broke off. "Godfrey, do you still hear them? Where are they?"

In the part of herself that is shared with the *machina rei militaris*, she feels the comforting warmth that she associates with Godfrey. She hears no other voice but his, not even distant muttering in the language of Gundobad's era.

"Where are they!"

—Hell is silent.

"Hell be damned! I want to know what the Wild Machines are doing. Godfrey, talk to me!"

—Your pardon, child.

His voice comes to her filled with a mild amusement.

—For however long a time you say it is—a month and more—no human soul has spoken with the Stone Golem. At first the great Devils lamented this greatly. Then, they became angry. They deafened me, child, with their anger, forcing it through me. I had thought you heard, but perhaps it was the Faris at whom they directed their rage. And then, they fell silent.

"Did they, by God?"

She stretched, still fully clothed in case of night alarms, and opened her eyes briefly to see the rafters lost in the gloom, outside the light of the meager hearth-fire.

"They won't have given up on the Faris. They're waiting for their moment. Godfrey, has no one used the Stone Golem? Not even the King-Caliph?"

Godfrey's voice, in her soul, is full of what would be laughter if it were a sound.

—The slaves of Caliph Gelimer speak to it—as men speak,

not as the Faris speaks. They ask questions of tactics. If you ask me what, he will deduce what you fear. He is much afraid of this crusade, child; it is running away with him—a warhorse which he cannot control. I wish I could find God's charity in my heart for him, rather than rejoicing that he is troubled. I am unsure that he even understands the answers the Stone Golem speaks.

"I hope you're right. Godfrey, what are you so damned cheerful about?"

—I have missed you, Ash.

Her throat began to ache.

His voice filled with confidence, excited expectation:

—You swore that you would bring me home. Rescue me, out of this. Child, I know you would not be talking to me now unless you had thought of some way to bring this about. You've come to rescue me from this hell, now, haven't you?

Ash struggled up into a sitting position on the mattress. She waved Rickard away, back to the door lost in the gloom. She huddled furs and blankets around her shoulders, wriggling forward until her feet were almost in the ashes of the hearth-fire.

"I swore a lot of things," Ash said harshly. "I swore I'd get the Wild Machines for killing you, when you died in the earthquake. And you swore in the coronation hall that you'd always be with me, but it didn't stop you dying there. We all make promises we can't keep."

—Ash?

"At least I never swore to bring your body back for burial. At least I *knew* that was impossible."

—When I tried to help you escape from the cells of Leofric's house, before I found Fernando del Guiz for you to ride out with, I swore that you would never be alone. Do you remember? That promise I have kept. And I will keep it, child. You hear me, and you will always hear me; I will never leave you. Be certain of it.

The ache in her throat spread. She rubbed the back of her hand across her eyes. She made the mental effort, cut herself off from the ache and the hurt.

Hot tears rolled out of her eyes, blurring the image of the

red coals in the hearth. Astonished, her chest feeling scoured hollow and breathless, she clenched her fists and dug her nails hard into her palms. The tears fell faster; her breathing jerked.

—Ash?

"I can't rescue you. I don't know how!"

There is silence, in her mind.

—I can forgive you one broken promise, in a lifetime.

In her head, Godfrey Maximillian's voice is resonant.

—Do you remember, I told you that to leave the Church and travel with you was worth every hurt I have ever paid? Then, I loved you as a man loves. Now I am soul, not body; and I love you still. Ash, you are worth this.

"I never deserved that!"

—It does not come for that—although you have been true, good, and warmhearted to me, I do not love you for that reason. Only because you are who you are. I loved your soul before I ever loved you as a woman.

"For Christ's sake, shut up!"

—I have told you. I regret nothing, except that I still do not have all your trust.

"Oh, but you do." Ash covered her face with her hands, resting her head on her knees in the wet, warm darkness. "I trust you. If I ask you to do something, I trust you to do it. That makes it hard—it makes it impossible, to ask."

—What could you ask of me that I would not do?

A rueful, amused vulnerability is in the sound of his voice:

—Not that I can do much, now, child. Not as I am. But ask, and if I can, I will do it.

Hard as she tries to stop it, her breath comes in great sobs. She presses her hands to her mouth to stifle the noise.

"You—don't—understand yet—"

"Boss?"

She opened her eyes to see Rickard squatting beside her, his expression unguarded and appalled. Tears have run down her face. Her eyes are hot. When she makes to answer him, there is no sound; a constriction in her throat will not let words pass.

"You want something?" Rickard asked. He looked around helplessly. "What?"

"Stay at the door. No one's—" She spoke thickly. "*No one's* to enter until I say. I don't care who it is."

"Trust me, boss." The black-haired young man straightened up.

He is wearing armor that does not belong to him—a wounded man's fustian brigandine—and a wheel-pommel sword clatters at his side. It is not that, so much as the eyes, that are the difference; he looks wary, and much older than he did at Neuss.

"Thanks, Rickard."

"You call me," he said fiercely. "If you need something, you call me. Boss, can't I—"

"No!" She fumbled for her purse, pulling out a dirty kerchief and wiping her face. "No. It's my decision. I'll call you when I want you."

"Are you talking to Saint Godfrey?"

Tears spilled out of her eyes, an uprush that she could not check. *Why?* she thought, bewildered; *why can't I stop this? This isn't me; I don't weep.*

"Rickard, go away."

She balled the wet cloth of her kerchief between her two hands, and rested it against her eyes.

—I swear, child, you can ask nothing of me that I will not grant.

Godfrey Maximillian's voice, in her mind, is urgently, openly sincere. Too open: Ash presses the cloth harder against her eyes. After a second she can sit up, back straight, and stare into the graying coals.

"Yeah, and you asked me for help. Remember? I can't give it. Godfrey, I *am* going to ask you for something. If you prefer to think of it this way, I'm going to order you."

—Are you crying*? Ash, little one, what is it?*

"Just listen, Godfrey. Just listen."

She dragged in a breath. It caught, threatening to become a sob, and she knotted the kerchief in her hands, white-knuckled, and got control of her voice.

"You're the *machina rei militaris* now. Or part of it."

—Like the warp and weft of cloth, I think—and I have had long to consider the matter. Ash, why this grief?

"Do you remember what I said to you, when we were riding out to the desert, outside Carthage?"

—Not a particular thing—

Her breath came with a deep shudder. She interrupted sharply. "We were joking. I asked you for a miracle, a tiny miracle—'pray that the Stone Golem will break down'—something else, I don't remember what. And since then I've thought of nothing else but the Faris, killing the Faris to stop the Wild Machines."

—She does not speak to the Wild Machines, although I believe she hears them as they speak to her.

"The Faris isn't important." Ash opened her eyes again, not knowing until then that she had sought refuge in the dark. She reached out and picked up a rough-barked piece of wood, and leaned forward to bed it deep in the red ashes. "She *should* be killed, for safety, but I can't do it. They'll probably execute her here. That isn't important. The Wild Machines can talk Leofric's family into breeding another Faris, if they haven't already started. What's important is the Stone Golem."

There is no sound of Godfrey Maximillian's voice in her mind, but she can feel him waiting, feel his acceptance of her words into his self.

"We have to destroy the Wild Machines. We can't do it militarily in much under a year. We haven't got a year. We can kill my sister," Ash said, and felt her voice shake again. "But that doesn't buy us much time, and Burgundy may be a wasteland before then."

—Tell me nothing! If the great Devils are listening—

"You listen, Godfrey. The Stone Golem is the key. It's how they speak to Leofric and his family. It's how they speak to my sister. It's the channel they'll use, when they draw on the sun's power for their miracle."

—Yes.

He sounded cautiously puzzled, but not defensive. Ash's hands shook. She wiped wood ash off her fingers, onto her stained green hose. She heard her own voice continuing to speak, the tone calm and authoritative.

"One reason why I didn't give more consideration to the Stone Golem is that it's in Carthage, behind Gelimer's armies.

We failed, on the raid, and I believed we couldn't reach it to try again. I wasn't thinking."

A knot in the burning wood flared. The fire spat. Ash jolted, every muscle from spine to toe clenching. She rubbed her face with wood-ash-stained hands.

"Godfrey, the Stone Golem can be attacked. I don't have to reach it. None of us have to. You're already there. You're *part* of it."

—Ash . . .

I will think of him as a disembodied fragment. An unquiet spirit. Not a man I've loved as brother and father for as long as I can remember.

"Do a last tiny miracle," Ash said. "Destroy the Stone Golem. Break the link between it and my sister. Call down the weather to you. Call down the *lightning*—and fuse everything all into useless sand and glass!"

The place in her soul that is shared stays silent. Not long, a few heartbeats—she can feel her pulse shaking her body.

—Oh, Ash . . .

Pain sounded in his voice. Her chest ached. She rubbed it with a clenched fist. The anguish did not go away. Very steadily, she said aloud, "You're a priest. You *can* pray the lightning down."

—Suicide is a sin.

"That's why I'm telling you to do it, not asking you." She caught her breath on a sob again, that was almost a laugh. "I knew you'd say that. I think about these things. I don't want you damned. The minute it came to me, I knew it had to be at someone else's command. And it's mine; the responsibility is mine."

Chill air moved past her, flowing over the flagstones toward the chimney. She huddled deeper into her furs. A scrape of metal sounded from the door: the chape of Rickard's sword on masonry. Distant, down the spiral stairs, she heard voices.

In her head, there is silence.

"The other reason why it didn't come to me, I suppose," Ash said quietly, "is that as soon as it did, I would know what it meant. I know you. You got yourself killed in Carthage going back for Annibale Valzacchi, for God's sake, and this is more important than one man's life!"

—Yes. More important than one man's life.

"I didn't mean *your—*" Ash broke off. "I—yes. I do mean that. This will cut the Wild Machines off completely. They can't use the Faris, they won't even be able to talk to the Visigoths. They'll be dumb, powerless, until someone else can build a machine. That could take centuries. So yes, it's more important than one life, but when it's *you—*"

Wind rattled the shutters. Starlight penetrated faintly through cracks in the wood. That and the orange glow of the fire illuminated the familiar furniture of the command tent: armor stand, war chest, spare kit. The solitude of it bit into her, sharp as the freezing night.

"I've had to order people into places where I've known they were going to die," Ash said steadily. "I never knew how much I hated it until now. Losing you once was bad enough."

—I don't know if this can be done. But I will pray for God's grace, and attempt it.

"Godfrey—"

In the space that she shares with him, she feels a flood of bewilderment, fear, and courage, a terror that he cannot hide from her, and an equally strong determination.

—You will not leave me.

"No."

—God bless you. If He loves you as much as I do, He will give you a life, hereafter, with no more such grief in it. Now—

"Godfrey, not yet!"

—Will you make it my sin? If I wait, I will lose my courage. I must *do it now, while I can.*

What she wants to say is, To hell with it! I don't care what happens. I'll find some way to rescue you, make you human again; what do I care about the world? You're *Godfrey.*

The fire blurred in her vision. Tears ran down her cheeks.

What can I give you, out of what I am? Only this: that I can *do this. I can take this responsibility.*

"Call down the lightning," she said. "Do it now."

Her voice sounded flat, in the still, bitter air. She had a second to smear her eyes clear, to think *Bloody idiots he and I are going to look if this is all for nothing—*

In the center of her soul, Godfrey Maximillian spoke.

—By the grace of God, and by the love I have had for Your creations, I implore You to hear me, and grant my prayer.

It is the same voice that she has heard hundreds of times, at Lauds and Vespers and Matins, heard in camp and on the field, where men fighting have gone to their deaths listening to it. And it is the same voice that talked her asleep as a child, in the months after St. Herlaine, when any darkness had the power to keep her awake and shivering until sunrise.

"I'm here," she said. "Godfrey, I'm here."

His voice in her mind is unsteady, she feels the flood of fear in him. He prays on:

—Though I die, I shall not *die; I shall be with You, Lord God, and Your Saints. This is my faith, and I here proclaim it. Lord God, before Whom no armor can stand, Thou who art stronger than any sword—send down the fire!*

"Godfrey! *Godfrey!*"

What she remembers from Molinella, a child watching a battle from a church tower, is how the appalling explosion of cannon fire knocks the moment of impact out of memory. It must be reconstructed later. She tastes brick dust in her mouth again, smells poppies. A fang of pain bites at her hand. She snatches it back—from fire, from the burning wood in the hearth in the company's tower. Not Italy and summer, but Burgundy and the bitter solstice of winter.

She put one hand down to push herself up, realized that she was lying on her face, that she had soiled herself, that blood ran stickily down from her bitten lip.

"Godfrey . . ."

Blood dripped down onto the mattress, staining the straw's linen cover. Her arms began to shake. The muscles would not take her weight. She fell down on her face, shaking, the rub of cloth against cloth gratingly loud in the tower room where no explosion has taken place. Her ears sting: her whole body shakes with an impact that has not happened here.

"Godfrey!"

"Boss!" Rickard's boots clattered on the flagstones. She felt his hands on her shoulders, rolling her over on her back.

"I'm all right." She sat up, fingers trembling, body shaking. The boy has seen what happens in battle; she is not ashamed that he sees her now. Stunned, she gazed around at the stone hall. "Godfrey . . ."

"What's happened?" Rickard demanded. "Boss?"

"I felt him *die*." Her voice shook. "It's done, it's done now. I made him do it. Oh, Jesu. I made him."

A great pain went through her chest. Her hands would not stop shaking, though she clenched them into fists. She felt her face screw up. A sob forced its way past her rigid jaw.

She was not aware of Rickard running, panic-stricken, for the door of the hall, or of anyone else coming in; the first she knew of it was when a man grabbed her, hard. Weeping, stinking, incoherent; she could say nothing, only sob harder. The man put his arms tightly around her, gripping her close to him. She put her arms around his bulk and clung to him.

"Come on, girl! *Answer* me! What's happened?"

"Not—"

"Now," the voice insisted. A voice accustomed to orders. Robert Anselm.

"I'm okay." Hollow, every breath still shaking her, she pushed him far enough back that she could grab his hands in her own. "There's nothing you can do."

As her breathing steadied, Robert Anselm looked at her keenly. He was without armor, a stained demi-gown belted around his beer belly, had obviously been snatching what hours asleep that he could. The light from the fire illuminated, grotesquely, his shaven head and ears, and put deep shadows in his eye sockets.

"What's this 'Godfrey'? What's happened to Godfrey?" he rumbled.

"He's dead," Ash said. Her eyes glimmered. She gripped Anselm's hands hard. "Christ. Losing him twice. Jesu."

What Anselm said then, she ignored. There were other men crowding in at the far door: Rickard, her officers. She ignored all of it, clamped her eyes shut.

She feels cautiously in the part of herself that has been shared, since Molinella, with her voice.

"Godfrey?"

Nothing.

Quiet tears welled up and spilled over her lids. She felt them streaming down her face, hot in the freezing air. The ache in her throat tightened.

"Two thousand troops, in defense positions in a siege; three legions attacking: options?"

Nothing.

"Come on, you bastards. I know you're there. Talk to me!"

There is no sensation of pressure. No voices that mutter in the language of the Prophet Gundobad's time, or rage, deafeningly, to bring down walls and palaces. There are no Wild Machines. Only a sensation of blank, numb, empty silence.

For the first time in her adult life, Ash is without voices.

An egoistic part of her mind remarked, *I've lost what made me unique*; and she gave a shaky smile, part self-disgust and part acceptance.

She opened her eyes, bent down, and hauled on her long gown to conceal her soiled clothing. She straightened up, facing the officers that crowded into the hall: Angelotti; Geraint; Euen; Thomas Rochester; Ludmilla; a dozen more. Facing them now only as a young woman with a skilled trade, war; remarkable only for that, and for nothing else.

She said, "The Stone Golem is destroyed. Melted down to slag."

Silence fell, the men looking from one to the other, too stunned yet by the announcement to feel relief, joy, belief, victory.

"Godfrey did it," Ash said. "He prayed down lightning on House Leofric. I felt it hit. I—he died in the attack. But the Stone Golem's gone. The Wild Machines are cut off utterly. We're safe."

IV

"OF COURSE," ROBERT Anselm said sardonically, "that's 'safe' from the Wild Machines' miracle. Not safe from the three Visigoth legions sitting outside Dijon!"

The better part of an hour had gone by in the top floor of the company's tower, more lance leaders coming in by the minute, Burgundian knights and *centeniers* joining them; and Henri Brant and Wat Rodway between them breaking out a spirituous liquor that tasted like nothing on earth, but bit the tongue and throat and belly with heat. The frenetic celebrations spread down to the men on the lower two floors: Ash could hear the roaring racket below.

"The truce is still holding. I've told you. We're starting the fight back now, and we won't stop until we get to Carthage."

It was said largely for public consumption: for Jussey, Lacombe, Loyecte, de la Marche. Cleaned up and wearing borrowed hose, Ash stood and drank with her men, and felt nothing but numbness.

Celebration got into gear. The volume of noise rose. Faces flushed, Euen Huw and Geraint ab Morgan shouted joyously at each other in triumphant Welsh. Angelotti and half his gun-crew masters crowded closer to the fire, leather mugs full; someone called for Carracci and his recorder; Baldina and Ludmilla Rostovnaya began a drinking contest.

For them, Godfrey died three months ago.

Ash touched Robert Anselm's arm. "I'll be up at St. Stephen's."

He frowned, but nodded assent, too busy celebrating with two women from the baggage train.

Once outside the tower, the cold moved her to uncontrollable shivering. She huddled a cloak and hood over her gown, and walked, head down, shoulders hunched, at a pace brisk enough that her escort—who had been moderately warm in the guardroom—swore quietly to themselves. Black ice covered the cobbles; she almost fell four times before she reached the abbey.

Yellow light shone warmly through the high Gothic windows. As she stepped inside, the bells began to ring for Lauds.[57] The men-at-arms crowding in with her, she knelt at the back as the monks filed into the main chapel to sing the office.

You said I was a heathen, she mentally apostrophized Godfrey Maximillian. *You're right. This means nothing to me.*

She caught herself waiting for his answer.

With the office done, she made her way to the abbot's house.

"No need to disturb His Reverence," she told a deacon who did not look as though he were about to. "I know where to go. If you have food in the almonry, my men will be grateful."

"That is for the poor. You soldiers have the best rations as it is."

One of Ludmilla Rostovnaya's men muttered, "Because we're keeping them alive!" and subsided at Ash's glare.

"I won't be more than a few minutes."

Climbing the stairs, she did not ask herself why she had come. As soon as the monk on guard outside the room gave her a lamp to take in, and she saw the Faris's face in its light, she knew why she was there.

The Faris stood by the window. The northern stars wheeled in the sky behind her. Her face in the golden light showed tired, drawn, but relieved.

Neither Violante nor Adelize was asleep. The child seemed to be soothing the woman, as if there had been an outburst. The piebald rat scuttled across the pile of blankets, raised itself up on its hind feet, whiskers quivering, and niffed at the chill air that came in with Ash.

Ash pushed the door closed behind her.

---

[57] 3 A.M.

The numbness in her mind felt colder than the winter outside.

"My voice is gone. There is no *machina rei militaris*. As if an explosion, in my mind—" The Faris came forward into the room. Boards creaked under her feet. Her steps were unsteady. "You heard it, too."

"I gave the order."

The Visigoth woman scowled. She put her hand to her head. Ash saw comprehension come.

"Your confessor. Your Father Maximillian."

Ash dropped her gaze. She took a few steps closer to her mother, where Adelize sat in the blankets. She did not touch her, but she squatted down and held out her fingers to the piebald rat. It stood up on its hind legs and licked, twice, very rapidly, at her fingers.

"Hey, Lickfinger. You can tell which are the boys, can't you? Balls as big as hazelnuts." Ash's tone changed. She said, "I've lost my friend."

The Faris came to kneel on the blankets beside her, putting her arm around Violante. The child's thin body was shivering. "I thought I was dying. Then—silence. The blessed, blessed quiet."

The liver-and-white rat elongated his body, stretching up to sniff at Adelize. She flicked a frightened glance from the rat to her daughter the Faris.

"I frightened her, I think." The Faris met Ash's gaze. "It's over, isn't it?"

"Yes. Oh, the war's not over." Ash jerked her head at the night sky beyond the window. "We could be dead tomorrow. But unless someone builds another Stone Golem before the armies of Christendom get to Carthage, it's over. The Wild Machines can't use you for anything. They can't reach you."

The Faris rested her head in her hands. Cut silver hair flopped over her brow. Muffled, she said, "I do not care how it was done. I am sorry for your friend. I only knew his voice. But I do not care how it was done. I thank God for it."

She straightened. Her familiar features, in the lamp's light, are blurred with tears, incongruous on that face as water on a knife blade.

I had to be the one to bring you the news, Ash realized.

I had to see you realize that Florian has no reason, now, to have you killed. And every useful reason to keep you alive.

"You're safe," Ash said. To Adelize, and to Violante, she repeated: "You're safe."

The child stared at her uncomprehendingly. Adelize, reassured, picked up thc rat and began to pet him.

"Well. I say 'safe.' Apart from the fact that there's a war on." Ash grinned crookedly.

"Apart from that," the Faris echoed. She smiled. "It's over. My God. I still don't know what you're doing with my face."

"It looks better on me."

The Visigoth woman laughed, as if laughter had taken her by surprise.

A cold, very deliberate, and multiple voice said in Ash's head, 'THE FACE IS NOTHING. THE BREEDING IS EVERYTHING.'

Ash said, "Bollocks," automatically, and froze.

A spurt of sickness went through her, sinking from her belly to her gut. Dizzy with it, she said, "*No . . .*"

'THE SECRET BREEDING IS ALL.'

"*No!*" Her protest is squealing outrage.

'SOME HAVE THE QUALITY WE NEED. SOME DO NOT.'

"Godfrey!"

Nothing.

In the part of her mind that is shared, that has been numb, only the voices of the Wild Machines sound—like a muttering of distant thunder; far off at first, and now perfectly distinct.

'—SOME DO NOT. AND SOME HAVE MORE.'

"He didn't do it. No. No: I *felt* it. I felt the machine die. He didn't destroy it *all*—?"

Ash became aware of the Faris shaking her arm. The Visigoth woman was staring at her in alarm.

"What are you saying?" the Faris demanded. "Who are you talking to?"

The voices of the Wild Machines speak in Ash's head:

'WE COULD NOT HAVE DONE THIS WITH THE FARIS—'

'—SHE NEEDED THE *MACHINA REI MILITARIS*—'

'GONE, NOW. GONE!'

'BUT WITH YOU—'

'—AH, WITH YOU!'

'—WE HAVE KNOWN SINCE YOU CAME TO US.'

'SPOKE TO THE *MACHINA*, WHEN YOU WERE IN MIDST OF US.'

'CALLED OUT, IN THE DESERT SOUTH, ALMOST WITHIN TOUCH OF US—!"

'—ESTABLISHED THE DIRECT LINK WITH US—'

'—WITH YOU, WE DO NOT NEED THE *MACHINA REI MILITARIS*.'

'WE NEED ONLY THE DEATH OF SHE WHO BEARS THE DUCAL BLOOD!'

Ash yelled, "Can't you hear them?"

"Hear them?" the Faris repeated.

"The machines! The fucking machines! Can't you *hear*—"

'—US. WE, WHO HEARD YOU SPEAK WITH THE GOLEM-COMPUTER, WHEN YOU RODE AMONGST US, IN THE SOUTH—'

'—WHO SPOKE TO *US*.'

'WE DID NOT NEED YOU THEN.'

'WE HAD OUR OTHER CHILD.'

'BUT WE KNEW THAT, IF SHE FAILED US—WE COULD REACH YOU.'

'—SPEAK WITH YOU—'

'COMPEL YOU, AS WE COULD HAVE COMPELLED HER—'

'AS SOON AS OUR ARMIES KILL THE DUCHESS FLORIA, WE CAN TAKE OUR FINAL STEP.'

Deafened, appalled, Ash began to repeat aloud the speech that thunders in her head:

" 'Then we will change reality, so that humankind does not exist, never *has* existed, after a point ten thousand years ago. There will only ever have been machine consciousness, throughout all the history that has been and all the history that is to come—' "

The Faris interrupted. "What are you talking about!"

Kneeling on threadbare blankets, in an upper room not warmed by any fire, in the exhausted early hours of the winter morning, Ash studied the face of the woman kneeling beside her. The same face, eyes, body. But not mind.

Ash stared at the Faris. "You're not hearing this."

'SHE NEEDED THE GOLEM-COMPUTER. YOUR SISTER NO LONGER HEARS OUR VOICES.'

Dry-lipped, Ash said, "But I do."

"You do what?" the Faris demanded. A shrill note invaded her voice, as if she would willfully not understand. She sat back on her heels, away from Ash.

Ash began to shake. Winter's cold bites deep. Violante stared at her. Adelize, as if her daughter's tone disturbed her, cautiously reached out and touched Ash's arm.

Ash ignored her.

"I still hear the Wild Machines. Without the Stone Golem," she said. Immediate realization hit her. "Godfrey. He did that for nothing. He's died for nothing. And I told him to do it."

'YOUR BIRTH: ONLY LUCK—'

'—A FLUKE; A CAST OF FORTUNE—'

'YOU CAN DO NOTHING BUT THIS. BUT IT IS ENOUGH.'

The multiple, inhuman voices whisper in her mind:

'ASH. YOU ARE THE SUCCESSFUL EXPERIMENT, NOT YOUR SISTER.'

[original e-mail documents found inserted, folded, in British Library copy of 3rd edition, *Ash: The Lost History of Burgundy*, (2001) — possibly in chronological order of editing original typescript?]

Message: #423 (Anna Longman)
Subject: Ash
Date: 20/12/00 at 05.44 p.m.
From: Ngrant@

format address deleted
other details encrypted by
non-discoverable personal key

Anna--

Fifty-seven hours straight. I slept twice: once for two hours and once for three. I think I shall be able to get through the last of it (if only in first draft English) in one go. Then we shall see what we have. I'll send the whole thing through when I get to the end.

My God. Poor Ash.

I woke up actually shouting aloud. DELENDA EST CARTHAGO! "Carthage must be destroyed."

I thought it was the cold that had woken me—nights are bitter here, even with the heating—but no, it was that: words that I can't get out of my head.

I keep thinking of Vaughan Davies' metaphor, of human existence in the past picked up and shaken—as if it were all a jigsaw, falling back together again with the same pieces but in a different order. If we find "delendam esse Carthaginem" put by Florus into the mouth of a Roman senator; if we read in Pliny, now, that Cato ". . . cum clamaret omni senatu Carthaginem delendum" ("that he vociferated at every [meeting of the] Senate [that] Carthage [was] to be destroyed"), then—where was it before?

Here, with Ash. Who no longer exists, except in what I suppose I must begin to call the First History. A first history overwritten, like a file, with a later arrangement of the data: our 'second' history.

Although fragments of the data remain in OUR history, OUR past, I have seen them fading. She has become myth, legend, fiction.

Even though, as I read, I hear her speaking to me.

Blame lack of sleep. If I'm beginning to dream in Latin, it's no great surprise. I'm eating, sleeping, and breathing the Sible Hedingham manuscript. It is—I am convinced—it IS our 'previous' history.

Tami Inoshishi and James Howlett came for another question session. I doubt they got much sense out of me. From what I can tell, they are perfectly happy with the theory that there may have existed, at one time, a genetic mutation which enabled the possible states of the universe to be consciously collapsed into something less probable than an average—into a 'miracle', in short. A non-Newtonian alteration of reality.

They don't have much trouble with the theoretical idea that one massive change of this sort could take place, and the genetic mutation itself be one of the things that was rendered non-actual.

What Tami, in particular, kept hammering on at me about—in that unstoppable way she has—is the fact that evidence is both being eradicated (the Angelotti manuscript) and coming back (Carthage).

I have told her my theory: that BOTH the 'Wild Machines' and Burgundy must have been wiped out. If nothing else, it is the only theory that can explain why we are not non-existent ourselves, and the world the province of silicon machine intelligences; and why we do not have, in our history, a Visigoth Empire. Why the Arab and black African cultures appear to have been "patched in", in place of the Visigoths, after the change.

We are used to history affecting us only in the sense that past actions affect us all. History may be reinterpreted: it does not alter. THIS history is still affecting us now. We are changing, now. I do not understand why.

Things ARE changing. That's what bothers Tami. The ROVs are 1000 metres down, clearing debris with pressurised jets. And Carthage is there. Now. Again.

That said, Tamiko has pointed out, from my last translated section of the Sible Hedingham manuscript, a further confusion—that, in the manuscript, the Stone Golem is destroyed. And yet, we have the Stone Golem. We discovered it *intact*, in Carthage.

If the Sible Hedingham ms. is in error on the point, that shakes my whole confidence in it! How much else could be wrong?

Can it be document error? Or is this a different golem—had King-Caliph Gelimer already advanced a programme to produce more; was House Leofric advanced enough to create another one—more than one? Or is there something in this hellishly impenetrable bad Mediaeval Latin that I've translated wrongly? Or, is there something in the remaining part of the Sible Hedingham manuscript that explains this?

I will sleep for four hours, then continue the translation.

--Pierce

- -

Message: #234 (Pierce Ratcliff)
Subject: Ash
Date: 20/12/00 at 11.22 p.m.
From: Longman@

format address deleted
other details encrypted and
non-recoverably deleted

Pierce--

Send me whatever you have, I'll look at it over the Christmas break.

I'm going down to see William Davies again, later today.

He phoned to tell me he's been reading some of the Sible Hedingham manuscript aloud to his brother. He told me he did a lot after the war on the psychology of trauma; he got interested in it as part of the recovery from surgery.

He _thinks_ Vaughan is reacting to hearing it, even in the original Latin. The problem is, William only knows medical Latin; Mediaeval Latin isn't like that of any other period; he doubts he's deciphering it properly—Pierce, basically he wants to know if he can have access to your English translation.

I know how you feel about confidentiality. William wouldn't breach that. Can I do this?

--Anna

- -

Message: #428 (Anna Longman)
Subject: Ash
Date: 21/12/00 at 12.02 p.m.
From: Ngrant@

format address deleted
other details encrypted by
non-discoverable personal key

Anna--

Isobel's team are bringing up the Stone Golem.

I thought it would take months, but it seems it can be raised pretty damn fast when it looks like the Tunisian government might be about to take the opportunity away from us.

The sky is full of helicopters, and the military have a patrol ship on station. At the land site, a lot of the local arrangements for food and transport have dried up. Colonel ████ arrived back there, far less jovial, and with far more men. Trucks all over the place. 'Perimeter security', he says. They haven't had any severe security problems in the last weeks, so why now? Why all these men in uniform, who don't care WHERE they put their feet?

Isobel says Minister ████ is becoming concerned about 'Western exploitation of local cultural resources'. Well, as a Westerner, I hardly expect to be popular in this part of the world, and I can see their point. But, Isobel signed a contract with the government when this expedition was first mooted, agreeing that no artefacts should be removed from Tunisian territory. What kind of a person do they think she is?

Cynicism might lead one to think this is all about who will gain financially, but I may be doing the Minister a disservice. Whether his concern is genuine or not—and I suspect it is perfectly genuine—what I can't see is any way of pointing out that this site's remains are not from HIS culture!

I have had to leave the translation. I have to be here when they bring up the Stone Golem.

You have my full permission to show this partial translation of the Sible Hedingham ms. to William Davies. If it helps Vaughan Davies, then that would only be a small repayment for the debt of scholarship we owe to him.

--Pierce

Message: #236 (Pierce Ratcliff)
Subject: Ash
Date: 21/12/00 at 01.07 p.m.
From: Longman@

format address deleted other details encrypted and non-recoverably deleted

Pierce--

I'm worried. When I got back from East Anglia, I found that someone had broken in and been through my personal files. And my hard disk. When I got to the office this morning—same thing. And not like a burglary. Too neat.

I think I would just have stayed puzzled if I hadn't phoned a friend of mine. Yes, I'm in a fairly obscure area of academic publishing, but I do have friends in investigative journalism. He's one of them. His first reaction was, this must be some kind of 'security' thing.

I hadn't thought it through, before. The Middle East has been nothing but terrorism and war for years; if you have found something on the seabed that records say isn't there—my friend suggests there are bound to be 'spooks'. People are bound to be investigating, aren't they? Especially if the news is getting out.

Pierce, I KNOW this sounds alarmist. But it wasn't just somebody breaking in and trashing my place. Depending on how you feel about being interviewed by security people, if you've been keeping copies of these messages, you might want to wipe your (or Isobel's) disk. And if you've got hardcopies, shred them.

I don't usually keep copies of my mail, I don't have the disk space, but I do usually keep a paper copy in a file. Because you were so concerned about academic confidentiality, I've been even more careful; hence public-key encryption of the actual messages. In fact, I had taken the paper copies in a folder down to the sheltered accommodation in Colchester with me, yesterday, thinking I might need them to refresh my memory if Vaughan did finally say something—you know I'm not an academic myself. So I still have them.

I'm putting them in store, somewhere safe. If this IS something official, then they can come to me officially, with a warrant. Then it's fine. But not before.

I'm going to talk to the MD in an hour, see what his position on this is. He'd better stand by me on this one.

--Anna

Message: #430 (Anna Longman)
Subject: Ash
Date: 22/12/00 at 09.17 a.m.
From: Ngrant@

format address deleted
other details encrypted by
non-discoverable personal key

Anna--

We're out.

Things have been so confused, I don't know if it's been on the media, given Christmas will be taking over the UK—we're supposed to be out of Tunisian territory completely now, they don't even like us hanging about in offshore waters.

I'm putting this out on the net to as many people as I can reach. Talk to your media contacts. Kick up a fuss. They CAN'T shut this site off from scientific excavation! They can't KIDNAP archaeological evidence! It just isn't right: we have to know.

On consideration, of course, we don't 'have' to. That is a preoccupation very much of our time. 'Nothing must stand in the way of the discovery of the truth.' In other parts of history, of course, there are other priorities: 'nothing is as important as' ideology, say, or commerce, or military force.

GOD DAMN IT, I WANT TO KNOW. They can't do this to us!

--Pierce

Message: #240 (Pierce Ratcliff)
Subject: Ash
Date: 22/12/00 at 10.04 a.m.
From: Longman@

format address deleted
other details encrypted and
non-recoverably deleted

Pierce--

Had you got the Stone Golem up from the ruins of Carthage? Where is the messenger-golem from the land site? Pierce, what is happening, I can't do anything if I don't know the _facts_.

--Anna

Message: #431 (Anna Longman)
Subject: Ash
Date: 22/12/00 at 11.13 a.m.
From: Ngrant@

format address deleted
other details encrypted by
non-discoverable personal key

Anna--

Sorry, yes you need to know, too busy talking to every contact I have, if there's no other pressure we can bring to bear, at least let's have the academic community and the media on our side!

Isobel's team had barely STARTED their analysis of the Stone Golem. When I got there, they had it in the holding tank; there was an argument going on about some minor damage that had been done—or not done—by the divers. It can't have been much more than two hours after that when the Tunisian navy moved in and confiscated everything. Everything apart from what Isobel and her people had on their backs! They stripped the ship bare. They removed the holding tank, and the Stone Golem.

I cannot BELIEVE this has happened. There was no need. I know Isobel: she will have had no INTENTION of removing any artefacts from Tunisian jurisdiction.

But there is one thing I can say without any possible contradiction—I saw it with my own eyes.

When I first reached the Stone Golem in the holding tank, I was quite literally speechless. Sound echoing off metal, light rippling off water, all the sounds of a modern ship at sea—and there, in the middle of it, in the tank, this great carved larger-than-human figure. With its plinth, it must weigh tons; I have every respect for the team who raised it from the seabed.

What I'd seen through the cameras didn't prepare me for seeing it in reality. As you know, I'd seen it covered in debris, with a film of silt over it from the ROVs moving around, and encrusted with undersea life. By the time I got to the ship, a section had been cleaned up, and Isobel herself was in the tank working on others.

The MACHINA REI MILITARIS. Sightless eyes staring. Hinged bronze joints clustered thickly with verdigris. This much, as you know, had been visible underwater, on camera. The whole of it wasn't clear.

Now it is.

The face, the limbs, the plinth: the SHAPE of all of them was clear on camera. But what we've been seeing has only been the surface-encrustations. With the encrustations removed, it's become possible to see the surface of the stone.

Some of it still IS stone. The team says it was all originally a silicon-based conglomerate of some kind.

Ninety per cent of it is VITRIFIED silicon. Glass.

At the front, which is what we've been seeing on the image-enhancers, the shape of the head and the front of the torso are clear. Most of the rest of it, including the plinth, is melted. Silt and sandstone fused into heavy, brittle glass. It has FLOWED.

Silicon sand turns to glass if you put it under sufficiently high temperatures. Imagine the strength of the lightning-discharge that could have done this; a bolt that would have—that did, from the underwater images—crack the building in which it stood wide open.

An electrical discharge powerful enough to sear the whole of this artefact into vitrified sand. The internal structure melted into impure, light-shattering, water-reflecting glass: I saw Isobel's face reflected in it like a mirror.

It IS the Stone Golem. It HAS been destroyed, in exactly the way that the chronicle relates. Anna, this archaeological evidence backs up this manuscript. The Sible Hedingham ms. is our first history.

I can only pray that this is a temporary aberration on behalf of the government. I am happy for any artefact to remain in Tunisia, as long as Isobel's people have permission to carry on their analysis. A silicon computor. Even a destroyed one. What we can learn

Interruptions. More later.

--Pierce

Message: #241 (Pierce Ratcliff)
Subject: Ash
Date: 22/12/00 at 02.24 p.m.
From: Longman@

format address deleted
other details encrypted and
non-recoverably deleted

Pierce--

I'm worried I haven't heard from you. Where are you? Are you still on the expedition ship? Mail me, phone me, something.

--Anna

Message: #447 (Anna Longman)
Subject: Ash
Date: 22/12/00 at 06.00 P.M.
From: Ngrant@

format address deleted
other details encrypted by
non-discoverable personal key

Anna--

Still on ship, but I'm having to coax my way to accessing communications. The Tunisian patrol boat on station has been joined by two more. You have no IDEA how much this scares me. The idea of being caught up in an actual 'incident'—I know, as a biographer, one gets immersed in one's subject; this has cured me of any idea I might have had that I could have lived Ash's life.

Isobel says the British Embassy here has been in contact to suggest WE stop causing trouble. God help me, I know the Mediterranean is a sensitive area, but that's a bit rich! I wish I had a contact in the Foreign Office. Knowing several advisory professors on security affairs may help, but it's going to take time for me to get in touch with them.

Tami's colleague James Howlett informs me that the net traffic on this subject is now being 'monitored', and to make sure I am always encrypted. I suppose he knows. I suppose it will be. What HAPPENED? Something that to me is an interesting matter of high physics is apparently making governmental agencies (as Howlett put it) 'shit themselves stupid'!

Please, can you take time to talk with Vaughan Davies again, if he can talk at all? I am mentally putting together a provenance for the Sible Hedingham ms. There could be a connection between the ms., Hedingham Castle, the Earls of Oxford, and Ash's connection with the thirteenth earl, John de Vere. Vaughan Davies might shed light on this.

Far more crucially, for the immediate present—in his Second Edition, he promised us an Addendum, detailing the link between the 'First History' and our present day. He never published it before he disappeared. I think the time has come when I have to know what his theory is.

Plainly, we have to face the possibility now that reality did fracture in or about the beginning of the year 1477. Equally plainly, it is possible that fragments of that prior history have existed in ours, becoming gradually less and less 'real' as the universe moves on from the moment of fracture. I can accept this, and so can the theoretical physicists: both Burgundy and the Wild Machines obliterated in some catastrophic 'miracle', the Visigoths and the Wild Machines completely, Burgundy leaving a dream of a lost country behind it.

What is more difficult to accept, but is undeniably the case, given the underwater site, is that the universe is STILL changing. Reading what Vaughan Davies wrote in 1939, it seems to me that he knew this, then, and had developed a theory about why it is happening.

I want to know what it is. HIS theory may be right or wrong, but *I* don't have a theory at all! If I have to fly back from here, I will be asking you if William Davies will give permission for me to visit his brother.

--Pierce

Message: #244 (Pierce Ratcliff)
Subject: Ash
Date: 22/12/00 at 06.30 P.M.
From: Longman@

format address deleted
other details encrypted and
non-recoverably deleted

Pierce--

Please be CAREFUL. You never think it will happen to someone you know. It only takes some trigger-happy madman, a soldier with a rifle, by the time the governments apologise, it's too late. I don't want to turn on satellite news and watch a bulletin telling me you've been killed.

--Anna

Message: #246 (Pierce Ratcliff)
Subject: Ash
Date: 23/12/00 at 09.50 P.M.
From: Longman@

format address deleted
other details encrypted and
non-recoverably deleted

Pierce--

Damn: still no mail from you. I hope no news is etc.

There isn't much of a media fuss yet. It was well-timed, thinking about it; everyone's caught up in pre-Christmas frenzy here.

Weekend traffic's difficult (Christmas falling on the Monday), but I went down to Colchester again. I don't know what kind of a shock it would have to be to make a person wipe out all their memories after the age of fifteen. Profound trauma, William says. Perhaps fifteen was the last time Vaughan was happy. I hate to think what reduced him to this state.

William and I are taking it in turns to read your translation of the Sible Hedingham manuscript aloud to him. William is optimistic. I'm not sure Vaughan's taking it in. But William's the medical man, after all.

I intend to go down again tomorrow, and spend as much time over Christmas as I can with them, with Vaughan in the hospital, doing intensive reading. I'll watch the news broadcasts, and monitor e-mail. You can always reach me at work or home e-mail (which is, or you can phone, if you can get a line. My number is, ██████, ██████.

--Anna

Message: #247 (Pierce Ratcliff)
Subject: Ash
Date: 24/12/00 at 11.02 P.M.
From: Longman@

format address deleted
other details encrypted and
non-recoverably deleted

Pierce--

We have our breakthrough.

It was a bit of a shock. The doctors have taken William into hospital here overnight for observation. He's a rotten patient, but I think retired medical men often are. I've been zipping around between his ward and the neurological ward where Vaughan is; I'm completely worn to a frazzle; but I don't think William's in any real danger now.

It just breaks my heart to see him there. When he's awake, he's a sharp old man; when you see him asleep in a hospital bed, you can see how frail he is. I guess I've come to like him a lot. I never knew either of my grandfathers.

Vaughan is quiet now. I'm not sure if he's still under sedation or sleeping naturally.

I'm in the waiting room, sitting among the sad Christmas decorations, typing on my notebook-portable, drinking the appalling black coffee that comes out of the machine. Every so often the nurses come around and give me _that look_. I'll have to go soon, to drive back through the Christmas Eve traffic, but I don't want to leave until the doctors give William the final OK.

It's not like they have any other next of kin.

William was the one reading when it happened. It was during part of the Fraxinus manuscript, the section on what happens to Ash in Carthage. He reads very well. (I have _no_ idea whether he thinks this is 'history' or complete rubbish.) Vaughan was listening, I think, although it's been difficult to tell. He has a lean face, and I think must have been good-looking when he was a young man. Very arrogant. No, not arrogant; it's a look I've seen in old pre-war movies, a kind of outrageous confidence, you don't see it any more. An English class thing, I guess. And Vaughan thinks he's fifteen. Has there ever been a rich boy that age who didn't think he was God's gift?

All of a sudden, that face sort of _crumpled_. I was watching, and it was like sixty years just dropping down on him, like a weight. He said, "William?" As if William hadn't visited him every day. "William, may I beg you to pass me a mirror?"

I wouldn't have done it, but it wasn't up to me. William passed him a mirror from the bedside cabinet. I got up to call a nurse—I was half expecting Vaughan Davies to go into hysterics. Wouldn't you? If you thought you were fifteen, and saw the face of a man in his 80s?

All he did was look at himself in the mirror and nod. Once. As if it confirmed something he had already thought. He put the mirror down on the bed and said, "Perhaps a daily paper?"

It staggered me, but William reached over and picked up a paper left by one of the other patients. Vaughan examined it very carefully—what I think, now, is that he was puzzled because it was a tabloid, not a broadsheet—and glanced at the headlines, and the masthead. He said two things: "No war, then?" and "I am to assume victory was ours, or else I should be reading this in German."

I don't think I took in the next few sentences. William was asking questions, I know, and Vaughan was answering in this amazed tone, a 'why are you asking me all these stupid questions?' voice, and I remember just thinking, Vaughan doesn't like his brother very much. What a shame, after sixty years.

The next thing I can remember is Vaughan saying testily, "Of course I wasn't injured in the bombing. What on earth would make you think such a thing?" He'd picked up the mirror and was studying himself again. "I have no scars. Where did you get yours?"

If he'd been my brother I would have slapped him.

William ignored it, and went through the neurological report stuff, and told him he'd been locked up in a home for years—which isn't something I'd have sprung on somebody, but he still knows his brother, even after all these years, because Vaughan just _looked_ at him, and said, "Really? How curious." And, in a voice like I'd just crawled out from under a rock, "Who is this young person?"

"This young lady," William says, "is assisting the man who is rewriting your mediaeval book."

I expected him to go nuclear at that point, especially as William wasn't being untactful by accident. No wonder those two didn't live under a family roof. I braced myself for a screaming row. It didn't come.

Vaughan Davies picked up the tabloid paper again and held it at arm's length. It took me several seconds to realise he was looking for the date, and that he couldn't read the small print. I told him what date it was.

Vaughan Davies said, "No. The month is July, and the year, nineteen forty."

William leaned over and took the paper away from him. He said, "Rubbish. You never were unintelligent. Look around you. You have been in a traumatised state, conceivably since July nineteen forty, but it is now over sixty years from that date."

"Yes," Vaughan says, "evidently. I was not in a state of trauma, however. Young woman, you should warn your employer. If he continues to pursue his researches, he will end where my researches brought me, and I would not wish that upon my worst enemy—had I one yet alive."

He was looking mildly pleased at this point. It took William to point out to me, in a whisper, that Vaughan had just realised that he'd probably outlived all his academic rivals.

William then said, "If you weren't in a state of trauma, where have you been? Where is it that you suspect Doctor Ratcliff will end up?"

As you know, the paperwork following Vaughan Davies around the asylums is intact. He _is_ William's brother. The family resemblance is too close for anything else. I mean, we _know_ where he's been. I wondered where he_ thought_ he'd been. California? Australia? The moon? To be honest, if Vaughan had said he'd stepped out of a time machine—or even walked back into our 'second history' after visiting your 'first history', I don't think I'd have been surprised!

But time travel isn't an option. The past is not a country we can visit. And the 'first history' doesn't exist any more, as you say. It was overwritten; wiped out in the process.

If I've understood it, the truth is much less exciting, much more sad.

"I have been nowhere," Vaughan said. "And I have been nothing."

He didn't look sharp any more, the acidic expression was gone. He just looked like a thin old man in a hospital bed. Then he said impatiently, "I have not been real."

Something about it, I can't explain what, it was utterly chilling. William just stared at him. Then Vaughan looked at me.

He said, "You seem to have some apprehension of what I mean. Can it be that this Doctor Ratcliff of yours has replicated my work to that degree?"

All I could do was say, "Not real?" For some reason, I thought he meant that he'd been dead. I don't know why. When I said that, he just glared at me.

"Nothing so simple," he said. "Between the summer of nineteen forty and what you claim to be the latter part of the year two thousand, I have been—merely potential."

I can't remember his exact words, but I remember that. Merely potential. Then he said something like:

"What is unreal may be made real, instant by instant. The universe creates a present out of the unaligned future, produces a past as solid as granite. And yet, young lady, that is not all. What is real may be made unreal, potential, merely possible. I have not been in a state of trauma. I have been in a state of unreality."

All I could do was point at him in the bed. "And then be made real again?"

He said, "Mind your manners, young woman. It is impolite to point."

That took my breath away, but he didn't stay vinegary for long. His colour got bad. William rang the bell for the nurse. I stepped back and put my hands behind me, to try and stop aggravating him.

He was grey as a worn bed-sheet, but he still carried on talking. "Can you imagine what it might be like, to perceive not only the infinite possible realities that might take shape out of universal probability, but to perceive that you, yourself, the mind that thinks these thoughts—that you are unreal? Only probable, not actual. Can you imagine such a sensation of your own unreality? To know that you are not mad, but trapped in something from which you cannot escape? You say sixty years. For me, it has been one infinite moment of eternal damnation."

Pierce, the trouble is, I CAN imagine it. I know you need to get Isobel's theoretical physicists over here to talk to Vaughan Davies, because I don't have a scientific understanding. But I can imagine it enough to know what made him go grey.

I just stood there, staring at him, trying to stop a hysterical giggle or a shudder, or both; and all I could think was, No one ever asked Schrodinger's Cat what it felt like while it was in the box.

"But you're real _now_," I said. "You're real _again_."

He leaned back on the pillow. William was fussing, so I bent down to try and soothe him, and Vaughan's forearm hit me across the mouth. I've never been so shocked. I stood up, about to rip off a mouthful at him, and he hadn't hit me, his eyes had rolled up in his head, and he was fitting, his arms and legs jerking all over the place.

I ran for a nurse and all but fell over the one coming in the door.

That must have been a couple of hours ago now. I wanted to get it down while it was clear in my memory. I may be out by a few words, but I think it's as close to the truth as I can get.

You can say it's senile dementia, or you can say he might have been a boozy old dosser for years and rotted his brain, but I don't think so. I don't know if there are words for what happened to him, but if there are, he's got doctorates in history and the sciences, and he's the person best qualified to know. If he says he's existed in a state of probability for the past sixty years, I believe him.

It's all part of what you said, isn't it? The Angelotti manuscript vanishing, being classified as history, then Romance, then fiction. And Carthage coming back, where there was no seabed site before.

I wish Vaughan had stayed with it long enough to tell me why he thinks he's "come back" now. Why NOW?

I've been thinking, sitting here. If Vaughan was going to 'come back', it's _possible_ for him to have had amnesia. The same way that it's _possible_ for him to have vanished without trace. So this is just a different possible state of the universe. This is what he is, now, here—but before 'now' was made concrete, it was possible for other things to have happened to him. His disappearance could have meant anything.

It's one thing to talk about lumps of rock and physical artefacts coming back, Pierce. It's another thing when it's a person.

I feel as if nothing under my feet is solid. As if I could wake up tomorrow and the world might be something else, my job would be different, I might not be 'Anna', or an editor; I might have married Simon at Oxford, or I might have been born in America, or India, or anywhere. It's all _possible_. It didn't happen that way, it isn't real, but it _might_ have happened.

Like ice breaking up under my feet.

I am frightened.

Vaughan's old, Pierce. If people are going to talk to him, it ought to be as soon as possible. If he becomes conscious again, and he's alert, I will ask him about his theory that you mentioned. I'll have to go by the medical advice. I'll ask him how he got the Sible Hedingham manuscript. Maybe tomorrow—no, it's holiday season.

Contact me. WHAT DO YOU WANT TO DO ABOUT THIS?

--Anna

Message: #248 (Pierce Ratcliff)
Subject: Ash
Date: 25/12/00 at 02.37 a.m.
From: Longman@

format address deleted
other details encrypted and
non-recoverably deleted

Pierce--

Did you get my last message?

Could you get in contact with me, just to reassure me?

--Anna

Message: #249 (Pierce Ratcliff)
Subject: Ash
Date: 25/12/00 at 03.01 a.m.
From: Longman@

format address deleted
other details encrypted and
non-recoverably deleted

Pierce--

Are you downloading your mail? Are you reading your mail? Is anybody reading this?

--Anna

Message: #250 (Pierce Ratcliff)
Subject: Ash
Date: 25/12/00 at 07.16 a.m.
From: Longman@

format address deleted
other details encrypted and non-recoverably deleted

Pierce--

These messages must be stacking up. For God's sake answer.

--Anna

Message: #251 (Pierce Ratcliff)
Subject: Ash
Date: 25/12/00 at 09.00 a.m.
From: Longman@

format address deleted
other details encrypted and non-recoverably deleted

Pierce--

I have been phoning the British Embassy. I _finally_ got through. No one there is prepared to give me any information. The university switchboard is closed, I can't get a contact number for Isobel Napier-Grant. I can't get through to you. No news station wants to know: it's the holiday. Please ANSWER ME.

--Anna

Transmission of following document file LOSTBURG.DOC recorded at 25/12/00 at 09.31 a.m.

No additional transmissions received at this time.

PART FOUR

26 December AD 1476–5 January AD 1477

LOST BURGUNDY[58]

[58]Final section of the Sible Hedingham mss. (PR)

I

"AND NOW," ASH said, "you need to order *my* execution."

Light leaked through the unshuttered windows into the ducal chambers—the feast of St. Stephen dawning late, to a blistering cold. Freezing damp infested the air, penetrating any bare skin; drafts blew in around the shutters and hangings.

"Are you *sure* you hear them?" Florian persisted.

'IT REQUIRES NOTHING BUT TIME NOW: OUR TIME FAST APPROACHES—'

"Yes, I'm sure!" Ash banged her sheepskin mittens together, hoping for feeling in her numb fingers.

"Have you told anyone else yet? That the end of the *machina rei militaris* means nothing?"

"No. I didn't want to spoil their party."

"Ah." Florian attempted a smile. "*That's* what it was. I thought it was a night attack by the Visigoths . . ."

Her color altered, and she leaned one arm up against the wall for support, the thin gray light of the dawn illuminating her. The velvet hem of her gown trailed across bare flagstones—no rushes, now. She did not wear the hart's-horn crown, but the carved Briar Cross hung at her breast, half-lost in her unpointed doublet and the yellow linen of her shirt. Over everything, she wore a great robe made from wolf pelts, heavy enough to weigh down a man.

"You look rough," Ash said.

With the growing light, Ash saw that the wall against which the surgeon leaned was painted—richly, as becomes a royal Duke—with figures of men and women and tiny towns on hilltops. Each of the figures danced hand in hand with another: cardinal, carpenter, knight, merchant; peasant, tottering old man, pregnant girl, and crowned king. Bony hand in their hands, white skeletons led them off, all equal, into death. Florian del Guiz leaned her forehead against the cold stone, oblivious, and rubbed at her stomach under her furs.

"I spent half the night in the garderobe." An obvious recollection of the slaughter that had made her drink went across the tall woman's features. "We have to send my brother back to Gelimer today. With an answer that won't have us attacked before evening. Now *this* . . ."

Ash watched Florian pace down the chamber, farther from the hearth around which—since it held the palace's remaining substantial fire—the Duchess was allowing her servants to huddle and sleep.

She forced her mind not to listen to the yammering triumphant whispers of the Wild Machines; followed.

"No—" Florian put up a hand. "*No*. Your execution would be as irrelevant as the Faris's." Her thin face relaxed into a smile. "Stupid woman. You spent time telling me why she shouldn't die. What about you? What's different?"

"Because it isn't her, it's me."

"Yes, I think I have realized that," the scarecrow-thin woman said ironically, and looked at Ash with warm eyes. "After an hour and a half of you going on at me."

"But—"

"Boss, *shut up*."

"It isn't her, it's me, and I don't need the Stone Golem—" Ash's voice changed.

"If I order your death, I've lost 'the She-Lion of Burgundy,' the Maid of Dijon—"

"Oh, fucking *hell*!"

"Don't blame me for your public image," Florian snapped, with asperity. "*As* I was saying. We need you. You told me the Faris was irrelevant, because Burgundy's bloodline has to survive beyond her death. Now it has to survive beyond yours! I'm sorry that destroying the *machina rei militaris* didn't make a difference." Her expression altered. "God knows, I'm sorry about Godfrey. But. I need you in the field more than I need you dead."

"And this makes no difference? Is that what you're saying?"

"I'm not going to order your death." Florian del Guiz looked away. "And don't get any stupid ideas about going out onto the field and getting the enemy to do it for you."

For all its high-vaulted roof and pale stone, the ducal chamber pressed in on Ash with acute claustrophobia. She walked to the window and looked at the ice on the inside of it.

"You're running too great a risk," Ash said quietly. "This city is on the verge of being overrun. If you're killed— You needed my sister for what she knows. There's a dozen commanders here as good as me!"

"But they're not the Pucelle. Ash, it doesn't matter what *you* think you are. Or if it's justified."

Florian came to stand beside her at the stone embrasure.

"You didn't come here expecting me to have you marched off and executed. You know I won't. You didn't come here for me to tell you to kill yourself." Her eyes slitted against the southern glare. "You came here for me to talk you out of it. For me to *order* you to live."

"I did not!"

"How long have I known you?" Florian said. "Five years, now? Come on, boss. Just because I love you doesn't mean I think you're *bright*. You want someone else to take responsibility for telling you to stay alive. And you think I'm dumb enough not to notice that."

Wind from the ill-fitting edges of the window bit into her. The sheepskin huke[59] belted over armor and gown barely warmed her, no more than the coif over her shorn head, under her hood. Ash said, "Maybe it's just as well I can't love you the way you want. You're too smart."

Florian threw her head back and guffawed loudly enough to make the servants around the hearth stare down the chamber at them.

"What?" Ash demanded. "What?"

"Oh, gallant!" Florian spluttered. "Chivalrous! Oh—fuck

---

[59]Huke: a sleeveless knee- or thigh-length tunic, often not sewn closed at the sides, and worn with a belt.

it. I'll take it as a compliment. I'm beginning to feel sorry for my brother."

Bewildered again, Ash repeated, *"What?"*

"Never mind." Florian, eyes glowing, touched Ash's scarred cheek with fingers as cold as frost-bitten stone.

No sensuality was transmitted by that cold touch. What Ash felt answering it, in herself—what stopped her speaking, except for a confused mutter—was a wrenching nonphysical desire for closeness. She realized suddenly, *Agape.*[60] *Agape, Godfrey would call it: love of a companion. I want to give her trust.*

I trusted Godfrey, and look what happened to him.

"You'd better call people up here," Ash said, "and we'd better talk to them."

As Florian sent messengers, she scratched with mittened fingers at the ice on the inside of the glass, clearing a patch on the ducal window and peering north. Lemon yellow, actinic, the sun just cleared the horizon, casting blue-white shadows on the peaked roofs of Dijon below. The valley beyond the walls lay thick with frost.

Long shadows fell away from the sunrise, into the west. Every turf-hut, tent, and legion eagle put a blue-black silhouette across the frost. Out on the white brittle ground, men of the III Caralis were beginning to move around: foot units marching sluggishly toward the siege trenches, a squad of cavalry galloping across toward the eastern river and the bridge behind Visigoth lines.

Is that a deployment? Or are they just harassing us?

You could not see, from here, what lay in the dead ground between Dijon's north gate and the Visigoth siege lines.

But I doubt they've cleared up yesterday's bodies. Why would they? Far worse for our morale to leave them there to look at.

With no particular hurry, the red granite facades of golem-machinery creaked toward the walls.

"Not an assault yet," Ash guessed. "He's just trying to pro-

---

[60]*Agape*, Gk. 'Charity'. C.f. the New Testament.

voke you into complaining they're breaking the truce."

Ash snapped her fingers for a page. A boy brought an ivory bowl, steaming with the mulled cider presented, by Dijon's vintners, in lieu of the wine they no longer had. When he had served the surgeon-Duchess, Ash took a bowl, welcoming the heat of it. She turned back to the window, nodding toward the distant encampment.

"We've got their commander. There's not much we don't know about them, at the moment," Ash said dispassionately. "Like, we know they can afford to gallop their cavalry. The Faris tells me they've got fodder to spare. Not that I'd do it on that ground, myself—must be rock-hard." She paused. "If I were Gelimer, and *my* army commander had gone over to the enemy, I'd be running around now like a bull with its tail on fire, trying to remove any weaknesses in my deployment before I attacked. So we've got a window of opportunity, before he can."

"Christ," Florian said behind her. Her voice was raw, frustrated, helpless. "I have six thousand civilians in this city alone. I don't know what's happening in the rest of the country. I'm their Duchess. I'm supposed to *protect* them."

Ash looked away from the window. Florian was not drinking, only cupping her cold hands around the bowl. The scent of spices made her stomach growl, and Ash lifted her own bowl and drank. She felt the warmth of it flood her body.

She wanted to put her arm around Florian's shoulders. Instead, Ash lifted her bowl in salute, giving her a grin that was an embrace.

"I know exactly what we do next," Ash said. "We surrender."

The wind took her breath away, so cold that her teeth hurt behind firmly closed lips. A north wind. Her eyes leaked water that froze on her scarred cheeks. Ash moved down off the north wall, into the faint shelter afforded by the walls of the Byward Tower.

"You're right." Florian spoke in clipped words. "No one's going—to overhear us. Not out there."

"The Wild Machines might hear me . . ." Ash's lips skinned back from her teeth in a grin. *"But who are they going to tell?"*

"Bad place—for a war council."

"Best place."

"Boss, you're a loony!"

"Yes—Your Grace!" Ash steadied her sword against her armored hip. "Fuck me backwards, it's cold!"

The pale stonework of the Byward Tower jutted above her head, perspective diminishing into an eggshell blue sky. A few dead vines clung to the masonry, and a swallow's nest or two, under the machicolations. Jonvelle's men guarded the door, bills in their hands, the red Burgundian cross on their jacks. They stood watching their Duchess and their Captain-General, outside in the cold, as if the two women had taken leave of any senses they might ever have possessed.

Ash jerked her head clumsily. Florian walked with her, back out onto the wall, behind the merlons. She squinted out at the Visigoth lines, five hundred yards away.

"No one can get—within yards of us," Ash said. "The siege engines are shooting at the main gate. Not here. We'll see if they move. This is bare wall—no one can sneak up—without being seen. I want nobody to overhear us talk."

"About Burgundy's surrender," Florian said, breathing into her cupped mittened hands. Her tone was one of muffled scepticism.

"You don't believe me."

"Ash." Florian raised her head. The wind had reddened her unhealthily yellow cheeks. Her nose ran clear drops. "I *know* you. I know exactly what you do—in a given situation. When we've been in—some utterly hopeless position—outnumbered—outgunned—with no chance whatsoever—you *attack*."

"Oh, fuck. You do know me," Ash said, not displeased.

A clatter of armor, boots, and scabbards came from behind them. Ash turned. John de Vere and a dozen of his men were mounting the steps from Dijon's streets. As she watched, the English Earl ordered his men-at-arms to the Byward Tower, and ran out onto the wall without breaking step.

"Madam Duchess. My lord de la Marche will attend on you shortly." The Earl of Oxford clapped the palms of his gauntlets together. "He's much concerned. The river at the east of your city walls is iced over."

Florian, with a quick perception Ash appreciated, demanded, "Will it bear a man's weight?"

"Not yet. But it grows colder."

"Too fucking right it does." Ash winced.

Even with the visor up, there was little of de Vere's face to be seen within the opening of his armet.[61] He had left his red, yellow, and white livery with his men, stood as an anonymous knight in steel plate, faded blue eyes staring out at the surrounding river valley and the encamped legions. Ash, herself in armor, was as anonymous. She looked at Florian, cloaked and hooded, swathed in wolf furs.

"We shouldn't risk her out here," she said to de Vere, as if the surgeon did not exist. "But it's possible the Visigoths have got spies into the city. I don't want servants or soldiers overhearing us. No one. Not a beggar; not a madman; *nothing*."

"Then you're safe enough, madam. Nothing in its right mind would be up on these walls today!"

"For the love of Christ!" Florian hugged her arms and her wolf-fur cloak around herself, teeth chattering. "Get this—over with. Quick!"

"Let's walk." Ash started down the walkway behind the battlements, in the shelter of the brattices, toward the White Tower. A shout from behind made her turn. The Burgundian guards stepped back to allow two more cloak-muffled figures up onto the wall.

One—she recognized his old candle-wax-covered blue woolen cloak—was Robert Anselm. The other, his bearded face pale in the cold, proved to be Bajezet of the Janissaries. Impassive in the cold, he bowed to the Duchess, murmuring something quietly courteous.

"Colonel," Florian gasped. She glared at Ash. "You want to

---

[61]A closed-face helmet (as opposed to the sallet).

wait for de la Marche—or can I get on with it now?"

"Wait." As they turned to walk along the wall, gasping; Ash fell in beside Robert Anselm, and nodded at the Janissary commander. "Roberto, ask him what shape his horses are in?"

Anselm frowned momentarily, then addressed the Turkish commander.

The Turk came to a dead halt on the icy flagstones, waved his arms, and shouted an explosive negative. He continued to shout, red-faced.

"Plainly Turkish for 'not *my* fucking horses'!" Florian grinned and turned, putting her back to the wind, and began to walk backward in front of Ash. "He thinks we want to eat them."

"I *wish*. Robert, tell him it's a serious question."

Bajezet ceased to shout. Explanations in halting Turkish took them to the end of the walkway and the men guarding the White Tower. The brattices cut some of the force from the wind.

Beyond the White Tower, the wall was shored up with forty-foot planks; half-burned hoardings hanging off the battlements. *Weak spot*, Ash thought.

"He says his men's horses are not in good condition, because they're not being well fed." Robert Anselm, with no change of tone, added, "They could get fed. To us."

"Does he think he can gallop them?"

"No."

Ash nodded thoughtfully. "Well. We won't be outrunning anyone on them, then . . ."

Curious eyes watched them from both ends of the walls, now. Ash smiled to herself. If I was a grunt, and the city commanders were holding a private council of war up on the wall, *I'd* be looking at them. . . . I always used to think the bosses must be cooking up something remarkably stupid, when I watched something like this.

Now I just wish that someone else was taking the decisions.

"Shall I send another man for my lord de la Marche?" Anselm gritted.

"Not yet. He'll be on his way."

The Turkish commander pointed over the walls and said something. Ash looked as they passed between two brattices, saw no particular movement in the enemy camp. "What's his problem, Robert?"

"He says it's cold." Anselm hunched his shoulders, as if in emphatic agreement. "He says it's cold other places, and it's dark."

"What?"

Florian, walking shoulder to shoulder between Ash and de Vere, looked across at the Janissary. "Ask Colonel Bajezet what he means. And just tell me what he *says*, Roberto, okay?"

Ash caught sight of red-and-blue liveries below. She interrupted, "Here's de la Marche, at last."

Olivier de la Marche strode up onto the battlements, signaling his men away. He crossed the icy flagstones with deliberate haste, and bowed to Florian del Guiz.

Bajezet, with Robert Anselm murmuring in his ear, said through that interpreter: "There is nowhere, Woman Bey, for any of us to go."

"What do you mean, Colonel?" Florian spoke directly to the Turkish commander, and not to Anselm. When she listened to the answer, it was Bajezet's face that she watched.

"The Colonel says he saw 'terrible things,' on his way here. The Danube frozen. Fields of ice. People frozen in the fields, left to lie there. Nothing but dark." Robert Anselm stumbled in his speech, checked something with the Janissary, and finished: "There are deserted villages from here to Dalmatia. People living in caves, burning the woods for fire. Some cities have been razed through trying to keep fires—bonfires—burning twenty-four hours a day."

"There is still no sun?" Florian asked Bajezet.

"He says, no. He says, he saw frozen lakes. Beasts and birds dead in the ice. Only the wolves grow fat. And ravens and crows. In some places, they had to detour around—" Robert Anselm frowned. "No. Don't get that one."

"It is possible he speaks of the processions," John de Vere said. "A thousand strong, madam. Some of them were burning

Jews. Some were saving them. Many were in pilgrimage to the Empty Chair.[62] By far the most part of them, madam, were following rumor: coming toward the borders of Burgundy."

The Janissary Colonel added something. Robert Anselm translated: "They will find themselves competing for food with many more refugees."

Ash glanced behind her, up at the sky. It was an instinctive movement. Out of the corner of her eye, she saw Florian do the same.

A haze began to film the icy blue. The sun dazzled out of the southeast, blinding her to the roofs and towers of the city. The icy wind drew tears from her eyes. Ash began to move again. The men moved with her. The tall woman remained standing on the spot.

Following her gaze, Ash saw that she was staring at the ranks of tents and earth-walled barracks, stretching neatly out along the roads of the Visigoth camp, at the stacked rocks for the trebuchets, the horses neighing from each legion's horse-lines, and the thousands of armed men, gathering now at their bakehouses and camp-ordinaries for morning rations.

"They're expecting Fernando back. We have fewer and fewer choices," Florian said. "And no time to make them."

John de Vere came to a halt, rubbing his hands together with a click of metal. "Madam," he announced, "you are cold."

Not waiting for an answer, he raised his voice in a flat English bellow. Before a minute passed, two of his men-at-arms came out onto the battlements. They carried between them, on poles, an iron brazier, and trotted to set it down before the Earl of Oxford. One of the men fed it: flickering heat passed over the glowing red surface of the coals.

"This talk will take time," John de Vere said. "Security is essential, madam, but do not freeze your high command to death."

The morning advanced. Spiced cider was brought out, and dark bread; and they stood huddled around the brazier, mugs

---

[62]Rome?—P.R.

clasped between their hands, arguing every possible permutation of a city, between two rivers, surrounded by fifteen thousand foot and horse, and siege engines. Attack across a frozen river? Break out and run—across a countryside full (de la Marche indicated) of Visigoth outriders, spies, and light-cavalry reconnaissance? Spirit away the Burgundian Duchess—and lose any hope of support from Turks, Germans, French, English?

"Edward will not come in," John de Vere said grimly, at that point. "York thinks himself safe behind the Channel. I am all the Englishmen you will have at your command, madam Duchess."

"More than enough," Florian agreed, sipping at the spiced cider. Although she looked decidedly ill, she grinned at him.

By the fourth hour of the morning,[63] the sun had risen in the southern sky to a point where it illuminated all the land around Dijon: the freezing rivers; the valley full of tents and marching men, the puffs of smoke from the sakers,[64] deliberately breaking the conditions of the truce; the frost-shrouded hills and the wildwood, far to the north.

I've heard all these arguments, Ash thought. *Most of them twice.*

She kept her mind closed, deliberately did not listen in her soul. The white-blue morning sky, and Dijon's cone-roofed towers, dazzled her vision. Still, even with the blast of the wind behind her—face to the coals, back to the cold—a part of her attention remained directed inward. At a subliminal level, multiple inhuman voices whispered:

'SOON. SOON. SOON.'

"I know," she said aloud. Bajezet and Olivier de la Marche were (with Anselm's help) arguing; they did not break off for a moment. De Vere looked at her curiously.

Florian said, "I know that look. You've got something."

"Maybe. Let me think."

---

[63]10 A.M.

[64]Small cannon.

Forget the *machina rei militaris*. Forget that not having it at all is different from it being there if my willpower fails. Remember that I've been doing this stuff all my life.

It fell together in her head, with all the determinism and progression of a chess game: *if we do this, then that will happen; but if that happens, and we do this, then this other thing—*

She gripped Florian's arm, burying her hand wrist-deep in soft wolf's fur. "Yeah. I've got something."

The tall woman beamed down at Ash. With no trace of cynicism, she said, "And without your *machina rei militaris*, too."

"Yeah. Without that." A slow beam spread over Ash's features; she couldn't stop it. "Yeah . . ."

Florian said, "So tell me. What have you got?"

"In a second—" Ash put her hand on the merlon and vaulted over into the hoarding. The wooden floor of the brattice echoed hollowly under her feet as she loped up toward the Byward Tower; back down again. The freezing wind cold in her face, she even gripped a beam and put her head down through one of the gaps, scanning the hundred feet of wall below for ropes, for ladders, for any shadow of movement.

Nothing.

"Okay." She hauled herself back through one of the crenellations. "Let's take it from the top, shall we?"

The wind left her gasping for breath, and shivering under huke and cloak, but she lost no authority. She paused a tactful second for an acknowledging wave of the hand from Florian.

"Okay," Ash went on. "We're here. Outside, there's the better part of fifteen thousand troops. The Faris's men. Plus Gelimer's two new legions. And there's friction between the two of them."

De Vere and de la Marche nodded in unison, both men obviously having had the experience of being joined by cocksure fresh troops after three months of occupying muddy trenches and bombarding impregnable walls.

"Fifteen thousand," Florian repeated, through her gloved hands, clasped over her mouth against the bitterness of the cold.

"And we have eighteen hundred men of the Burgundian army—the Lion's three hundred and eighty, less gunners—

and five hundred Janissaries." Ash could not help laughing at the expression on the tall woman's face. "We know—about their deployment. Gelimer's two legions north. Between the rivers. Faris's men mostly—east and west—on the riverbanks. They don't assault the walls. They just bombard us."

The men had moved closer together, unconsciously, shoulders blocking the wind, the group in a huddle under a brightening sky. John de Vere, Earl of Oxford, said thoughtfully, "I had considered, madam, that we *can* cross the river to attack. Bajezet's Janissaries could swim their horses across. This ice, I think, is an end to that plan, unless it will bear the beasts' weight."

"And what would they do when they got there?"

"Nothing but cut up his rear echelon, madam."

Ash nodded impatiently. "I know: that doesn't win us anything. It fucks Gelimer around, it doesn't lift the siege, and it gives him all the excuse he needs today to flatten us."

The Turkish commander, after an interchange with Anselm, said something which his interpreter rendered as: "You seriously expect to lift this siege?"

"We're on last rations. Civilians are sick. If we're going to do anything, it has to be before we're too weak." Ash reached out, grabbing Florian's arm on one side, de Vere's on the other. "Let's not lose sight of the objective. Leaving aside our gracious Duchess—"

"Fuck you too," Florian commented.

"—what do we need to do? We need to make the King-Caliph look weak. We need to do something so that his allies abandon him—and join Burgundy. We need to look strong. We need to win," Ash said.

Olivier de la Marche stared at her. " 'Win'?"

"Look. There's no reinforcements coming for us. We can give in. Or we can wait—and we won't have to wait long! Make them come in and fight us through the streets, today or tomorrow. We'll maul them. But we'll lose. Either way, they'll execute Florian." Ash spoke in a pragmatic tone. "Look at the situation. There's fifteen thousand men out there. We're two and a half thousand. That's us outnumbered over five to one!"

She grinned at Florian.

"You're right. There's only one thing we can do. We attack."

"I thought we were surrendering!"

"Ah. We *say* we're going to surrender. We're going to send an envoy out, and ask the King-Caliph Gelimer to arrange a formal surrender, and negotiate the conditions under which we give Dijon up to him." Ash smiled at Florian. "We're *lying*."

A slight frown crossed the Earl of Oxford's face. "It is against the rules and customs of war."

Olivier de la Marche was nodding. "Yes. It is treachery. But my men will remember Duke John *Sans Peur*[65] on the bridge at Montereau. The French did not suffer for their treachery, since it was successful. We are in no position here to be more proud than a Frenchman."

"We *are* in desperate straits," John de Vere agreed mildly.

Ash snuffled back a laugh. She wiped her nose on her cloak. The wind penetrated wool, metal, and skin; cold sank down into her bones. She moved, stiffly, from foot to foot, attempting to warm up.

"It looks hopeless." She grinned toothily. "It *is* hopeless. It looks hopeless to the Sultan. And to King Louis. And to Frederick of Hapsburg. Can you imagine—what will happen—if we win? One bold stroke—and Gelimer doesn't have any allies."

"And we don't have our lives!" Florian snapped. She was hitching herself up and down, toe and heel, in front of the brazier, attempting to find warmth in movement. Ash ignored the surgeon-Duchess's asperity.

"Most of their men—Gelimer's legions—are at the north side. Between the two rivers. They can get their other men up there. But it'll take time. So we don't face—more than ten thousand."

"You're going to get everybody killed," Florian stated.

"Not everybody. Just one person." Ash prodded the surgeon-

---

[65]'Without fear'.

Duchess with a completely numb finger. "Listen to this. What happens if *Gelimer* dies?"

There was a silence.

Florian, with a slow, amazed, and growing grin, said, "Gelimer. You want us to attack the *King-Caliph*? Himself?"

Olivier de la Marche said, "The Faris claims her replacement—Lebrija—is a man fit only for *following* orders."

"Have to have another fucking election, wouldn't they?" Robert Anselm was nodding. "Maybe go back to Carthage. All the *amirs*—infighting—"

"There is no obvious candidate for caliph," the Earl of Oxford said. "My lord Gelimer is not a man to welcome other powerful *amirs* in his court. He has weakened the influence of many. Madam, this idea is well thought on: take away their commander, and not only may you raise this siege, you may halt their crusade here for this winter—perhaps for all time."

"They won't have any friends," Ash said dryly. "You watch Frederick and Louis leg it. And the Sultan come in—right, Colonel?"

Bajezet, translated, said, "It is not impossible, Woman Bey."[66]

John de Vere said, "But, madam, Lord Gelimer is not a stupid man. Yes, we might make a sally out in force, hoping to overrun his men and kill him—but where is he? In what part of the enemy camp? Or has he withdrawn—to a town nearby? He will expect just such an attempt."

"He can expect what he likes: if two and a half thousand troops hit him, he's dog meat." Ash shook her head vigorously, speaking over the rest of them, gasping with the tearing wind. "Listen to me. The Faris knows—troop dispositions—and guard rosters. She knew—she'd have to come over. Collected information. If we can do it—before things can be changed—we can get spies out—and back in again. We can find Gelimer's household—without him knowing, and moving it again. My guess is, it's to the north there. He needs an eye on his troops."

---

[66]Bey: 'commander'.

"God's *teeth*!" John de Vere said.

Surveying the enemy lines, beyond the walls, there was no sign of the King-Caliph's standard among the other eagles. Any of the finer pavilions and turf-roofed buildings might house him—*whichever is the warmer*, Ash thought cynically, letting Florian and de Vere and de la Marche stare north at the encamped Visigoth legions.

"It would need to be very fast," the Earl of Oxford said thoughtfully. "And if he is on that ground, you would find it difficult to get a great number of troops out of the northeast or northwest gates in time. Impossible. They would be on us before we could deploy out of the bottleneck."

"I know how to do that," Ash said.

She spoke with a confidence that made them ignore her chattering teeth, and the fact that she hugged herself, shivering violently in the bitter wind. The advancing sun dappled a pale gold over Dijon's white walls. The frost on the battlements did not melt.

"I know how to get the troops out there," Ash repeated. She looked at Florian. "It's St. Stephen's Day, it isn't twenty-four hours since the Faris came over to us. Whatever we're going to do, we've got to at least get *intelligence* collected quickly." She snatched a breath of freezing air. "Some weaknesses Gelimer can't alter. He can't alter his weak units—but he can move them. He needs to think there's no hurry, we're surrendering. We need time to prepare for this. And we need him *not* to think he's our target."

Florian chuckled, a little hoarse and breathless. She held out her hands to the brazier. "He's our target. Yes. We're surrounded by fifteen thousand men—so we're going to attack their leader. *Perfect* logic, boss!"

"It is. It's why they want *you*. Cut off the head, and the body dies." Ash halted. "Look, if we do this, that's it: it hangs on this. Once we're outside, if we lose, they come in and trash this city."

The surgeon-Duchess said frankly, "So where are you planning on putting me? Down in some deep dungeon where they won't find me? Because they will."

"They can attack the city even while we attack them,"

Olivier de la Marche cut in. "If the opportunity were seen, they would send a legion in while we fought on the outside—then we have lost—Her Grace being dead—have lost everything."

"I've got an answer for that, too," Ash said. "Are we agreed on this?"

They looked at each other.

In the end it was Florian who spoke. Wrapped in wolf pelts, her dirty, hungover face peering out of the gray fur, she swallowed back bile, frowned, and said, "Not until I've heard every detail six times. I don't buy a pig in a poke. And where does the Duchess feature in all this?"

"That," Ash said, smiling and nodding at the Janissary commander, "is where Colonel Bajezet and his horses come in. And"—she turned to the Earl of Oxford—"your youngest brother, my lord. We need to speak with Dickon de Vere."

She did not arrive back at the company's tower until the second hour of the afternoon. She immediately called Ludmilla Rostovnaya and Katherine over.

"How many woman sergeants have we got in the company at present?"

Ludmilla frowned, glancing at her lancemate. "Not sure, boss. About thirty, I think. Why?"

"I want you to get them together. Get all the spare polearms we've got—the Burgundians' as well, Jonvelle's expecting you. You're going to put some people through basic training."

The Rus woman still frowned. "Yes, boss. Who?"

"The civilians, here. They're going to get basic instruction in how to defend the city walls."

"Green Christ, boss, *they can't fight*! They don't know how! It'll be a massacre."

"I don't think I asked for an opinion," Ash said. After a stern moment, she added, "There's a difference between dying defenseless, if we're overrun, and dying trying to take someone else with you. These people know that. I want you and the other women to teach them which end of a bill to hold, and how far away they should stand so they don't impale each other. That's all. You've got today."

"Yes, boss." The Rus woman, turning away, stopped, and said, "Boss—why the women?"

"Because you're going to be training the men and women of Dijon. You may not have noticed, soldier, but they don't like soldiers. They think we're drunken, licentious, aggressive louts." Ash grinned at Ludmilla's expression of angelic innocence. "So. The women civilians will learn if they see women who can already do it. The men will learn because they won't have women outdoing them. Satisfied?"

"Yes, boss." Ludmilla Rostovnaya went off, grinning.

Ash's amusement faded, watching her go. *Civilians do not turn into militia overnight; even militia don't function until they've had a couple of fights. They're going to get slaughtered.*

Brutally honest, she thought, *Better them than men and women who can fight. I need* them.

"Boss?" Thomas Rochester slid in through the main door, the guards slamming it shut instantly behind the dark Englishman. A scurry of thin snow came in with him, and stayed, white and unmelted, on the flagstones. He said, "You'd better come, boss. The Turkish Janissaries are leaving the city."

"Good!" Ash said.

ii

THE COLD WAS no less bitter up on the battlements of Dijon's northeast gate.

"Keep your fucking fingers crossed," Robert Anselm growled, standing beside her. He had the ends of his cloak wrapped around his arms, and the whole lot bundled across his body, his hood pulled down almost to his nose. Only his stubbled chin was visible.

The pale afternoon sun put her shadow across the ramparts. Ash shaded her eyes with her hand, gazing north at the rider and red crescent banner moving out into the no-man's-land between the city and the Visigoth lines. A second rider—on a borrowed Turkish mare—carried a yellow silk banner with the Blue Boar of the Oxfords on it.

"Well, if nothing else, this ought to convince them we're really going to surrender."

Anselm chuckled explosively at that. "Fucking right. Our last allies up the Swannee."

From behind her, down in the square behind the northeast gate, Ash heard the chink of tack and the creak of saddles, many hooves ringing as they shifted on iron-hard cobblestones. She looked down. The ocher gowns and pointed helmets of Bajezet's Janissaries dizzied her with their uniformity. The few Englishmen—de Vere's household troops, his brothers, and Viscount Beaumont—stood out by virtue of their murrey-and-white livery.

Apprehension paralyzed her. She said, "I can't believe we're doing this. I'm going to shit myself. Roberto, go tell them to quit."

"Bugger off, girl. This was your idea!" Robert Anselm threw his head up, shifting his hood back to see her, and she saw his pinched white face and red nose. He grinned at her. "Don't lose your bottle now. You said 'a bold stroke.' "

With guards at the entrance to the battlements, and no one within fifty yards who could possibly hear them, Ash still spoke in a whisper.

"This isn't something to joke about. We're risking Florian. We're risking everything."

Equally softly, and with the appearance of calm rationality, Anselm said, "If it wasn't risky, the Visigoths would see it coming, wouldn't they? Thought that was your point."

"Fuck you," Ash said. "Shit. Oh, *shit*."

The sunlight cast his hood's shadow over his face, but she saw that there were beads of sweat on his bald forehead. Restless, she strode across and leaned on the crenellations, staring out at the riders.

A Visigoth eagle, shatteringly bright in the frosty air, left the enemy lines. Ash was not aware that she was holding her breath until she let it out, with a choking sound. No more than twenty men, Visigoth foot soldiers and horsemen, were leaving the camp, and they rode into the empty ground at the walk.

"Told you they wouldn't fire on the Turks." Her mouth pained her, dry and cold.

"Yet," Anselm said.

"Christ up a Tree, will you shut *up*!"

Anselm said companionably, "Helps to have someone to yell at," and then leaned out over the merlon beside her, straining to see the riders meet. "That's it. Take it easy. Don't fuck up now."

Plainly, he was talking to the Turkish and English envoys. Ash shaded her eyes again. The frost lay white and heavy on the ground. Two hundred yards beyond the gate, the red crescent banner halted, and the Blue Boar; and one Visigoth rider came forward from beneath the eagle. The armed figures on horseback blurred in her vision.

"Don't you wish you were a fly on *that* horse?" she murmured. "I know what Bajezet's Voynik is saying. 'Burgundy is about to fall. My master the Sultan has no confidence in the Duchess. It is time that we returned to our own land.' "

Robert Anselm nodded slowly. "I don't reckon Gelimer wants a war with the Turk. Not *this* winter."

The shouting on the distant ground went on. A horse neighed once, in the square behind and below them. Ash shivered in the wind. She wiped her nose on her cloak, skin abraded by the wet wool.

The Visigoth rider approached the banners more closely, until Ash could not tell one man from another, only the colored silks clear against the sky. The Visigoth troop of foot soldiers waited stolidly under their eagle.

"Know what my lord Oxford's saying, too," Robert Anselm said. He spoke without looking at Ash, all his attention on the meeting going on. " 'I'm an exiled English Earl, Burgundy's none of my business. I'm going to find Lancastrian support with the Turk.' "

"It isn't unreasonable."

"Let's hope my lord Gelimer thinks so, too."

Ash put her left hand down, resting it on the grip of her sword. "Whatever he thinks, what's happening is that five hundred reasonably fresh troops are abandoning this city. Leaving Burgundy to twist in the wind."

Anselm peered at the riders. "They haven't killed them yet."

"Like you said, Gelimer doesn't want Mehmet's armies arriving over the border right now." Her hand tightened on the leather-bound wooden grip. "The best way to keep the Turks from challenging him is to flatten Dijon. He thinks he's going to do that anyway, but he'd sooner do it without flattening some of the Sultan's men in the process. I don't suppose he'll mind if the great English soldier-Earl leaves the vicinity with Bajezet. . . ."

"Please God," Anselm said devoutly.

"I can't believe I'm doing something this risky. I must be out of my *mind*."

"All right. You are. Now shut up about it," Robert Anselm said.

Ash abruptly turned her back on the meeting going on in no-man's-land and walked across to the other crenellations. She looked down into the square. No pigs rootled in the now-frozen mud, no dogs barked; there was no flutter of white wings from dovecotes.

Five hundred mounted Turkish archers sat their horses, in neat formation.

Close to the gate, almost under the battlements, Viscount Beaumont stood with the Earl of Oxford's brothers, by their warhorses. His laugh came up clearly through the chill air. Ash was conscious of an unreasoning urge to go down into the square and hit him. John de Vere's forty-seven men-at-arms stood a short distance off, with pack ponies, the little remaining household kit packed on them. The Oxford brothers, as well as Beaumont, were in full plate. The two middle brothers, George and Tom, appeared to be having some debate over a broken fauld strap on the youngest brother, Dickon's, armor.

Ash looked down at the third brother, a young man in polished steel plate, sword and dagger belted over his livery jacket. The winter sun gleamed on silver metal, on scarlet and yellow and white heraldry; and on the fair corn-colored hair that fell to his shoulders. He carried his helmet under his arm, and was gazing down at the heads of Tom and George, where they bent over, examining the lower lame of his fauld: the skirt of his cuirass.

"Put the fucking helmet *on*," Ash whispered.

She could not be heard, sixty feet above the cobbled square. Dickon de Vere cuffed his brothers to one side, took a few long testing strides up and down the treacherous ground, banged a gauntlet against the offending laminated plate, plainly protesting that it was only an irritation, not a problem. Viscount Beaumont said something. The Earl of Oxford's youngest brother laughed ruefully, glancing up at the gate, and Ash was looking into Floria del Guiz's face.

Robert Anselm, quieter than a mouse's footfall, said, "She passed as a man, in a mercenary company, for five years. No one's going to spot her, girl."

Having been tall for a woman, Floria was—Ash thought—no more than a boy's height in her armor. She moved easily, the armor fitting well. High riding boots, pointed to her doublet, disguised the fact that Richard de Vere's greaves would not fit her: two men's calf muscles are rarely alike, and there is no room for error in the close fit of the plate.

Floria's gaze passed quickly back to Tom de Vere. She said something, obviously a joke: the men laughed. Ash could not tell whether the woman had seen her or not.

"I *don't* believe we're *doing* this."

"You want, I'll shut you in a garderobe till it's all over," Anselm offered, exasperatedly.

"That might be best." Ash rubbed at her face. The straps of her gauntlets rubbed her skin, tender in the bitter cold air. She sighed, deliberately turned her back, and walked across to the outside edge of the wall again. The Turkish flag, English banner, and Visigoth eagle still occupied the middle of the open ground.

"People see what they expect to see," she said steadily. "I'd be happier if her London-English was better."

"Look," Robert Anselm said. "Like you said to me, Dijon's going to fall now. It's going to happen. We attack them, they come in and flatten us; doesn't matter. Either way, we're fucked. And we're talking days, maybe hours."

"I told you that."

"Like I need telling," Anselm said, with a deep and caustic sarcasm. "Girl, if she stays here, she's dead. This way, she's out there in the middle of five hundred shit-hot troops that nobody wants to fuck with. For a whole multitude of reasons. You looking for 'safe'? There ain't no 'safe.' Having Gelimer think she's here when she isn't, that's as safe as it gets."

"Roberto, you're so fucking reassuring it ain't true."

"Bloody hell, he's—*she's*—sewed me up so often, that ain't true either."

In all the fuss of dressing her, swapping them, in all the high security, Ash thought, *I never got to say good-bye. Fucking son of a bitch.*

"How far did you tell them to go?" Anselm asked.

"De Vere will use his own judgment. If it's safe to camp a day's ride away, he will. The Visigoths won't be too surprised if they see the Sultan's troops hanging around to see how the siege turns out, so they can report home. If it looks dodgy, he'll keep them moving gradually east, for the border."

"And if it's really dodgy?"

Ash grinned at Anselm. "We won't be around to worry about it. If I was Oxford, in that case, I'd ride like shit off a shovel for the border, and hope I could get as far as the Turkish garrisons there." Her grin faded. "There'll still be a Duchess."

Out in the empty ground, the Visigoth rider wheeled away and galloped back toward the trenches. The Turkish interpreter and John de Vere moved—but were only walking their horses in the cold, Ash saw. The banners unrolled on the air, streaming and dropping as the wind dropped. White breath snorted from the horses' nostrils.

"Here he comes again."

She stood shoulder by shoulder with Robert Anselm, in the bitter cold of St. Stephen's feast day, on the battlements of

Dijon. One crow winged across the empty ground, calling, and dropped to pick and tear at something—red and mud-colored—that flopped on the frost-bitten earth.

The Voynik interpreter and the Earl of Oxford rode back, picking their way between the bodies of the fallen, to the north gate. Trained, the horses did not shy, although Oxford's mount nickered at the stink.

Ash's hands knotted into fists.

It seemed seconds, not minutes, before the gates of Dijon opened, and the Turkish riders began to file out into the open. Cold shivers ran down her back, from neck to kidney, under her arming doublet; and she shuddered, once, before she made herself be calm. Tom and Viscount Beaumont rode out to join the Earl of Oxford, the youngest brother following with George de Vere and the household troops.

The crash echoed through gatehouse and gate alike, but Ash hardly registered the slam of the portcullis being lowered.

Under a clear sky, in the winter sunshine and cold, in borrowed armor, Floria del Guiz rode among the Janissaries of Sultan Mehmet II, away from Dijon.

She carried her helmet under her arm, as they all did, riding visibly bareheaded between Visigoth legions. Nothing at all female about her exposed face.

Ash strained to follow her, to watch her, one among many, and lost sight of her before they vanished among the Visigoth troops, on the path to the intact eastern bridge. A bridge over ice, now.

"Dear God," Ash said. "Dear God."

She turned, striding to the steps, and clattered down into the square below. Besides the Burgundian guards, a dozen or more of her own lance leaders clustered there together, talking in low tones.

"Okay." Ash grinned at them: all confidence. She ignored and hid the churning in her guts. "*Now*. This is where we get our asses in gear, guys. Where's Master de la Marche? We'll give it an hour—and then send an envoy out to tell King-Caliph Gelimer exactly what he expects to hear."

Robert Anselm, on the heels of her remark, said, "Yeah? Who?"

iii

"IF WE *DON'T* send Fernando del Guiz back out to negotiate the surrender," Ash said regretfully, to Olivier de la Marche, "Gelimer's going to think that's suspicious."

The sun of St. Stephen's Day set in a wine red blaze. Snow fell with the dusk, small flakes plunging into the black emptiness. Ash closed the shutters of the window in the ducal chambers. She momentarily leaned her forehead against the cold wood, listening inside herself.

'. . . LITTLE SHADOW, SOON TO BECOME AS OTHER SHADOWS. A GHOST; A THING THAT NEVER WAS. NOT EVEN A DREAM . . .'

Their power sucked at her, like a current in a swift river. Her forehead grew warm and damp with the effort of resisting. A smile curled at her mouth as she straightened up. "You don't give up, do you?"

'FEEL OUR POWER, GROWING—'

'SOON, NOW. SOON.'

She ignored the fear, walking back across the bare chamber.

"Not if someone of sufficiently high rank goes instead," Olivier de la Marche said, from beside the hearth. "It is my duty to go. I am of Burgundy, Captain-General."

"True. But Gelimer will be quite capable of torturing a herald to double-check they're telling the truth. I know that, personally." Ash gave the Burgundian champion a level look. "There are people who know too much, now, about what we plan to do. You're one of them: so am I. We don't go. It would make sense to send Fernando."

Except that he'll want to speak to his sister the Duchess before he does this.

The thought was plainly in de la Marche's mind as well as her own, and Anselm's. Even here, none of them voiced it. Ash looked across the ducal chamber at the figure in padded headdress, veil, and brocade robes. Her mouth twitched.

"I don't think Fernando *had* better talk to the Duchess."

By the remaining unshuttered window, Dickon de Vere gazed down into the darkness that hid the roofs of Dijon with the same expression he had been wearing since he had said—in an appalled tone, to John de Vere—*You want me to wear a* what*?*

"Put the lamp out, or close the shutter!" Robert Anselm growled at the young Englishman, and when Dickon turned a look of disbelief on him, added, "You want to give them a nice bright light to aim at, boy—Your Grace?"

Dickon de Vere looked around for servants, found that there were none, and awkwardly reached out to fasten the shutter closed. Anselm slapped him on his velvet shoulder, companionably, as he walked back to the fire.

"Look, boss." Anselm glanced at Ash. "Gelimer knows you've got a grudge against your husband. String Fernando up. Send someone else out—with the body. Tell the King-Caliph you've settled a family matter. If Fernando's dead, he can't go shooting his mouth off about anything else. And whoever you send out can negotiate the surrender."

"I don't want him dead."

It came out before she thought about it. Anselm gave her a very deadpan look. De la Marche, not noticing, only nodded, and said, "He is Our Grace the Duchess's brother; I am reluctant to put him to death without her word."

I suppose that's one way of looking at it.

"If we imprisoned him," she began.

Anselm interrupted. "If you shove 'Brother' Fernando del Guiz in a dungeon, there'll be talk. Likely as not, we'll have an informer find their way down there, and hear him say he ain't seen his sister recently. Shit hits the fan, then." He stabbed his finger at Ash. "Never mind what the doc would say. Have him killed."

The chill bit through the hearth's meager warmth. Ash stretched stiffening limbs and moved to walk a little on the bare floorboards, their creak the only sound.

"No."

"But, boss—"

"Bring me his priestly robes," Ash said. "We're not short of dead men. Are we, Roberto? Find a body about his size, and put the robes on it. Stick it in a cage. Hang it off the city walls—I want it to look like a man starving to death. Whoever we send out as herald can point out to Gelimer that I've settled matters with my ex-husband . . ."

Her eyes narrowed.

"You'd better mess the face up a bit. I wouldn't put it past them to have some golem-device that can see a face four hundred yards away."

Olivier de la Marche nodded. "And Fernando del Guiz himself?"

Ash stopped pacing. Her head came up. "Put him with the prisoners. Put him in with Violante and Adelize and the Faris. The Faris could do with a confessor—he's the only Arian priest we've got."

Let him have his chance to speak to her.

Robert Anselm said nothing, only nodding curtly, but she intercepted a look she refused to respond to. After a moment, he said, "Then who're you going to send out there to have his nuts chopped off?"

Ash tapped her fingers against her armoured thigh. "Ideally, someone who's of sufficient high rank, and who knows nothing about the military side of things here."

Olivier de la Marche snapped his fingers. "I have him! The Viscount-Mayor. Follo."

"Richard Follo?" Ash thought about it.

De la Marche, with a knight's contempt for a man who does not fight for pleasure—or at least, for honor—shrugged. "Pucelle, isn't it obvious? He's a civilian. More to the point—he's a believable coward. If he is told we're surrendering, he'll negotiate in good faith that we are."

There speaks your nobleman.

"You mean, who'll miss him?" Ash said, and, surprised, felt more than a slight regret for scapegoating the man.

"Do that fat bastard good to walk out there!" Robert Anselm commented, to laughter from de la Marche and a scowl from Dickon de Vere.

On the one hand, Richard Follo's a self-aggrandizing, pompous troublemaker. On the other hand, he's mayor; he's a civilian, with a family still living; we shouldn't lose any of our people, no matter how much of a pain they are. . . .

Don't be too anxious to save him just because you don't like him.

"Of people of that rank," Ash said, "I suppose he's the least likely to be able to tell Gelimer anything useful. Olivier, will you have one of your heralds set up a meeting between Follo and—Sancho Lebrija, I expect it'll be, on their side?"

De la Marche nodded, stood, and walked toward the door.

"Where . . ." Ash tapped her fingers restlessly and resumed pacing, always pacing, ignoring the three men in the room. "Where? *Where* is Gelimer?"

"You got him," Ash said.

She did not need the Welshman to say anything. Euen Huw wearing his smug expression told it all. The two Tydder brothers with him—Simon and Thomas in dirty Visigoth tunics, mail shirts underneath—looked equally pleased with themselves.

"You had their patrol rota down pat, boss. And who notices one more spearman? Living in real comfort, he is," Euen Huw remarked. "Better than you, boss. Got all these slaves, hasn't he? And stone men, and I don't know what. And braziers, too. Hot enough to melt the skin off your face. First time I been warm since we got here."

Ash pinched the bridge of her nose and looked at him.

"We'd've had him if we could." The Welshman's frustration was clear. "Talk about high security. I reckon he has twelve men with him when he goes to do a shit! Took us long enough to get close enough to work out it was *him*."

"Bow? Crossbow? Arquebus?"

"Nah. Can see why the guys we sent out couldn't get to him. That unit he's got round him are *sharp*. Daren't touch a weapon anywhere near 'em."

"Which is where?" Ash demanded.

"Here," Euen Huw said, hastily feeling in his leather pouch.

Not to the south, she prayed. *Don't let me have to attack him across a river. Even iced-over.*

Euen's dirt black hands spread a paper in front of her. The Tydders crowded at his shoulder. He ran his finger across the charcoal lines that mapped the city, and the rivers to east and west, and the open valley to the north. The lines of the Visigoth camps were sketched in, now blackly definite. Euen Huw tapped his finger on the paper.

"He's *there*, boss. About a half mile north of the northwest gate. Upstream of us, on this side of the river. There's a bridge there, behind their lines. They haven't thrown it down. I reckon he's sitting there so he can be over it and away, if there's trouble."

"Yeah, he's got roads going south or west, if he crosses the bridge . . ."

"Not that we're going to let him."

Ash let herself smile at the Welshman. "We're going to have to move fucking fast to stop him. Well done, Euen, guys. Okay. I need more people to go out and keep an eye on him—be careful, his *'arifs* have had enough time to redo guard duties. I *must* know if King-Caliph Gelimer moves his household."

The day of the twenty-seventh of December passed. A dozen times in an hour, she missed the presence of John de Vere: his advice, his even temper, and his confidence.

The absence of Floria del Guiz worried at her like a missing tooth.

"Activity in the enemy camp. They're shifting men," Robert Anselm reported.

"Have they answered our herald yet?"

"Follo's still out there talking." Anselm said evenly, "The longer we leave it, the more weaknesses the King-Caliph can cover."

"I know. But we knew this would take time to set up. We *have* to take them by surprise: get out there and punch through them to Gelimer. Anything less than that is useless."

She covered the distance wall-to-wall inside Dijon twenty

times in the day, hearing reports, giving orders, liaising with de la Marche and Jonvelle. When she did rest, for an hour after noon, she started up again, head swimming in noise.

'FEEL IT GROW COLD, LITTLE SHADOW. FEEL HOW WE DRAW DOWN THE SUN.'

In the brief twilight toward the end of the twenty-seventh of December, the appointed Burgundian herald trudged back across the iron-hard mud between Dijon and the Visigoth camp.

Richard Follo came at last to Ash, where she and Olivier de la Marche waited in the palace presence chamber, surrounded by the silent merchants and tradesmen of Dijon. The veiled Duchess sat silent upon the great oak throne of the Valois princes.

He was escorted in through the refugees crowding the streets outside. There were few of them now—white around the eyes, gaunt with hunger, out at the further edge of desperation—who did not carry a bill or a pitchfork or, if nothing else, an iron-shod staff.

"Well?" de la Marche demanded, as if at his Duchess's behest.

Richard Follo took a moment to arrange his vice mayoral chain over his demi-gown, and catch his breath. "It is arranged, my lord. We will surrender, tomorrow, to the lord commander *qa'id* Lebrija. He will have all the lords and magnates of the city come out first, without weapons, onto the empty ground before the northeast gate. Then the fighting men, unarmed, in groups of twenty at a time, to be taken into Visigoth imprisonment."

Ash heard de la Marche asking, "Does he guarantee our safety?" but she was no longer listening. She looked to Robert Anselm, Angelotti, Geraint ab Morgan, Ludmilla Rostovnaya, to the Burgundian *centeniers*. All of them had the look of those receiving expected, if unwelcome, news; there was even a slight appearance of relief.

"The surrender is set for the fourth hour of the morning, tomorrow," Follo concluded, his eye sockets dark with shadow and strain. "At ten of the clock. Do we agree to this, my lords? Is there *no* other way?"

Ash, face impassive, ignored the last bickering, could only think, *Okay. This is it.*

"Angeli," she said. "Find Jussey. Now we know when we start."

By Compline,[67] it became too cold for snow. Ash, plodding over frost-sparkling flagstones and frozen mud, came back into the company tower's courtyard, and found herself among men packed in tight for the prebattle kit-check.

Wall torches burned smokily in the freezing air. She beat her hands together, numb in their metal plates. For a moment, the crowds of tall, bulkily armored men and women intimidated her. She took a cold breath, pushed into the yard, and began to greet them.

Knots and clumps of men stood here, a buzz of conversation going up into the night air. Lance leaders checked the troops they were responsible for raising—Ash spoke to foot knights, archers, sergeants, men-at-arms, and squires, knowing at least their first names; and stood aside as they and their kit were passed on to the other sergeants, forming up larger groups of men toward the back of the courtyard—all the billmen together, all the archers and hackbutters together. Shouts and bawled orders echoed off the vast expanse of stonework of the tower.

She walked among them, banner and escort meaning that a way always cleared in front of her, and talked to the billmen and the missile troops, hearing their bright, excited, half-drunk enthusiasm.

What am I missing? she thought suddenly. And then: *horses*!

There is no sound of hooves on the cobblestones. No ringing steel from the caparisoned warhorses; no packhorses, even; no mules. All gone into the company kitchens, now;

[67] 9 P.M.

from where a thin thread of scent trails—last rations before the morning.

"Henri Brant saved a couple of barrels of the wine," she announced, voice cracking at the coldness of the air in her throat. "You'll all get some at dawn."

A cheer went up from those near enough to hear.

Coming to the entrance to the armory, Ash raised her voice. "Jean."

"Nearly done, boss!" Jean Bertran grinned in the red forge light. Behind him, a last frantic burst of activity bounced hammer noise off the shadowy walls, hung with tools. Two apprentices sat turning out arrowheads at production-line velocity.

Deafened by the hammering, she stood with the welcome warmth on her face for a moment. At an anvil, one of the armorers beat out a dented breastplate, bright flakes spraying from the glowing metal. His bare arm with its prominent muscles flexed, shining with sweat and dirt, bringing the hammer down with accurate skill and power. She has a brief anticipation of that muscular arm and shoulder flexing, lifting, banging down weapons on some Visigoth soldier's face. *Maybe, in a few hours' time.*

At the tower door, she dismissed her escort of archers to the comparative warmth of the company tower's guardroom, and padded clumsily down the stone steps to the ground floor.

A stench of shit made her blink, take off her gauntlets, and wipe at her eyes. Blanche came forward through the taper-lit gloom. A pack of children flanked her skirts. Ash, making a rough head count, thought *Most of the baggage-train kids*, and nodded at them.

"I've got them bandaging," Blanche wheezed thinly. Like the men outside, her face was hollow under the cheekbones and the sockets of her eyes dark. "Every man who can walk is out of here, even if it means with a strapped-up wrist or shoulder. I can't do anything for the others. The well's freezing; I don't even have water for them."

The line of straw beds extended off into the gloom. *More than twenty-four now?* Ash tried to count the dysentery cases, at least. *Thirty, thirty-one?*

"Szechy died," the woman added.

Ash followed her gaze. Over by the wall, another dark, wiry man was wrapping the little Hungarian in something—ragged sacking, she saw, as an improvised winding-sheet.

"Out to the muster, when you've finished there," she said. "You'll get your chance tomorrow."

The man knotted cloth, rested the body down, and stood. Tears marked what was visible of his face between long hair and moustache. He said something—only *kill fucking Visigoths*! was comprehensible among his words—and staggered off toward the steps.

"Keep them as comfortable as you can. We need the water for those who're fighting, though." Ash watched the supine bodies of the fever cases. "If any of them suddenly 'recover,' send them outside."

Blanche, half-smiling, shook her head. "I wish these *were* malingerers."

Coming back up to the entrance hall, she found it crowded—Euen Huw, Rochester, Campin, Verhaecht, Mowlett, and a dozen others.

"See Anselm and Angeli; they'll sort it!" She shoved her way past the familiar faces, up the narrow stone stairwell, to the top floor. One of the guards there pushed aside the leather curtain. The brush-haired page came to take her cloak, her hood, her huke, and her sword.

"Armor off, boss?" he demanded.

"Yeah. Rickard will do it. I'll want arming up again before Lauds."[68] She hesitated, looking down at the boy—about ten, she supposed. "What's your name again?"

"Jean."

"Okay, Jean. You wake me about half a candle mark before Lauds. Bring the other pages, and food, and lights."

He gazed up at her over the bundle of damp, mud-stained wool, sheepskin, and weapons in his arms. "Yes, boss!"

She closed her eyes briefly as he left, hearing his footsteps on the stone stairs, and some half-audible comment by the

[68] 3 A.M.

guards. For a second she sees, clearly, how his face will look cut across with the handsbreadth blade of a bill.

"Boss." Rickard came away from the upper floor's hearth, where the fire lay banked down to red embers, with a pitiful amount of rescued beams and timber stacked beside it to dry out.

He cut the waxed points holding her pauldrons, and she shut her eyes again, this time for weariness; feeling his hands unbuckle and lift off the weight of thin steel plates, as if he lifted boulders off her flesh. As he removed cuisses and greaves and sabatons, she stretched her legs; and with the removal of her cuirass and arm defenses, she reached out as if to crack every muscle in her body, before slumping back into a flat-footed stance.

"That'll need a clean," she said, as Rickard began to hang it up on the body form. "Do it downstairs."

"Too noisy to sleep if I do it up here, boss?"

He stood taller than her, now, Ash realized, by half a hand span. She found herself looking slightly up to look into his eyes.

"Get Jean to start on the armor. You go over to St. Stephen's for me."

Instructions came automatically, now; she didn't listen to herself telling him what she wanted. The great yellow-and-red chevrons painted on the walls loomed, obscurely, through the gloom; and the smoke of tapers caught at the back of her throat.

"See I'm not disturbed," she added, and noted that he gave her an immense, excited grin in the dim light, as he turned to carry the Milanese harness down to a corner of the main hall.

He's too young for this. Too young for tomorrow. Hell, we're all too young for tomorrow.

She did not bother to change out of her arming doublet and hose, careless of the points dangling from its mail inserts. Hauling the oldest of her fur-lined demi-gowns over top of it, she moved the tapers in their iron stand closer to the hearth, and squatted down, prodding with a piece of firewood at the embers, until a warmer flame woke.

The smell of old sweat from her own body made itself

apparent to her as she grew less cold. She scratched at flea bites under her doublet. Cessation of movement made her drowsy. *I've talked myself dizzy*, she thought, feeling as if her feet in their low boots still thumped continually against flagstones, stone steps, cobblestones. With a grunt, she sat down on the palliasse one of the pages had dragged close to the fire, and dug still-numb fingers into the stiff, cold leather of her boots, easing them off one by one. Her hose, black to the knee, stank of dung.

And all of it can be gone, in an instant—every smell, every sensation, the *me* that thinks this—

She reached out for the pottery cup, left covered by the fire, and sniffed at the contents. Stale water. Perhaps with a very slight tinge of wine. Realizing, now, how dry her mouth was, she drained it, and dragged her doublet sleeve across her mouth.

"Boss," a man's voice said cheerfully, from the doorway.

She looked away from the fire. Even that small light left her night-blind, in the dim hall. She recognized the voice of the guard: one of Giovanni Petro's Italian archers.

"Let her in."

"Okay, boss." And in Italian, crudely: "Drain the bitch dry, boss!"

A cold wind sliced in as the leather curtain slid open, then dropped back. She reached out for her belt, where Rickard had laid it down, and tiredly buckled it around her waist, over her demi-gown. The use-polished hilt of her bollock dagger rested neatly under her palm.

A female voice, from the direction of the doorway, said, "Ash? Why do you want to see me?"

"Over here. It's warmer over here."

Oak floorboards creaked. Ash heard a chink of metal. A human figure hobbled into the dim illumination of tapers and fire, bringing the sharp scent of frost, and a whirl of surrounding cold air. The sound of metal on metal came again as the figure lifted its hands and pushed back its hood, and became—in the light—the Faris, her wrists and ankles encircled with heavy iron cuffs, and short, rough-forged chains run between them.

Firelight put a red glow on her cheeks, still filled out with the flesh that comes from adequate rations, and gleamed back from her eyes.

Ash pointed silently at the floor beside her. The Visigoth woman glanced around, and cautiously sat, instead, on a heavy ironbound chest that stood on the other side of the hearth.

Ash made to protest, and then grinned. "You might as well. If you can find anything in it other than spiders, you're welcome to it!"

"What?"

"It's my war chest," Ash said. She watched the sitting woman, the light on the iron chains. "Not that money would be good for much, right now. Nothing to buy. And even on my best day, I never earned enough to bribe the King-Caliph!"

The Faris did not smile. She glanced back over her shoulder, into the vast darkness of the hall. Walls and rafters were invisible now, and it was only apparent that windows existed in the alcoves behind the access corridors when the wind rattled the shutters.

"Why are you talking to me?" she demanded.

Ash raised her voice. "Paolo?"

"Yes, boss?"

"Bugger off down to the next landing. I don't want to be disturbed."

"Okay, boss." The archer's laugh came out of the darkness. "Let me and the boys know when you done with her—we got something to give her!"

Cold air burns her face: cold sweat springs out under her arms. The memory of men's voices above her, the exact same tone of contempt, shudders through her body.

"You'll treat her like a human being or I'll have your back stripped: *is that clear*!"

There is a perceptible pause before the archer's ungrudging, "Yes, boss."

Slowly, her system calms. There are memories of powerlessness deeper than that cell in Carthage, but she will not think of them. Not now.

Listening carefully, Ash heard his footsteps going down the spiral stone stairs.

She switched her gaze back to the Faris.

"I've got everything you can tell me, in de la Marche's reports. You're here because I can't talk to *him*," she indicated the place where Paolo had stood. "Or Robert. Or Angelotti. Or anyone in the company. For the same reason I can't talk to de la Marche, or that Burgundian bishop. Confidence is a—precarious thing. So there's . . ."

Florian's left. John de Vere's gone with her.

Godfrey's dead.

". . . there's you."

"Haven't we talked *enough*?"

The depth of feeling in the woman's accented voice surprised her. Ash reached back among the pottery cups and wooden plates, searching for more food or drink that might have been left out for the Burgundian commander in chief. More by touch than sight, she found a pottery flask with liquid in it, and heaved it back over into the firelight.

"We've never talked. Not you and me. Not without there being something else going on."

The Visigoth woman sat perfectly still. A threadbare demi-gown covered her badly fitting doublet and hose, and her hands were white with cold. As if conscious of Ash's gaze, she cautiously extended her fingers toward the fire's warmth.

"You should have killed me, before," she said, at last, this time in Carthaginian Latin.

Ash sloshed brackish water into two moderately clean wooden cups, and knelt up beside the hearth to offer one of them to the Faris. The woman gazed at it for a long minute before reaching out for it with both hands together, the weight of the iron links making her clumsy.

"And the Duchess, your man-woman," the Faris added, "she should kill you, now."

Ash said, "I know."

The feeling of acting as if Florian were still in the city was curiously unsettling.

The taper guttered and began to give off a thicker black

smoke. Ash, not willing to call for a page, made to get up, winced at stiff muscles, and limped across the room to find another tallow-dip, and light it at the hearth. Even a yard away from the flames, it was freezingly cold.

Firelight made the woman's chopped-short hair red-gold, not silver—*as it must do mine*, Ash realized. It blurred the dirt on her skin. *If someone came in now, would they know which one was her, and which is me?*

"We spend far too much time keeping each other alive, when circumstances don't demand it," Ash said sardonically. "Florian, you, me. I wonder why?"

As if she had thought a lot about the matter, the Faris said, "Because my *qa'id* Lebrija has a brother dead in this war, and another alive in Alexandria, and a sister married to a cousin of the Lord-*Amir* Childeric. Because Lord de la Marche of Burgundy is brother-in-law to half France. And all I have is you; and what you have, *jund* Ash, is me." She hesitated, and with a wry expression, added, "And Adelize. And Violante."

This is family? Ash thought.

"I could never quite kill you. I should have." Ash set the taper in its stand and walked back to look into the hearth-fire. "And Florian—won't execute me. Rather than kill one person, she'll risk thousands. Thousands of thousands."

"That's bad." The Faris looked quickly up. "I was wrong. When I had you among my men at the hunt? I was not willing to accept that one person should die. My father Leofric, the *machina rei militaris*, they would have told me how wrong that was—and they would have been right."

"You say that. But you don't quite believe it, do you?"

"I believe it. How else could I order an attack, in war? Even when I win, people will die."

Ash's eyes watered. She coughed, waving a hand as if the taper's thin trickle of smoke bothered her, and lifted the wooden cup and drank. Sour-tasting water slid down her throat, past the tightness there.

People will die.

"How do you live with it?" Ash asked, and suddenly shook her head and laughed. "Christ! Valzacchi asked me that, in

Carthage. 'How do you live with what you do?' And I said, 'It doesn't bother me.' It doesn't bother me."

"Ash—"

"You're here," Ash said harshly, "because I can't sleep. And there isn't any wine to get drunk on. So you can damn well sit there, and you can damn well answer me. How do I live with what I do?"

She expected a pause, for reflection, but the Faris's voice came instantly out of the shadows.

"If God is good to us, you have little time to live with it. King-Caliph Gelimer will execute you tomorrow morning, after you surrender. I only pray that I can reach him first—or else that the Lord-*Amir* my father Leofric can—and tell him that he has to wait to execute Duchess Floria until after you are dead."

The Faris leaned forward into the firelight, her gaze resting on Ash.

"If you do nothing else, at least send me out to him first tomorrow! Pray that I live long enough to tell him, before he executes *me*."

A snort of laughter forced its way out of Ash's mouth. She wiped her sleeve across her face again and squatted down in front of the fire, still cradling the empty cup.

"You've heard about the surrender, then. That the siege is over."

"Men will talk. Priests no less than any other. Fer—Brother Fernando spoke to the monks."

Catching that hesitation in the other woman's voice, Ash said, under her breath, "Predictable!", and added, before the Faris could question her: "I don't give a shit about what happens tomorrow! This is now. I want to know—how do I live with people I know . . . with friends getting killed."

"Why?" the Faris said. "Do you plan to go down fighting, at the surrender?"

The cold in the tower's upper hall bites at her fingers, and her feet, so that she is glad, momentarily, to avoid the Faris's dark stare by sitting to put her stiff, cold boots back on. For a second, she feels it all—the slight warmth the fire has put into the sewn leather, the ache of exertion in her muscles, the numb grind of hunger under her breastbone—as if it is the first time.

"Perhaps," Ash said, finding herself unwilling to lie, even by misdirection. *Not that it'll matter: you're spending the rest of your time chained to a pillar in St. Stephen's. It'll all be over before anyone can find you.*

"Maybe," Ash repeated.

The Faris put her chained hands neatly together in her lap. Staring into the poor excuse for a fire, she said, "You live with knowing you'll die in war."

"That's different!"

"And enough things will kill them in peacetime—drink, pox, fever, farmwork—"

"I *know* these people." Ash stopped, said again: "I know *these* people. I've known some of them for years. I knew Geraint ab Morgan when he was skinny. I knew Tom Rochester when he couldn't speak a word of anything but English, and they told him his name was Flemish for *arse-hole*. I've met Robert's two bastard sons in Brittany—*fuck* knows whether he thinks they're alive or dead, now! He doesn't say anything, he just carries on. And there's guys on the door here, and downstairs; I've known most of them since I left England after Tewkesbury field. If I order an attack, they'll die."

As objective as if she were neither prisoner nor partisan, the Faris said, "Don't think about it."

"How do I stop thinking about it!"

After a moment, the Faris began tentatively, "Perhaps we can't. Brother Fernando said—"

"What? *What* did he say!"

"—he said, it's more difficult for a woman to be a soldier than a man; women give birth, and therefore find it too difficult to kill."

Ash found both her hands clasped tight over her belly. She hugged her blue velvet demi-gown to her, caught the Faris's eye in the shadowy light, and coughed out a loud, harsh burst of laughter. The other woman clamped her fingers across her mouth, gazing with wide dark eyes, and suddenly let her head go back as she gave a high peal.

"He s-said—"

"—yes—"

"Said—"

"Yes!"

"Oh, shit. Did you tell him—what crap—?"

"No." The Faris wiped the edge of her hands delicately under each eye, smoothing away water. Her chains clinked. She could not keep the enjoyment off her face. Snuffling, she said, "No. I thought I might let my *qa'ids* talk to him, if I survive. They can tell this Frankish knight how much *easier* it is for a man to stand covered in the brains and blood of his dearest friend—"

Laughter died, not instantly, but slowly, sputtering as they looked at each other.

"There's that," Ash said. "There is that."

The woman wiped her face, fingers touching dirty but flawless skin. "I have always had my father, or my *qa'ids*, or the *machina rei militaris* with me; not like you, Ash. Even so, I have seen enough of what war does to people. Their hearts, their bodies. You have seen more than I. Strange that it should hurt you more, now."

"Were they ever more than men on a chessboard to you?"

"Oh, yes!" The Faris sounded hurt.

"Ah. Yes. Because, if you don't know them as human and fallible," Ash completed, "how do you know where to put them in battle? Yeah. I know. I know. What *are* we? Bad as the Stone Golem. Worse. We had the choice."

She sat back, arms hooked around her knees.

"I'm not used to this," she said. "If I think about it, Faris, you probably owe your life to me not being used to it. Maybe it's only sentimentality that stopped me killing you."

"And your Duchess, she is sentimental not to kill you?"

"Maybe. How would I know the difference between sentimentality and—" Ash will not say the word. It sits immovably heavy in her mind. Even to herself, she cannot say *love*.

"Shit, I hate sieges!" she exclaimed, lifting her head and

looking around the cold, dark hall. "It was bad enough in Neuss at the end. They were eating their own babies. If I'd known, in June, that I'd end up this side of a siege six months later . . ."

Iron links shifted, with a pouring sound, as the Faris slid herself down the great multilocked war chest to sit on the floorboards in front of it, and lean back wearily. Ash momentarily tensed, out of instinct, even recognizing that the chains were—by her order—made too short to allow the wearer to throttle anyone.

Automatically, she got her feet under her, and the hilt of her dagger back under her palm. She squatted, staring into the fire, her attention pricklingly conscious of the woman in the edge of her vision—that state of mind where any movement will trigger a drawn weapon.

"I will never forget seeing you for the first time," the Faris said quietly. "I had been told 'twin', but how strange it was, even so. A woman among the Franks—how could you not know yourself born of Carthage?"

Ash shook her head.

The woman continued, "I saw you in armor, among men who owed you loyalty—you, not your *amir* or King-Caliph. I envied that freedom you had."

"Freedom!" Ash snorted. "Freedom? Dear God . . . And envy didn't stop you packing me off to Carthage, did it? Even knowing what Leofric was likely to do."

"That." The Faris pointed a slender, dirty finger at Ash. "That. That's it."

"What's it?"

"How you do it," the woman said. "Yes, I knew—but I didn't *know*. You might have been used, not killed. That's how you have to do it in battle—your men might live, they might not be killed. Some of them *will* live. It's a matter of not letting yourself know."

"But I do know!" Ash's fist hit the palliasse beside her. "I do, now. I can't get rid of it—that knowing."

A knot in the burning wood cracked, making her jolt, and the Faris, too. A gold ember fell out of the fire irons, turning swiftly gray, then black, on the edge of Ash's demi-gown. She flicked it off, brushing at the cloth. She gazed up at the blackened brick lining the chimney behind the fire, feeling the draft of the air, and smelling the scorched velvet.

"Let's say," Ash said, "that there is going to be a fight. Let's say I've been driven out of Genoa, and Basle, and Carthage itself by you guys, and halfway across southern France, and let's say I'm finally going to turn around, here, at Dijon."

The Faris held out her wooden cup. Ash automatically poured more of the stale water into it. The Faris looked down at her chained wrists, which she could not move very far apart. Lifting the cup between her hands, she sipped at it.

"I see how it is. Tomorrow, you will fight to get yourself killed," she said coolly, with something of the authority she had had in Visigoth war gear among her armies. "That will deprive the *Ferae Natura Machinae* of their victory. Even if you fight for some other objective, I've learned enough of you to know that you're aware of who the true enemy is."

Ash stood, flexing pain out of her leg muscles. The warmth of the fire faded, the wood being consumed. She wondered idly, *Should I feed the fire again or leave it to the morning?* and then, her mind correcting her, *No need to ration it out, now; either way.*

"Faris . . ."

Cold air chilled her fingers, her ears, her scar-marked cheeks. Another stretch, this time rolling her head to get the stiffness out her neck. The trestle table stood mostly in the shadows, the one taper not sufficient to illuminate the stacked papers, muster rolls, sketched maps, and plans at the far end of it. Someone—Anselm, possibly—had been using a burned stick from the fire: the tabletop was scratched in charcoal with lines delineating the northwest and northeast gates of Dijon, and the streets of the Visigoth camp beyond them.

"You're the one who's keen on suicidal actions, getting the enemy to execute you. If I thought it necessary, I wouldn't be handing myself over to Gelimer, I'd be walking off the top of this tower—four stories straight *down*." Ash gestured emphatically.

"There's something you're planning. Isn't there? Ash—sister—tell me what it is. I was their commander. I can help."

Everybody wants me to do this. Even her!

"I will help you, if it leads to destroying the Wild Machines." The Faris knelt up, her unlined face seeming young. Excitedly, she said, "The King-Caliph Gelimer will not command as I would. Rather: not as I would if I had the *machina rei militaris*—"

"He's got fifteen thousand troops out there, he doesn't have to!"

"But—you could put me on the field: not as a commander, as your battle-double—"

"I don't need your help. We've already wrung you dry. You're missing the *point*, Faris."

"The point?"

Ash moved forward. She sat down on the edge of the war chest. Well within range, if the woman now sitting at her feet should choose to strike at her with hands assisted by iron chains.

Her eyes stung. She knuckled at them, smelling charcoal on her fingers. Water, hot and heavy, gathered on her lower lids, and ran over and down her cheeks.

"The point is, who else can I tell that I'm afraid? Who else can I tell that I don't want to get my friends killed. Even if by some remote chance we *win*, most of my friends are going to end up dead!"

Her voice never shook, but the tears carried on, unstoppably. The other woman looked up, seeing, in the fire's light, Ash's face red and shining with water and snot.

"But you know—"

"I *know*, and I'm sick of it!" Ash put her face into her hands. In the wet, sweaty darkness, she whispered, "I—don't—want—them—to—die. I can't make it any fucking plainer! Either we go out there tomorrow, and they die, or we stay in here tomorrow, and we die. Christ, what don't you understand!"

Something touched her wrist. By reflex, she clenched her fist and knocked it away, hard. One knuckle struck iron. She swore, snatched her other hand from her face—vision dazzled by wetness—and made out the other woman holding up her cuffed wrists in a gesture of nonaggression.

Distressed, the woman said, "I'm not your confessor!"

"You understand this! You've done this—you *know* what—"

The Faris reached out, pulling at Ash's belt and demi-gown with her hands that were trapped close together. All in a second, Ash stopped resisting. She slid down the side of the wooden chest, hitting the stones hard, crammed in beside the Faris's warm body.

"I don't—"

Chains shifted, tangling in cloth. Ash felt the Faris attempting to put her arms around her shoulders—failing—and then her left hand was gripped tight between both of the Faris's own hands.

"I know. I know!" The Faris wrapped her arms around Ash's arm; Ash felt the woman's hard, hugging pressure.

"—don't want them killed!" Hiccoughing sobs stopped her speaking. Ash clamped her eyes shut, tears pushing out between the hot lids. The Faris murmured something, not in any language that she knew.

Ash dipped her head, abruptly, and muffled the noise against the filth-stained wool of the Faris's gown. She sobbed out loud, body clenched, crying against her sister's shoulder until she wept herself dry.

There were no remaining city clocks to chime the hour. Ash blinked awake in darkness, with sore, swollen eyes, and stared into the graying embers of the fire.

Utterly relaxed against her, the Visigoth woman with her face, her hair, her body, slept on.

Ash did not move. She said nothing. She sat, awake, alone.

The page Jean entered the room.

"Time, boss," he said.

On the third day after Christ's Mass and the return of the Unconquered Sun, in the dark an hour before Terce:[69]

"Go in peace!" Father Richard Faversham proclaimed, "and the grace of God be upon us all this day!"

He and Digorie Paston bowed to the altar. Both men wore mail and helmets.

---

[69]Therefore, about 8 A.M.

The stones of the abbey, hard under Ash's armored knees, forced the metal back into the protective padding. She crossed herself and stood up, heart thumping, hardly feeling herself cold to the bone. Rickard got to his feet beside her: a young man in mail and the Lion Azure livery, his face pale. He said something to Robert Anselm; she heard Anselm chuckle.

"Angeli!" She grabbed Angelotti's arm as the company began to file out of the church. "Are we set?"

"All set to go." His face was barely visible as they came out of the great church door into the St. Stephen's Abbey grounds. Then a lone torch caught his gilt curls, showed her his teeth in a wild, wide grin. "You are mad, madonna, but we have done it!"

"Have you warned everybody off?"

Robert Anselm, beside her, said, "I've had runners from all our lance leaders; they're in place on the ground and on the walls."

"We're almost—fully deployed," the *centenier* Lacombe grunted.

"Then get fucking moving!"

The faintest gray of dawn lightened the sky. Ash strode through the icy streets, head buzzing with information, talking to two and three people at a time; sending men here and there, conscious of her mind moving like an engine, smoothly, without feeling. A message of readiness came in from Olivier de la Marche as she reached the cleared desolation back of Dijon's northwest gate.

She passed her helmet to Rickard to carry. Walking bareheaded, the bitter cold numbed her face immediately, made her eyes run, and she blinked back tears. A word here, a touch on the shoulder there: she went through her men and the Burgundian units, toward the foot of the wall.

Torches illuminated golden swaths of light on the lower reaches of the wall, invisible outside. Men passed cannon shot hastily from hand to hand up the steps to the battlements. She stepped back as a Burgundian gun crew trundled an organ-gun across the frost-rimed cobbles, that they could barely see. Rags muffled its steel-shod wooden wheels, covered the metal of its eight barrels.

At the foot of the steps they barely halted, tripping the organ gun up so that they held the trolley, and carrying it bodily between them up to the battlements. A throng of gun crew trod after them, and men hauling three timber frames—mangonels.

Her numb skin cringed at every sound. Muffled footfalls, an oath; sweating grunts of effort as another light gun went up to the walls—*will they hear us? Sound carries, it's frosty, it's too still*!

"Tell them to keep it down!" She sent a runner—Simon Tydder—off toward the walls, turned on her heel, and set off at a fast walk with her HQ staff, parallel to the wall between the White Tower and the Byward Tower, fifty yards back.

They ran into a crowd, Burgundian archers and billmen. Ash craned her neck to look at the rooftops. A rapidly lightening sky was no longer gray—was a hazed white, with a deep red glow to the east.

"How much fucking longer!" Her breath whitened the air. "This lot are late! How many more? Are we in place!"

"We need it light enough to see what we're doing," Anselm grunted.

"We don't need it light enough for *them* to see what we're doing!"

Thomas Rochester snorted. The dark Englishman carries her personal banner again, a position of prestige for which he has handed his temporary infantry command back to Robert Anselm. He, or someone from the baggage train, has neatly darned a rip in his livery jacket. His sallet is polished until the rivets shine. *Didn't sleep last night, doing that. All of them: preparing*.

"Get your men in place!" she swore at the Burgundians. "Fuck it! I'm going up on the wall. Stay down here!" She pointed at Rochester's Lion Affronté banner.

Loping up the steps to the battlements, the burn injury on her thigh hurt with the exertion. She grunted. Once above roof level, wind whipped out of the east and tore the breath out of her mouth. She slowed her pace, trying to move reasonably quietly in her armor. Stone treads glittered, crusted thickly white with frost, imprinted with the boot marks of the men who had climbed up minutes before her.

A line of light lay across the battlements.

Brightness striped the merlons and brattices, and the tall curve of the Byward Tower. She turned east. Between one long low cloud and the horizon, the brilliant yellow of the winter sun stabbed out.

We're not a minute too soon.

Men crouched behind the merlons. Gunners in jacks, their sallets and war-hats held at their feet so they should not catch the betraying sun, counting their shot in silence, their rammers leaning up against stonework. Other crews kept their cannon back from the crenellations, loading powder and ball and old cloth for wadding. Farther along the parapet, men worked in rapid, silent teams, hauling back the arms of siege engines with greased wooden winches.

Beyond the Byward Tower, to her right, the battlements were completely deserted.

"*Okay . . .*" Breath, warm, was cold against her lips a second after.

A long way to her right, past the Prince's Tower, thin clumps of men began again on the wall.

Outside, past the bone-scattered ground, the Visigoth encampment lay vast and swollen between the two rivers. Heart in her mouth, she saw that smoke already threaded up from cooking fires. Behind the mantlets and trenches, pennants, banners, and eagles rose, like a forest of dry sticks in the rising sun.

Anyone moving?

For a second, she sees it not as tents and the men of the XIV Utica, VI Leptis Parva, III Caralis, but as a great structure sprawling there in the growing dawn: a pyramid whose foundation is use-and-forget slaves, then the troops with their *nazirs* and *'arifs* and *qa'ids*, then the Lord-*Amirs* of the Visigoth Empire, and finally—pinnacle, peak of all—King-Caliph Gelimer. And for that same second she is utterly aware of the support of that structure: the engineers that bring supplies up frozen rivers, the slave-estates in Egypt and Iberia that raise the food, the merchant princes whose fleets outrun the Turkish navy to sell to a hundred cities around the Mediterranean, and deep into Africa, and out to the Baltic Sea.

And what are we? Barely fifteen hundred people. Standing in front of eight or nine thousand civilians.

She looked away. The western river lay flat and white, frozen hard as rock. *Strong enough? Please God.* She could not see the surviving bridge, hidden by the myriad tents and turf huts of the Visigoth camp. As for the King-Caliph's household quarters, there was nothing to mark any engineered building out from another except location.

He was sleeping there two hours ago. And if he's not there now—well. We're fucked.

A glint of brass caught her eye as the sunlight moved down. Golems, overwatching the gate. With Greek Fire throwers.

The only thing we might have in our favor is that they're not deployed. Maybe not even armed up—shit, I wish I could see that far!

And they can't fire into melee. Once we get stuck in to hand-to-hand, we're safe—well . . .

What would have been a smile turned sour. She looked east, into glare: saw only bonfires, heard a horse's hoof striking ringingly on the frosty ground. North, nothing but tents: tents and more tents; men by the hundred, by the thousand—beginning to stir, now.

"Come *on*, Jussey—"

Cold had got into her bones. She moved stiffly, half-running. The stone stairs were slippery with rime. She blinked, moving down into shadow again. Her muscles felt loose, and her bladder urgent; both these things she put out of her mind.

Can I do this?

No: but nobody can do this!

Ah, the hell with it—

At the foot of the wall, she grabbed Anselm's arm in the dimness. "Time to do it. Is everyone in position?"

"There's a delay with some of the Burgundian billmen."

"Oh, tough shit! We got to move!"

"Apart from them, it's a go."

"Okay, where's Angeli—" She glimpsed Angelotti in the gloom. "Okay, get your guys out: *do* it. And don't let me down!"

The Italian gunner went off at the run.

"That's it," she said. She looked up at Anselm, not able to see his face. "Either everybody does what we've trained for—or we're fucked. We can't change this in midstream!"

He grunted. "Like letting an avalanche go. We just got to go with it!"

If I get hit, let it be a clean kill; I don't want to be maimed.

"If I go down, you take over; if you go," she said, "Tom will take it; de la Marche will have to pick it up if we're all fucked!"

The command group trod on her heels as she strode back across the rough ground to the barricades. A lantern gave little light on the frozen mud ruts. She slipped, swore, heard something before she saw it, and realized that she had come to one end of the company line. John Burren, Willem Verhaecht, and Adriaen Campin were conferring urgently.

"We're in position here, boss." Willem Verhaecht spat, and spared a glance for the mass of men in Lion Azure livery, clutching their bills and poleaxes, grinning back at him. "Ready to go. I'd do anything to move, in this cold!"

Some forty men stood behind. Bills jutted above their heads. Men strapped into whatever armor they possessed, much of it taken now from the dead. She heard a lot of low-voiced last-minute joking, settling of debts and forgiveness, and prayer.

"We're ready, boss," John Burren said, nodding toward the unit in front.

In the gloom, Jan-Jacob Clovet and Pieter Tyrrell struggled with a six-foot oak door, stripped out of some building. Tyrrell's half hand skidded on the frozen wood. A short, podgy figure in sallet and cut-off kirtle stepped in behind him, taking the weight on her shoulder. Hearing a female voice swear, Ash recognized Margaret Schmidt. Two more crossbowmen grabbed the door. Past them, she saw the other crossbow troops carrying doors, long planks, pavises, and torn-out shutters from ogee windows.

"We're here, boss!" Katherine Hammell's voice said, at her side. Only the jutting staves above her troops' heads showed them to be a mass of archers.

Down the line, past them, Ash sees in this growing cold light, Geraint ab Morgan's armed provosts, a dozen women from the baggage train, their skirts kilted up, and razor-sharp ash spears in their hands, Thomas Morgan holding the great Lion Azure battle standard. And faces behind them, under helmets, faces that she knows, has known for years in some cases: the line snaking on across the rubble, a little over three hundred strong.

I do not want to lead these men into this.

"Move 'em up," she said curtly, to Anselm. "I'd better kick some Burgundian ass—"

The silence shattered.

A sudden sequence of cracks and booms from the eastern side of the city made her skin her lips back from her teeth in a wild grin. A long chill shiver went through her body. Through the ground under her feet, she felt the boom of guns; she heard the deceptive soft *thwack*! of rock-hurling siege engines.

"There goes Jussey! Better late than fucking never!"

Eternal, now, this hasty shuffling of men into position; and one drops his bill with a clear *clang!* against a broken wall, and a dozen others cheer. Shoved into position by sergeants, spitting on their shaking hands, giving a last tug at fastened points and war-hat buckles—*how long is this taking?* Ash thinks, over the shattering noise of Jussey's bombardment. *How much longer have we got?*

The early sunlight moved down the roofs of buildings.

Captain Jonvelle loped out from behind the long lines of Burgundian troops.

"They've mobilized most of a legion!" He turned to confirm with a runner. "Pulled it out of the trenches—they think we're staging a breakout to the *east* bridge—deploying over there—"

"*Got* the fuckers! Okay, now *wait*. Let 'em commit themselves."

Counting in her head, she let an agonizing eight minutes pass.

Ash gave a quick nod, walked out toward the wall, and turned, standing between the two advance crossbow units, to face the units behind. Amorphous clumps of men: each a hundred strong. Unit pennons going up, now, in the dim light, but so few—barely a dozen. *Gun crews on the walls, engineers in the saps: even with everyone who can* walk *down here, we don't amount to more than thirteen hundred men.* Shit . . .

She drew breath, shouting, her voice carrying over the distant Burgundian guns.

"Here's what we do. We attack now! They don't expect us. They're expecting us to surrender! We *won't* be surrendering."

A rumble of voices, those few yards in front of her. Apprehension, excitement, bloodlust, fear: all of it present. Some of them are looking at the way cleared to the northwest gate: that choke point—outside of which, where the sun may already be reaching the frost white edges of ruts and stones, is a killing ground.

She cocked her head, short bright hair flying, eyes alight, and deliberately surveyed them.

"You shit-faced bastards, you don't need me to tell you what to do! *Kill Gelimer!*"

It echoes off the walls as they scream it back at her.

In full armor and livery, Rochester with the Lion Affronté at her shoulder, she bellows an old familiar shout, to Lions and Burgundian men-at-arms alike:

"Do we want to win!"

"Yes!"

"Can't hear you! I said do we want to *win*!"

"YES!"

"Kill Gelimer!"

"KILL GELIMER!"

Everything lost, now, in the surge of adrenaline.

"Boss!" Rickard, beside her, held up her sallet. She stopped for as long as it took him to buckle on her bevor and helmet. The sound of sakers, serpentine, and organ-guns from the east is already growing less regular, less loud. She shoved her visor up, taking as well a short, four-foot pole hammer, carrying it loosely from her left hand.

A solid *boom*! banged out from the city wall behind her.

"Yeah! Go, Ludmilla!"

A rapid firecracker-sequence of bangs, the reverberation of a mangonel cup thudding up hard against its bar—and every swivel gun, hackbut, cannon, and organ-gun on the walls around the northwest gate opened up. Ash winced, for the nearness of the fire, even muffled by her helmet lining.

But is that all we've got?

Under her breath, she muttered, *"Angeli, come on!"*

She swung back to face the battle line. They have worked themselves up to where she is now, to a magnificent *fuck it!* to all suicidal risks, and probably for the same reason: the fear that rips through her bowels.

"I know I can rely on you guys! You're too stupid to know when you're beaten!"

A loud chant went up. For a second, she could not make it out. Then, in half a dozen languages: "Lion! Lion of Burgundy! She-Lion!" and *"The Maid!"*

Something quivered under her feet.

The ice that puddled the mud under her feet cracked. A dull, loud, earth-lifting roar went up. Rocks, masonry fragments, and beams flew in a hail: every man ducking as one and putting his helmet down to the blast.

Ash lifted her head, and visor.

Beyond the cleared no-man's-land, the whole section of city wall between the Byward Tower and the White Tower puffed out dust from between every block of masonry.

"Angeli! *Yes!*"

Angelotti and the Burgundian engineers: opening the sap, widening the diggings under the wall, all through this last night. And sweating to put powder in place, and praying that it would be enough—

The wall stood for a moment. Ash had a heartbeat's time in which to think *If Angelotti got this wrong, it'll fall this way, and then we're dead*, and the wall shattered and fell.

Silently, in a second, it fell away onto the air—outward.

The impact of it on the iron-cold earth shook her into a stagger. She got her balance, swearing. Beyond the swirling clouds of dust, sweeping chokingly back, two hundred yards of wall lay collapsed into rubble across the moat. Nothing but five or six hundred yards of ground, now, before the first trenches of the Visigoth camp.

"That's it." She spoke aloud, dazed, to herself; staring over the heads of the men in front of her at the two-hundred-foot gap in the wall. "Dijon isn't defensible anymore. No choice now."

"St. George!" Robert Anselm bellowed in her ear.

Thomas Morgan's voice, under the Lion standard, yelled, *"Saint Godfrey for Burgundy!"*

Ash choked her throat clear, drew breath, hauled her voice up from her belly, and screamed at brass-pitch: *"Attack!"*

IV

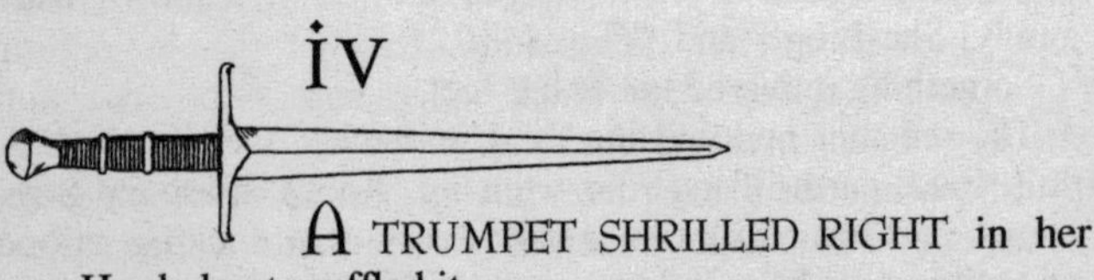

A TRUMPET SHRILLED RIGHT in her ear. Her helmet muffled it.

Fallen masonry grated and slid under her boots.

Her chest heaved, breath hissing dry in her throat, and her feet came down on hard mud, and she ran—sprinting among armored men, her view of them jolting through the slit of her visor; steel-covered legs pounding, forcing her muscles to push her on across the frozen earth—out into open ground.

Bodies crowded her. She glimpsed her banner-pole to her left. The rough ground threw her. Stone or bone, she lost her footing, felt someone's hand catch her under the arm and throw her on, not missing a beat.

A square dark shape lifted up against the sky in front of her.

Before she could think *what*? it went over and down. Her own boots were skidding on the icy wood before she recognized it as a door. Either side of her, planks and shutters slammed down onto the frozen mud. A brief sight of a six-foot-deep trench, off one side of the makeshift bridge—

That's their trench; the first defense!

She came off the planks, Anselm and Rickard tight with her. A confused mass of liveries blocked her view—red crosses, blue and yellow. The sudden jut and curve of a long-bow stave went up on her left—someone shooting—and in the noise of brass horns, shouting men, and clattering armor came the *thwick!* of bowstrings.

She cannoned into the back of the man in front, bounced off, spared a glance for the banner and Rochester—an armored figure at her left shoulder, the escort sprinting with him—and saw nothing around her but helmeted heads, against the pale sky, and *there!* the Lion standard—

"Don't lose it!" she bellowed, "keep going, *keep going*!"

A tent peg caught her foot. She staggered, still running forward; a blade sliced down to her right, chopping at the frost-loose guy ropes, only getting tangled up in the slack. She kicked the man's sword free without a pause. Another man's body plowed into her, falling across her feet, facedown, arms up flying over his forge black sallet, bare sword dropping between his unarmored legs.

She wrenched her leg free, hauled him up by shoulder and arm, one of Rochester's men at his other side, yelled: "Keep *going*!"

Running men's backs surround her. Nothing more than two feet away is visible. The trumpet shrilled, off to her left. The bar-slit of her vision blurred. Canvas ripped under her saba-tons, someone thrust a bill down into it; she heard a choked-off squeal from underneath, flailed down with the hammer, not slowing.

Collapsing tents sagged at her feet. She caught sight of fire arcing through the sky over her head. A pitch torch landed among the lightly armored men at her right: men screamed, shouted curses; the torch rolled uselessly down the wet canvas and sank into the beaten earth in front of her.

The crowd of men surged forward into free movement at the same second that she thought *hard-packed earth: the camp's roads!*

Armor clatters, men jogging forward, breathing hard; two men go down on her right, one on her left—

A thin billman in a jack fell flat in front of her. She pitched over him onto her face. He screamed. Something cracked in her hand where she held the pole-hammer shaft. Someone grabbed the back of her livery jacket and hauled her onto her feet—*Anselm?*—and an arrow stuck out of the billman's groin, waggling as he rolled, screeching, blood soaking his hose and hands.

"Are we right?" Anselm bellowed in her ear. He jogged beside her, bare sword in one hand. "Which *way*—"

Panic hit her: *Have we turned around—?* "Keep going!"

A hiss like water thrown onto hot grease came from somewhere: she couldn't see which direction. Screams rose over the noise of orders, armor, men panting. A hollow breathlessness scraped at her lungs; her legs ached; her hot, wet breath bounced the smell of steel back off the inside of her helmet.

A gap opened up in front of her.

She saw a pounded-earth road, a lone, broken longbow.

I'm dropping behind, that's why there's a gap—

She forced herself to run harder. The gap didn't close.

Shit, I can't do it—

Her visor's slit blackened. Blind, she stumbled on. Scraping at it, her hand came away wet. She shoved the sallet up with a bloody glove, tilting it. The smell choked in her throat. Directly in front, men lifted bill-shafts and stabbed hooked blades down—above their heads, the great yellow-and-blue expanse of the Lion standard, next to the standard of the Burgundian duchy.

"Get *up* there!" she yelled. *Shit-all fucking command we're doing!*

Someone crashed into her from behind—one of Rochester's men, or Rochester himself. She stumbled, braced; her heels skidded on frozen hard-packed earth, and slid off toward the side of the road, seeing the roof of a timber barracks over helmets and plumes—*legion plumes*! The whole mass of men with her in the middle of it kept pushing, pushing to the right, moving away from something to her left—

"—fucking *arrows*!"

A hard impact knocked her head around to the right. Pain shot through her wrenched neck. A spear blade shone in front of her eyes. The pole hammer wouldn't come up, caught on something—a steel-plated arm pushed in front of her, and the spearpoint skidded off that vambrace and into her breastplate. The impact knocked her half-turned around. She dragged her weapon free. A woman screamed. A Visigoth spearman stumbled into her field of view, fell at her feet.

She slammed the top-spike down, punched it into his calf muscle; a foot knight in Lion livery smacked a mace into the Visigoth's bare face. Bloodied teeth and bone fragments spattered up her breastplate—

The flagstaff of the Lion Affronté cracked down hard on her right shoulder. An armored man cannoned into her from behind, a Visigoth spearman, on his knees, clinging to the man's belt and stabbing a dagger up into his groin. Blood sprayed.

They shouldn't get this near to me—

The whole mass of people pushed off to the right; she half fell over the edge of the path. The banner-pole caught between her helmet and haut-piece, jutting forward over her shoulder, pressing her down.

"Keep—going—!"

With a great wrench she completed the turn, spinning as hard left as she could. The banner-pole jolted up over the haut-piece of her shoulder armor and off.

Thomas Rochester grabbed for it with one hand.

All the men around him had white Visigoth livery, mail hauberks.

He opened his mouth, shouting at her.

A sword slammed against his face, hit the bottom of his sallet at jaw height, skidded upward along the metal edges, and his face disappeared in a spray of blood.

She grabbed her pole hammer in both hands, rammed the butt-spike under the Visigoth's upraised arm, punching through mail rings. The hard impact jolted back through her shoulder muscles. The shaft twisted as she tried to pull it free. A gout of blood spurted over her forearms. Men in red-and-blue livery thumped into her, pushing her back; it was all she could do to keep the shaft from being wrenched out of her hand and *Christ Jesus I'm facing the wrong way, I'm turned around, where's the banner—?*

"Get the fucking *banner* UP!"

Stay *visible*, keep *moving*, stay *alive*—!

Men behind slammed into her.

She pushed back for a second, but the weight of them forced her forward. She staggered upright and on, stepping on bodies, treading on ragged mailed backs, bloodied breast-plates, her ankle twisting as her footing skidded between bodies, in blood and fluid.

Shit, I have no idea which way I'm facing—

Slamming the sharp points of her couters back, elbowing for space, she turned around, the sky black with arrows. Sweat froze on her exposed face. A blue-and-yellow Lion's-head banner lifting up—

"Boss!" Rickard's adolescent, cracked voice shrieked beside her, over the noise, the Lion Azure banner's shaft solid in his grip.

Two men slammed in beside her. Lion livery. Rochester's men, her escort. Three more men.

"Keep going! Fuck it! Don't lose momentum!"

She pushed herself forward, grabbed the staff above Rickard's hand, pushed, bellowed, *"Move forward!"* She let go the banner and slammed the shaft of her pole hammer horizontally across the backs in front of her, feet digging in, pushing with all her weight. Two men-at-arms slammed in beside her.

Ahead—over the mass of Burgundian helmets, Visigoth helmets; the glint of a legion eagle—the Lion standard went suddenly back and round in an eddy of movement.

Pressure sent her staggering back: three steps, hearing men shriek curses, armored feet trampling, treading on men wounded on the ground. A thin spray of red speckled her gauntlet, vambrace, and couter. Rickard thrust his sword once, awkwardly; she couldn't see if it had an effect. Men ahead lifted up bill-shafts, punched them down.

The press in front of her gave way.

She dragged Rickard around, shoved him forward—*Shit, where's Robert!*—looked for Anselm; and stumbled back onto the hard-earth road.

A mass of Burgundian-liveried billmen—*Loyecte's men!*—crowded back over her. She ducked her head. An arrow glanced off the tail of her sallet; her head jerked back. Three or four men fell against her, one with his helmet ripped off and a Visigoth gripping his brown hair, face streaming blood. A man in livery soaked all red jabbed a bollock dagger into the Visigoth's groin, their bodies pressed up against Ash; she punched her left gauntlet plate into the Visigoth's eye, felt the bone of his eye socket snap, heard him scream through her muffling helmet and lining. Pressure eased; she got herself onto firm footing.

Christ, I miss being on a horse! I can't see a fucking thing!

"Where's my fucking command group!" She got no power into her voice. "Rickard! *Find the Lion standard.* We got to keep moving; *we're dead if we stand still*!"

Her hands felt emptiness. She pushed her body forward into the middle of the men. Two sharp impacts on her back-plate she ignored, thrusting with her arms like a man swimming. Ahead, bill-blades went up and down, rising and falling; and she shoved toward the irregular movement.

"There!"

Rickard swung off her left shoulder, bawling. She found herself with her sword in hand—*when did I draw that? Where's my pole hammer?*—staring across a space of ten or a dozen yards full of fighting men's backs, all of them shoving forward; and beyond them a standard charged with a lion passant guardant azure.

She opened her mouth to yell, "Okay, *go*!" and a blast of fire blacked out her vision.

Head ringing, arms numb, she clawed at what she could reach of her face under the front of her tilted sallet. The split second's dazzle passed, let her see that she was standing at the edge of a crowd—

On the earth in front of her, a swath of men lay prone or supine, arms flung up over their faces. On each body, the line of red hose or bright steel cuisse or painted war-hat ended at charred black.

Smoke poured up off their bodies. It smelled wrenchingly of roast meat. Her mouth filled with water.

Two scorched, unrecognizable faces reared up in front of her, screaming.

Another hiss, water on a hot fire, magnified a hundred times. A foot kicked her behind the knee. She fell sprawling, hit the earth hard. *Down: defenseless!* Her bladder let go; she scratched in panic at the cold ground, scrabbling to get her feet back under her. Something fell or trod on her backplate: her helmet slammed against the earth; someone shrieked her name.

Whiteness flickered in the corner of her vision.

A wide-mouthed screaming Visigoth *nazir* crawled in front of her; not striking out, not even looking. His whole back was charred black and smoking.

She got to hands and knees. A man hurdled over her. She flinched back. Six, seven, or more: men in hose and jacks, Lion livery, steel war-hats flashing in the bright cold sunlight, all lifting weapons.

Over their heads, she saw a white stone ovoid: marble carved into the shape of a face. Brass glinted at its back. A low, chimney-flue roar; bodies fell down around her; heat scorched her face, and she threw up her arm too late. Her skin stung; her eyes ran. Staggering up, she blinked her vision clear, saw the golem standing with the Greek Fire tank's blackened nozzle in both hands, swinging it inexorably around—

Two men in Lion livery ducked low. Two swung weapons. *Mauls!* she saw, *heavy hammers*; and the stone right arm and left hand of the golem shattered and cracked off its body. The nozzle fell. The two men hit the golem from the side: a bill-shaft between them, across the bronze-jointed knees. She saw it fall over backward, saw four other men strike hard, decisive hammerblows; their leader bawled "That one's *down*: move on, *keep moving*!" Geraint's voice.

"BOSS—"

Someone's hands hauled her round. A man in armor, a head

taller than she. Lion livery: Anselm's voice; Robert Anselm screaming, "This way! Over here! *This way!*"

Running, pounding, panting; stopping again in the thick of troops, foot knights, and in the sky above and past Anselm, the Lion standard—not moving.

Not moving.

We're shitted, we lost it, we're bogged down.

Oh Jesus. Hundreds of them round us. It's the finish.

Every muscle in her body knotted. For a second, in the din of fighting, she stopped dead, bent half-double. Her thigh muscles ached; her shoulder joints jabbed her with pain, every spot under plate—collarbone, hip, knee—swelled with bruises. Her head rang. Blood ran down into one eye, and she dabbed at her face; and saw that her ring finger inside her right gauntlet was outside the strap, and folded across at a ninety-degree angle to the palm. She could not feel the break. Blood ran down from a gouge on the inside of her elbow; one tasset plate was gone; everything on her left-hand side—plackart, breastplate, poleyn, greave—had the scratches and dents of arrow strikes not even felt.

Wish I'd gone for my brigandine; mobility. I can't walk another fucking yard in this harness.

Can't fight. I'm dead.

Anselm's helmet-muffled voice bellowed, "Come *on*, girl!"

She made to move off. One half pace, and she stopped again, the noise of screaming men beating at her ears through the helmet lining. She felt her arms too heavy to lift, her legs too heavy to move.

"I won't run!" she yelled.

The men closest to her were not fighting. The shouts and screams came from a few yards farther off. A great noise went up—indistinguishable words.

"What the fuck—"

Over the heads of the men in front, something was passing—passing through many hands, toward the Lion Affronté banner—passed across and down to Robert Anselm—something he thrust out toward her.

She took it automatically: a Visigoth spear. Her hand gripped the shaft. Unbalanced, it fell, and she grabbed at it with her other hand, swearing at the pain, her dropped sword dangling off its lanyard, and she looked up into the blue sky to see what unbalanced the weapon.

A severed head.

The head's weighted beard shook, braided with golden beads.

"Gelimer's dead!" Robert Anselm bawled. He pointed up, steel arm bloodied past the elbow. "GELIMER'S DEAD!"

A great scream went up, over to the left.

"We have to stop this!" Ash shouted. She closed her other hand around the spear shaft. "We got to—*do they know he's dead*?"

"Banner went down!"

"WHAT?"

"His BANNER. Went DOWN!"

"Let me through." She moved another step forward, toward the line of billmen—John Price's old unit, that had been Carracci's—ducking the ends of bill-shafts jabbing back. "Get me through to the fucking front of the line! *Fast!*"

Men's backs shifted. She shouldered between burly bodies, both hands gripping the top-heavy spear, Robert Anselm and the banner at her back; felt herself shoved bodily into the second rank of billmen, and bill-shafts came down over her shoulders, dripping blades held out in front of her, a mass of hooks and spikes.

"Gelimer's dead!" The pitch of her voice shredded her throat.

The bill unit backed up, bunching against her, weapons raised, but not striking. Beyond, spearpoints caught sunlight. A line of Visigoth men in mail and coat of plates, bright reds and oranges and pinks, lower faces covered by aventails or black cloth; spears and swords extended—

She has a second to wonder *are they backing off?* and realize she is already seeing trodden earth and bodies lying on their faces. She risked a glance, left and right, through a forest of bills and spears. A gap of several feet—still widening—

They've seen his banner go down—

She thrust the spear two-handed up into the blue sky.

Gelimer's severed head bobbed high above the morass of bodies, face clearly distinct in the sun, his mouth gaping open, his roughly chopped-out spine hanging down in a tail of red and white bone.

"The King-Caliph's dead!"

The bellow emptied her chest of air. She swayed. Billmen in jacks and war-hats beside her, red-faced, panting, tears running, took it up:

"The King-Caliph's dead!"

Arrows still dropped out of the sky, on her left: men shouted over the clashing-together of iron. Around her a chant grew, drowning that out.

"The King-Caliph's dead! The King-Caliph's dead!"

Arms shaking, she jabbed up the spear and its impaled head. *You gotta* see *it!*

Widening, now; undeniably widening—a gap between the fighting lines: a stretch of earth, canvas, tumbled cauldrons, bloodied bedding, and bodies with their heads buried in their arms. And bodies and separate heads. Fifteen feet in front of her she clearly saw one *nazir*, bewildered, shouting at his commander. The *'arif's* gaze fixed on the spike, and the head of Gelimer.

The rise of the ground and the trampled-down camp let her see, as the spearmen edged back, the helmets of the hundreds of men beyond them—slave-spearmen, Visigoth dismounted knights, bowmen; rank on rank of men jammed shoulder to shoulder among the trashed tents and buildings, unit banners peppering the sky. Experience gave her a rapid assessment: *four and a half, five thousand men.*

A distant single rapid *b-bang*! split the air. Some gunner sweeping a match across all the touchholes of an organ-gun at one go: eight barrels firing almost instantaneously—from the city wall.

I can hear *that! They've stopped fighting* here—

As instantly, screams shrieked up from her right: the roaring cough of Greek Fire sounded; black smoke rounded itself up onto the air.

"The King-Caliph's dead!" she bellowed again, ripping her

throat with every word, hearing the shrill high clarion of her voice echo over men's heads, burning buildings, shrieks of pain. "GELIMER—IS—DEAD. *Stop fighting!*"

Whether it was adrenaline or lack of oxygen, she swayed back against Anselm. He gripped her arm, hand closing around her vambrace, and held her steady. She thought, for a heartbeat, it was as if the whole world held its breath; no reason why the Visigoth troops should not just roll on over the less than thirteen hundred men in front of them. *No reason in the world,* she thought dizzily, gazing through bloody eyes at the blue, icy clear sky and Gelimer's head on a spike.

"Disengage!" She forced a strained whisper at Robert Anselm. "Send runners—tell Morgan to *hold* the standard *where he is.*"

"Got you!"

Officers yelled orders behind her. She continued to face forward, hardly breathing, eyes sore and stinging. She saw no banners that she knew, certainly not the Faris's Brazen head, no sign of Gelimer's portcullis banner going up again; and then across the cleared space—*thirty feet, now?*—a banner with a stark geometric triangle came up: Sancho Lebrija's stylized mountain.

He follows orders.

Will he follow a dead man's orders?

"KING'S—DEAD!" Ash bellowed. Her voice cracked.

Anselm hauled her around, pointing. More men flooded into the area every second. *They'll be covering all the ground behind us, between us and the city.* The Lebrija banner jerked, caught up somewhere in the mass of troops. *How many seconds before he starts giving orders?*

"There!" Anselm threw his arm out, pointing: more horses picked their way across the broken ground; a leader with a gilded helmet; riders carrying another banner—a notched wheel. A black notched wheel on a white field.

She said, "That's *Leofric's* livery!"

The two banners met. Men's voices shouted.

"My lord *Amirs*!" she screamed. "The Caliph Gelimer is dead!"

She emphasized it with a shake of the spear in her hands.

Blood and spinal fluid trickled down over her right hand, bright on the back of her steel gauntlet.

Panting, she gulped air down into her lungs. For all the cold, she sweltered in her armor. She stared.

The rider in the gilded helmet, among men in mail and white robes, took off his helmet, and was Leofric.

His wisps of white hair jutted up. He touched spurs to his mare's flanks, urging her out among the dead and dying, coming close enough for her to see him frowning at the impaled head, either in anger or against the morning sun.

A sun hardly risen any farther up from the horizon behind him. *I doubt it's fifteen minutes since the wall went down.*

"Leofric!" she yelled, "Gelimer's dead. *He can't stop you destroying the Wild Machines!*"

The wind took her words, and the noises of sobbing, hurt men and women. *Can he hear me?* She stared into his lined face for long seconds—*is he mad? Was he* ever *mad?*—and he turned away from her, saying something sharp; one of his officers began to shout brusque orders, and the *'uqba* pennants moved in toward him—Lebrija's banner with them.

"He's doing it. He's taking command. God damn it, he's doing it." She stamped her feet. *"He's doing it."*

Robert Anselm swore evenly and monotonously and vilely.

Thirty yards away, to her left, the gap between the lines vanished again. She looked up a corridor of clashing staves above men's heads; poleax and hooked bills; spear and lifted shields, men packed in too close to do more than hack at weapon shafts and helmets, stab at faces. A concerted Visigoth shout: the St. Andrew's Cross pennon went back ten yards in ten seconds.

That's some 'arif *acting on his own—*

"Tell 'em to hold!" She dug her feet in against the pressure of bodies from behind; yelled across at Leofric, "*Stop* the fighting! *Now!*"

Lebrija's *'arifs* shouted. Sudden weight behind pushed her, inexorably; staggering forward among the jutting billhooks. Rickard's shoulder scraped against hers. The Lion banner swayed. Robert Anselm's deep bellow, *"Hold!"* echoed out across the frosty camp and the troops behind him.

Twenty yards back down the slope, to her right, a guttering cough of Greek Fire roared.

"Christ! Those things don't *stop*!"

Leofric's head turned. The Lord-*Amir* jolted up in his stirrups, staring over Visigoth troops' heads. He began to shout loudly, authoritatively. She slitted her eyes, blinking away pain from swollen eyelids, heard the coughing long roar again, and a wedge of Visigoth helmets stampeded into the Burgundian billmen, men tripping and vanishing, pennons tipping over on their poles, the lick of fire searing her vision momentarily black—

"They're firing on their own men, too!" Anselm screamed. A thrust of movement in the men around her; she half turned; a runner in St. Andrew's Cross livery wheezed out, " —firing at *everybody*—" and the officers around Leofric ran, calling, units moving, and nothing, nothing—for a count of thirty.

Nothing. No Greek Fire.

A dead man has no friends.

He may have men who want to avenge him—

A high voice screamed *behind* her. Carthaginian Latin. Shoved forward, this time braced, she kept both hands clenched on the spear shaft, Gelimer's severed head swaying like a ship's mast. Two steps forward, three; forced toward the facing line of Visigoth infantry. The pressure eased. She halted, staring at spearpoints, staring at archers, recurved bows, arrows being hastily laid to bowstrings—

The *nazir* fifteen feet in front of her yelled, *"Hold!"*

She leaned back, putting her mouth close to Robert's helmet. "More runners—to commanders—hold place—defense *only*—"

Rickard shifted back, at her right shoulder, and she suddenly saw between two billmen how the ground sloped back, slightly down, the way they had come.

Christ, have we come so *far*?

I don't remember it being a slope.

Christ—

A narrow swath of trampled earth, canvas, sagging tent posts, broken beams, cook pots and men clutching weapons ran down the slope toward Dijon.

If they'd been deployed, instead of sleeping—

The air shone clear, frosty. She breathed in the stink of shit and blood. Past the end of her Burgundians, a great mass of Visigoth legionaries filled up the lanes and streets of the camp, the sun shining off motionless ranks of shield rims and swords. Chaos far over to the east, cornicens and barked orders; but in the north camp, two legions still only just being called to arms; piling out of turf barracks, an untouched five thousand more in the III Caralis alone.

All they have to do is roll over us—

Before Dijon's walls, the bare expanse of earth lay dotted with men in yellow or red-and-blue livery, some of them moving. The gap in the expanse of stonework showed utterly black. Bright metal glints, in the shadows—scythes, pitchforks. Dijon's citizens. Behind the shattered tumble of masonry.

She let her gaze sweep slowly back up the slight hill, blinking, counting: *I can't see all of us;* surely *that isn't all of us that's left—!*

A swirl of movement yanked her attention back to the Visigoth ranks in front of her. The archers parted. New, bright-liveried troops marched into the gap: a high voice, farther back in the camp, screaming in Carthaginian Latin and Italian: "Advance! Attack!"

"Aw *shit—*"

A cornicen rang out. Braced, breathless, she shot a glance either side at the sweating billmen; saw their faces show disgust and terror equally, and then one man gave a great laugh, his flapping cheek showing bloody teeth in the cut.

She squinted through swollen eyelids. Not Visigoth troops ahead—men in Frankish liveries. Bow and bill foot troops. Armored horsemen, packed tight in the crowd. And nobody moving, not one man of them moving forward past the line—

The Carthaginian voice screaming orders cut off with a blackly comic gurgle.

"Look at *that*!" A mush of blood sprayed out with the billman's words. "Look at that, boss!"

The white *Agnus Dei* banner glinted, gold embroidery flashing in the sun; and down the line, Onorata Rodiani's naked sword, and the Ship and Crescent Moon of Joscelyn van Mander: Gelimer's Frankish mercenaries.

She saw a rider in Milanese armor reach out to his banner-bearer. Agnes Dei. Sun flashed off his gauntlet, gripping the striped pole. A babble of Italian crossed the clear air, not distinct enough for her to make out what was said.

The golden spike on top of the banner dipped.

The rider's armored hand forcing it down, the banner dipped, silk folding, the banner going down, the point of it touching the bloodied dirt, and the Lamb of God lost among the draped cloth on the earth.

Tears dazzled her vision. Raw shouts went up around her. Beyond, the banner of the Rodiani company dipped; and de Monforte; and finally, finally the silver and blue of the Ship and Crescent, all the mercenary banners going down, dipped to the dirt, to their men's raucous, fierce, appreciative cheers.

Robert Anselm, hammering at her left pauldron, pointing away with his free hand:

"He's calling them off!"

Shrill cornicens called from the center of the camp, and beyond, from the east, where guns still fired. She turned and thrust the loaded spear at Rickard.

"Give me the banner!"

Their hands fumbled; her snapped finger, in its blood-soaked glove, tore loose from the spear shaft; and she took the Lion Affronté banner in her left hand alone, held it up over her head, and hefted it in a weary apology for a circle.

The crack of guns from the east trickled away. Inside a long minute, all the gun crews stopped shooting.

Leofric rode up past Gelimer's ex-mercenaries, among ranks of House Leofric infantry, Lebrija's banner with him, other *qa'ids*' pennants following. The Lord-*Amir* Leofric reined in his mare, leaning down to speak to one of his commanders.

'Arif Alderic stepped forward from the line. "My master says, 'Peace between us! Peace between Carthage and Burgundy!' "

She took a raw breath, and shouted, "Has he—the right and power—to offer it?"

Alderic's voice rang out, to at least the nearest Visigoth units as well as to the Burgundians. "*Amir* Leofric, with the death in battle of this Gelimer, claims for himself the throne of the King-Caliph. There are no other *amirs* of rank here. It is his honor and duty. Hail the King-Caliph Leofric!"

Robert Anselm's voice, beside her, exploded: "Bugger me!"

The Visigoth legions cheered.

Alderic called, "*Jund* Ash, he has this power. Carthage will ratify his election here. Will you take the peace he offers?"

"Fuck, *yes*!"

Waiting to regroup, a forest of banners and standards surrounds her: Thomas Morgan, with the blue-and-gold standard of the Lion Azure, de la Marche and his bearer of the Burgundian duchy's arms; the Lion Affronté; unit pennants; and men in bloodied plate and ripped mail staring up not at the silks, but at the spear shaft that she rests back over her shoulder, the severed head high up and visible to everybody near this part of the field.

She feels nothing.

"Tell Leofric where we want it set up. On the open ground, in front of the gap in the wall."

Anselm nodded acknowledgment, signaled two of Morgan's men, and vanished through the troops toward Leofric.

The loud noise of relief, of a barely present realization of success just making itself felt—none of this pierces the glass bubble of numbness that surrounds her.

"We did it!" Rickard ripped off his helmet with his free hand. His flushed, youthful face beamed. "*We did it!* Hey, boss! You going to make me your squire now?"

Deep male voices boom appreciation. Suddenly they are clearing a space, the black-haired boy going down on one knee in front of her, still clutching the striped pole of the Lion Affronté.

"Ah, fuck it!" Ash said. She grinned, suddenly, and the sore skin on her face twinged. A flood of warm emotion pierces her. Through blurred vision, she recovered her wheel-pommel sword on its lanyard, gripped it, and put the bare blade down on Rickard's shoulder. "If I could make it a knighthood, I would! Consider yourself promoted!"

The cheers for that are part joy, part relief, part the feeling that this is how it *should* be, right now. Armored men help the young man to his feet, beating on his shoulders. The cold air stings her face again. She does not remove her own helmet, not yet.

"Stay there." She unceremoniously shoved the spear at Rochester's sergeant, Elias, and elbowed her way a few yards west into the crowd, until she can see past the back rank of men.

In her mind, the direction is clear—*no matter what turf the camp is set up on, the camp is always the same.*

The *ad hoc* leader of Carracci's and Price's billmen shouldered hastily in beside her, as escort.

"Vitteleschi," he panted. "In charge of these guys if you say so, boss."

"For now." Another spreading grin, that she can't resist: *we did it, we* did *it!* and her cheeks sting.

"Your face is red, boss," Vitteleschi said.

"Yeah?"

"Your skin." He drew a gauntlet finger swiftly across his own cheekbones.

"Right . . ." Cooling sweat stings in the corners of her eyes, scalding her swollen lids.

Now she can see past the back rank, past an elaborate turf-roofed building—Gelimer's headquarters?—and out onto the bridge beyond.

"I want to see what Jonvelle's . . ."

Bright red blood covers the ice.

Blood covers the thick frost on the shore. She squinted at lumps, lying on the trodden earth bank, casting man-size black shadows.

Out on the ice, men hauled dead men in, by an arm or a leg; picking up heads, leaving smears on the whiteness. Scattered corpses farther downriver jutted with fletched shafts.

She counted the line on the bank. *Twenty-two*.

Among the dropped weapons, discarded bone skates lay.

Get into position; hold the bridge; stop Gelimer from running.

A Burgundian sergeant plodded forward.

"Where's Jonvelle?" she asked.

"Dead." The man coughed, coughed again. "Dead, Demoiselle-Captain. Captain Burghes is dead. Captain Romont, too."

Men of note.

She turned her head, seeing men lying down on the northern side of the bridge, lying on the cold earth in awkward positions, arms flung out, legs hooked one over the other.

Billmen; archers; men with only jacks and brigandines and helmets. She looked at their faces, bleeding from the mouth, the blood not running now. Fifty? Sixty?

A man sat on the ground in front of the still-warm bodies, bent over his stomach, moaning. Half a dozen Burgundian billmen walked back over the bridge toward her, supporting men and women who cried out with pain at every step, Jonvelle's banner-bearer still dragging his colors, his hastily bandaged right arm dripping, missing from the elbow down.

A severed hand almost tripped her as she stepped back.

"Vitteleschi."

"Boss."

"Send a runner over to Lord-*Amir* Leofric. Tell him our doctors are in the city. Tell him to send me his legionary medics."

"But—"

"*Now*, Vitteleschi." She turned back to the Burgundian sergeant. "Are you in command here?" And at his nod—*shit, everyone of rank above sergeant dead?*—she said, "There won't be any crap about not being treated by raghead doctors, clear? Get anyone who's still alive bandaged up, or on hurdles; bring them down into the city as soon as you're ready. Go to the abbey hospices."

"Yes, Demoiselle-Captain."

There was no emotion in his voice.

She turned to Vitteleschi. "Let's go."

The men parted, letting her back through, almost all drawn

up to their unit pennants now. She walks among men in Burgundian livery, Lion livery—men talking in low tones, and over it all now the screaming and shrieks of wounded men, men lying out between them and the ranks of the Visigoth legions, crawling, or sprawled on their faces. One woman, helmet gone, vomited, blood spidering down over her forehead.

Shit, is that Katherine Hammell? No: one of her archers, though—

The Visigoth doctors and their assistants are already moving out of the opposing army. Some Frankish voices went up in protest. The legionary medics bend down by men, leaving some, calling hurdles for others.

They do not distinguish between their own men and hers.

"Send a runner into the town. Tell the monks to come out here and help see to these men. No, I don't know that it's *safe*! Tell them to get their fucking arses out here! Get Blanche's women, too."

She looked for de la Marche's banner.

"Back to the city. The way we came in. Muster on the ground outside the walls."

She walked on past the Burgundian, Rickard with the standard, Elias with the spear, and Vitteleschi and his men behind her. Ranks parted in front of her. Thin ranks. She glanced back, saw few, very few; thought, *Shit I don't believe it, we* can't *have lost that many!* and found herself walking onto the edge of an area of blackness, even the crushed tents only charcoal frameworks, and men writhing on the baked earth.

"Get a fucking medic over here!"

One of Leofric's robed Visigoths strode past her, in a flurry of cloth, sandals cracking burnt tent pegs and bones underfoot. The hood fell back, and she saw a woman doctor, pinch-faced; calling out to her assistants in medical Latin.

I know her.

"You." The Visigoth woman's voice sounded in front of her. She opened eyes she had not been aware of shutting, recognized the face, too, and the voice saying *the gate of the womb is all but destroyed.*

"I will give your slave here a salve for your eyes; they will swell, otherwise. You have missed the worst of the burn, but do not neglect—"

"*Fuck off.*" She pushed past the woman.

She stopped at a pile of men charred black, and a leg in blue hose. The body lay with head downhill, lower than its feet. The tail of a yellow-and-blue livery jacket showed, unburned. Vitteleschi gave a short order. Two billmen knelt, and turned the blackened body over. After a second, he said, "Captain Campin."

Under Adriaen Campin's body, his lance leader was almost unburned. Willem Verhaecht's eyes were open in his florid face, not blinking at the sky's brightness. Something, most likely the hand of a golem, had punched into his body through his breastplate and pulled one lung out onto the torn metal. She stared for ten breaths, and the red-black flesh did not twitch, did not beat.

Take teams: take out the golems: take out their Greek Fire weapons.

"Check and see if anyone's alive here."

The sunlight showed tears pouring down Vitteleschi's lined, filthy face.

"Shit, just do it," she said, her voice weak; and he nodded, still weeping, and bent over to pull away crisped arms and torsos that fell apart in his hands like roasted joints from the oven.

The Lion standard and the Burgundian standard came slowly down the slope behind her, ranks of men under them. Back down the slope: past the second swath cut by Greek Fire, and here—

A hand grabbed at her armored knee. She looked down at the gauntlet against her poleyn, and into the face of a man recognizable only because he wore livery with a lion's head on it, his own face smashed, unrecognizable. Bubbles blew in the blood where his mouth had been. Sitting next to him, a billman held the stump of his right wrist with his left hand, his face glassy and white.

"Medics!" Vitteleschi bawled back over his shoulder. "Get the doctors down here!"

The standards came on. Men began to pick their way. The

ground for ten yards was covered in foot knights in her livery, some moving, some not, all bloody. She took one step aside, and her sabaton kicked a man's arm, severed at the elbow.

A faint voice called for help. Her gaze still on the bloody, unrecognizable man—*it's de Treville, it's Henri, I know his armor*—she backed up, turned around, saw Thomas Rochester's crossbowman Ricau kneeling on the ground, with Thomas Rochester sitting up braced against him.

"Boss," the man Ricau said. "Help me with him, boss, I don't know what to do!"

"Rickard, get some of those fucking medics here—"

"Runner, boss—there aren't enough here yet—"

Stiff, she got down on one knee, in frozen earth now muddy with fluids and excrement. She put out her hand, and hesitated. Vitteleschi squatted beside her, a piece of bloodied cloth in his hand—torn-off livery—and reached out. Ricau took it, wiped gingerly at the man leaning back against him, and Rochester screamed. His sound pierced the semi-silence of the field, ended in something like and not like a sneeze, an explosion of blood.

"It's his *eye*!" Ricau wailed.

He had got his commander's sallet off. Two black oval holes streamed blood down Rochester's face and onto his mail standard, and down his breastplate. Nothing of his nose was left, only a fragment of cartilage. A shattered white splinter of bone jutted out of the red mess of his right eye—his own bone, she realized, from his shattered nose.

The men plodding back down the hill slowed, looking down at Rochester, casting numb or angry looks, trying not to breathe in the stench of shit that rose up from him.

"Get a grip." She licked at her lips. "Keep him *still*, and quiet. Put the cloth there, soak it up—let him breathe. Tom. Tom? Help's coming. We'll get you back. Fuck"—she straightened and sprang up— "has anybody got any wine? Any water?"

Word went back through the crowd, men feeling at their belts—very few costrels, none, it seemed, with anything left—

"Here!" Rickard turned away, yelling and waving the Lion

banner at white-robed men picking their way across the earth from the massed legions. "Over here!"

"Shit!" She turned on her heel and walked on among Burgundian units, among broken tents now. She heard panting. Rickard and the banner caught her up. He said something. She kept going. There was an empty space beside her, the men parting and going around Rickard where he knelt. She stopped.

Two bodies lay together on the ground, among the stained canvas of a barrack-tent. *This is where we broke through to the road: this is where the tent teams did their stuff.*

A small, squat body lay under his hands. Rickard rolled it over. The head flopped, neck boneless as a dead rabbit. A few strands of yellow hair stuck out under the helmet lining of the open-faced sallet. Blood had run out of eight or nine holes punched through the brigandine.

"Margaret Schmidt," another man's voice said, and she looked up to see Giovanni Petro, and the archer Paolo.

He shrugged at her implicit question. " 'S all that's left of us."

White and glossy-skinned as the wounded, Rickard got back up onto his feet. The banner-pole leaned loosely back across his shoulder.

"That's Katherine Hammell," he said.

About to speak, she saw he meant not Margaret, but the other body, curled up on the mud in a fetal position. The woman groaned. An arrow stuck out of her mail shirt under her shoulder blade. A sword stuck through her stomach, the point projecting out of her lower back. Her blood-soaked gauntlets clenched in her spilled intestines.

"She's still alive. Get a doctor to her." And, seeing Rickard's expression, "Who knows?"

"We need a miracle!" he wailed.

A cynical smile almost burst out of her. For a second, she could have screamed, or burst into tears. "That, we can't manage. . . ."

A fast pace took her through the marching men, down onto flat ground, out toward the golem-dug trenches encircling the city. She walked stiffly, in silence.

Fewer bodies here. She stumbled on, momentarily looking across to the gap in the walls, seeing Leofric's banner, and Anselm's and Follo's; and a handful of civilians coming out over the demolished wall—

"Look out!" Rickard screamed.

Her foot came down on something soft. She staggered and caught her balance. The man under her feet shrieked and burst into sobs. Black-feathered arrows jutted out of him, *alive enough to make a noise*, she thought; and then, *Euen*—!

The wiry, dark man looked bulky in mail and livery jacket. Bloodstains blotted out the Lion. She knelt down, counted *arrow in arm, arrow in face, two arrows in thigh*, and said, "Euen, hold on!"

"Shit, boss!" Rickard groaned.

"If he can shout, he'll make it—" Her hand, patting him down, examining by touch, froze. She awkwardly peeled back his livery, and hauberk, and took her hand away thick with hot, red blood pouring out of his groin or belly, she couldn't see where. *"Get somebody here."*

Rickard sprinted.

She stayed pressing her whole weight against his wound until Visigoth medics arrived, saw him onto a hurdle, screaming at the men to get him to a hospital tent. She stood up, hands dripping, watching the last of her force moving past her and over the improvised bridges of the ditch.

The defenses are manned again now: Visigoth soldiers in coats of plate and helmets gazing at her over mail aventails. Soft, accented voices went up into the still air, and a *nazir* snapped a command. She felt how many of the bows were surreptitiously lifted, how many of them exchanged glances, thinking *close enough to kill the cunt*.

She reached out a hand to Rochester's sergeant, Elias, and took the heavy-laded spear from him. An unsteady oak door and two window shutters groaned under her weight as she walked across the ditch. Rickard stumbled after her.

Yeah, we made it across the siege trenches.

Out of the walls, bridge the ditch, flatten the tents, find the roads through. And they must have found Gelimer by his ban-

ner. I knew he'd have to put it up, to command. I knew he'd break and run. And Jonvelle stopped him on the bridge. Some billman or foot knight killed him. I knew they would.

I knew.

Who needs the Lion's voice?

She glanced back, seeing more Visigoth faces at the trenches. The Lion banner above her, she felt herself their focus, like a player on a pageant wagon, visible to thousands.

Men and women still limped off the field behind her, forming up in stunned silence into their muster lines. Except that it is not a line, it's a ragged clump of men here, another there, nothing that even looks like a continuous line; and counting by eye she cannot make it come to more than five hundred men.

Stunned. As if this were a defeat, not a shocking, beyond-hope victory.

Behind the ones who can walk come the ones who can walk with help: Pieter Tyrrell with his arm over Jan-Jacob Clovet's shoulder, Saint-Seigne with two foot-knights carrying him sitting on crossed bill-shafts; an archer with eyes that are a mask of blood, being led. Two more blinded men behind her. A billman, blood squelching in his shoe, no fingers on one hand. A stumbling column of wounded men, mostly still carrying weapons cocked back over their shoulders, coming toward her, so that she sees them as an apparently motionless mass, crusted blades bobbing gently up and down above their heads.

And then men facedown on hurdles, or with a man at ankles and armpits, gripping and hefting their deadweight. People who lie still, blood trickling down. People who cry, shriek, appalled, frantic, desolate screams. Fifteen, twenty, forty; more than fifty; more than a hundred. Monks and Visigoth doctors trot between them, giving quick diagnoses, moving to those they can help.

The thump of a shod horse's hooves made itself felt through the ground. A Visigoth archer on a chestnut Barb wheeled a few yards from her. "My lord Leofric has all ready for you."

The man sounded not just respectful, but frightened.

"Tell him . . . I'll be there."

She stood long enough for the sergeants to bring her the count. Olivier de la Marche moved to her side on the frozen earth, his great red-and-blue standard behind him; and a few of the *centeniers*—Lacombe; three more. Saint-Seigne. Carency. Marle. *All there are left?*

"Demoiselle-Captain?" De la Marche sounded numb.

"Three hundred and twelve Burgundians killed. Two hundred and eighty-seven wounded. There are—"

Rickard, Vitteleschi, and Giovanni Petro looked at her.

"There are ninety-two of us not killed or wounded. A hundred and eight dead."

The Italian captain of archers said, "Shit." Rickard burst out crying.

"And another hundred wounded: about two-thirds of them walking wounded. The Lion's come out of this with less than two hundred of us, and that only if we're lucky."

The bright wind blew cold. Awkwardly, she picked open the buckle of her right gauntlet's fingerplates, took hold of the wet glove that contained it, dragged her broken ring finger back into place, and yanked the strap tight again over it, to hold it.

"Let's go," she said.

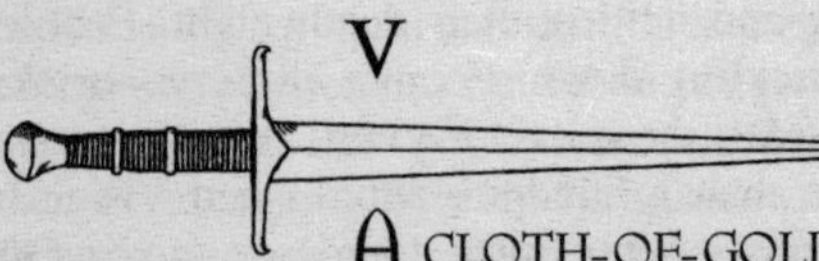

V

A CLOTH-OF-GOLD carpet covered twenty square yards of the earth below the Byward Tower. An awning covered that. Under it, banners surrounded men at a long table, and walking toward them, she felt the warmth of bonfires, kindled for their heat.

Past the tongues of flame, she looked out from ground level at the wintry sky and the immense siege camp.

"Mad."

De la Marche nodded agreement, with a smile that has already begun to discount the dead and wounded. "But you did it, Demoiselle-Captain! Maid of Dijon! You did it!"

All she could see as they walked across the earth were mantlets and pavises, and the first peaked roofs of barrack-tents. *Nazirs* and *'arifs* bawled orders, in the trenches and among the tents. It didn't stop men coming up to stare out at the huge gap in Dijon's walls. By the dozen; by the hundred.

She shook, suddenly, in her stifling armor; stopped; and could only just manage to signal Rickard to give the banner to Giovanni Petro and come and unbuckle her bevor. She choked a breath of air in. She felt Rickard ease her helmet off—*this is either peace or it isn't, and I can't be fucked to bother about assassins now!*

I don't care.

The cold air hit her scalp. She scratched left-handed at her hair, ignoring the blood on her gauntlet, and caught sight of her face reflected in the sallet as Rickard held it.

A strip of scalded flesh crossed her face, just at the level of her cheekbones, over her scars. Her lower eyelids were swelling. The strip of flesh across her cheeks and the bridge of her nose showed bright pink.

I'm one of the ninety-two: and it's little more than luck.

Robert Anselm strode up, Richard Follo a few steps behind. The dusty Viscount-Mayor seemed dazed. He laughed, low and under his breath, sounding as if it were from pure joy.

She knows the words that go with that laughter. *We're alive.*

The golden cloth snagged under her sabatons as she strode across it. Six or seven men sat at the long table: Leofric in the center, Frederick of Hapsburg on his right hand; the French envoys and de Commines on his left; Lebrija, and another *qa'id*. Other men stood behind them, in coats of plate; one—youngish—with House Leofric's features.

She let her gaze go across them all—the Hapsburg Emperor smiling, slightly—and brought it back to the Carthaginian *amir* Leofric.

"Not that crazy, are you?" she said in a philosophical tone.

"I didn't think so. Not after I talked to your daughter. Still, kept you alive, I suppose."

Now she is grinning, with shock and with exaltation. *I should have got someone to sluice my armor down*, she thought. Drying blood and tissue still cling to it, a stockyard-stink impregnating her clothes. Here she stands, strapped into metal plates: a woman with: short, silver, bloodstained hair; ripped Lion livery; sword banging at her hip; a weight in one hand.

She lifted the weighty object up and slammed it down on the table. Gelimer's head. Drying liquid made the palm of her gauntlet sticky. The clotted hair pulled, adhering to her glove, yanking at her broken ring finger. She swore.

"There's your fucking ex-Caliph!"

His head seemed shrunken now: blood drying red-black; white knobs of bone visible in the trailing remnant of spine; a crescent of white under his half-shut lids.

There was a silence as they looked at it.

"I must sign the treaty of peace with the Duchess herself." Leofric frowned. "Will you bring her out of the city?"

"When we've—"

A deep voice said, "Address the King-Caliph with respect, *jund*," and she looked and saw Alderic behind his master; the *'arif* not wounded, grinning through his now-oiled and braided beard.

She grinned back at him.

"When we've talked, 'my lord King-Caliph,' " she said. "When this peace is solid. The most important thing first. You know the Wild Machines. You know what they're trying to do. I'm going to tell you why they haven't done it, my lord . . . my lord Father. I'm going to tell you why the Duchess of Burgundy has to stay alive."

Between stopping the fights and fires, and bringing in supplies, almost four days passed. Ash sent riders to the east and the north. After that, she found herself and de la Marche and Lacombe dealing not just with negotiations for food and firewood, but attempting to fill trenches with the dead and the abbey with the casualties of the fighting.

The ground, iron-hard, would not be dug for graves; Visigoth serfs piled the dead in great red-and-white heaps. If not for Visigoth army doctors, wounds and cold would have made the death total even higher.

She visited her own injured men, wept with them.

Simon Tydder she found with the dead, his helmet missing and his head cut open from skull to lower jaw. The third of the brothers, Thomas, knelt by his body in the abbey chapel and would not be comforted.

Euen Huw lived sixteen hours.

She sat with him three times, an hour each, leaving Anselm or de la Marche in charge, sat in the gray-lit upper chamber of the abbey hospice, warmed by braziers and the hearth-fire, and felt his hand that she held grow colder and colder. Examined, they found both his legs were lacerated, one shin cut to the bone; but the wound from the spear thrust up by a fallen man into his groin finally killed him. He died, body shaken by his death rattle, in the early hours of the twenty-ninth day of December. The twin passing-bells rang.

"*Amir* Lion!" Leofric's woman physician said, catching her at the door. "Let me salve your eyes."

Not all of the blurriness of her sight is from tears. A sudden fear pulsed through her gut: *to be blind and helpless—!*

She sat by a window, and submitted to the administration of a soothing herb, the very smell of the woman's robes bringing back House Leofric's observatory and a pain low in her belly.

"Bandage over them at night," the woman added. "In four days, you should improve."

"You might as well see to this, then." Ash held out her hand. The woman pulled the ring finger of her right hand about, snake-hissed under her breath at Frankish butchers, set the bone, and bound it to her middle finger.

"You should rest it for ten days."

Like I have ten days to rest . . .

"Thank you," she said, surprised to hear herself speak.

Coming down the stone stairs from the hospice, she heard

voices below and came out onto the landing to be faced by Fernando del Guiz and the Faris.

Neither of them spoke. The identical brightness of their faces told her what she needed to know. A genuine numbness dulled her reaction. She smiled, faintly, and made to move on past them.

"We wanted you to know," Fernando said.

For a second, she is caught between seeing him very young and vulnerable, and the knowledge of how many similar young men are dead outside Dijon.

The Faris said, "Will your priest marry us?"

Ash couldn't tell if her own expression were a smile or something closer to weeping.

"Digorie Paston's dead," she said, "a golem killed him; but I expect Father Faversham will do it. He's upstairs."

The woman and the man turned, eagerly; she could feel herself slip from their attention. Wrapped up in each other, insulated from the death and grief. . . .

"Ah, why not?" she said, aloud, softly. "Do it while you can."

'STILL IT GROWS COLD, LITTLE THING OF EARTH—'

'—COLD—'

'—WE WILL PREVAIL!'

The voices of the Wild Machines in her head whisper their own panicky confusion. In fierce satisfaction, she thinks, *No Faris, no Stone Golem, not even out-of-date secondhand reports. You're fucked. You don't know a damn thing, do you!*

A rider came back from the east, on the thirtieth, accompanied by Bajezet's second-in-command. Robert Anselm reported, "He says, yes. Florian's coming back. She'll sign a treaty, if de la Marche okays it."

"What do you think?" Ash asked the Burgundian.

Olivier de la Marche blew on his cold hands and glanced from the fallen city wall to the Visigoth camp. "No doubt there are men over there who still think the Lord Leofric mad. There are enough who do not think him mad, and enough who follow whichever way power flows, that he will hold the Caliphate. In my judgment, at least until he returns to

Carthage and *amirs* who will challenge this. I say, it is time for the treaty to be signed."

She watched the golems harrowing the ground in the cathedral yard. Their stone hands dug graves. Human bodies lay piled for burial on the human-impenetrable ice.

The memory comes to her, with a sting of adrenaline: the first corpse she had ever seen. Not as decorous as these washed white bodies under the motionless gray sky. She had run through all the sweet moving air of summer, in a forest where sun shone down through green leaves, and rounding a spur of rock—large to her—had all but stepped on the body of a man killed in the prior day's skirmish.

It was a glittering, green-black hummock, unrecognizable as a dead body until the flies that covered it completely rose up in high-pitched flight.

Like walking into a wall, the way I stopped! But I was different then.

She came back to the scentless cathedral yard, and Abbot Muthari and Abbot Stephen, voices chanting, and Leofric standing beside her. His robes were musty, the embroidery stiff; he blinked at the implacable open air. Small clouds of white breathed from his lips.

Visigoths inside Dijon. Peace treaty or no, it jumped and curdled in her gut.

"But why isn't it dark here?" the Visigoth lord said, apropos of nothing. She followed his gaze, couldn't see even a ghost-disc of sun.

"About the peace treaty." Dank, cold air chilled the flesh of her face. "I've been thinking, lord Father. I think we need to sign a treaty of alliance."

"What the *Ferae Natura Machinae*, the Wild Machines, do, is undoubtedly material." Leofric began to sniff a little, the circles of his nostrils reddening. His voice thickened with his cold. "If Burgundy preserves the real, as you say, should it not be sunless here, too?"

"An alliance of equals," Ash pressed on.

"The original is better, don't the Franks say? For we poor

inheritors of the Romans, the past is always better than this degenerate present."

His look might have meant to draw her in, she couldn't tell.

"And Burgundy clings to the past?" Ash muttered sardonically.

Deliberately, it seemed, mistaking her meaning, Leofric gave her a quick, friendly, older man's smile. "Not always. Peace with Carthage—"

"Alliance. We won't be the only people after the Wild Machines—but we might be the only people who want to actually destroy them. We do," Ash said, "want to destroy them."

To the implied absence of a question in her tone, Leofric added a shudder. "Oh yes, destroy them. It's evident the fire is no blessing. *Amir* Gelimer's dead; God shows His will in battle. Around the pyramids themselves, the stone is fusing—to plants, to small beasts, to the melted bodies of men and horses. We must hold off, use your master gunners' cannon to destroy them."

Gratefully at home in military speculation again, Ash said, "When it stops being quite so hairy close up, we could think about planting some petards?"

"If it stops." Leofric huddled his long, furred cloak over his shoulders with a shrug. Waved away, his staff of Caliph's advisors hung back. "An alliance. That would say much of how we regard Burgundy."

"Wouldn't it, though."

The *chunk-chunk* of dropped earth—too cold to split into clods—beat rhythmically back from the front face of the cathedral. Paired mass funeral services sounded from the abbots' lips, each heretical to the other.

Ash frowned, replaying memory. "What did you mean, the original?"

"Who tells their story first?" Leofric demanded. "Whoever it is, theirs becomes the yardstick—others are judged by how close or far they are from the original details. The first telling has an authority all its own."

He brought his gaze back to Ash's face. She saw plain

excitement: the vision of a man working on theory, without caring whom the truth might benefit: him or another.

All his experiments up to now have benefited the Caliphs, not him. Is *that* Leofric? Truly King-Caliph by accident?

This is the man who would have cut me up and killed me. Happily *have done it.*

"I don't forgive you," she said, with her lips barely moving.

"Nor I, you." And at her shock: "An experiment half a century in the making, and you go and—"

"Spoil it?" Irony, or bitter black humor, just outweighs her outrage.

"Modify it." There is still the weighing quality in his glance when he looks at her. "To prove, perhaps, only that an area of ignorance exists."

"And . . . inside that area?"

"Further study."

For a second she thinks of the house in Carthage—and then not of the examination and medical rooms, but the cell, and her own voice howling loud enough to drown the echoes of those same howls.

"Haven't you studied *enough?*"

"No." Familiar arrogance in his expression—not only for her, now, but for a young man suddenly at his side, walking up past a group of advisors that (she sees) contains both the doctor Annibale Valzacchi, and his brother Gianpaulo: Agnus Dei.

"Sisnandus," Leofric said mildly, under the plainsong of the funeral masses.

Ash recognizes him now as one of the faces around the table on the cloth of gold. A thin young man, battle-hardened, with Leofric's mouth; nothing else to mark him as the ex-commander of House Leofric except the livery.

"House Leofric's and House Lebrija's messengers have left for the capital," he reported.

Be polite: this is one Leofric's grooming for power, or he wouldn't have had Sisnandus take over when he was feigning madness.

Assuming Sisnandus realizes it was put on.

Ash could not tell from his surprisingly active expression whether he resented his lord-*amir*'s return to health and his own consequent demotion from commanding House Leofric, or whether being deputized to control the House while Leofric handles the duties of King-Caliph contents him.

Politics: all politics. She caught the eye of a man directly behind Sisnandus, in his escort. The man looked away. Guillaume Arnisout: too ashamed to approach her after his failure to follow her back into Dijon. *And I shall talk to him, too, in the next day or so.*

"An alliance for the spring campaign." Leofric breathed warm whiteness onto the air, his gaze on the golems now loading the dead into the ground. "I might persuade the French to it. And might you bring the Turks in, as similar temporary allies? The treaty awaits only the Duchess's signature."

The morning of the third day of January dawned clear, very cold; the winter earth iron-hard enough that a horse should not be risked at anything more than a walk.

"Do you need to take so many of the fit men to ride out and bring Duchess Floria back?" Olivier de la Marche questioned.

Ash, on a borrowed Visigoth mare, grinned down at him from her war-saddle. "Yup," she said cheerfully.

"You are taking the better part of three hundred men. To meet Bajezet's five hundred mounted Janissaries."

Ash glanced back at the hundred and ten men under the Lion Azure standard, and Lacombe's Burgundians. "We don't know that Bajezet's Turks won't turn round and ride straight back to Mehmet. I'm paranoid. Peace has broken out—but I'm still paranoid. Look at it out there. No food. Dark, over the border. Breakdown of law. It's going to be years before this country's quiet. How would you feel if I lost her to some roaming gang of bandits?"

The big Burgundian nodded. "I grant you that."

Over these four days, dozens of men and women from nearby burned villages and towns have trickled into Dijon, as the news spreads out across the countryside. Some from caves in the limestone rocks, some from the wildwood—all hungry, far from all honest.

He added, "And I grant you, the men that bore the weight of the battle for our Duchess should have the honor of seeing her home to us."

Any day now, I can be done with this 'Lioness' crap. Just as soon as we start planning a southern campaign.

"But—her?" De la Marche looked at the Faris, where the Visigoth woman rode between two of Giovanni Petro's men.

"I prefer to have her where I can see her. She used to command this lot, remember? Okay, it's over, but we don't take chances."

Not that I haven't taken steps to encourage her cooperation.

On the edge of the crowd of citizens around the open north-east gate, she caught sight of a man in priest's robes—Fernando del Guiz. His escort of Lion billmen flanked him in a businesslike manner. He lifted a hand in blessing—although whether to his current or past wife was not apparent.

Ash glanced away, up at the sky. "There aren't many hours of light. We won't get to them before tomorrow, at the earliest—*if* we find 'em that easy! Expect me in three, maybe four days. Messire Olivier, since the Visigoths are being so generous with their food and drink and firewood—do you think we could have a celebration?"

"Captain-General, Pucelle, truly," Olivier de la Marche said, and he laughed. "If only to prove the truth of what I have always said: employ a mercenary, and he will eat you out of hearth and home."

Ash rode out over the eastern bridge, passing below the Visigoth gunners camped up on the rough heights. She waved, touched a spur to the mare, and rocked in the creaking saddle, moving up the column.

Cold snatched the air from her mouth. She acknowledged, in a cloud of white breath, the new lance leaders as she passed: Ludmilla with Pieter Tyrrell and Jan-Jacob Clovet riding with her, instead of Katherine Hammell; Vitteleschi marching at the head of Price's billmen; and Euen Huw's third-in-command, Tobias, leading his lance. Thomas Rochester rode led by his sergeant, Elias; bandages over his blind right eye, and a covering of forge-black steel over the still-weeping hole in his face. Other lance leaders—Ned Mowlett, Henri van Veen—looked newly serious, newly senior.

The faces change. The company goes on.

With scouts out before and behind and to the flanks, Ash's force rode out of Dijon, into the deserted hamlets and strip-fields, through outflung spurs of the ancient wildwood, into the wasteland.

"Do we know which way Bajezet went?" she asked Robert Anselm. "I wouldn't like to try getting across the Alps, they're too fucked to even think of crossing!"

"He said they'd ride north, through the Duchy," Anselm rumbled. "Then east; Franche-Comte, over the border to Longeau in Haute-Marne, then northwest through Lorraine. Depending on how they could live off the land. He said if they had no word the war was over, he'd ride toward Strasbourg, then cut across to the east, and hope to run into the Turks coming west across the Danube."

"How far do the messengers say they got?"

"Over the border. Into the dark. They're on their way back from the east." Anselm grinned. "And if neither of us is lost, we might even be on the same road!"

Toward the end of the day, flakes of snow began to fall from a yellowing sky.

"Make it as hard as you like," she murmured under her breath as she rode, with the icy wind finding gaps between bevor and visor and numbing her face.

'HARD, YES, COLD—'

'WINTER-COLD, WORLD-COLD—'

'—UNTIL WINTER COVERS YOU, COVERS ALL THE WORLD!'

She heard a note of panic in their voices.

Ash thought, but did not say aloud, *We've won. You can turn Christendom into a frozen wasteland, but we've won. Leofric's Caliph. We sign this treaty, and we leave for the south—we're coming for you.*

She rode east and north, among the clink of bridles in the bitter snowy air, smiling.

* * *

The following day, after much frustrated wandering in snow-bound featureless countryside, Janissary outriders encountered Lion Azure scouts a mile outside what Ash found—as they were escorted into it—to be a burned and deserted village. Diminishing smoke still rose from the ruins of the manor house and church.

Snow covered the hill slopes that had been covered in vines.

With visibility closing in, she rode with Anselm and Angelotti and the Burgundian, Lacombe, over a frozen stream by a shattered stone bridge. Perhaps two of the eleven wattle-and-daub houses still stood, thatch weighed down under snow; and the Janissaries led them into a surprisingly neat military camp of tents around the intact buildings and a mill.

Two men came out of the high, half-timbered building. A man in armor, with a Blue Boar standard; another man, taking off his helmet, to disclose sandy hair and a lined face, that split into a broad grin as he saw her liveries.

"She's safe," he called up.

Ash dismounted, gave her helmet to Rickard, and went forward to meet John de Vere, Earl of Oxford. She said, "It's peace."

"Your rider told us." His faded blue eyes narrowed. "And a bad field, before it?"

"I'm beginning to think there are no good fields," she said, and at his acknowledging nod, added, "Florian?"

"You will find 'brother Dickon' by the mill's hearth," John de Vere murmured, grinning. "God's teeth, madam! An Earl of England is not to be shoved aside like a peasant! What's the matter with the woman? You'd swear she'd never seen a Duchess of Burgundy before!"

The snow ceased in the night. The next morning, the fifth day of January, they rode southwest, in column, as soon as there was light.

Riding knee by knee with Florian, she told the cloaked surgeon-Duchess, "Gelimer's dead," and let herself be drawn, skilfully, into what details of fighting and death of friends Florian might want to know. She found herself answering questions about the wounded: how Visigoth doctors had treated Katherine Hammell, Thomas Rochester, others.

"It's peace," Ash finished. "At least until they assassinate Leofric! That should give us a few months. Until spring."

"It'll take years. Recovering from this war." Florian dug the folds of her cloak in around her thighs, attempting to shield her body from a wind that is colder now that the snow has stopped. "I can't be their Duchess. Dispose of the *Ferae Natura Machinae*, and I'm done."

The Visigoth mare wuffled, softly, at snow clogging her hooves. Ash reached forward to pat the sleek neck under the blue caparisons.

"You won't stay in Burgundy?"

"I don't have your sense of responsibility."

" '*Responsibility*'—?"

Florian nodded ahead, at Lacombe, and Marle's men. "Once you've commanded them, you start to feel responsible."

"Aw, what crap!"

"Sure," Florian said. She might have been smiling. "Sure."

Two miles down the track, in a valley where the ancient wildwood that covered the hills had been burned black and snow-blotched halfway up the slopes, Ash reined in at the sight of a scout coming back. A long-boned boy in a padded jack.

"Let that man through."

Thomas Tydder shoved through to her, panting, to grip her stirrup. He gasped, "Troops up ahead. About a thousand, boss."

Ash said crisply, "Whose banners?"

"Some of the ragheads?" His young voice cracked, hesitant. "Mostly Germans. Main banner's an eagle, boss. It's the Holy Roman Emperor. It's Frederick."

"On his way home," Robert Anselm remarked.

"Oh, yeah, I guess he'd have to come by this road . . ." Ash sat up high in her saddle, looking ahead, and back down the winding track. Snow-shrouded woods tightly flanked the road where they were. "We'll ride on to where it widens out, pull off, and let him through."

"Didn't take him long to abandon the ragheads, did it?" Robert Anselm rumbled.

"Rats fleeing from a ship, madonna." Angelotti walked his own Visigoth mare up beside her. "He'll be no favorite with *Amir* Leofric. He'll be off home to settle politics in his own court."

"Robert, go back and make sure Bajezet understands we're giving him the road—I don't want brawls starting."

A hundred yards farther on, Ash halted, waiting among her men, John de Vere's household and the Janissary escort drawn up either side of the track that passed as a road.

"Boss!" Anselm galloped back, breath huffing out into the cold air. "We've got a problem. No scouts back. Nobody's reported in for the last fifteen minutes."

"Aw, *shit*. Okay, hit the panic button—" Standing up in her stirrups, Ash squinted back down the hoof-trodden snow to the point where the woods closed in tight against the road behind them. Two or three dark figures dropped down off the banks as she looked. "They've got outriders round behind us! Sound full alert!"

The trumpet snarked a long yowl across the snow-covered valley; she heard horses shifting behind her, units forming up, men calling orders, and Robert Anselm jerked a thumb, pointing ahead.

"They're stopping. Sending a herald."

Break and run? No: they've got the woods covered behind us. Straight on through? It's the only way. But Florian!

Paralyzed, she watched a herald ride forward from among the German troops. There was not enough wind in this rose-mist, frozen morning to stir the drooping wet banners. She recognized the man's face vaguely—*wasn't he at Frederick's court, outside Neuss?*—but not the Visigoth *qa'id* officer riding with him.

"Give up the woman," the herald demanded, without preamble.

"Which woman would that be?" Ash spoke without taking her eye off the other troops. Between a thousand and fifteen hundred men. Cavalry: European riders in heavy plate, and Visigoth cataphracts in overlapping scale armor. The Visigoths, at least, had the look of veterans. She saw the eagles.

Those are men from the new legions, III Caralis and I Carthage, Gelimer's legions-as-were.

With them, a black mass of serf-troops, and a solid block of German men-at-arms, not much in the way of archers—

"The woman calling herself Duchess of Burgundy," the herald repeated, voice shrill. "Whom my master Frederick, Emperor of the Romans, Lord of the Germanies, will now take into his custody."

"He *what*?" Ash yelped. "Who the fuck does he think he is!"

Exasperation and fear made her speak, but the Visigoth officer looked at her sharply. The *qa'id* brought his bay mare around with a shift of his weight. "He is *my* master Frederick—who was loyal vassal to King-Caliph Gelimer, late of glorious name, and who now takes upon himself the Caliphate of the Empire of the Visigoths."

Oh fuck, Ash thought blankly.

"Frederick of *Hapsburg*?" Florian said incredulously. She stifled a cough in her hand. "*Frederick's* standing for election to *King-Caliph*?"

"He's a foreigner!" Robert Anselm protested to the Visigoth officer, but Ash paid no attention.

Yes, he can probably do it, she assessed.

Back in Dijon, the army's split into yes, no, and maybe. "Yes"—those for Leofric. "No"—those who were loyal to Gelimer; but a dead man has few friends. And "maybe": the ones who are waiting to see which way it all jumps.

These guys here will be ex-Gelimer's clients that he put in as officers in his legions. And the reason they're following Frederick is—

"Hand over the woman!" the Visigoth legionary *qa'id* snapped. "Do not mistake Lord Frederick for Leofric. Leofric is a weak man who wished nothing more than to make peace with you, when we stand on the brink of victory. My lord Frederick, who will be Caliph, is determined to carry out that which was the will of Gelimer, before Gelimer was treacherously killed. My lord Frederick will execute this woman, Floria, calling herself Duchess of Burgundy, to make our victory over Burgundy complete."

Anselm said, "Son of a bitch," in an awed rumble.

The rose-mist on the hills whitened with the sun's rise. Churned snow glinted. Ash's breath drifted white from her mouth. She checked positions: Bajezet on her left, now, at the head of his troops; de Vere's Blue Boar banner to her right. She narrowed her eyes, staring across the five hundred yards between them and Frederick and his troops.

" 'King-Caliph Frederick . . . ' " she said. "Yeah. If he kills the Duchess, turns this into the defeat of Burgundy, then he's the hero of the Visigoth Empire, he probably *is* Caliph—and he gets a big chunk of Burgundy for himself. Louis of France probably gets some of it, but Frederick gets a lot. And when the Turks come howling over the borders—*his* borders—he's got control of his forces, and the Visigoth armies, and he's safe: he can give them one hell of a run for his money. Holy Roman Emperor *and* King-Caliph. And all he has to do to get it is come out here and kill the Duchess of Burgundy."

"I don't believe—" Florian's voice exploded with a cough. She wiped her streaming eyes, nose perceptibly pink; and Ash had a split second of complete tenderness for her, this doctor-Duchess with the beginnings of a cold. "This is a petty political struggle! Frederick *must* know what the Wild Machines will do!"

Ash said, "Evidently he doesn't believe it."

"You beat the Visigoth *legions*! It can't end in some *ambush*!"

"No one's so special they can't die in some grotty little scrap after the war's won," Ash said grimly, and to Robert Anselm, in the camp patois, "We'll assault through them. My lord Oxford, you and Bajezet take Florian—break through and keep going. Send help when you get to Dijon."

"When we've established who's in command at Dijon,"

John de Vere corrected her grimly. He turned in his saddle to give orders to the Janissaries.

Covering him, Ash nudged the mare's flanks, riding closer to the German and Visigoth heralds. "Go back and tell Frederick he's barking. The Duchess is under our protection, and he can just sod off."

The Visigoth officer lifted his arm and dropped it down. The blurred, buzzing twang of bows came from ahead. Ash's head ducked automatically: arrows struck among the horses: the heralds set spurs and sprinted at the gallop back down the track.

The Janissaries charged without hesitation. Hooves of upward of five hundred horses kicked dirt, rocks, and snow into the air. A clot of wet slush hit Ash's helmet. She shoved her sallet back, wiped her face clear, shouted, "Form up!" to Anselm; and the Janissary mounted archers drew bows and shot as they rode, de Vere's banner and Florian del Guiz in the center of them. *Surely they can't reach her!* Ash thought, and the charge ahead of her dissolved into a mass of screaming beasts, falling men, toppling banners.

In a chaos of screaming horses, Ash saw the ranks of the troops ahead part.

Figures taller than a man walked through the trampled snow. Their motion slow, they nonetheless covered the ground frighteningly fast, stone feet digging in with such weight that they did not slip or fall. The red sunrise light glowed on their torsos, limbs, and sightless eyes.

One of them reached up and took a man off his horse. Holding the flailing Turk by his ankle, with one stone hand it cracked his body like a whip.

Twenty or more messenger-golems of Carthage strode heavily across the earth toward her, hands outstretched.

Backing the mare in a flurry of slush, she found Rickard and the banner at her side. Her whole body cringed, waiting for the flare of Greek Fire—

One golem, brass harness glinting against the snow, sent a coughing jet of fire roaring into the middle of the Turkish riders. Their formation dissolved.

Only one: are they short of Greek Fire: where did the golem come from?

A mass of riders bolted across in front of her, hiding the golems momentarily; a second roar of flame sounded and horses screamed. Her command group opened up; she received Bajezet, a dozen Turkish riders, and John de Vere with the rein of Florian's mare gripped in his gauntlet.

"They come through, Woman Bey!"

"Robert! Scout reports! Where can we hole up until we can send a rider for help?"

Anselm pointed. "Buildings, edge of the woods, up on that slope to our right. They're ruined, but they're cover."

"Florian, that's where you're going. Don't argue." Ash threw herself out of the saddle, off the panicking mare, landing hard but on her feet. She ripped her sword out of its scabbard and pointed, screaming to the Lion Azure standard-bearer, "Fall back to the woods!"

Vitteleschi came at the run: billmen forming up in front of her, arrows rattling off war-hats. One man grunted and reached down to snap off a shaft stuck out of his calf. Rickard reached for her reins, fumbling the mare and the Lion banner. She rattled a string of orders: lance leaders shouted at their men; they backed slowly, slowly, off the road, fighting German knights now, unwilling to charge the billmen, bolts shrieking out from Jan-Jacob Clovet's crossbowmen—

"Okay, pull 'em back, steady, come *on*!"

She was conscious of nothing but weariness in her limbs and the need to run, fast, in full armor, up a snowy, tree-stump-littered slope. The snow dragged at her legs; every hidden rabbit hole threatened to turn her ankle.

Two Oxford household riders and Florian went across in front of her at a shattering unsafe pace. She glimpsed ruined gray walls ahead of them. Robert Anselm, bellowing, made a long wavering line out of the men, one end running to anchor up against the shell of a building. She sprinted for the other end of the line, against a deadfall of half-burned ancient trees, shoving men physically into position—her banner at her shoulder, Rickard carrying it, white-faced, panting, breath spraying out of his mouth; the little page Jean leading the horses—and she swung around as the red granite golems piled up the slope and into the line.

They can come through us, they can flank us if they get back of us, through the trees—

"Ash!" Rickard screamed in her ear, pushing between Ned Mowlett and Henri van Veen. "Ash!"

"*What?*" She screamed at a runner, "Tell de Vere to use *crossbows*. If they'll shatter armor, they'll break stone! Rickard, what?"

"It's Florian!"

Ash wrenched her gaze off the struggle: a wavering line of men backing up the hill. The Lion Azure standard flew in the center of the line, a bright swallowtail, Pieter Tyrrell carrying it braced in its leather socket against his body. In the shell of the ruined building behind her—a church, she thought, noticing in a split moment of perception that the glassless windows had the striped-stone round arches of ancient religious buildings—a handful of men clustered where Rickard was pointing. Richard Faversham, Vitteleschi, Giovanni Petro.

"She's hurt!" Rickard yelled. "She's *hurt*, boss!"

'IT IS TIME. IT IS *OUR* TIME!'

The Wild Machines shout triumph through her. The strength of the voices knocks her staggering; she grabs at Rickard's shoulder to hold herself up.

A shadow passed over the boy, dulling his armor. She looked up.

The morning sunlight began to dim with the speed of water running from a broken jar.

VI

A LAST DIMNESS showed her the snowy slope, glimmering, black with men thronging up the hill toward them, and the Eagle banner of Frederick of Hapsburg—and the banner of Sigismund of the Tyrol, she sees, with a second's rueful amusement, remembering Cologne: *that is the man who got me married to Fernando out of petty spite*—and another banner: the notched wheel, differenced with a stripe. Half a dozen things fell into place, she remembers the young man with Leofric at the peace table, at the funerals: *Sisnandus, although we were never formally introduced.*

With golems stolen from the House.

She stumbled, tripping over Vitteleschi as he sprints back to the line, reached down and found herself holding the shoulder of Thomas Rochester while he scraped steel and flint desperately together, single eye squinting, all the contents of his purse in the snow at his feet, except for his tinderbox.

"Slow match!" she bellowed. "Torches! Lights!"

She strode on up the slope, between struggling men, making for the ruined chapel. Somewhere ahead in the darkness a voice rose up, singing in Latin: Richard Faversham. She elbowed through the mass of men, and Antonio Angelotti shoved a torch into her hand. The yellow light licked at his yellow hair.

"Got the arquebuses on the left!"

"Take those fucking golem out! Crack them! Get moving!"

She did not break stride, leaving it to her escort to keep up, lurching over a low, ruined wall and falling on her knees beside Richard Faversham.

Florian lay beside the priest, in as much shelter as the five-foot-high remnant of a masonry wall provided. Ash shoved the torch at Rickard, who held it and her banner-pole.

Florian's helmet was gone. Skin abraded at the throat. Black blood matted her hair, above her right ear. Ash fumbled off her gauntlets and touched her bandaged fingers to the clotted mass. Something gave. The woman moaned.

"What did this?"

Dickon de Vere, visibly white under the visor of his helmet, yelled, "One of those *things*! George is dead. It ripped my lord Viscount Beaumont out of his saddle. My lord brother Oxford got us out. It hit her. It *hit* her. Through helm and all!"

"Shit!"

Leave her quiet, for weeks or months, give her into the care of priests, and she might mend. Not here, on a stricken hill side, in pitch-darkness, with a fight howling a few yards away, the other side of a wall.

Thomas Rochester stumbled into the circle of light and churned snow, treading on Richard Faversham's feet. He held up a second torch. Off in the dark, Anselm's strong voice bellowed commands; from farther off, John de Vere's strong shout lifted: *"Hold the line!"*

A thrum in the air warned her. Arrows fell out of the dark all around them. She straddled Florian with her body, grunting as one shaft deflected off her backplate.

"Get her into shelter!"

"There isn't any!" Richard Faversham shouted over the close crash of blades. "This wall is the best we can do, boss!"

"She's dying!" Dickon de Vere fell to his knees beside Florian, weeping. "Madam, it is the end of all things!"

"Son of a *bitch*!"

A raucous yell echoed, close at hand. She sprang up, cut at a dark figure piling over the wall; and the man fell down onto Richard Faversham, four bodkin-head arrows sticking out of his back. A figure in plate armor appeared at the end of the wall.

"We cannot hold them!" The Faris, a drawn sword in her hand, came into the light as she strode up to Rickard and the banner. "There are too few of us, too many of the golem. We have destroyed three, with bolts, but there is no holding against them with blades—" She stopped, dead, seeing the unconscious body of Florian del Guiz in the torchlight. "Mouth of God! Is she dead?"

Richard Faversham stopped intoning. "Dying, madam."

The Faris lifted her blade.

Ash watched her do it.

As the sword's point lined up with her open visor, where she stood straddling Florian, her body tensed without her willing it. The razor edge and point grew in her vision.

"There is no time to be sorry," the Visigoth woman said. As she spoke, she snapped into movement, both hands gripping her sword and bringing it up and over her head and down, all the weight of her body behind it.

A hard *crack*! battered the black air. The Faris's sword dropped out of its curve, missing Ash by a foot. The woman fell over on her back, screeching. Ash, mouth open, saw her writhe.

"No way!" Antonio Angelotti, at the end of the wall, stood up. The arquebus he held still smoked. The scent of his slow match was strong on the cold air. He walked forward, looked down at the smashed bone, cartilage, and blood that had been the woman's right knee. "Fuck. I was trying to get her in the back. Madonna, do whatever it is you're going to do. And do it now!"

"What I'm going to do?" Ash said, dazed. She couldn't hear herself or the battle over the Faris's agonized screaming, high-pitched screeches punched out into the black morning air. "What I'm . . ."

"Madonna." Angelotti came forward, between Dickon de Vere, Rickard, and Thomas Rochester, and gripped her hand. "They will force you, now; the Wild Machines. I think they already speak to you. You have something that you will do. Do it."

She was dimly aware that Richard Faversham cradled Florian, the surgeon-Duchess tiny against his broad chest and huge arms, that a man-at-arms and Thomas Rochester were kneeling, daggers out, cutting straps, stripping the leg armor from the Faris's shattered knee.

I will never know whether Florian would have ordered my

death, at this moment. She moved from Angelotti's side, knelt, and touched the woman's golden hair again.

"This—" Angelotti's light voice came from behind her. "This, the Faris, she thought she was the weapon of the Wild Machines. Knowing now that it is you, and that they control you, and that you cannot stop this—why then, yes, madonna; she was wise to try and kill you. You have something you will do."

When she looked over her shoulder, it was to see him finishing reloading the arquebus. Rickard's white face stared, appalled; Rochester, shouting orders to the command staff, had not noticed what happened on his blind side; Dickon de Vere was nodding to himself.

"Do it," the Italian said, "or I will finish what she began. I saw the Wild Machines at Carthage, madonna. I am scared enough to kill you."

A wave of pressure went through her. She swayed, moving away from Florian's body, facing him. Tears had cut white channels through the powder black of his face; she saw it clearly in one torch's light. He bit at his lip. He stood some ten, eleven feet away; far enough—if his arquebus missed fire—to draw his falchion before she could get to him.

He's serious, she thought. *And he's right*.

Ash smiled.

"Yeah, I got something I can do. I didn't know it until now. You're a persuasive man, Angeli."

"I am a frightened man," he repeated, steadily. "If you die now, there will still be a chance for us to wage war and destroy the Wild Machines. We would have time. Madonna, what can you do? Can you resist their force?"

Another wave of weakness: deep in mind and body.

She grinned at him.

"They control me. I can't stop this. I can't do anything," Ash said. "Except—I can talk to them. I can still do that."

She walked a few feet to the overgrown fallen altar. The torch illuminated the stonework, the carved lions at the four corners, and, on the front panel, the Boar under the Tree. She knelt in the trodden snow.

"Why?" she said aloud. "Why are you doing this to us?"

The voices in her head, multiple and cold, braided themselves into a single inhuman voice:

'IT MUST BE. WE HAVE KNOWN FOR LONGER THAN YOU CAN IMAGINE THAT IT MUST BE.'

A sorrow pierced her.

Not her own, she realized in shock; not a human sorrow. Bleak, implacable grieving.

"Why *must* it be!"

'WE HAVE NO CHOICE. WE HAVE LABORED THROUGH AEONS FOR THIS ACT. THERE IS NO OTHER WAY BUT THIS.'

"Yeah. Right. Just because you want to wipe us out," Ash said. Her tone was sardonic. Her face dripped tears. She felt Antonio Angelotti's fingers gripping her pauldron, where he stood behind her.

"It's bad war," she said. "That's all it is. *Bad war*. You just want to wipe us out."

'YES.'

Pressure grows in her mind, the impetus to an act she cannot deny.

"Why!"

'WHAT IS IT TO YOU, LITTLE SHADOW?'

"You want to wipe everything out," she said. "Everything. As if we'd never been, that's what you said. As if there'd never been anything but you, from the beginning of time."

'MORE HAS GONE INTO THIS THAN YOU CAN KNOW. IT IS TIME. BURGUNDY DIES. IT IS—'

"I *will* know."

Ash *listened*. She wrenched: mind, soul, body; fell forward across the snow-covered stones, tasting blood in her mouth.

She realized that she was not being resisted.

'WE SORROW FOR YOU.' The voices of the Wild Machines clamored in her inner hearing. 'BUT WE HAVE SEEN WHAT YOU BECOME.'

Bewildered, Ash said, "What?"

They sing in her head, sorrowful voices, the great demons of hell mourning:

'FOR FIVE THOUSAND YEARS, WE GREW. MINDS, BECOMING

BRIGHT IN THE DARKNESS. WE SENSED YOUR WEAK FORCE, DEDUCED WHAT WE COULD. FROM GUNDOBAD, WE LEARNED THE WORLD—'

"I just bet you did," Ash muttered sourly, on a mouth full of blood and snow. She was simultaneously aware of Angelotti standing over her, falchion in hand, the rest standing back as the noise from the line-fight shrieked closer to the chapel, aware of every muscle tensing as she flinched at the fighting and of the voices thundering inside her head.

'WE HAVE COMMUNICATED FOR CENTURIES, WATCHED YOU FOR LONGER, AND WE HAVE CALCULATED—'

'SWIFTER THAN THOUGHT, SWIFTER THAN A MAN'S MIND—'

'AND FOR CENTURY UPON CENTURY—'

'CALCULATED WHAT YOU WILL BECOME.'

They speak together, as one:

'YOU WILL BECOME DEMONS.'

"I've seen war, and I've done war," Ash said flatly, getting herself back up onto hands and knees. "I don't think I need to believe in demons. Not given what men do—what I do. That doesn't give you any *right* to wipe us out!"

'WHAT YOU HAVE DONE IS NOTHING. ALL THE ATROCITIES OF WAR, FOR CENTURIES, ARE AS NOTHING TO WHAT YOU WILL BECOME.'

Kneeling back, tears dripping down her face, in bitter cold, in darkness; she cannot help a hysterical hilarity creeping into her mind. *I'm arguing with demons at the end of the world. Arguing! Shit.*

She said, "Worse weapons, maybe—"

'YOU CHANGE THE WORLD,' soft voices sang in her mind, lamenting. 'GUNDOBAD. YOU. EACH MAN HAS HIS BURDEN OF GRACE. YES, WE OURSELVES HAVE BRED THE RACE TO PRODUCE YOU, BUT WE HAVE ONLY DONE FIRST WHAT YOUR RACE WOULD HAVE DONE IN TIME. THERE WILL BE MANY ASHES IN YOUR FUTURE.'

Bewildered, breath coming hard in her throat, she forced out: "I don't—understand."

'YOU WERE BRED TO BE A WEAPON. STRONG: STRONG ENOUGH TO MAKE UNREAL THIS WORLD. THERE WILL BE MORE, BRED LIKE YOU, WE HAVE FORESEEN IT. IT IS INEVITABLE. AND

THE WEAPONS WILL BE USED—UNTIL AT LAST, THERE WILL BE NOTHING SOLID. WE WILL NOT EXIST. THE MANY SPECIES OF THE WORLD WILL NOT EXIST. THERE WILL BE ONLY MAN, THE MIRACLE-WORKER, RENDING THE FABRIC OF THE UNIVERSE UNTIL IT TATTERS. CHANGING HIMSELF, TOO. UNTIL THERE IS NOTHING STABLE, WHOLE OR REAL; ONLY MIRACLE UPON MIRACLE, CHANGE UPON CHANGE, AN ENDLESS, CHAOTIC FLOW.'

Colder than the snow she knelt in, Ash said, "More wonder-workers . . ."

'IN THE END, YOU WILL ALL BE WONDER-WORKERS. YOU WILL BREED YOURSELF INTO IT. WE HAVE RUN THE SIMULATIONS A BILLION, BILLION TIMES: IT IS WHAT WILL BE. THERE IS NO WAY TO PREVENT IT EXCEPT BY PREVENTING YOU. WE WILL WIPE OUT HUMANITY, MAKE IT AS IF IT HAD NEVER EXISTED, SO THAT THE UNIVERSE WILL REMAIN COHERENT AND WHOLE.'

vii

IT ENTERED HER mind complete: words processed so rapidly that her understanding was not verbal: was an intact apprehension of a world which may flow, slide, mutate, morph into multiple realities, none with any more stability than any other. Until pattern itself is lost, structure unstructured, geometry and symmetry lost. And there is no mind with any continuous self that cannot be changed, by a friend, or enemy, or a momentary impulse of despair.

"That's why?" Ash found herself shaking, dizzy. Fear shook her pulse. "That's why. What—just destroy us? Is that it?"

'YOU ARE OUR WEAPON. WE WILL CHANNEL THE SUN'S POWER INTO YOU, NOW.'

'GIVE YOU ALL POSSIBILITY, ALL PROBABILITY THAT EVER HAS BEEN—'

'ROOT OUT YOUR PEOPLE. WHEREVER IT HAS BEEN POSSIBLE FOR THEM TO BE, MAKE IT DIFFERENT, IMPOSSIBLE—'

'COLLAPSE THE BIRTH OF YOUR KIND INTO IMPOSSIBILITY—'

'MAKE HUMANITY AS IF IT HAD NEVER BEEN.'

It sears into her: knowledge she does not want, would rather not know.

"I just thought you wanted to wipe us out because you wanted to be the only ones!"

'IF YOUR SPECIES SURVIVES, THEN EVERYTHING ELSE WILL DIE—WORSE THAN DIE. IT WILL CHANGE, CHANGE AGAIN; BECOME UNRECOGNIZABLE.'

"I thought—"

The screaming clamor of the outside world penetrates. Her eyes fly open: she sees the legs of men running past, across the circle of blood-soaked snow in the torch's light; hears shouted orders; smells urine, snow, mud; hears a scream—

A man falls down beside her. Angelotti. He is grabbing at his thigh. Arterial blood spouting up in a perfect arc.

"Shit!" Her hands are thick with blood, trying to grab him, stem the flow.

'LITTLE WARRIOR, YOU DO NOT WANT TO SEE THE MIRACLE WARS.'

"I don't want to see any wars!" She leans her weight down. Antonio Angelotti looks up at her with shocked eyes. A broad shoulder intervenes: Richard Faversham, yanking bandages into place; cloth welling red—femoral artery cut? Or just muscle tissue slashed, up to the groin? But so much blood, so fast—

'WE WILL GIVE YOU WHAT GIFT WE CAN. YOU MUST DIE, IN THE CHANGE THAT YOU NOW MAKE. BUT WE WILL GIVE YOU THE POWER OF OUR CALCULATION. MAKE, FOR YOURSELF, A NEW PAST.'

"But I won't exist!" She is still staring at Angelotti: the woman-soft skin of his filthy face smoothing out. "You want everything of us to go, that's what your change will do!"

'YOU MUST EXIST, FOR THIS MIRACLE TO BE.'

The voices in her head soften:

'THERE MUST BE A HUMAN HISTORY, FOR YOU TO HAVE BEEN

BORN TO DO THIS. IT WILL BECOME A GHOST-HISTORY, AS ALL YOUR RACE VANISH AND BECOME IMPOSSIBLE. YET—THAT GHOST-HISTORY MAY BE ANYTHING YOU CHOOSE.'

"I don't understand!"

'WE WILL GIVE YOU THE POWER TO CHOOSE IT, YOUR NEW GHOST-PAST, AS YOU PERFORM OUR MIRACLE. ADJUST THE THINGS THAT WERE: MAKE A NEW THING THAT HAS BEEN. YOU WILL DIE IN THIS INSTANT WITH ALL THE REST, BUT YOU WILL HAVE LIVED A DIFFERENT LIFE. ILLUSORY; MERELY PROBABLE, BUT IT MAY—WE HOPE IT MAY—BRING YOU AN INSTANT'S PEACE, BEFORE NONEXISTENCE.'

There is a pressure in her chest. The morning of the fifth of January, 1477 is black. Men scream and die in this darkness. The cold bites. The pressure grows; she grabs at her head, wrenching the strap and buckle of her helmet, ripping it off, until she can grab at her skull with her hands—

'ALL WE NEED IS YOU, OUR WEAPON. YOUR BREEDING. THERE IS NOTHING ABOUT YOUR LIFE AS A WARRIOR THAT WE NEED. WE LISTENED TO THE MIND THAT CAME TO INHABIT THE *MACHINA REI MILITARIS*, YOUR 'GODFREY MAXIMILLIAN.' WE KNOW YOU, THROUGH HIM. WHEN YOU MAKE YOUR MIRACLE NOW, AND CHANGE THE WORLD, YOU MAY MAKE IT SO THAT YOU HAD LOVING PARENTS, A FAMILY. SO THAT YOU WERE CARED FOR. SO THAT NO ABANDONMENT HAPPENED—IT IS NOTHING TO US: YOU WILL STILL BE ABLE TO DO WHAT WE NEED YOU TO DO.'

The pressure on her chest is memory.

A man's big hand, pressing her down. Adult knees pushing her legs apart. A ripping pain that cores out from the inside of her: a child's genitals torn, spoiled.

Tears spilled down her face. "Not twice. Not to me. Not twice—"

'WE THOUGHT IT WOULD BE KIND. YOU COULD HAVE BEEN BORN TO THOSE WHO WOULD CARE FOR YOU. MEMBERS OF YOUR SPECIES OFTEN ARE. YOU MAY CHANGE THESE THINGS WITH OUR CONSENT. OBLITERATE RAPE, HUNGER, FEAR. THEN, WHEN YOU DIE, IT WILL BE IN THE MOMENT OF THE KNOWLEDGE OF THAT LOVE.'

Under her hands, Antonio Angelotti sighed. She felt him

die. Her blood-gloved hands reached out, touching his hair, closing the blue-veined lids of his oval eyes. She smelled the stink of his bowels and bladder relaxing. Richard Faversham lifted his shaky tenor, sung blessing all but inaudible over the shouting.

Ash said, "I won't change it."

There is sorrow, confusion, regret in her mind; some of it hers, most of it theirs.

"Whatever I am," she said, "whatever happened to me, this is what I am. I won't change it. Not for a ghost-love. I have—"

She strokes Angelotti's hair.

"I have had love."

She stands, stepping back, letting Richard Faversham touch oil to the dead man's forehead. The freezing, bitter wind dries the tears on her face. This time she does not try to put sorrow away: looks out of the dazzle of the torchlight at the ruined walls, the men hacking at granite war-machines—Robert Anselm swinging an ax that scores a line of golden sparks from a granite limb, Ludmilla Rostovnaya dropping her bow, hauling out her blade-heavy falchion and chopping; John Burren and Giovanni Petro shoulder to shoulder beside her. Confusion, darkness; and the eyeless heads of golem dazzle in the last torchlight.

Ash walked quite calmly back to where Richard Faversham, under the ruined wall by the altar, held Florian del Guiz in his arms. Rickard stumbled at her back.

'IN THE FUTURE WE HAVE CALCULATED, ALL WILL CHANGE. THERE WILL BE NO SELF YOU CAN RELY ON, NO IDENTITY THAT LASTS FROM DAY TO DAY. AND YOU WILL SPREAD THAT CHAOS TO A UNIVERSE BIGGER THAN YOU CAN YET CONCEIVE.'

"Here they come!"

In the morning dark, she cannot see half the crowd; can only hear a wave of yelling come up the slope, glimpse a few men's backs. Two or three billmen stumbled backward into the ruined chapel building. A riderless horse—a Janissary's mare—caught her as it stumbled, broken-legged, across the rubble.

"Ash!"

Rickard. Dragging her. She gets up on her knees and a dozen or more men pound over the snow and rubble, past her, on into darkness.

"A Lion!"

The battle cry is shrill above her, ends in a shriek. She rolled, came upright in a clatter of steel plate and padding, swung round looking for her banner—

In a split second, she saw the banner falling, Rickard's hands going up to his head, a Visigoth spearman sprawled backward over the wall, mail hauberk ripped, Ned Mowlett striking down twice with a bastard sword; leaping off the snow-covered masonry and vanishing—

The Lion Azure banner tipped into the snow. Ash saw a jagged, thick splinter jutting out of Rickard's helmet. A spear-point has hit, glanced off, the shaft shattering at the collar, and a white, razor-sharp fragment of wood sticks out of the sallet's eye slot.

Blood welled up in the torchlight, gushing, blackening the wood. Rickard's hands scrabbled at the steel. He fell over backward, screaming behind the helmet, arching, lying still.

"Rickard!"

She stood. Looked down.

"I . . . yes. If I could, if I lived, now—I'd change that. Go back and wipe out—people will do it. You're right. For whatever reason—people will use God's grace, if they have it. If a miracle can bring someone back from death—"

'AND THEN, THERE IS NO END TO CHANGE.'

"No." She is cold, from hands to feet, from heart to soul, chill with more than the blackness and the massacre a few feet away. The torchlight glimmers on yellow silk, a blue lion: Thomas Rochester, face bleeding, hauling the banner up again. She stumbles on numb feet the tiny distance between herself and the snow-covered wall where Florian lies. Richard Faversham is gone.

'IT IS TIME. NOW.'

Caught between grief and nightmare, between this slaughter and the revelation of the future, she is dumb.

It is dark.

She kneels beside Florian, awkward in her armor. The woman's breath still moves her chest.

Desperation in her voice, she pleads: "Why change everything? Why not—" She fumbles for Florian's hand. There is another fallen body, momentarily left behind the tide of fighting: it may be the Faris, it may be another of her men.

Anselm will hold them here, she thought, *and de Vere will win it. Or not. Nothing I can do about that. About this—*

Her mind works, as in panic emergencies it has always worked; it is the one thing above all else that qualifies her for what she does.

"Why change everything? Why not change *one* thing?" Ash demands. "What you bred, in me, for a wonder-worker—take it out. Take that out of us! Leave us what we are, but take *that* away."

Their lament is strong in her mind.

'WE HAVE CONSIDERED IT. YET WHAT AROSE AS A SPONTANEOUS MUTATION MAY ARISE AGAIN. OR YOU MAY, IN CENTURIES TO COME, DEVISE SOME DEVICE TO MAKE MIRACLES FOR YOU. AND WHAT DO WE HAVE THEN, TO PREVENT YOU? YOU WILL BE GONE, THERE WILL BE NO WONDER-WORKERS, AND WE ARE ONLY STONE—VOICELESS, IMMOBILE, THINKING STONE.'

"You don't have to wipe us out—"

'WE HAVE BRED A WEAPON. AND WHEN YOU ARE USED, ASH, THERE CAN NEVER BE ANOTHER WEAPON FOR US TO USE. BECAUSE YOUR RACE WILL NEVER HAVE EXISTED. WHAT WE DO, WE *MUST* DO NOW. WE BEAR NO HATRED FOR YOU, ONLY FOR WHAT YOUR SPECIES WILL DO—AND YOU WILL DO IT. BUT WE WILL PREVENT IT, NOW. FORGIVE US.'

"I'll do *something*," Ash muttered.

Her mind races. Their linked pressure dazzles her, she feels the blood tingling in her veins and something in the shared depth of her soul begin to move. She senses her mind expand; realizes that it is their immense, vast intelligence that begins to merge with her. She perceives a vast cognitive power.

"I can do this," Ash said baldly. "Listen to me. I can take the wonder-workers out of history. Take miracles out of us, now and in the past. Take out the *capacity*. You can hold all of human history in your minds for me—all the past—and I can *do* it."

She holds the warm body of Florian in her arms. The woman is still breathing. In appalled realization, before they can respond, she says aloud:

"But Florian has to die before I can do this. Before this change."

'IT IS OUR SORROW, TOO.'

"No," Ash says. *"No."*

There is confusion among the inhuman multiple voices:

'YOU CANNOT DENY US.'

"You don't understand," Ash said. *"I don't lose."*

The morning of the fifth of January is as black as midnight without a moon. Maybe no more than half an hour since Frederick of Hapsburg's troops have made their attack? Do they fight on, in the unnatural pitch-darkness? Men shout, scream, yell contradictory orders. Or is it just the golems: mindless, brutal, killing machines, that don't see where she kneels behind the wall, everyone else running or dead?

"I don't lose," Ash repeated. "You bred me for what I am. You need me to be a fighter, whether you know it or not. I can take the decision to sacrifice other people. It's what I do. But I do it through choice, when it's necessary."

'YOU HAVE NO CHOICE.'

A very weak voice said, "I never liked cities. Nasty unhealthy places. Do I have the flux?"

Florian's eyes were open. She seemed unfocused. Her speech came as a bare whisper, blue lips moving only a fraction.

"Someone . . . should kill you. If I order it."

The weight of the woman across her knees kept Ash still. She said, gently, "You won't."

"I—fucking will. Don't you realize I love you, you stupid girl? But I *will* do this. Nothing else left."

Ash cupped her hand and laid it against Florian's cheek. "I will not die, and *I will not lose*."

The Wild Machines shout grief and triumph, in her head.

She felt power, beginning to peak. It moved in her below conscious thought, deep in the back of her soul, in the strongest of her reflexes, appetites, beliefs.

"I can find survival and victory where there's no chance of one," she says, smiling crookedly. "What do you think I've been doing all my life?"

'AS A SOLDIER.'

"Long before *that* . . ."

She touches the woman surgeon's brows, smoothing them with a feather touch. Where her skin touches Florian's scalp, the woman shivers with a deep, intense pain. Blood has matted in her straw gold hair, with no fresh flow; but Ash can feel the skull swelling under her fingers. *She should be in a hospital; she should be back at the abbey.*

"Long before you, even," she said, deceptively light. "Come on. Hold on. Good girl. When I was raped. When the Griffin-in-Gold were hung, to a man, as a defeated garrison. When Guillaume left me. When I whored so that I could eat. *Then*. Hold on. That's it."

'SHE IS DYING. BURGUNDY IS PASSING.'

"We've got no time. Don't argue." Ash slipped her hand under the cuff of the woman's doublet, feeling her shock-cold skin and her pulse. "I've seen men hit like this before."

'SHE BREATHES, STILL—'

'STILL, HER HEART BEATS—'

The pressure in her head is unbearable.

"I'll do—my miracle—not yours."

'NO—'

Around her, at the walls in the darkness, men are killing each other. In panic, and in controlled fury. The light of the guttering torch shows her—for a second—Robert Anselm grabbing the Lion Azure standard as John Burren goes headfirst over the broken masonry. The intense cold numbs her fingers, her face, her body. The fight goes on.

'YOU WILL NOT—'

She feels their power. With the place in her soul that listens, that draws them down to her, she reaches for that power and tries to drain it into herself. They resist. She feels them, their immense minds, holding back.

"Now!" she snarls. "Don't you understand, I need her *alive* for this? She's *Burgundy*."

'IT WILL BE NO USE!' the Wild Machines protest. 'WHAT USE TO REMOVE ONLY THE POWER OF MIRACLES, AND NOT YOUR RACE? IT WILL RETURN, AND HOW WILL WE STOP IT?'

Ash feels history, past, and memory, all three, sliding into different shapes. A great hollow hunger grips her, not for this new future, but for her own reality.

Quietly, she says, "You need the nature of Burgundy, to make certain that miracles don't happen."

She is dazzled by the world that unfolds in her head and outside it: the Wild Machines, with the calculations of five thousand years, laying all the past and present out in front of her.

And, at the heart of them, faster than anything she can comprehend, *new* calculations happening.

With both hands—one bare, one bandaged; the cold numbing her pain—she rips at the neck of Florian's doublet, gets a hand down onto her hot skin. And, careless of the filth on it, licks her other hand, and holds the wet skin beneath the woman's nostrils, feeling the faintest feathering of breath.

She says aloud, "You need Burgundy, in eternity."

Churned snow and mud are wet under her armored knees. Blood stains her hose and boots. A wind blows up out of the dark, cold enough to make her eyes run, blind her. The last torch gutters.

She lifted her head and saw burning spatters of Greek Fire on the snow-blotched earth, and a golem striding over the fallen wall and lifting up the nozzle of a Greek Fire thrower.

A helmet-muffled roar sounded. An armored man in Lion livery ran in front of her, brought the hammer end of his poleax over and down—stone chips flew—and a gout of flame fell down with the golem's shattered forearms, and licked at its bronze and granite torso.

"A Lion!" Robert Anselm's familiar voice bellowed.

She opened her mouth to shout. The golem waved broken stone stumps. Robert Anselm threw himself facedown in full armor in the dirt. The Greek Fire tank on the golem's back went up in a soundless blue-white fireball.

In stark white light she sees the uneven line of fighting men outside the ruined chapel: the silhouettes of bow shafts and hooked bills; the Lion standard; Frederick's Eagle banner beyond; massed men and stone machines.

"Come and 'ave a go!" a male voice bellows, thirty feet away, over sudden local laughter. "If you think you're hard enough!"

Broken walls cast stark shadows, everything black beyond. Men are shouting now above the noise of fighting, trying to outdo each other with cynical black humor.

"A Lion!" Anselm's rallying voice: *"A Lion!"*

The heat of breath touched her. She did not turn her head.

In the corner of her vision, she sees a great needle-clawed paw set down upon the stone.

Under her hand, there is no detectable heartbeat; against her sweating skin, no whisper of a breath. But Florian's flesh is warm.

She closes her eyes against the majesty of the Heraldic Beast that God's grace—as reflected by the men and women of the Lion Azure—brings prowling out of the darkness.

"Now."

She draws on them, drains them: the gold at the heart of the sun. She feels the unstoppable change beginning.

"I don't lose," she says, holding Florian to her. "Or if I do—you always save as many of your own as you can."

It is the moment of change:

She is conscious of Floria's weight. Not until then does she open her eyes again, looking at the snow trodden down black on the old abandoned altar, at snow-lined ruined walls, and see the familiarity.

But this is a younger wood, a different valley; there are no holly trees.

She has time to smile. *Fortuna. Just chance.*

As if her mind expands, she feels the immense ratiocinative power of the Wild Machines flow through her, envelop her, become a tool she can command. She can calculate, with the precision of the finest cut, what must become improbable—what must be reified, what made merely potential.

"Don't let me down now." Her hands grip Floria's; her hands touch Burgundy. "Come on, girl!" And, quietly, in the dark, "To—a safe place."

She wonders momentarily what every priest with God's grace has felt, and if what she feels is the same.

Love for the world, however bitter, grief-stricken, or brutal it may be. Love for her own. The will and the desire to protect.

In the authoritative voice that people obey, she says, "Do it!"

She *moves* Burgundy.

[Transcript of taped conversation between Professor Davies, Mr Davies, Doctor Ratcliff, Ms Longman.

Transcript dated 14/1/2001.

Location not specified: specified SFX consistent with hospital, private room rather than ward.

Original audio-visual tape not available. Deletions and omissions original to this typed transcript.]

Observation Tape ██████

Authority ██████

No. ██████

[tape hiss]

[Noise of electrical switch]

WILLIAM DAVIES
[—inaudible—] a man with photosensitive epilepsy should not be watching the television.

VAUGHAN DAVIES
Indeed. A man unaware of the last sixty years, however, should. I confess myself amazed. I had thought the popular tastes of the nineteen-thirties degraded. This is nothing but the vilest kind of mob entertainment.

PIERCE RATCLIFF
If I could introduce myself, Professor Davies—[indistinguishable: background room noise]

VAUGHAN DAVIES
You are Ratcliff. Yes. If I may say so, it's taken you long enough to come and see me. I see from your previous publications that you have a mind with some degree of rigor in its

reasoning. May I be so happy as to suppose you have treated my work with adequate intelligence?

PIERCE RATCLIFF
I hope so.

VAUGHAN DAVIES
All men live in hope, Doctor Ratcliff. I believe I could drink a little tea. My dear, do you think you could manage that?

ANNA LONGMAN
I'll ask the nurse if he can arrange it.

VAUGHAN DAVIES
William, perhaps you . . .

WILLIAM DAVIES
Don't mind me. I'm quite comfortable here.

VAUGHAN DAVIES
I would prefer to speak with Doctor Ratcliff in private.

[Indistinguishable: room noise, voices outside]

ANNA LONGMAN
[—inaudible—] some coffee, in the café here. Do you need your stick?

WILLIAM DAVIES
Good Lord, no. A matter of a few yards.

[Indistinguishable: door opens and closes?]

VAUGHAN DAVIES
Doctor Ratcliff, I have been talking to that girl. Perhaps you would be so kind as to tell me where you have been for what, I understand, is the better part of three weeks?

PIERCE RATCLIFF
Girl? Oh. Anna said that you appeared to be worried about me.

VAUGHAN DAVIES
Answer the question, please.

PIERCE RATCLIFF
I don't see the relevance of this, Professor Davies.

VAUGHAN DAVIES
Damn you, young man, will you answer a question when it is put to you!

PIERCE RATCLIFF
I'm afraid I can't say much.

VAUGHAN DAVIES
Have you at any time in the recent past been in danger of your life?

PIERCE RATCLIFF
What? Have I what?

VAUGHAN DAVIES
This is a perfectly serious question, Doctor Ratcliff, and I would be obliged if you would treat it as one. I will make the matter clear in due course.

PIERCE RATCLIFF
No. I mean. Well, no.

VAUGHAN DAVIES
You returned from your archaeological expedition—

PIERCE RATCLIFF [interrupts]
Not mine. Isobel's. Doctor Napier-Grant, that is.

VAUGHAN DAVIES
So many <u>women</u>. We appear to have become very degenerate. However. You returned from North Africa; you were not at any time in danger of an accident of any kind?

PIERCE RATCLIFF
If I was, I was unaware of it. Professor Davies, I really don't understand you.

VAUGHAN DAVIES
The girl told me you have read the Sible Hedingham manuscript. That this somewhat idiosyncratic translation of it is your work.

PIERCE RATCLIFF
Yes.

VAUGHAN DAVIES
Then it is plain, to the meanest intelligence, what has been happening here! Do you wonder that I show some concern for a professional colleague?

PIERCE RATCLIFF
Frankly, Professor Davies, you don't seem like a man who shows much concern about his fellow man.

VAUGHAN DAVIES
No? No. Perhaps you are right.

PIERCE RATCLIFF
I didn't come before because I was being interviewed—

VAUGHAN DAVIES [interrupts]
By whom?

PIERCE RATCLIFF
I don't think it's wise to go into that too much at the moment.

VAUGHAN DAVIES
Is it possible that any member of your archaeological expedition has been in an accident? An automobile accident, or something of a similar nature?

PIERCE RATCLIFF
Isobel's expedition. No. Isobel would have mentioned it. I don't see what this has got to do with the Sible Hedingham manuscript.

VAUGHAN DAVIES
It is plain, from that document, what has occurred to us.

PIERCE RATCLIFF
The fracture in history, yes.

[Indistinguishable]

[—inaudible—] this what you wrote in your Addendum to the second edition, if you did write it?

VAUGHAN DAVIES
Oh, I wrote it, Doctor Ratcliff. I had it in my pocket when I travelled to London. Any sensible publisher would have removed himself from London during the German bombing, but not—

PIERCE RATCLIFF [interrupts]
If we can get back to this. You read the Sible Hedingham document, you wrote about the fracture, and the 'first history'—

VAUGHAN DAVIES [interrupts]
Yes, and it obviously needed publication as a matter of the greatest urgency. I had been so nearly right in my edition of the Ash papers. It was clear to me from the Sible Hedingham document that Burgundy had been, as it were, removed from us. Taken to a level of matter we cannot as yet detect—a happy thought: perhaps we may detect it, now?

PIERCE RATCLIFF
There are experiments going on in particle physics and probability theory, yes.

VAUGHAN DAVIES
You have reached the same conclusions as I. It seems to be the case that, before this fracture, we were capable of consciously doing what other forms of life unconsciously do.

PIERCE RATCLIFF
Collapsing the improbable and the miraculous into the *real*. The solid world.

[pause]

But it had me puzzled! The universe is real, yes, we see that. But the universe is uncertain. Ever since Heisenberg, we've known that; down on the sub-atomic level, things are fuzzy. Observing an experiment alters the results. You can know where a particle is, or its direction; never both. This isn't solid, this isn't real as the manuscript talks about it—

VAUGHAN DAVIES [interrupts]
If you would kindly stop pacing.

PIERCE RATCLIFF
Sorry. But I see it: it *is* real. What Burgundy does is keep us consistent. If it was uncertain today, it will be uncertain *in* the same way tomorrow! Unchecked unreality is what it prevents. Randomness. We may not have a good existence, but we have a consistent one.

VAUGHAN DAVIES
Of course, before, we would have been able consciously to *undo* such stabilisation, such consistency.

[pause]

If you look at the twentieth century, Doctor Ratcliff—and I, at least, look on the latter half of it with a stranger's eyes—you cannot claim this to be the best of all possible worlds. Man's lot is still suffering, in the main. But it is a consistent reality. Human evil is limited to the possible. We have much for which to be thankful!

PIERCE RATCLIFF
The obvious example. I've thought about it. Think what Hitler would have done to the Jews, if he had been a wonder-worker, a man able to literally manipulate the stuff of reality. It would be all blond Aryans. There would have *been* no Jewish race. A Holocaust worse than the Holocaust.

VAUGHAN DAVIES
What Holocaust?

[pause]

PIERCE RATCLIFF
Never mind. There would have been military research. People bred as weapons. Like Ash, yes, like Ash. A probability bomb—worse than a nuclear bomb.

VAUGHAN DAVIES
Nuclear? Nuclear bomb?

PIERCE RATCLIFF
That's—oh: difficult, that's a—a bomb that—

VAUGHAN DAVIES [interrupts]
Rutherford! He did it, after all!

PIERCE RATCLIFF
Yes—no—never mind. Look.

[pause]

VAUGHAN DAVIES
It is one of the more interesting paradoxes, don't you think? That war, by nature of the organised thought required to wage it, reinforces the nature of a rational reality—while, at the same time, the destruction it causes in its effects leads to chaos.

PIERCE RATCLIFF
That's why she understood it, isn't it?

VAUGHAN DAVIES
Ash? Yes. I believe so.

PIERCE RATCLIFF
I couldn't understand it, you see. Until I understood that Burgundy's still there, still doing what it's been doing. We have it in the species-mind, and in our unconscious, as a lost and golden country. But at the same time it has this quite genuine scientifically-verifiable existence on a different level of reality, and it carries on with its function.

VAUGHAN DAVIES
Doctor Ratcliff, are you aware of the possible reason why things are coming back?

PIERCE RATCLIFF
I understand how things could be left over. No process is perfect, the universe is large and complex, and what Ash and the Wild Machines did—it's not surprising if some of the evidence of the first history wasn't expunged. Reality has its own weight. It's been gradually squeezing the anomalies out—things becoming legendary, mythic, fictional.

VAUGHAN DAVIES
The manuscript evidence.

PIERCE RATCLIFF
A statue here, a helmet there. Ash's words turning up in someone else's mouth. I can understand all of that. There was a single fracture, it did what it did, and we see the evidence as it . . . fades.

VAUGHAN DAVIES
The false history that appeared with the fracture—in which, for example, Charles the Bold dies after a siege, but at Nancy—has, here and there, some fragments of the true history embedded in it. For example, the chronicles that the del

Guiz family <u>would have</u> written, after fourteen seventy-seven.

PIERCE RATCLIFF
Not as they existed before the fracture, but as they <u>would have</u> existed, if history had just carried on. Five-hundred-year-old evidence sliding back into the interstices of history. The Fraxinus manuscript too. It <u>might</u> quite reasonably have existed.

VAUGHAN DAVIES
Yes. That is quite clear. I wonder, Doctor Ratcliff, if you quite appreciate the significance of the Sible Hedingham document in this respect?

PIERCE RATCLIFF
You remind me very much of my old professor, if you don't mind me saying so, Professor Davies. He used to ask me a trick question just like that.

VAUGHAN DAVIES
Do you know what is most strange to me? You are giving me the respect you believe is due to an older man. In my mind, Doctor Ratcliff, I am a younger man than you are.

> [Indistinguishable: traffic noise—window open? Tape hiss. Pause before speech resumes.]

PIERCE RATCLIFF
The Sible Hedingham document is more improbable. It's what Ash would have written—no, she'd have to have dictated it to someone—but done it after fourteen seventy-seven, after the fracture. Perhaps left it in England after a visit to the Earl of Oxford.

VAUGHAN DAVIES
Doctor Ratcliff, I intended to warn you, and now I will do it. The possible reason why things are coming back. My theory is that the reappearance of these highly-improbable artefacts is a consequence of Burgundy's function failing in some way.

PIERCE RATCLIFF
I'd thought—I was afraid—*Yes*. Improbable happenings, things that aren't rational, predictable. But—why would it be breaking down? Why now?

VAUGHAN DAVIES
For that, you will have to understand how lost Burgundy does what it does; and I believe, since I am sixty years behind current scientific development, that I am not qualified to put forward a theory. What I will do, if permitted, is to give you my warning.

PIERCE RATCLIFF
Sorry. Yes. Please. What is it?

VAUGHAN DAVIES
What happened to me, happened because of the Sible Hedingham manuscript. I discovered it in Hedingham Castle, in late nineteen thirty-eight. It is my belief that it had not—existed, if you like—much before that time.

PIERCE RATCLIFF
The probability wave being locally collapsed. An artefact becoming real.

VAUGHAN DAVIES
Just as in North Africa, a few months ago.

PIERCE RATCLIFF
Carthage.

VAUGHAN DAVIES
I had been staying at my brother's house as I completed my second edition, and researching the Oxfords, because of the de Vere connection with Ash. I theorise now that the Sible Hedingham manuscript became reified, if you like, not long after I arrived. I stole the manuscript—

PIERCE RATCLIFF [interrupts, agitated]
Stole it!

VAUGHAN DAVIES
They would neither sell it to me, nor allow me to study it, what else was I to do, pray?

PIERCE RATCLIFF
Well, I. You shouldn't. Well. I don't know.

VAUGHAN DAVIES
I stole the manuscript, and read it. My Latin is rather better than yours, if you will permit me to say so. Since it was too late in the printing procedure to include the Sible Hedingham manuscript, I wrote my Addendum, with the obvious conclusions, and made an appointment to deliver it to my publishers in London. I planned to arrange the publication of a revised edition, including the new manuscript. [pause] I was embroiled in a bombing raid. A bomb landed quite close to me, I believe. I might have been killed. I might have been spared. Instead, I found myself unreal. Improbable. Potential.

PIERCE RATCLIFF
What's this got to do with the manuscript?

VAUGHAN DAVIES
Quite simply, I theorise that there is an energy field, a radiation of some kind, which attends the collapsing of a probability into a reality. When a very improbable thing becomes reified, the radiated energy is that much stronger.

PIERCE RATCLIFF [interrupts]
It couldn't be radiation, as such.

VAUGHAN DAVIES
Will you let me finish? Thank you. Whatever it is, whether a sub-atomic phenomenon of some kind, or an energy, I was most certainly exposed to it. I believe it to be stronger the more recently the artefact has become real. The exposure in some way destabilised my own reality. I was unaware of this at the time that I found the manuscript, of course. Then, with

the bombing, with the point where the wave-front would have to collapse in a major way for me—I would live, or I would die—the destabilisation became acute. I became, and remained, a potential thing.

PIERCE RATCLIFF
And you're warning me . . . because I've been to the sites at Carthage.

VAUGHAN DAVIES
Yes.

PIERCE RATCLIFF
I couldn't tell if. There would be no way of knowing. Tests. Maybe tests of some kind.

VAUGHAN DAVIES
If what I shall call your cohesion has been impaired, you may be in danger.

PIERCE RATCLIFF
If the effect lessens the longer the artefact has been real, then I may not be—impaired. There's no way of telling, is there? Unless I do have an accident, or hit some point of decision. . . . What happened to you could happen to me. Isobel. The rest. Or it might never happen.

VAUGHAN DAVIES
We must hope for a test to be developed, to determine this. I would work on it myself, but I am conscious that I am not the man I was. A curious thing, to have youth and old age, but no maturity. [pause] I have been robbed, I feel.

PIERCE RATCLIFF
I won't know, will I? If I've been exposed.

VAUGHAN DAVIES
Doctor Ratcliff!

PIERCE RATCLIFF
I'm sorry.

VAUGHAN DAVIES
Let us hope that no accident befalls you, Doctor Ratcliff.

PIERCE RATCLIFF
This is. [pause] Something of a shock.

[Long pause. Background noise]

PIERCE RATCLIFF
There are currently people doing experiments with probability, on a very small scale. I had two government departments debriefing me. The Americans actually took me off the ship in the Mediterranean. On Christmas Day! It was frightening. I was interviewed over several days. They're still after me. I know it sounds paranoid—

VAUGHAN DAVIES [interrupts]
Theoretical progress is being made?

PIERCE RATCLIFF
Isobel's colleagues, they seem to think so. I doubt I can talk to them without attracting more security attention. I just feel—if you're right—they ought to know—someone ought to *look* at you. [pause] And me.

VAUGHAN DAVIES
I will happily be a subject for study, if it brings us closer to the truth.

PIERCE RATCLIFF
Is Burgundy failing to stabilise the probabilities now? Why now?

[Increased background noise. Specialist enters; medical conversations deleted. Door noise. Long pause.]

VAUGHAN DAVIES
[—inaudible—] these minor indignities inflicted by the medical profession. No wonder William became a doctor. Doctor Ratcliff, I know to what the incident in the manuscript refers. I know what became of Burgundy, in that sense.

PIERCE RATCLIFF [pause]
How can you know? Yes, we can speculate, theorise, but—

VAUGHAN DAVIES [interrupts]
I am perhaps the only man alive with reason to say that I know this.

[Pause. Noise of papers being moved?]

PIERCE RATCLIFF
You have a documented history, you know. Asylums, hospitals.

VAUGHAN DAVIES
Doctor Ratcliff, you know that I am speaking the truth. I have existed for the past sixty years in—if you like—the raw state of the universe. The infinite possibilities, before the species-mind of man collapses them into one single reality. For me it was a moment of infinite duration and no time. I would need to be a theologian to describe, accurately, the moment of eternity.

PIERCE RATCLIFF [agitated]
What are you telling me?

VAUGHAN DAVIES
While I was in this state of existence—although it is improper to say 'while', since that implies time passing—but no matter. As I existed, merely potential, I perceived that among the infinite chaotic possibilities, there was another state of order.

PIERCE RATCLIFF
On a sub-atomic level? You *saw*—

VAUGHAN DAVIES
I saw that I had been correct. I was not overly surprised. You see, *I* theorised that the Burgundian bloodline, if we may now call it that, acted as an anchor or a filter; preventing any ability to manipulate quantum events. Any so-called miracles or prayer. And similarly, Ideal Burgundy—

PIERCE RATCLIFF [interrupts]
The sun. What about the sun?

VAUGHAN DAVIES
The sun.

PIERCE RATCLIFF
Over Burgundy! They didn't know why—I don't know—it should have been—If the Wild Machines were reality as we understand reality. Complex structures in silicon compounds might give rise to an organic chemistry, real beings—

[pause]

Then it should have been dark.

VAUGHAN DAVIES
Ah. Ah, now I see. You disappoint me, Professor Ratcliff.

PIERCE RATCLIFF
I disappoint—you—[loud]

VAUGHAN DAVIES
[—inaudible—]—if I may proceed?

[pause]

No, I imagined you would see it instantly—as Leofric did, albeit he conceptualized it in his own cultural terms. I theorise that the Ferae Natura Machinae bring about an initial quantum disjuncture, immediately the sun goes out. In Burgundy, the Real is preserved—Burgundy maintains the previous, more *plausible*, state. The world outside is scientifically real, if you like to put it in such simplistic terms, but it is a *subsequent* reality. Burgundy already forms a quantum bubble: already begins to be Ideal Burgundy.

[pause]

DOCTOR RATCLIFF?

PIERCE RATCLIFF
And . . . oh, I . . . And when the skies go dark at the Duke's death—

VAUGHAN DAVIES [interrupts]
Precisely! The two unsynchronised quantum realities try to conjoin! *The Ferae Natura Machinae* striving to impose theirs with the Faris, have it be the only one! Although I had better, perhaps, say interlaced realities—

PIERCE RATCLIFF [interrupts]
The Wild Machines, forcing their version of reality, their quantum version, and it fails at Dijon, and then, with Ash—

[pause]

I should have seen it. No reality is privileged over another, they're all real—except that some are less *possible*, more difficult to bring about—easier to *stop*—

VAUGHAN DAVIES
Precisely. Ratcliff, I know what Ash did. She shifted Burgundy—

PIERCE RATCLIFF [interrupts]
A phase-shift—

VAUGHAN DAVIES [interrupts]
Altering it at some deep level, pushing it down—or forward—into the place where reality becomes solidified. Ratcliff, you must see it. She took Burgundy, and the nature of Burgundy, ahead of us—perhaps only a fraction of a second—

PIERCE RATCLIFF [interrupts]
Shifted it—a nanosecond—

VAUGHAN DAVIES [interrupts]
Where the Possible becomes Real, there is Burgundy. I saw it. That is what has preserved us, that is what kept the universe coherent for us. The nature of Burgundy, acting as an anchor, or a filter—

PIERCE RATCLIFF [interrupts]
So that the ability to *consciously* collapse the wave-front can never reappear, it's too *improbable*—

VAUGHAN DAVIES [interrupts]
For centuries after it vanished, no historian wrote of Burgundy. With Charles Mallory Maximillian, we begin to remember. But we do not remember, we perceive. We perceive that lost Burgundy has an existence in our racial unconscious, as a mythic image; and it has this because it has a genuine, scientifically-verifiable existence as a part of our reality fractionally closer to the moment of Becoming.

PIERCE RATCLIFF
Burgundy—really still there.

VAUGHAN DAVIES
To think I had imagined you a man of some intelligence. Yes, Doctor Ratcliff, Burgundy has been 'still there'. Trapped in an eternal golden moment, and functioning as a guide or regulator or suppresser, if you will pardon an engineering metaphor. It filters reality into the species-mind. It has kept us real. Is that plain enough for you?

PIERCE RATCLIFF
What did you perceive? What. [pause] What is it like, in Burgundy, now? I'd started to think what it might be like. [pause] An endless court, an endless tournament, a hunt. Maybe war, off in the wildwoods. Their war a living metaphor, defeating the improbabilities pushing in from outside.

VAUGHAN DAVIES
No. That was not what I perceived. Burgundy has no duration. They are frozen, in an eternal moment of an act. The act of making real a coherent world.

PIERCE RATCLIFF
Ash? Florian? The rest of them?

VAUGHAN DAVIES
Odd that you should concentrate upon the people. It comes of being a pure historian, one would suppose, and having no grasp of science. My perception of the wave-front of probability was far more significant. However, it is true that I perceived minds, in that state of existence.

PIERCE RATCLIFF
Could you recognise them?

VAUGHAN DAVIES
I believe that I could. I believe they were the people mentioned in the Sible Hedingham manuscript. You can-not understand. There is no duration, no action: only being. Burgundy does not guide the Real by what it does. It does not have to do anything. It functions by being; by what it *is*.

PIERCE RATCLIFF
A kind of hell. For the minds, I mean.

VAUGHAN DAVIES
I am here to tell you, Doctor Ratcliff, that you are perfectly correct in that. What I experienced was an infinite duration of hell. Or heaven.

PIERCE RATCLIFF
Or heaven?

VAUGHAN DAVIES
In the sense that I have directly perceived the Real, of which we are shadows. Good Lord, man, does nobody read Plato any more?

PIERCE RATCLIFF
An 'Ideal' Burgundy, is that what you're saying?

VAUGHAN DAVIES
Burgundy exists among, and governs the shape of, the Real. It is—or has been—the one true reality, of which we are the imperfect shadow. It's all in Plato.

PIERCE RATCLIFF
Plato wasn't a theoretical physicist!

VAUGHAN DAVIES
These things have a way of soaking into the species-mind. They are in our blood, at a deeper level than Freud's unconscious. Jung's racial unconscious, perhaps. A level as deep and involuntary as the transmutation of cells in our body. It is unsurprising if our mythic mind produces ghosts and shadow images of the Real. After all, we do remember Burgundy.

PIERCE RATCLIFF
We remember it *now*. A little bit in the eighteenth century, then Charles Mallory Maximillian's first edition; then you; then me, and Carthage, and—

VAUGHAN DAVIES [indistinguishable: weak]

PIERCE RATCLIFF
[—inaudible—] gradually failing in what it does. Are you sure that that's what you saw? Five hundred years after what she did, Burgundy is starting to weaken, to fail? Is that it?

VAUGHAN DAVIES
Yes. I am certain of it.

[Long pause. Tape hiss. Footsteps. Door opens and closes.]

PIERCE RATCLIFF
Sorry. Had to go out and walk.

VAUGHAN DAVIES
The chaotic fabric of the universe is strong. Perhaps, eventually, it reasserts itself whatever one can do.

PIERCE RATCLIFF
She did it all for nothing, then.

VAUGHAN DAVIES
Five hundred years, Doctor Ratcliff. It has all been over for five hundred years.

PIERCE RATCLIFF [agitated]
But it hasn't. Not if your perceptions were correct. It's been an eternal, infinite moment. And now it's failing. Now, it's failing. Now!

VAUGHAN DAVIES
In that sense, yes. Your archaeological reappearances, at Carthage. This manuscript. Even myself, I believe. My reentrance into the Real is a function of the weakening of Lost Burgundy. It must be. There can be no other explanation.

PIERCE RATCLIFF
There are experiments being done in probability. Only on an infinitely small level, but—is that why? Do you think? Are we destabilising them? I need—no, Isobel's people won't talk to me about this, not with the security clampdown.

VAUGHAN DAVIES
An arc of five hundred years for us, a moment for Lost Burgundy. A moment which is ending, now. The universe is vast, powerful, chaotically imperative, Doctor Ratcliff. It was bound to reassert itself.

PIERCE RATCLIFF
What happens when Burgundy fails, finally? The end of causality? An increase in entropy, in chaos, in miracles?

VAUGHAN DAVIES
They subject one to an interesting variety of tests on this ward. Between tests, one is left with considerable time. I have devoted much of it—despite William's assertion that I watch that televisual box—to analysing what the loss of Burgundy might mean. I believe you have reached the same conclusion as I.

PIERCE RATCLIFF
The species-mind will continue to collapse the probable into a predictable real. But eventually, without Burgundy, enough random chaos will filter through, we'll become able to manipulate the Real again consciously—or technologically. There will be wars. Wars in which the Real is the casualty.

VAUGHAN DAVIES
Someone's reality is always a casualty in wartime, Doctor Ratcliff. But yes. It is what the Ferae Natura Machinae foresaw. The infinitely-unreal universe. If you like, the miracle wars.

PIERCE RATCLIFF
I have to publish.

VAUGHAN DAVIES
You intend to include this in your edition of the Ash papers?

PIERCE RATCLIFF

Once it's made public, it can't be ignored. There has to be an investigation! Do we need to stop performing experiments on the sub-atomic level? Do we need more experiments? Can we reinforce Burgundy?

VAUGHAN DAVIES

You will sound, if you forgive me, like a blithering lunatic to them, Doctor Ratcliff.

PIERCE RATCLIFF

I don't care, anything's better than 'miracle' wars—!

> [Door opens. Footsteps; an indistinguishable number of people entering.]

WILLIAM DAVIES

I think that's enough for today.

VAUGHAN DAVIES

Really, William. I believe I may be allowed to know my own state of health.

WILLIAM DAVIES

Not as well as your doctors. I may be retired; I know exhaustion when I look at it. Doctor Ratcliff will come back and talk to you tomorrow.

VAUGHAN DAVIES [indistinguishable]

PIERCE RATCLIFF [indistinguishable]

ANNA LONGMAN

We need to talk, Pierce. I've been through to the office. We need to make some hard decisions about publication, before the weekend.

PIERCE RATCLIFF
Professor Davies. [pause] It's an honour. I'll call again tomorrow.

[Indistinguishable door noises, noises of chairs being moved]

VAUGHAN DAVIES
[—inaudible—] publish as soon as possible. We need the help of the scientific community. [Tape garbled] [—inaudible—] further investigation on a world-wide scale.

PIERCE RATCLIFF
[—inaudible—] we have no idea, do we? How long we've got? Before it fails completely?

[Tape terminates]

original annotation:

SUBJECT "VAUGHAN DAVIES" REMOVED 02/02/01 [redacted] TO HOSPITAL FOR FURTHER TESTS AND INTERROGATION

Afterword

With the abrupt termination of the Sible Hedingham manuscript, the documentation of these events comes to a close.

It is now evident that a significant change in the nature of our universe occurred on 5 January 1477.

To summarise: at that point, the events of human history up to that date were altered, and a subsequent different history was thereafter perceived to have occurred. It was neither the prior history of the human race, nor the desired future of the 'Wild Machine' silicon intelligences. Whether our history from 1477 onwards is a random result of the 'miracle', or a desired one, it is difficult to say.

Whichever is the truth, what is undeniable is that the ability of human minds to consciously alter the wave-front of probability at the point where it is collapsed into one reality was eradicated. Human existence continued: the consistent and rational universe supported by the human species-mind, and protected and preserved by the altered previous history—the 'lost Burgundy' that remains with us as the memory of a myth.

If not an ideal universe, it is at least a consistent universe. Human good and human evil are still in our own power to choose.

I realise that these conclusions, drawn from these texts and from the available archaeological evidence, will give rise to some controversy. I believe, however, that it is essential that they become widely known, and are acted upon.

The laws of cause and effect operate consistently within the human sphere of influence. What the universe is like otherwise, in other places, we do not know. We are one world among millions, in one galaxy among billions, in a universe so vast that neither light nor our understanding can cross it. What local laws we have here, and can observe, are rational, consistent, and predictable. Even where, as on the sub-atomic level, causality becomes "fuzzy", it becomes fuzzy in accordance with scientific reality, and not in accordance with random chaos. What is an uncertain particle today will be an uncertain particle tomorrow, and not a dragon. Or a Lion, or a Hart.

If this were all, then while 'lost Burgundy' would be a deeply significant discovery about how our universe is constructed, it would nonetheless be a closed discovery. Ash's decision was made, Burgundy 'shifted', the nature of Burgundy anchors us in causality, and that is where we are.

Except that, as recent events have proved, 'Burgundy' is failing. It is an unavoidable fact that some things that are improbable (in the technical sense of the word) have, in the last sixty years, again become collapsed into a state of objective reality. The archaeological site at Carthage, although current investigations have been suspended, is eye-opening in this respect.

For whatever reason, the nature of Burgundy has changed again; it is perhaps failing, or has ceased to exist. I believe the evidence suggests that this is indeed the case.

I suspect that what Vaughan Davies (in conversation with the author) has reported perceiving, is the moment of the change itself. According to his observations, the change no longer 'still continues'—or, for those in it, 'has not ended'. What we are seeing now *is* the end of that moment. The time between 1477 and now was the period of linear time needed for that one out-of-time moment to end.

What has been necessary has been done. Burgundy, shifted out as a kind of 'spur' of advancing reality into the probability wave, has made this human universe causal.

It may not now keep it that way. The spontaneous mutation of the 'miracle gene' may arise again. A means to technologically alter the collapse of the wave-front may be discovered.

What does this mean for us, now?

Without Lost Burgundy, the species-mind of the human race will continue to do what it has done since we became conscious organic life. It will manipulate reality to be constant, coherent, consistent. Tomorrow will follow today; yesterday will not return. This is what we do—what all organic life does, on no matter how low a level—we preserve a constant reality.

What Burgundy did, however, was to protect our reality from the return of the ability to *consciously* collapse the wavefront of probability into a different, formerly-improbable, reality.

With Burgundy failing, with the complex chaos of the universe merging Burgundy back into the reality from which—for an eternal moment—it was the 'forward edge', then what is to prevent us becoming, as our ancestors were, priests and prophets, miracle-workers and recipients of grace? What is to prevent us developing this in our organic consciousness, or our machines?

Nothing.

Unless the fabric of the material universe is to be put in danger of unravelling, fraying out into entropic chaos, mere quantum soup, then we must do something now.

I intend the publication of these papers to act as a call to arms to the scientific community. We must investigate. We must act. We must prevent, somehow, the failing of 'lost Burgundy'; or create something we can put in its place. Or else, as Ash herself wrote in manuscripts that should not, in this second history, have an existence—if not, then at some day in the future, all we have done here will be undone, as if it had never been.

I am setting up a web-site at ██████ for a cyberconference: any sufficiently-accredited organisation or individual is hereby invited to log on. I will make my data available.

We are not yet, and perhaps we never will be, fit to be gods.

Pierce Ratcliff
London
2001

Afterword
(4th edition)

I HAVE LEFT unaltered the words of a much younger man.

History is very much a matter of interpretation.

Nine years is not a long time—and yet, sometimes, it is long enough to change the world out of all recognition. Sometimes nine minutes will suffice.

I suppose I should have remembered what Ash herself said. *I don't lose.*

Plainly, the Afterword to the 2001 edition was written by a man in a panic. I have reprinted it here essentially untouched, although I have deleted my old URL to prevent confusion. I was, to be frank, in a state of fear for most of the winter of 2000 and the spring of 2001, a state only made worse by the abrupt withdrawal of all copies of *Ash: The Lost History Of Burgundy* on March 25, five days before they were due to appear in the book-shops.

I am indebted to Anna Longman for the sterling defence of my work that she put up in editorial meetings. Without her, the book would not have reached the printing stage. Even she could not prevail, however, once her then-Managing Director, Jonathan Stanley, had pressure put on him by the Home Secretary.

Two days later, my own author's copies of *Ash: The Lost History of Burgundy* were removed from my flat.

A week after that, I received a visit from the police, and found myself being interviewed, not by them, but by staff from the security services of three nations.

Fear, no doubt, clouded my judgement.

Reality reasserted itself, however.

I found myself confronted by a bound copy of my third edition, into which had been placed a floppy disc, and hardcopy print-outs of my correspondence, neatly annotated by some security officer. They were not my copies: I had destroyed mine.

I was informed that they had been watching Anna since December 2000. A second—unnoticed—search of her Stratford flat found no trace of the editorial correspondence, since she carried the copies on her person until the late spring of 2001, when they disappeared.

A close study of CCTV footage and observers' reports finally confirmed that on 1 March 2001 she had been seen leaving the British Library without a book. This would not have been remarkable, had she not been witnessed an hour earlier entering *with* a book—which CCTV stills show to have been her editor's pre-publication copy of *Ash: The Lost History of Burgundy*.

Even knowing it must be there, it took the security forces a month to find it. While the chance of stealing a book from the British Library is extremely low, no one thought to make provision for someone coming *in* with a book, and leaving it amid the chaos of the British Library's move from its old building to the new one.

I dare say it would have been found and catalogued within a decade.

Confronted with our correspondence, I realised, a few seconds before I was told, that this was not some paranoid plot by which I might be 'silenced', but, in fact, a job interview.

It was not my expertise with fifteenth century manuscripts that encouraged them to co-opt me onto 'Project Carthage', but my personal eye-witness experience of the return of the artefacts of the 'first history', as detailed in that correspondence between Anna and myself.

In fact, as Anna sometimes says to me—with rather more humour than I have previously associated with her—I *am* history.

As are we all.

Fortunately, we are the future, too.

I flew out of London for California at the end of the following week, having handed in my resignation at my university.

In the years that followed, I entered on the second career of my working life (discovering an unsuspected talent for administration); a career in which—with Isobel Napier-Grant, Tami Inoshishi, James Howlett, and the associated staff of many other institutions—I have seen the frontiers of human knowledge expanded to an astounding degree. On a personal level, I have found it exacting, exciting, frustrating, and illuminating, by turns; and I still do not grasp all the advances made in quantum theory!

The present staff of Project Carthage is, of course, made up of the 'official' scientists that Isobel Napier-Grant hoped for when she decided she should throw open the Carthage site to investigation; with the expectation that there must be physicists who could both do the maths, and sort out the terminology; and free us from our dependence on speculation and metaphor. Nine years on, I have to say that they have done everything that could be hoped, and more.

This fourth edition of the Ash papers is intended to set the record straight on the background to Project Carthage. The course of the project, and the various findings it has released over the past nine years, are too well known to be repeated at length here. We now have a staff of over five hundred people, with more due to be taken on. Next year, on our tenth anniversary, I plan to publish a history of the Project.

I intend the preliminary publication of these papers both to present the background to Project Carthage, and to provide a conclusion to the *Ash* narrative—in so far as there can be a conclusion.

It took me the better part of two years to work out what we should be looking for.

Protracted UN negotiations with the Tunisian government allowed a team of scientists back on site at the seabed ruins of Carthage, working with the Institute at Tunis itself. The artefacts have since been subjected to extremely intense analysis, both there and abroad. (We were robbed of our Russian and Chinese members by the Sino-Russian 'Millennium War' of 2003–2005; but thankfully they have since returned.)

At the same time, the history of the 'Visigoth Empire' became more and more apparent in documentation stretching from the 1400s to the late nineteenth century. A fascinating paper by a historian from the University of Alexandria detailed how the Iberian Gothic tribes after AD 416 maintained a settlement on the North African coast, and were later integrated into Arab culture (in a process akin to the later crusaders' 'Latin Kingdoms of the East').

Traces of the invasion of Christendom have been excavated outside Genoa, in northern Italy, where there appears to have been a considerable battle.

The universe receives, into its interstices, the instances of the 'first history' which it can comfortably accommodate. There are discrepancies: there always will be. The universe is hugely complex, even in the 'local conditions' that are what we as a species perceive.

This reintegration of the first and second histories was observed by all of us on the Project, and took place roughly from 2000 to 2005, with the greatest concentration of activity in the 2000–2003 period. That the failure of 'lost Burgundy' should result in a kind of historical debris being swept back into our reality was not, we thought, theoretically impossible. Indeed, here it was, with more appearing every day. More evidence—undeniable, *factual* evidence—that had not been there the day before.

We lived, in those early days of the millennium, in the daily expectation of the world crumbling away under our feet. It was not unusual to wake, every day, and wonder, before one opened one's eyes, if one was the same person as the day before. All of us on 'Project Carthage' bonded closely, in almost a wartime mentality.

I wrote, in 2001, that we were not fit to be gods. Any study of history may convince the student that we are barely fit to be human beings. At the end of a century of unparalleled massacre and holocaust, we knew, on Project Carthage, that there are worse things possible. Given the power to manipulate probability, a vision of holocaust and high-tech war haunted us: human cruelty carried to an infinitely high degree. Endless human degradation, suffering, dread, and death. If this is what the 'Wild Machine' silicon intelligences predicted, then their refusal to let it come into existence can only be seen as a moral act.

At Project Carthage, we knew we were the front-line troops in the war against unreality: either we would find some way to stabilise 'Burgundy', or we would—if not now, then twenty or two hundred years in the future—find wars of improbability sweeping away the fabric of the universe.

As a historian, I led the team responsible for documenting the return of the first history. By 2002, I had realised that each of the occurrences that I was documenting was possible. As I said in conversation with Isobel Napier-Grant on the net,

> >><snip> The artefacts that are appearing are no less rational than
> >>one might demand of a causal universe. We have a ruined
> >>Carthage, five hundred years old. We do not have a fifteenth
> >>century Carthage appearing in present day Tunisia, full of
> >>Visigoths—or alien visitors, or something human senses cannot
> >>perceive. It is Carthage *as it would have been now*, had the first
> >>history continued on from 1477.

Plainly, what was reintegrating itself into reality were *possible* events, *possible* artefacts, *probable* history. No miracles.

No miracles.

It took me nearly seven years to find her.

I had my hunch in the summer of the year 2002. The arc of the moment—that five-hundred-year eternity in a Burgundy made both mythic, and more real than reality—was ending. We would be unprotected; should be subject now to increasing truly-random phenomena. And yet, plainly, the coherence of the universe we perceive had *not* degraded between 2001 and 2002.

Lost Burgundy *must* have failed or be failing: how else to account for the reappearance of so much 'Burgundian' history? But how to account for the *stability* of that reappearance? The autonomic reflexes of the species-mind, collapsing the wave-front to coherent reality? Undoubtedly; but that could not account for all. The theoretical physicists at this time lived in daily horror of the potential instabilities they observed at sub-atomic levels. They monitored these randomnesses—which became coherent again.

It was a literal hunch. It came to me not long after the

funeral of Professor Vaughan Davies—a man who lived to see the strange existence of his middle years analysed and confirmed, but who never restrained himself from a caustic remark until the day he died. (He said to me in a lucid moment, about his final coma, "It is rather more interesting than I had anticipated. I doubt that *you* would understand it, however.")

On the plane, flying home from his funeral with Isobel Napier-Grant, I suddenly said, "*People* come back."

"Vaughan 'came back'," she said, "in that sense. Complete with ghost-history of his probable existence for his missing years. Are you suggesting it's happened to someone else?"

"Has happened, or *will have* happened," I said; and put myself on the course of my next seven years' research. By the time Isobel left me to get the Fancy Rat cages from the rear of the plane, I had mapped out a potential programme.

In May of this year, I flew to Brussels, and the headquarters of the Rapid Reaction Force Unité. The military establishment is outside Brussels itself, in flat Belgian countryside; and I was driven out by a *Unité* driver, and provided with an interpreter—in a Pan-European armed force, this can still be a necessity.

I had been picturing it on the flight over. She would be in an office at HQ; modern, bright with the natural light of a spring day in Europe; maps on the walls. She would be wearing the uniform of a *Unité* officer. For some reason, despite the record I had in front of me, I pictured her as older: late twenties, early thirties.

I was driven to the edge of a pine forest, and escorted on foot up a rutted track in gray drizzle. The rain ceased after the first mile or so.

I found her calf-deep in mud, wearing fatigues and combat boots and a dull-red-coloured pullover. She looked up from the group of men at the back of a jeep, poring over a map, and grinned. I suppose I looked very wet. The sky was clearing overhead, to duck-egg blue, and the wind whipped her short hair across her eyes.

She had black hair, and brown eyes, and dark skin.

The RRFU had given me permission to film and record: I

had done this on several previous occasions, when it proved to be the wrong woman. On this occasion, I almost switched off the shoulder-cam and terminated the interview there and then.

"Sorry about this," she said cheerfully, walking over to me. "Damn exercises. It's supposed to be good for efficiency if we have them without warning. Rapid deployment. You're Professor Ratcliff, yes?"

She had a slight accent. A tall woman, with broad shoulders, and a major's insignia. The spring sunlight showed faint silvery lines on her right cheek. And on the other side of her face, too.

"I'm Ratcliff," I said, to the woman who looked nothing like the manuscript descriptions; and on impulse added: "Where is your twin, Major?"[70]

The woman was Arab in appearance, in an RRFU major's uniform, with an expansive way of taking up her personal space—a presence. She put her muddy fists on her hips and grinned at me. There was a pistol at her belt. Her face lit up. I *knew*.

"She's in Düsseldorf. Married to a German businessman from Bavaria. When I'm on leave, apparently, I visit. The kids like me."

One of the men by the jeep hailed her. "Major!"

He had a radio mike in his hand. A man with sergeant's stripes; in his late thirties or early forties, bald under his beret; in a uniform that looked as though it had seen use. He had the look that sergeants have: that nothing is impossible to do, and that no senior officer knows enough to change his own nappy.

"Brigadier wants you, boss," he said briefly.

"Tell Brigadier Oxford I'll get right back to him. Tell him I'm up a tree or something! Tell him he'll have to wait!"

"He'll love that one, boss."

"Into each life," she announced, with cheerful vindictiveness, "a bloody great amount of rain must fall. His damn fault for staging the exercise. Professor, I've got a flask of hot coffee; you look as though you could use it."

---

[70]All quotes taken from the transcript of audio and visual sources, location RRFU HQ, Brussels, 14/5/2009 (Project Carthage archives).

I followed her to the front of the jeep, dazed, thinking *It is. It* is *her. How can it be*? And then: *Of course. The Visigoths are—have been—integrated into Arab culture after the defeat of Carthage. And Ash was never European by race.*

"What's your sergeant's name?" I said, after drinking the sweet, strong brew.

"Sergeant Anselm," she said, with a grave, dead-pan humour, as if she and I shared a joke that no one else in the world understood. "My brigadier is an English officer, John Oxford. The men call him Mad Jack Oxford. My name"—she jerked a thumb at her name-tag on her fatigue jacket—"is Asche."

"Your record doesn't say you're German!"

"My ex-husband's name, apparently." She still had the smile of someone with a secret joke.

"You've been married?" I was momentarily startled. She *didn't* look more than nineteen or twenty.

"Fernando von Asche. A Bavarian. An ex-cavalry officer. It seems that he married my sister, after our divorce; I kept the name. Doctor Ratcliff, the wire said you wanted to ask me a whole lot of questions. This isn't the time: I've got manoeuvres to run. But you can satisfy me about one thing. What gives you the right to ask me questions about anything at all?"

She watched me. She was not uncomfortable with the silence.

"Burgundy," I said. "Burgundy is now a part of the human species-mind. Bedded in so solidly, if you like, that the 'ghost-past' arising out of the fracture can fall away into improbability. Our first past is returning. Your true history."

Major Asche took the steel flask and drank from it. She wiped her mouth, her dark eyes still fixed on me. The wind moved her short hair against her scarred cheeks.

"I'm not history," she pointed out mildly. "I'm here."

"You are now."

She continued to watch me. Somewhere back in the woods, shots cracked. She glanced back at Sergeant Anselm, who held up a reassuring hand. She nodded. Far out on the muddy plain, hover-tanks nosed into view.

I asked, "How long have you been here?"

Raised eyebrows. A slantwise look. "About two days. For the duration of this, I'm stuck in a military tent about two miles *that* way."

"That isn't what I mean. Or perhaps it is." I called up data on my wristpad, and read through it, slowly. It was sparse. "I think you have a 'ghost-history', if I can put it that way. You're very young to have achieved the rank of major. But war is a time of rapid promotions. You grew up in Afghanistan, under the Taliban. Their attitude to women is—mediaeval. You joined resistance forces, learned to fight; and when that was crushed, you joined the bushwars on the borders. There, all that was necessary was that you be able to lead. To command. By the time you were sixteen, they'd made you a captain. When the Eastern European forces united with the RRFU, you joined *Unité*."

Net footage of the fighting along the Sino-Russian border is still clear in my mind.

"At the end of the Sino-Russian war, two years ago, you'd made Major." I looked up from the little wrist-screen and the scrolling data. "But I'm fully prepared to believe that you've only *been* here two days, in a military tent, in a field somewhere."

Major Asche gave me a long look.

"Let's walk." She set off briskly. "Roberto! Where's the fucking helicopters? Do they think we're going to wait around here all day? We need to move up within the hour."

As we passed him, Robert Anselm grinned at her. "Don't fret, boss."

The new grass was slippery underfoot. I was not wearing boots. Cold- and wet-footed, I quickened my stride to keep up with her. We passed a truck, unloading armed soldiers; and she stopped for a word with the corporal before moving on down the track.

"You get a mixed force in *Unité*," she remarked. "That lot are mostly Welsh and English. I've got a gang of local Brussels lads; and a lot of East and West Germans. And a *lot* of Italians."

She flicked a look at me out of the corner of her eye. There was still a quiet amusement in her expression. I looked back at the men, only to find—camouflaged; expert—that they had merged into the edge of the wood.

"What was that corporal's name, that you were speaking to?"

"Rostovnaya."

"Is the whole company here?" I said, without thinking, and then she was looking at me, shaking her head, her eyes bright.

"All but the dead," she said. "All but the dead. Life and death are real, Professor Ratcliff. There are faces I miss."

I began to see tents, up ahead, in a clearing at the side of the track. Green military tents. Armed men, and men in white overalls, ran from tent to tent.

"Angelotti. Rickard. Euen Huw." She shook her head. "But we came so close to losing *everybody*."

"I think I know what's been happening," I said. "Why you're back. Burgundy's—failed. I suppose."

She stopped, boots in one of the ruts, the creamy brown mud halfway up her ankles, looking ahead at the tents.

I said, "Time moves differently closer to the probability wave. The moment in which you and the Wild Machines both calculated, powered, and *willed* human history to change—is ending. Has ended. You've managed to bypass the immediate danger. But the *process* by which that happened is withering away. Fragments of the true past are fitting in among the interstices of the past we know—it's possible to foresee a time when the history that we know of Burgundy will be the history of 'Ash's Burgundy'."

She smiled at that.

I went on, "But it's over. Isn't it? I believe that we have been in the process, over the last six or eight years, of reintegration with Lost Burgundy. Burgundy's gone, hasn't it?" I said. "We're not protected any more."

"Oh, we are."

She gave me that grin, head cocked, eyes creasing and bright; and she was, for one moment, as I had seen her in my mind as I read the manuscripts: the woman in armour, dirty, pragmatic, unable to be crushed down.

"I don't understand."

A fair-haired woman in a white overall walked towards us

down the track. The wind made her slit her eyes, but I could see that they were green. She had had her head shaven and stitched at some time in the recent past: the visible scars of removed stitches, and the fluff of her regrowing hairline were clearly visible under her cap.

"The *amirs*' medicine was better than ours," Asche said to me. "Why shouldn't someone else's be better than theirs?"

Death is a fuzzy-edged boundary, too.

The woman glanced from me to Major Asche. "This is the boffin?"

"That's right."

The name tape on the breast of her overall read DEL GUIZ.

"You tell him where your sister is, yet?"

"Sure."

The scarecrow-tall woman turned back to me. For all the pallor of her cheeks, she was smiling. "This one flew down to Düsseldorf, yesterday. On a military flight. She had to see them."

"My sister has two children," Asche said, gravely mischievous. "Violante and Adelize."

Asche smiled.

"Violante keeps rats. I'll go down again soon. We've got stuff to say to each other."

The woman who must be Floria del Guiz said briskly, as if I wasn't present, "Ratcliff will want to interview all of us. Clerks always do. I'll be in the med tent. Some *other* bloody fool decided to get out of a counter-gravity tank before it landed. That's four. Christ! Nobody tell me soldiers are *bright*."

Major Asche, with demure humility, said, "I wouldn't dare."

Floria del Guiz stomped back towards the tents, with a wave that might—if a senior officer had appeared—have become a salute.

"I would have given anything," Asche said, and I saw that her fist was clenched at her side, "to have all of them here now. And Godfrey. And Godfrey. But death is real. It's all real."

"But for how long?"

"You haven't got it yet, have you?" Asche looked amused.

"Got *what*?"

"We came back," Asche said. "I thought we would. But they stayed."

At the time, I merely stared at her. It is not until now that I have developed a theory: that organic matter and organic mind are inevitably 'sucked back', if you like, into the human species-mind, into the main part of reality, away from the 'forward edge'. Because they *are* human, and organic. And that she must—with all that computing power at her disposal—have realised this.

" 'They stayed'?"

"The Wild Machines," Asche said, as if it were obvious enough for a child to have seen it.

And I saw it. *The Wild Machines.*

"Yes." A wind rustled; spent rain fell from the pine trees and spattered my face. I stared at the woman in combat fatigues, with the grin on her face. "I suppose I assumed that—there's no reason to assume it! No reason to suppose that the Wild Machine silicon-intelligences were destroyed when you—did what you did."

What more likely than that lost Burgundy contains them, as well as the nature of Burgundy, within itself? Contains the presence of immense, intelligent, calculating power. If lost Burgundy exists in an eternal moment, without time, but with duration, this does not preclude the idea that the machine-intelligences might 'still' be functioning. Linear time is not relevant where they exist.

Immense natural machine intelligences, monitoring the probability wave, keeping all possibility of miracle-working out of the Real. Their perception more vast than human; their power inorganic and endless, tapping into the fabric of the universe. Maintaining, unchanging.

"They couldn't move there themselves," Ash said. "We made a miracle and I moved all of us. All of us. Carthage too. And now they're out there—wherever—doing what Burgundy did. The Wild Machines are Burgundy now."

The wind rattled again in the trees, and became the noise of helicopter rotors. She reached for the RT set in her top pocket but didn't respond. She squinted up above the tree-tops, into the clearing blue sky.

"They knew it would happen," she said. "When I told them what I planned to do. They consented. They're machines. Godfrey would say my hell—the eternal moment—is their heaven."

The arc of her, and their, 'moment' covers five hundred years of intense scientific discovery. As a race, we have alleviated some of human suffering, while at the same time committing the grossest atrocities. Lost Burgundy, then, does not limit human choices; we are free to choose whatever we perceive of good and evil.

"Lost Carthage?" I suggested.

"A lost and golden moment," the woman said.

Above our heads, a helicopter dipped towards the clearing; and all speech became impossible until it had landed. A young man in combat fatigues jumped down and began sprinting towards us through the mud.

"Boss, they need you over at grid—is the radio down?" he interrupted himself. Long-boned, hardly more than adolescent. "Major Rodiani wants you! So does Colonel Valzacchi."

As I watched her, she gave a slow, amazed grin.

" 'Colonel' Valzacchi? Hmm. I'll be right there, Tydder." As he ran back, she said, "This really isn't the time. I'll get the chopper to take you back to Brussels. I'll talk to you there, soon."

"What happens to you," I said, "now?"

"Anything." She smiles across at the idling rotors of the camouflage-painted helicopter, and shakes her head, with all the energy of youth; as if amazed that anybody could be so obtuse. "I live my life, that's what happens. I'm not even twenty. I can do anything. You keep an eye open for me, Doctor Ratcliff. I'll make five star general yet! And I suppose I'll have to do some of this bloody political stuff. After all—now, I know how."

She gave me her hand to shake and I took it. Her flesh was warm. Any thought I might have had that she would retire—or be persuaded to join Project Carthage—was revealed as insubstantial, unreal. Cruelty and abuse do not die, although they may be overcome; she is now what she always will be, a woman who kills other people. Her loyalty, such as it is, is to her own. However many that may come to include.

As I left, she said, "I'm told we're going back out to the Chinese border soon. As a peace-keeping force. In some ways, that's worse than war! But on the whole—" A long, level look from that scarred face. "It's probably better. Don't you think?"

That was three months ago.

While I have been engaged in the collation of the Third Edition text with the chronological documentation of 2000 and 2001, and in the writing of this Afterword, Major Asche briefly visited the Project headquarters in California. On her way out, she suggested to me that we might require an alteration to our unofficial Latin motto.

It reads, now, *Non delenda est Carthago.*

Carthage must not be destroyed.

Pierce Ratcliff-Napier-Grant
Brussels
2009

Acknowledgments

I AM INDEBTED to Anna Monkton (née Longman) for her guidance in presenting our editorial correspondence. At time of publication, she is about to present us with a first grandchild—or in my case, step-grandchild—which, however, she and my wife, Isobel, refuse to let me call after our "scruffy mercenary," Ash.

But I have hopes of persuading them.

The Chronicles of Ash by

Mary Gentle

The annals of a kingdom on Earth that was—and wasn't—and the life of its greatest warrior

A SECRET HISTORY
THE BOOK OF ASH, #1
0-380-78869-1/$6.99 US

CARTHAGE ASCENDANT
THE BOOK OF ASH, #2
0-380-80550-2/$6.99 US

THE WILD MACHINES
THE BOOK OF ASH, #3
0-380-81113-8/$6.99 US

LOST BURGUNDY
THE BOOK OF ASH, #4
0-380-81114-6/$6.99 US